Maggie Hope was born and raised in County Durham. She worked as a nurse for many years, before giving up her career to raise her family.

Also by Maggie Hope:

MAGGIE HOPE
Orphan Girl

EBURY
PRESS

7 9 10 8 6

First published as Lorinda Leigh in 1993 by Judy Piatkus (Publishers) Ltd.

This edition published in 2015 by Ebury Press, an imprint of Ebury Publishing
A Random House Group Company

The Random House Group Limited Reg. No. 954009

Addresses for companies within the Random House Group can be found at:
www.randomhouse.co.uk

A CIP catalogue record for this book is available from the British Library

The Random House Group Limited supports The Forest Stewardship Council®
(FSC®), the leading international forest-certification organisation. Our books
carrying the FSC label are printed on FSC®-certified paper. FSC is the only
forest-certification scheme supported by the leading environmental organisations,
including Greenpeace. Our paper procurement policy can be found at:
www.randomhouse.co.uk/environment

Printed and bound by CPI Group (UK) Ltd, Croydon, CR0 4YY

ISBN 9780091957384

To buy books by your favourite authors and register for offers visit:
www.randomhouse.co.uk

Chapter One

'You'll blooming well do what I say or you can get yourself up to the workhouse! Oaklands, that's where the other little bastards are! You impittent little basket, you're not going to turn out like your mother, not if I have the bringing up of ye!'

The hard, blue eyes of Auntie Doris Parker bored into Lorinda Leigh's uncomprehending head. Lorinda looked round the kitchen of the old terraced house: she looked at the table and chairs, scrubbed white with soda water daily: she looked at the piles of dishes waiting to be washed in the brownstone sink in the corner, then down at the stone-flagged floor which was sending icicles of cold shafting up through the thin leather of her boots.

What did Auntie Doris mean, she wondered through her misery, by the workhouse? Wasn't this a workhouse? Lorinda pushed the thought to the back of her mind. First of all she had to deal with the insult to her mother:

she wasn't going to let anyone get away with talking like that about her mam.

'My mother was a good woman! Me grannie said so!' Lorinda lifted her chin and stared fearlessly up at her aunt. 'She was taken down, that's what me grannie said!'

'Taken down, eh?' Auntie Doris grinned in jeering amusement and Lorinda hated her. Her small fists doubled up at her sides. 'They all say that, don't they?' Auntie Doris continued. 'But they don't all go gallivanting off to London and leaving their by-blows to God and Providence!' She glared down at the little girl, seeing the stricken look in the violet eyes, eyes which seemed too big for the thin, pale face. Long, black lashes lay over the white cheeks, hair just as dark curled over her shoulders. Doris Parker turned away and Lorinda was bewildered by the anger in her eyes. She watched dumbly as her aunt hung the apron on a hook behind the back door and took down her old black jacket, her shopping jacket.

'Just you get on with the washing-up!' Auntie Doris snapped. 'I've wasted enough time fetching you all the way from Durham and it's a scandal, the fares, a shilling and threepence for a little mite like you. Eight blooming miles, that's all it is from Durham to Bishop Auckland! And the station a mile from the market place. Eeh, well, I've the shopping to do and a meal to make before the ironworks turns out. Now, just you make sure it's all done by the time I get back.' She pinned on an enormous, black straw hat over her thin, grey hair and, picking up her basket from the table, swept out of the back door and down the brick-paved yard.

Lorinda stared after her stolid form as Doris turned into Finkle Street. The girl thrust out her chin mutinously though her heart felt like a lead weight and tears were close. Sighing, she pulled a stool up to the sink and climbed onto it. She jumped as the door opened again and Auntie Doris poked her head round it.

'An' another thing, I'm not having such a daft name as Lorinda in my house. Lorinda, indeed! I'll call you Ada like your mother, she never liked it but I think it's good enough, a nice, down-to-earth name. Yes. You'll be Ada from now on.' Banging the door decisively behind her, she went on her way to the Co-op, the Store as everyone called it. So she didn't see or hear Ada's protest.

Ada! What was wrong with Lorinda? Her grannie had told her she was named for her great-aunt, it was a family name and Auntie Doris knew it. But now Lorinda was to be Ada. Her cup of misery was full to overflowing. Blindly she put her mind to the washing-up.

Carefully she carried a ladle can half-full of hot water, steaming hot from the boiler, by the side of the black-leaded range, and poured it into the enamel bowl, going back for another as a full can was too heavy for her. Being so short, she had some difficulty in reaching the bowl but she managed it without mishap. Grating hard,

3

white soap with a handful of washing soda, she made a lather, just as her grannie had taught her. She began to wash the plates, steadfastly refusing to think about her grannie.

She looked up at the dingy, green-painted dado on the walls with the light-green distemper above it. Somehow the walls made her think of Durham Gaol, so bleak and forbidding when she walked past it with her grannie. There now! And she wasn't going to think about her grannie. Lorinda plunged her thin wrists and hands into the steaming water, wincing as the soda burned into a cut on her little finger. She had done that with the bread knife, when her grannie had first been taken bad. Lorinda had tried to tempt her appetite with bread and milk broily but it wasn't any good, grannie couldn't eat anything. And now . . . Lorinda concentrated on the plates, rubbing hard with the mop to get off the traces of congealed porridge, using her thumbnail for the stubborn bits. In spite of her resolve, memories kept intruding into her thoughts, causing her to sniff back the tears.

Lorinda's heart burned as she remembered Auntie Doris's sneering reference to her mother, who was, after all, Auntie Doris's own sister. Lorinda couldn't remember her mother at all; she could remember nothing before living in the little house in Durham City with her grannie. But Grannie would talk to her about her mam, telling her how she had gone south so that she could earn good money and be able to send for her daughter as soon as she could.

'We were all right,' Lorinda said aloud, talking to the plate in her hand. 'Me and Grannie were all right.' That's what Grannie always said. Grannie never made Lorinda feel she was a burden, not like Auntie Doris did.

'We're all right,' Grannie would say. 'I've got me bit of charring for the students up at the university. And I can always take in washing. A good washerwoman I am. And you're such a help to me, Lorinda. Your mam will send some money soon, you'll see; till then we'll manage.'

But me mam didn't send money home for us, Lorinda thought. And she didn't send for me or come back for me. Lorinda picked up a pint pot and scoured it with the mop. She had been sure that when the new century came her mam would come home. Everyone said that things would get better in the new century and Lorinda had looked forward to it eagerly. It was a bright promise, the new century.

But it was 1901 already and Lorinda was seven and a half years old and still her mam hadn't come for her. By now, her mam was like a character in a fairy story to Lorinda. She didn't come, not even when Grannie took to her bed and Mrs Armstrong came in from next door but one, and Grannie had to go to the fever hospital and Lorinda wasn't allowed to see her for fear of the fever. Then there was the awful day that Grannie died and

Auntie Doris Parker came, trailing Uncle Harry, bustling in and taking over the house and Lorinda.

Lorinda was lifted up to see her grannie in the coffin but it wasn't really Grannie, her grannie was gone. So she had to go too, with Auntie Doris and Uncle Harry with his sandy moustache and shiny, wet lips. He didn't say anything at all to her, simply looked at her and at Auntie Doris and then back at Lorinda.

'There's no help for it, Harry, we'll have to take her in.'

Auntie Doris was firm. There was only one boss in their house and it wasn't Uncle Harry, that was what Grannie used to say. 'Though why we should have to, I don't know,' Auntie Doris continued in an aggrieved tone of voice. They were picking over Grannie's things at the time to see if there was anything worth saving. 'Her mother should come for her really.'

'Yes please!' Lorinda breathed as she obediently packed her woven straw box after the funeral. 'Please come, Mam!'

So far this hadn't happened, which was why Lorinda was standing on a cracket at Auntie Doris's sink, in the kitchen of a boarding house in Finkle Street, with her tears going 'plop' in the washing-up water.

'Ada!' she said out loud and sighed. She had been proud of her pretty name; no one else in the street in Durham had been called Lorinda. Still, Ada was her mother's name and she comforted herself with the thought that she could still be Lorinda in her own mind. She sighed and wiped her eyes on the corner of her apron; she wasn't going to let Auntie Doris see her cry. Squaring her shoulders and lifting her chin, she got on with the work.

'I'll stick up for myself,' she said out loud. Grannie always said she should stick up for herself, not let anyone get her down.

Soon Auntie Doris was back and the rest of the day passed in a blur for the newly named Ada. She fetched and carried at her aunt's demands until her thin arms ached with tiredness.

'There's six men and a lad will be wanting their dinners at half past six on the dot,' said Auntie Doris, blowing a strand of grey hair back from her red face as she lifted an enormous iron pan from the fire and rested it on the fender. Uncle Harry was laying the tables in the front room where the lodgers ate their meals, presided over by Auntie Doris and Uncle Harry. 'You can eat your dinner in here,' she added. 'I don't want you in the front room, getting in the way, most like.' As she spoke she was dishing out huge platefuls of meat pudding, potatoes and cabbage. Deftly she piled them onto a battered tin tray and took them through the door into the hall.

Relief and delight shone in Ada's eyes. She had been afraid she wasn't going to get any dinner herself. Her stomach rumbled. After all, she hadn't eaten since leaving Durham that morning.

Auntie Doris was soon back in the kitchen for the jam roly-poly, shovelling it onto thick, white soup plates and smothering it in yellow custard.

'Let the bairn go in and sit at the table with us.'

Ada looked up to see Uncle Harry, who had appeared behind his wife. The wet ends of his moustache were sucked to a point and Ada stared at them, feeling slightly repelled.

'You mind your own business! She's my sister's brat, not yours!' came the sharp retort, causing Uncle Harry to shrug and back out of the kitchen ineffectively. Ada sat down at the kitchen table; she didn't mind where she ate so long as she ate. Her thin legs dangled inches from the floor and she propped herself up with her elbows on the table.

'Sit up straight! And mind you eat it all up! I cannot abide wasted food. While you're a good girl and do your work properly, you will get proper meals.'

To do Auntie Doris justice, the plate she set before the girl was piled high with meat pudding and potatoes and Ada tucked in with a will, relishing the thick, meaty gravy. Auntie Doris left her to it, going back into the front room with her tin tray loaded with plates of jam roly-poly.

Ada had eaten only a few mouthfuls when her head

drooped, the long, black lashes closing over the violet eyes. She woke with a start and propped her chin on her left hand, the elbow supported on the table. She tried another bite of the suet pudding doused in rich gravy but she was unequal to the task and inevitably her head sank lower and lower until it was cradled in her arm and she fell properly asleep. For she was still only seven years old and the momentous happenings of the day had been too much for her altogether.

A few minutes later the door to the passage opened and a boy of about fourteen came into the kitchen on his way to the lavatory in the back yard. His sandy eyebrows lifted in surprise when he saw the little girl sleeping peacefully at the table, her dark curls falling over her forehead and her hand clutched round a spoon over her rapidly congealing dinner.

Clumsy in his hobnailed boots he tiptoed to the back door, fearing to disturb her, but she was too sound asleep for that. He closed the door quietly behind him as he wondered who she was, surely not family; as far as he knew the Parkers had no children. The peaceful scene was changed as he came back into the house, the angry voice of his landlady rang out as he opened the back door.

'I told you to eat your dinner! Well, you'd better eat it now, cold or not or you'll get it for your breakfast. I don't hold with wasting food, I told you before!' Doris Parker was standing with her hands on her hips, her eyes glaring from a bright, red face as she bent over the child shouting her threats.

The boy closed the door and began the walk through the kitchen, away from the angry voice. But he stayed a moment, his attention arrested as the girl lifted large, violet eyes and stared back at her aunt. For all her small stature, her chin was set firmly and defiantly.

'I couldn't help going to sleep, could I? I was tired!'

'Don't you cheek me, just you do as you're told!' Auntie Doris raised her hand for a blow, she was admitting no excuses.

After a moment, Ada dropped her eyes and started to eat. She took a bite and chewed doggedly, looking up from her plate and letting her gaze rove around the room. Noticing the boy, she paused and looked curiously at him. He winked at her, rolling his eyes in the direction of Auntie Doris before grinning his support.

Ada smiled, revealing a missing tooth, and winked back, albeit inexpertly. She saw a red-headed, green-eyed boy, tall and well-built. He was dressed in old working clothes: a red-checked shirt which clashed violently with his carroty hair, together with an old and stained serge suit which looked far too tight for him. A good two inches of wrist showed beneath the cuffs of the jacket. His hands, though rough and scarred by manual work, were well-shaped and capable-looking. Ada had time to notice all this before her aunt butted in.

'Get on through with you, Johnny Fenwick. You know I don't like my boarders hanging about in the kitchen.' Auntie Doris had seen the latter part of this exchange and she wasn't slow to show her disapproval.

Undeterred, Johnny gave Ada a last sympathetic grin before returning to the front of the house. He pondered afresh on the presence of the girl as he went. There was something about her, a vulnerable yet defiant quality that disturbed him, and when Mrs Parker had raised her hand to the child he had felt instantly protective of her. Shrugging his shoulders – after all, he knew practically nothing of the girl – he climbed the stairs to his tiny room, which had been split off a larger one by shaky wooden boarding. Sitting on the bed, the only place there was to sit, he picked up an engineering manual from the tiny bedside table and was soon lost in his studies.

Meanwhile Ada bent her head over her food once more and managed with some trouble to finish her meal. She sat back in her chair, feeling bloated and uncomfortable, and looked up at Auntie Doris who was busy washing the dishes.

'Can I go to bed now, Auntie Doris?' The small voice with its humble plea came out with more pathos than Ada realised and her aunt was not completely insensitive.

'Well,' she said grudgingly, 'I suppose you will be tired. All right, get ready for bed. I'll get you a dish of water and you can get yourself washed. You'll sleep in here, I can't afford to give you a bed upstairs. I need them for the lodgers.'

Ada looked round in dismay; she couldn't see that there was anywhere to sleep in the kitchen. There was not even a settee – was she to sleep on the clippie mat on the floor? But she hadn't noticed that in the corner there was a red mahogany chiffonier sideboard. Auntie Doris pulled open the doors and revealed a fold-up bed.

'There are blankets and a pillow in the drawers. Now don't forget, when you get up in the morning you'll have to fold the bedclothes and put them away. Tidy, mind! You'll get up at five o'clock. I can't do with the bed out when I'm making breakfast for the boarders. Now run along to the netty, then you can get ready for bed.'

Obediently Ada slipped out of the back door and into the yard. There were two doors in the corner at the far end but from the coal dust on the step of the first one, the netty had to be the second, Ada reckoned. She stretched up to the latch and there it was, an ash closet with a scrubbed wooden seat and a large – very large – hole, and there was not a small one beside it as at Grannie's. She climbed up and sat, hanging on desperately, terrified she would fall in and thankful when she could clamber down at last. Well, at least it seemed to be for the sole use of the occupants of the house and not shared with the neighbours like the water closet they'd had in Durham

City. Quickly she pulled up her drawers and rearranged her skirt, shivering in the chill of the autumnal evening before scurrying back to the warmth of the kitchen.

Auntie Doris was pouring water into an enamel dish on the table. She scowled at the little girl. 'Wash properly, mind. Take your dress off first.' She brought white Windsor soap, a piece of flannel and a worn, rough towel and placed them beside the bowl.

Ada unbuttoned her brown cotton dress with its black crepe armband and sat down on the clippie mat to untie her tall boots. The laces were stiff and hurt her fingers.

'Eeh, man, howay here and I'll do it!' Auntie Doris was impatient with Ada and her hands were rough and horny, the veins standing out lumpily on the red skin. 'I want you in bed in five minutes,' she said.

Grannie's hands had been rough and red too, Ada thought, but Grannie was gentler somehow and Ada hadn't minded. Auntie Doris pulled off the boots, scratching Ada's skin with a jagged nail. Then, after Ada had washed, Auntie Doris pulled and tugged a metal comb through Ada's curls, forcing her head back and bringing tears to her eyes.

At last she was ready and could climb onto the lumpy mattress and pull the blankets up to her chin. The blankets smelled of the same soap she had used to wash her face, and the smell reminded her of Monday washdays when she had helped Grannie, catching the clothes as they came out of the rollers of the iron mangle. It was comforting somehow. Ada watched as Auntie Doris pulled a folding screen across the foot of the bed, hiding it from anyone going through the kitchen to the yard but not entirely screening the kitchen from Ada's gaze.

Tired as she was, she felt she wouldn't be able to sleep for everything was so strange. And any road, she thought forlornly, she had never slept in a kitchen before. She would be the only one downstairs! Her vivid imagination was already conjuring up dark shapes in the gloom. After Auntie Doris put out the gas it would be even darker, eerie and strange. Ada's heartbeat quickened. The gas went 'plop' as Auntie Doris turned it off and went out of the door, closing it firmly behind her. Ada squeezed her eyes tight shut.

'Matthew, Mark, Luke and John,' she prayed desperately, keeping her eyes closed in case she saw anything horrible in the shadows, 'bless the bed that I lie on.' But it was no good, without her grannie's soft voice intoning the prayer with her she couldn't remember no matter how hard she tried. A tear squeezed its way out of her closed lid and coursed down her cheek unheeded.

'Psst!'

The hiss made her jump rigid, her eyes starting open in alarm. It was a moment before she realised it was Johnny Fenwick peeping round the screen, a candle in one hand and a paper bag in the other. The glow from the candle made his face all light planes and dark hollows but it was definitely Johnny.

'I've brought you some pear drops.' He moved swiftly towards her as he whispered and put the bag of sweets on her pillow. Grinning, he backed away with a finger to his lips before she could find her tongue and thank him.

Wondering, she picked up the bag and its contents, sniffing. It was the familiar pear-drop smell, sweet and acidic at the same time. How did Johnny Fenwick know she loved pear drops more than anything? Hadn't her grannie bought them of a Saturday night and hadn't they sat before the fire sucking them together? Ada clutched the sweets to her and turned over onto her side. She relaxed, feeling better already, a lovely warm feeling overcoming her fears. She had a friend. Johnny Fenwick was her friend. Her eyelids drooped and Ada slept.

It was still dark when Ada woke. For a moment she was bewildered, not knowing where she was or what it was that had caused her to wake up. She peered fearfully round her at the gloom. As her eyes grew accustomed to it, there was enough light getting in the kitchen window to show her a grotesque shape at the end of the screen. Ada stared hard, trying to make out what it was. It looked like a huge head on hunched shoulders. The light outlined what seemed to be a large nose, long and bent. Ada stared hard at it, trying to make it out. She felt a new discomfort, she wanted to go to the lavatory but she was afraid to move in case she attracted the attention of the strange being.

The back door opened with a squeak of unoiled hinges and she heard heavy footfalls crossing the room; there was a pause before a flickering light was lifted and she saw the figure of a man through the gap between the screen and the wall. He was opening the door to the passage.

'Dafty!' Ada said it aloud, scolding herself, for as the man lifted his candle she had seen no monster but her own clothes which Auntie Doris had flung over the top of the screen, one sleeve jutting out and looking like anything but a nose! Sitting up in bed, Ada felt on the floor for her boots, pulling them on over bare feet.

Bye! She'd been lucky there, she thought in relief. What would Auntie Doris have said if she had wet the bed? Would she have been sent to the workhouse? Quickly she made her way to the back door in the grey light of predawn. The man, whoever he was, had left the bolt drawn so she got out easily enough.

The air was fresh and cold, making her shiver in her flannel nightie. She hurried as fast as she could, gasping as a blast of cold air from the hole in the seat hit her bare flesh. She raced back to the kitchen and jumped into bed. As she snuggled down into the warm cocoon of blankets, her elbow encountered something hard. Groping down, she found the bag of pear drops. Popping one into her mouth, she sucked luxuriously and thought about the boy who had given her the sweets, Johnny, Johnny Fenwick.

Doris Parker was also awake, lying beside her snoring husband. She was wondering if she had done the right thing in bringing her niece to live with them. In the half-light she stared at the framed text which had been her mother's and now hung on the wall opposite the bed; she couldn't make out the words but she knew they said, 'God Is Love'. She thought back to the time when she had embroidered it and given it to her mother for Christmas, she'd been so proud of it. But Mam had been absent-minded, too interested in the new baby, who had a snuffling cold. Her sister Ada was the first baby in the family to live more than a few weeks since Doris herself and Mam lavished all her anxious care on her.

The familiar jealousy flared in Doris's breast as she remembered Ada, her sister. It was Ada who got all the treats, Ada who had naturally curling hair and good looks and it was Ada who in the end came to nowt. Doris remembered the thrill of satisfaction she felt when she found out that Ada was expecting a baby. She turned over in bed and smiled; now she was in charge of the bairn.

The bairn was such a little stick of a thing for all her seven years, but she seemed strong enough. She'd pay for her keep all right. Doris's anger rose again as she remembered the spark in Lorinda's eye: she might be small but she showed the spirit of her flaming nowt of a mother. Doris grinned. She'd brought her down a peg or two calling her Ada.

'I'll bray that impittance out of her,' Doris said as she wearily got out of bed. 'I'll start as I mean to go on.'

'What? Eh?' Harry turned over and looked at her sleepily.

'I said nowt for you. Just you get yourself up and see to the breakfast tables, the men'll be down before we know it.' Doris poured cold water into the basin on the washstand and splashed it over her face and arms before drying herself on the rough towel which was hanging on the side rail. Aye, she'd soon train the lass to the work, it would ease her own burden.

Chapter Two

'Come on, you! Up you get!' The strident voice woke Ada from a pleasant doze, Auntie Doris sounded angry already and Ada sat up in alarm. Flinging the girl's clothes on top of her, the woman folded the screen and set it back against the wall, glaring sideways at her niece as she did so.

'Howay now, get yourself dressed, you don't want to be caught in your nightie, do you? The men will be coming through here in a minute.'

Auntie Doris turned up the gas in the mantle above the table and lit it with a match. Then she turned her attention to the range, raking out the ashes into the box underneath, screwing up yesterday's *Northern Echo* and laying it in the grate. She took sticks from the oven and criss crossed them over the paper, covering them with the still warm cinders and coal from the scuttle, all the time working at a furious rate and berating Ada while she worked for being slow.

'And don't forget to tidy the bedclothes away, neat and tidy now! Then I'll show you how to put up the bed.' She filled the kettle and put it to boil on the gas ring by the fire before turning to her niece with her hands on her hips.

Ada was scrambling into her clothes, pulling on her coarse, black stockings, pulling the legs of her drawers down over the stockingtops. She fumbled with the buttons of the dingy brown dress, managed them in the end, and then it was the turn of her pinafore. Tying the neat bow at the back as Grannie had taught her, she took a broken piece of comb out of the pocket and dragged it through her tangled curls, fastening them back from her face with a piece of black tape. Auntie Doris watched as Ada folded the blankets, pursing her lips as she struggled with their weight but not offering to help. At last the bedclothes were in the drawer and before long the chiffonier was back to looking like a sideboard again.

Uncle Harry shuffled into the kitchen, his pale eyes watering and his nose bright pink. He glanced briefly at Ada, who was standing uncertainly, not knowing what she was expected to do next, before going over to the range and holding his brown-spotted hands out to the fire. His wife grunted her impatience.

'For God's sake, Harry, show the girl how to set the

table. We haven't got time to stand about gormless! I'm too busy now to have you in here anyway.' Auntie Doris nodded her head purposefully to Ada, who followed Harry as he shuffled back to the front room without even bothering to answer his wife. Ada looked about her with interest. So far she hadn't been beyond the passage door and she had thought she was to be confined to the kitchen for ever.

The room where the lodgers ate their meals and spent their spare time was as dismal as the kitchen, she thought. Two square tables were covered in scratched and worn 'American oilcloth' and the chairs set around them were mismatched and ugly, though they were sturdy enough. A scrubbed wooden cupboard on the wall was the only other furniture; the only attempt at decoration was one picture on the wall, a cheap print of 'The Thin Red Line'. The red coats of the soldiers were faded to a dirty pink and brown spots of damp adorned the corners.

Uncle Harry drew back the thin brown curtains to disclose a thick lace, 'dolly-dyed' to a sickly shade of cream. Ada stood in a corner and watched him curiously as he turned up the gas jet and opened the corner cupboard. The room looked no more inviting for the extra light.

'Howay then, lass,' he said as he motioned her over. 'You get out the pots, they'll be down for their fodder before we know it.'

Ada came to his side obediently, waiting for him to hand down the pint mugs and knives and forks which she could see were in the cupboard. She looked up in surprise as he glanced quickly at the door before patting her bottom lingeringly. Her mouth dropped open as he put an arm around her thin body and squeezed her to him. She didn't know what to do or how to respond to him so she kept herself rigid. It was the first friendly touch she had had since she came to Bishop Auckland, but it didn't feel right somehow, not really friendly. Desperately uneasy, she just wished he would let her go.

'I'm your friend,' Uncle Harry said softly and his wet moustache brushed her cheek, making her skin shrink, 'I'll look after you.'

There was a noise in the passageway just outside the door and Uncle Harry released her abruptly, causing her to stagger a little. Ada took the mugs he handed down to her without looking at him and moved away to set the tables. Her face was red and she felt awkward and strange and very unsure of herself.

Suddenly the ache for her grannie was a hard lump in her stomach which refused to budge, a lump as heavy as lead. Her eyes blurred and she couldn't look at Johnny as he came into the room, closely followed by the other lodgers. Johnny paused, glancing curiously from Ada to her uncle. He could sense there was something wrong. But Ada brushed past him quickly, anxious to get back to the kitchen and the rough voice of Auntie Doris. At least she knew where she was with Auntie Doris.

Ada sat back on her heels and surveyed the front steps she had just finished scouring with sandstone. She thought they looked nice and clean but would Auntie Doris? Standing up, she took deep breaths of the cold early-morning air. It wasn't very often Ada got the chance to be out in the fresh air; Auntie Doris didn't like her to go out much. She'd been in Finkle Street for a month and she hadn't been to school yet. Ada liked school, she looked forward eagerly to starting a new one here in Bishop Auckland. If it was like the school in Durham she would soon make friends with the other girls, she knew. Maybe Auntie Doris would let her go next week.

'Are you not finished out there yet?'

Ada jumped as Auntie Doris came out into the passage and stood with her hands on her hips glaring at her.

'Yes. Yes, I am.'

Picking up her bucket and piece of sandstone, Ada hurried through the house. She emptied her bucket in the yard drain and then began washing up the breakfast dishes. By this time she didn't have to be told what the next job for her was, she had quickly got into the routine.

Auntie Doris was black-leading the range, her brush going rhythmically to and fro, to and fro. Ada looked at her sideways. She didn't seem to be in a really angry mood, just intent on getting the oven door to shine.

'Am I going to school next week, Auntie?'

The question sounded loud in Ada's own ears, and her heart pounded as she bent over the plate she was scrubbing clean of grease. Auntie Doris stopped buffing the oven door. She stood back and looked at her niece, her mouth set.

'No you're blooming well not!' she said flatly. 'You'll learn all you need to know here in this house.' She turned back to the range. As far as she was concerned the subject of school was closed.

Ada pressed her lips tightly together to stop herself from crying. She continued with the washing-up and after a while she no longer wanted to weep, she began to feel rebellious instead. Why shouldn't she go to school?

Everybody went to school. How would she ever be able to read and write if she didn't go to school? Auntie Doris was horrible, she had no right to stop her. She hated Auntie Doris. She glared her hatred behind her aunt's back. Auntie Doris continued with her work, serenely unaware of the feelings she had roused in Ada.

When the washing-up was finished, the draining board scrubbed down and the cloths wrung out and hanging on the brass rail above the range, Ada went out to sweep the back yard. Gradually she worked off her bad feelings towards Auntie Doris, there was nothing she could do to alter things now. She would leave it for now, but Auntie couldn't keep her off school for ever. Any road, if her mam came back for her – and Ada prayed every single night that she would – Auntie Doris would no longer have the charge of her. Mam would let her go to school, surely she would. Ada fell to dreaming about how it would be if her mam came back. They would go to live in Grannie's old house in Durham and Johnny would come to tea and she could change her name back to Lorinda. Bye, it would be lovely.

The morning of Ada's eighth birthday she was out of bed and had the screen put away and the bed back to a sideboard before Auntie Doris came down to the kitchen. When her aunt came in Ada smiled at her, waiting for her to say, 'Happy birthday'. She'd been a good girl and got on with her work. Surely Auntie Doris would know what day it was? But Auntie Doris merely grunted and went to fill the kettle at the tap over the sink. Ada waited. Maybe when the breakfast was ready Auntie Doris would give her a little present, a bag of sweets or something to mark the day.

In the dining room, setting out the tables, Ada glanced out of the window at the sun shining on the pavement. Dust motes hung in the air as a sunbeam came in and brightened the room. Ada felt optimistic: surely now she was eight Auntie Doris would let her go to school?

The lodgers began to filter in and take their places at the tables, most of them morose and taking little or no notice of her. Their minds were on the day ahead of them.

'Hello, Ada.' A softly whispered voice in her ear made her turn eagerly to Johnny with a wide, welcoming smile.

'Hello, Johnny. Do you know what day it is today?'

Johnny paused on his way to his seat and looked at her vivid face. Her cheeks were rosy with excitement and her lovely eyes sparkled.

'Er . . . May the twentieth?'

'No, silly! Well, yes, it is, but it's my birthday. I'm eight today.'

'Are you, pet? Happy birthday, Ada!' Johnny looked round the room at the older men. 'Did you know it was Ada's birthday today?'

They looked up. Seeing her shining face, most of them relaxed and wished her many happy returns. Two of them even reached into their pockets and brought out pennies for her. Ada was delighted.

'Eeh, thank you,' she breathed, clutching her pennies to her. It was such a long time since she'd had a penny of her own.

'I'll have a surprise for you tonight, Ada.' Johnny winked at her. Just then they heard Auntie Doris calling from the kitchen.

'Are you not finished in there, Ada? What the heck are you doing?'

Ada quickly slipped the pennies into her apron pocket and ran out of the dining room.

'What're you looking so pleased about?' Auntie Doris looked up from the table where she was dishing up the plates of porridge.

'It's my birthday today, Auntie.'

'Aye, well, I know that,' said Auntie Doris. 'What that has to do with anything I don't know. Howay, give us a hand.'

Ada's moment of happiness dimmed as she began to pile the plates onto trays and Auntie Doris took them through to the boarders. She was not going to let Auntie spoil it for her, she decided. Grannie had always made her birthday a special day and Auntie Doris was just being nasty the way she was sometimes. Anyway, she had Johnny's surprise to look forward to that night.

Uncle Harry was sitting at the end of the table drinking a mug of tea, but as his wife went out of the door he got up and moved towards Ada. He caught hold of her arm and drew her towards him, bending his face close to hers so that she could see the bits of porridge sticking to his moustache, wet and shining.

'Haven't you got a birthday kiss for Uncle Harry, then?'

'Let me go, Uncle Harry. I have to see to the bacon.' Ada felt sick as his hands began to wander down her back.

'Give me a kiss then.'

Ada closed her eyes and pecked him on the cheek. 'I

27

can hear Auntie Doris coming,' she said. Uncle Harry released her and sat down at the table as his wife came back into the kitchen.

Ada carried on with her work. She soon recovered her spirits, looking forward to the evening when Johnny would come back from work with his surprise, and planning what to do with her pennies. She would buy a present for Johnny when it was his birthday, she decided. Meanwhile she would hide them in the chiffonier drawer.

'When is it your birthday, Johnny?'

The evening had come at last and Johnny took advantage of the Parkers' presence in the dining room to slip out to see Ada under the pretence of going to the lavatory in the yard. He sat down at the kitchen table with Ada, a pleased smile on his face. He had brought her a bunch of ribbons, blue, red and green, to tie in her hair, and she kept glancing down at the parcel in her lap, delighted with the bright colours. Her dinner was hardly touched, she was so excited. Bye, it was lovely! She had thought she wasn't going to get any presents at all and here Johnny had picked the very things she loved. Though these, too, had better go in the chiffonier drawer.

'Not for ages yet, not till November. Bonfire night,' said Johnny. 'Now, are you sure you like the ribbons? I can take them back –'

'Eeh, don't be barmy, Johnny Fenwick! I love them,

I do. Thank you, Johnny, I've never had such bonny ribbons, I haven't.' There was the distant sound of the dining-room door opening into the passage and a shadow crossed her face. Quickly she slipped over to the chiffonier and stowed the lovely ribbons away before her aunt came in. When the kitchen door opened Johnny had disappeared down the yard and Ada was steadily eating her dinner.

'Howay then, get a move on!' Auntie Doris snapped. 'We want the dishes cleared tonight, you know, not tomorrow.'

Ada said nothing; she wasn't going to let anything spoil her pleasure in Johnny's thoughtfulness. Bye, he was a lovely lad, he was!

'Johnny, will you learn me to read? And maybe write my name?' Ada asked timidly. Her hopes of going to school were growing dimmer as the weeks turned into months. Johnny might help her, she thought and looked anxiously at him, afraid he wouldn't think much of her for not being able to read.

Johnny frowned. 'Don't you go to school, Ada? And it's "teach", not "learn".'

Ada blushed painfully, not only because she had used the wrong word but also because she was ashamed of the reason Auntie Doris gave her whenever she asked about school. She bent her head over the fork she had been polishing with ash from the grate and didn't speak until she had put down the fork and picked up a knife, rubbing hard on the blade.

'I've seen you watching the others go down the street to school. Why don't you?' Johnny went on.

Ada kept her head bent, she was near to tears. Just then they heard Doris Parker coming and swiftly Johnny went out and down the yard. Ada would get into trouble for talking to him and it wouldn't be the first time. For once, Ada was glad of the interruption; she rubbed harder and harder on the knife until it sparkled through the tears on her lashes.

'You not finished those knives yet?' Auntie Doris said sharply, glancing through the window at Johnny as he disappeared through the gate. 'You've been talking to that lad again, haven't you?' As she passed Ada's chair she brought her horny hand casually across the young girl's head, making her ears ring. Ada now had an excuse for the tears in her eyes. She finished cleaning the cutlery and took it to the sink to wash with soap and water. Johnny hadn't said he would *teach* her, she thought. She resolved to ask yet again about school.

'Please, Auntie, can I go to school?'

The question seemed to hang in the air and Ada waited hopefully for Auntie Doris's answer. Auntie Doris didn't reply for a minute and Ada began to think she wasn't going to.

'Well, if I can't go to school, can I go to Sunday

school?' Ada persisted. She had kept her star card showing her good record for attendance in Durham. She remembered that lovely day when she and Grannie went on the Sunday-school trip to Redcar. Bye, the sea was grand, and the sands and the Punch and Judy show. Her reminiscences were interrupted harshly by Auntie Doris.

'Go to school? How many times do I have to tell you you're not going to school? Nor Sunday school neither. I'll not have you shaming me by letting everyone know I've a bastard niece on my hands. What do you think the Sunday-school teacher will think?'

Auntie Doris's red face was glistening with sweat as she took the oven cloth from the brass rail over the range and opened the oven door. A great blast of hot air was let out into the kitchen and the smell of newly baked bread filled the room. She pulled a loaf tin out of the oven and expertly upended the loaf onto the cloth in her hand, tapping the bottom of it to see if it was ready. Satisfied, she brought out the rest of the batch and put them to cool on the table before turning back to Ada with her hands on her hips.

'An' I expect you don't go telling any busybody who has the impittance to ask why you're not at school that you live here. You're only visiting while your mam's away.' Doris Parker wiped her forehead with the oven cloth and glared at the girl.

Ada said no more. She was humbled as she was

reminded yet again of her origins; Auntie Doris was always doing that. She wondered why – Grannie hadn't minded her going to school, not even Sunday school. I must be really bad, she thought and carried on washing the knives and forks, her dark head bent over her work. I must be very bad not to be able to go to school. But as far as not telling anyone, well, she didn't see anyone very often, apart from the lodgers, that is. And Johnny was the only lodger who took much notice of her.

Summer slipped away and Ada stopped asking if she could go to school though she still hoped that some day she might. In the meantime Johnny brought her a slate and chalk and tried to teach her to write her name. The trouble was that they only had snatched moments together so Ada's progress was slow.

Johnny's birthday approached and Ada managed to slip out to the newsagent in Bondgate and buy him a tuppenny notebook. Carefully she wrapped it in the paper she had saved from the ribbons and early on the morning of his birthday she was in the dining room waiting for him. Johnny was always the first lodger down.

'Happy birthday, Johnny.' Ada felt suddenly shy as he came through the door. Hesitantly she handed over her present; maybe he had plenty of notebooks and didn't need another.

'Oh, Ada, you shouldn't spend money on me,' Johnny said helplessly, looking down at the cheap, paper-backed exercise book. 'You shouldn't really.'

'Do you not like it, Johnny?'

Johnny looked at Ada's crestfallen face. 'Oh yes, I do, I do really. It's just the thing. I can use it for making notes,' he said hastily. 'Thank you, Ada, it's lovely.'

Ada's face cleared and as the boarders filtered in she went happily back to the kitchen. The warm glow of satisfaction from giving Johnny a present he liked stayed with her all day.

Ada always woke up with a feeling of anticipation on Saturday mornings. On Saturdays, Auntie Doris and Uncle Harry always went for a 'lie-down' in the afternoons and Ada could look forward to being fairly free. Johnny would come into the kitchen, Ada would get out her slate and chalk and he would try to teach her a little. Sometimes they would just sit and talk, cosy beside the fire. Though Ada's workload had grown heavier as time went on and Auntie Doris succumbed to the damp northeast weather and stiffened with 'rheumatics', Saturday afternoons were easier.

One Saturday afternoon, just after her tenth birthday, she and Johnny were sitting at the table, Ada bent over her slate.

'Why don't you tell the kiddy-catcher you want to go to school? You must have seen him about, he's always out looking for truants.'

Ada looked up, biting her lip. It was true, even though she rarely got out without her aunt she had seen the truant officer employed by the Schools Board. He hunted among the mean streets of Town Head and walked down Newgate Street looking to left and right, in shop doorways and down the alleys. Auntie Doris always rushed her into the Store or some other shop, well to the back so they weren't seen. Ada would hide behind Auntie Doris's skirts as the small man in the black overcoat two sizes too big for him and clutching a large notebook peered round. The news that the kiddy-catcher was on the prowl spread like wildfire for he was usually preceded by a lookout, so few children were actually caught.

'I can't,' she said at last and bent over her work.

'I'll tell him if you like, I often see him,' Johnny offered, warming to the idea.

'Eeh, no, don't!' Ada cried in alarm, halting her laborious penmanship, pencil poised in the air.

'No, no, I won't.' Johnny hastened to calm her distress. 'But why not?'

'Just . . . I don't want you to.' Ada was ashamed to tell him of Auntie Doris's threats or about her mam running off to London or that she had no father. She was ashamed of being a bastard, too, though she still wasn't sure why it was her fault or even what it meant. The spectre of the workhouse or the orphanage down Escombe Road loomed large in her life. Auntie Doris would surely send her to one or the other if the kiddy-catcher came knocking at the door. She changed the subject.

'Will you show me how to write Lorinda?' She was hesitant, the forbidden name sounded strange on her tongue.

'Lorinda? Why Lorinda?'

'Oh, nothing, it's just that I used to be called that. Auntie Doris didn't like it.'

Johnny's face darkened. 'That woman!' he said savagely. Ada looked at him. Johnny didn't usually get angry. His green eyes were flashing sparks for a minute but he calmed down. I'll call you Lorinda if you like, I mean, just when we're alone.'

'Well, I don't know . . .'

'Anyhow, I'll write it down for you.' Johnny took the slate and printed the name, watching Ada as she copied it laboriously. The tip of her tongue peeped out of her mouth and her black curls tumbled over the slate, having escaped the piece of tape she used to tie them back. The ribbons were still safely hidden in the chiffonier.

Suddenly he stood up and made for the back door. Ada hurriedly took the slate over to the drawer of the chiffonier.

'Put the kettle on, lass,' Auntie Doris said as she came into the kitchen, puffy-eyed with sleep. 'Bye, I could do with a cup of tea.'

Chapter Three

'You can go down to the market when you've had your tea and get the messages in.'

'The market?'

'Yes, the market! You've not gone deaf, have you, lass?'

Ada paused in surprise from her task of setting the table. Normally, the only way she got out to the market was to sneak out when Auntie Doris was busy elsewhere. She stared at her aunt now. The older woman was sitting with her elbows on the table, resting her head in her hands.

'You can get cabbages and whatever else is cheap in the vegetables. They always bring down the prices before they pack up for the night.' Auntie Doris peered out through the kitchen window at the darkening yard and shivered, despite the blazing fire in the grate.

'I'm not looking forward to this winter, I can tell you,' she said, her voice dismal. 'Every year it gets worse.' Shaking her head, she turned on her niece. 'Where's that tea then?' she barked irritably. 'A body can be fair clammed waiting for you!'

Ada got on with her job, her head bent submissively to hide the excitement in her eyes. A thrill of anticipation ran through her. She loved the market with its bustling crowds, the miners and their wives in from the pit villages dotted around the outskirts of the town, the flaring, hissing carbide lamps lighting up their happy holiday faces. She couldn't help smiling in delight.

'And mind, no hanging about! Just get the messages and get yourself back here!' Auntie Doris had seen the smile and was frowning heavily, her voice sharp.

'Eeh, yes, I will, I'll be straight back. I'll run all the way!'

Ada was anxious now, maybe her aunt would change her mind and go herself. She mashed the tea and drank hers quickly, burning her mouth a little. She slid off the chair and fairly ran over to the door, reaching up for the shawl which hung on a hook, taking it down and tying it securely around her slight frame. Folding the shopping bags and placing them in a large basket, she was ready to be off. Auntie Doris sighed as she picked up the purse from the table by her side, the heavy leather purse which went everywhere with her.

'And mind, you be careful with the money!' She handed over two half-crowns and Ada pushed them deep inside the pocket of her pinafore. 'We've plenty of onions, the onion-seller was round last week. I expect some change, think on, but we need enough to last next week.' Auntie Doris pursed her lips and continued grudgingly, 'You can buy a penn'orth o' bullets for yourself, toffee maybe.'

Ada gasped with pleasure and her eyes sparkled. 'Oh! Eeh, ta, Auntie!' She danced over to the door. 'I'll get the best bargains I can, I will!'

Auntie Doris's voice floated after her as she ran down the yard. 'An' no talking to lads! I'll have no trouble in this house!'

Ada barely heard, though she nodded. Auntie Doris was always saying that and Ada hadn't the least notion what she meant by it. How could there be trouble in the house if she talked to a lad? Ada put it out of her mind; there was the exciting prospect of the market to think about. Happily she threaded her way through the crowds thronging Bondgate, the narrow street that led to the marketplace. The wind blew chill and the dark November night was already drawing in fast. The high, old buildings on either side channelled the wind, which was bitterly cold, but the crowds didn't seem to notice and neither did Ada. She herself was noticed, though; quite a number of people took a second look at the diminutive girl with the shopping basket almost as big as herself. The wind and excitement whipped up a rosy colour in her cheeks and her violet eyes shone as she came past the coaching inn into the marketplace.

Johnny, standing by the Town Hall, had seen her at once. He watched her for a while indulgently as she made her way round the stalls. He enjoyed her vivid expressions as she paused and looked all round her. There was something about the young girl that always tugged at him and he felt fiercely protective of her, bitterly resenting the life of drudgery she was forced to live. Now, seeing her happy and enjoying herself, he was happy too. Quickly he moved behind a plump stallholder as Ada turned in his direction, his tall, gangly figure ducking agilely. He wanted to watch her unawares for a while.

Bye! How she loved the crowds! Ada thought as she looked at the miners' wives and daughters in their weekend finery, the young girls jostling and laughing with the flat-capped young miners in town for the afternoon and evening. The lights from the stalls reflected the tall windows of the Georgian terrace to her right and the arched gateway leading to the bishop's castle loomed dark and heavy against the pools of light cast by the gas streetlamps.

It was the stalls themselves that really held her interest, though. The stallholders calling their wares, the piles of glistening boiled sweets and cinder toffee, and the wonderful smell from the penny dips and meat pies on a stall next to one piled high with cabbages and carrots.

Cabbages! 'I must get on or Auntie Doris won't let me

come again,' Ada muttered under her breath. If she did well, maybe Auntie would let her do the messages every Saturday afternoon. Maybe Thursday morning too, when the fishwives from Shields came and set their stalls up on the other side of the market square. Bye, she liked to see the fishwives from Shields and she liked the smell of the fish. It reminded her – what was it it reminded her of? Oh yes, the time when her star card was all filled up and she'd been able to go on the Sunday-school trip with Grannie. Ada struggled to remember that magical day and sketchily it came back to her.

The sea, bye, the sea was so big! The sands had stretched right along for miles and there had been fish-wives on the quay, gutting the herring and throwing them into big boxes. It was Redcar, not South Shields, but Ada imagined it was just the same. Grannie had bought some herring and they had eaten them soused in vinegar and baked in the oven. How could she have forgotten that day? Reluctantly, Ada sighed and turned to the serious business of the afternoon.

Bustling now, she did a round of the vegetable stalls, checking the prices, looking for a stall that had almost sold out and was ready to pack up for the day. The serious shoppers had already bought and the crowds were just idling now, filling in the time before the Eden Theatre or the pubs opened. Youths were whistling boldly at girls and girls were tossing their heads, pretending disdain.

'Tuppence a head, cabbages!' A red-cheeked woman in a sacking apron and with thin, grey hair tied back tightly in a skimpy bun encouraged Ada as she picked over the produce on the woman's stall. Critically, Ada pursed her lips in unconscious imitation of Auntie Doris and made as if to move away from the stall. She was small but she wasn't going to be taken for a neddy.

'Eeh, go on then, three ha'pence. An' you won't do fairer than that!' the woman called after her.

Ada turned back and started to pick over the vegetables importantly, choosing half a dozen cabbages. Give them plenty vegetables, Auntie Doris always said, then they wouldn't want so much meat. Eventually Ada had her bags full of carrots, cabbages, swedes, parsnips and leeks, but she turned down the Brussels sprouts as too dear. In the end she had to hoist the bags over her forearm rather than hold them in her hands or they would trail on the floor. But at last she was free to visit the toffee stall. Slowly, dragged down by the weight of the bags, she moved back along the line of stalls.

'Get your toffee here!' the stallholder was shouting as she wiped her hands on the bleached flour sack tied round her middle with a length of brown twine. 'All home-made, I made it meself the day wi' best butter and sugar!'

Ada quailed for a moment, eyeing the greasy, fair hair tied back with a length of the same twine, and the grimy marks on the flour sack. But the piles of cinder toffee, fudge and butter toffee, never mind the jars of boiled sweets, made her mouth water so much that she forgot about the dubious cleanliness of the toffee-maker as she pondered what to buy.

'Aren't you going to get pear drops?' The laughing voice behind her brought her from her rapt contemplation of the goodies.

'Johnny!' She swung round to look up at him with a broad, delighted grin. It was lovely to be able to share her happy evening with him. Then her smile became anxious and slipped a little.

'But you always buy me pear drops,' she blurted. 'And Auntie Doris said to buy toffee.'

'All right! All right! I'll still buy your pear drops.' Johnny pretended to grumble but his eyes were alight with amusement. He waited, watching her eager little face as she turned back to the stall deciding at last on cinder toffee. The woman wrapped the broken pieces in a twist of paper and handed it over to Ada who stowed it in her skirt pocket. Johnny was fascinated by her total absorption in what she was doing as she methodically arranged the straps of the heavy bag over one arm and picked up the basket with the other.

'I'll carry them for you,' he offered, taking the heavy shopping from her and lifting it easily. Though he was still thin and boyish, his muscles were already work-hardened.

'Well,' Ada said doubtfully, 'only till we get back to the gate.' She knew Auntie Doris would be angry if she saw them together and her aunt's parting stricture came back to her – Johnny was a lad and she wasn't supposed to talk to lads. Yet how could it hurt? She decided to forget about the warning and walked happily by Johnny's side through the thinning crowds up the narrow street of Bondgate and round the corner into Finkle Street.

'I'll go round the end of the street and come in the front door. Then there'll be no bother,' said Johnny. He was well aware of Ada's dilemma. Rather reluctantly he handed over the heavy shopping.

Ada nodded. Oh, Johnny was so understanding, he understood everything, she thought as she watched his tall figure rounding the corner, sighing happily despite the weight on her arms. She'd had a lovely, lovely time. She opened the gate and heaved her burdens up the yard.

'You're back then,' was all Auntie Doris said as Ada heaved the bags onto the kitchen table. 'It took you long enough.'

'Here's the change, Auntie,' Ada answered meekly, for nothing was going to spoil the day for her.

Later in the evening, when the work was done and Ada was sitting beside the kitchen fire toasting her toes and sucking a large piece of cinder toffee, she thought about Johnny and a warm glow enfolded her. Bye, he was nice!

43

A real nice lad. She felt so lucky to have him as a friend. He was a big lad and he didn't have to bother with a little lass like her but he was so kind. She smiled softly to herself as she gazed into the fire, completely forgetting to listen for footsteps in the passage.

'Ah, little Polly Flinders, eh?'

Ada jumped in her chair as Uncle Harry shuffled in, rubbing his hands together and stretching them out to the fire to warm them. His pale-blue eyes watered above his pinched, red nose and the hairs of his moustache were stuck damply together. He took out a large, brown handkerchief and blew his nose loudly before stuffing it back into the pocket of his grease-spotted, baggy trousers.

Ada gave him a guarded smile, sitting up straight in her chair, her muscles tensing and uneasiness lurking in her eyes. Uncle Harry didn't snap at her as Auntie Doris did; sometimes he helped her and spoke softly to her. When she had first come to live here she had craved affection and responded gratefully whenever it was offered but she didn't like the way Uncle Harry touched her. It was always there, a cloud at the back of her mind; he whispered things to her which made her feel hot and uncomfortable and once he had shown her a postcard with a picture of a lady with her clothes off.

'It's a secret,' he had said. 'Don't tell Auntie Doris.' Ada hadn't known what to say to him but she knew she could never tell her aunt anything like that.

'Haven't you got a hug for your uncle?' he said now. His voice was soft and persuasive and there was an intent look in his eyes which Ada had grown to know and fear. She looked instinctively towards the door which led to the passage, hoping her aunt would come. The door remained tightly shut.

'Yes, Uncle Harry,' she said, her voice almost inaudible. She stood up awkwardly, feeling cornered. As he wrapped his arms around her and hugged her, she stiffened, her slight body shrinking away from him, but it wasn't any good. He held her whole body against his so she could feel the buttons of his waistcoat sticking into her chest. His hand slid down to her bottom, squeezing and pressing. Ada closed her eyes tightly. Suddenly she was released and flung back into her chair, red-faced and damp-eyed. The door had opened and Auntie Doris had come in. But Auntie Doris was not looking at them; she went straight to the sink and took up the kettle.

Uncle Harry turned swiftly and faced the fire. 'Just having a bit of a warm.' He spoke over his shoulder while he thrust his hands deep into his pockets. Auntie Doris ignored him. She looked at Ada and jerked her thumb in the direction of the screen in the corner.

'Off to bed with you, you've a lot on your plate the morrow. Sunday dinner an' all, I want the fire going and the oven warming so that we can put the mutton in by nine at the latest. It'll want a good doing, it looks a bit tough but I got it cheap. A good and slow cooking and it'll be fine. An' you know we've got extra for dinner.'

Ada did not need to be told twice. She was all churned up inside and happy to get behind the screen to her sanctuary, where Uncle Harry never ventured. At least he hadn't yet. The thought niggled but she pushed it to the back of her mind. Uncle Harry was too frightened of his wife, she knew that. He wouldn't want to be caught behind the screen. She undressed quickly and slipped into the chiffonier bed as soon as she could, snuggling down into its safety.

She couldn't settle down to sleep, however. Her aunt and uncle were talking quietly together as Auntie Doris moved from sink to stove to table making cups of cocoa for them both. Ada heard the hiss of boiling water as it was added to spluttering milk and smelled the pungent aroma of rum as it hit the hot liquid.

'Well, another couple of months, Harry, then we'll be moving into Tenters Street.' Auntie Doris smacked her lips as she took a long sip of her cocoa.

Ada pricked up her ears in surprise as she heard this piece of news. Tenters Street? Tenters Street was quite a posh street, the houses bigger and more modern than the one they were in.

'Aye,' Harry answered. 'Well, I only hope you're right and we will be able to 'tice the theatre folk in. One thing's for sure, there's more money in them than there is in the men from the works. And any road, they'll be going to Middlesbrough now the steelworks are there.'

'Aye. We deserve to get on, though, we've worked hard enough. We will do better in a bigger house and theatre folk'll be cleaner, easier to see to than this lot.'

Ada lay in a turmoil at the news that they were leaving Finkle Street. Tenters Street was only just around the corner and a couple of streets away, but what about Johnny? Was he going with them? And what was that about the steelworks? Johnny worked at the steelworks.

It was a long time before Ada fell asleep. Apprehension flooded through her at the prospect of losing Johnny. She didn't hear the couple leave the kitchen and when she did sleep she dreamed of Johnny going away, walking down a long street and never coming back while she gazed after him with tears streaming from her eyes.

Next morning Ada was so busy that all thoughts of the move were driven from her mind. She had to mend and bank the fire against the oven side of the range until it was hot enough to take the rack of lamb, or rather old mutton, and watch the fire so that the oven didn't get too hot while the meat was cooking or too slow to cook it properly. All this while she had to attend to the great pan of porridge on the hob and the slabs of breakfast bacon in the frying pan. On Sundays, the meals were enormous as the men relaxed on their only day off.

Then there was the washing-up of the breakfast things to be done quickly to clear the way for the vegetables to be cleaned and washed in the brownstone sink. Twenty men were in to Sunday dinner, there were mountains of potatoes to peel, turnips and cabbage. Auntie Doris came in to beat up the great bowl of Yorkshire pudding mix and make the gravy. It was half past three before the washing-up was done and the house went quiet as the men went off to bed for their Sunday-afternoon sleep, replete with dinner on top of the beer they had drunk in the Sun earlier on.

Johnny was nowhere to be seen, he had gone out immediately after the meal. Ada wondered about it but she was so tired she felt only like flopping down on the chair by the fire and putting her feet up on the steel fender. She intended to keep awake listening for footsteps in the passage. She didn't want to be caught again by Uncle Harry. But within minutes she was fast asleep, her dark curly head pillowed on her arm as the shadows lengthened across the kitchen floor.

It was not until Monday teatime that Ada had a chance to talk to Johnny and then it was only a stolen moment. He slipped into the kitchen where Ada was eating her meal. Everyone else was in the front of the house.

'Ada, look – Lorinda,' he said softly and for once he sounded young and awkward, 'I have to tell you I'm going away at the end of the week.'

Ada stared numbly, her eyes enormous in her white face. She put down her knife and fork and moaned quietly. Johnny walked over to the table and sat down beside her.

'I have to go, pet, I have to go to Middlesbrough. It's the work, you know, I have to finish my apprenticeship in Middlesbrough, our Fred says so and he's the boss.'

Ada didn't answer, she didn't know what to say. She looked up at this boy who always seemed to be growing out of his clothes, big-boned and gangly he was, yet with the promise of strength in his frame. He was her only friend. She turned her gaze back to her plate and, picking up the fork, traced rings in the pile of mashed potatoes. Her eyes blurred as tears threatened.

'I'll come and see you when I can, I promise I will. Come on, it will be all right. Let's see you smile, Lorinda pet.' Johnny grinned at her, trying to cheer her up. Her worries always seemed to become his worries. He couldn't get this little girl out of his mind and he didn't know why it was. He too looked at her fork going round and round in the potato. Her foot kicked the leg of the table softly but compulsively. How could he leave her with the Parkers? Especially Harry Parker. His thoughts darkened.

'Listen, Lorinda,' he said, his face puckering earnestly – but how could he say it? How could he make her understand what he feared without disturbing her innocence?

'Johnny?' Ada gazed up at him, puzzled, her eyes large and dark in her white face.

'I wanted to say . . .' Again he faltered. She watched him carefully, trying to read his expression. His face flushed a painful dark red.

'Lorinda,' he tried again, 'I wanted to say . . . don't trust your Uncle Harry!' There, it was out. But he had to say it – Harry Parker was known as a dirty old man among the children round about the doors, even if not to the adults. They whispered and sniggered in corners about him. But Ada did not mix with other children, she didn't get the chance to hear the tales.

Ada's face flushed as darkly as his. She looked down quickly, remembering other times like Saturday evening. She felt dirty, guilty. What did it all mean?

'Uncle Harry?' she faltered.

'Just be careful. I mean . . .' His voice trailed off, in truth he wasn't sure what he meant. He only knew he couldn't bear to see the way the older man looked at Ada, especially when he thought he was unobserved. But in this Ada was beginning to know more than Johnny did himself. In fact, she felt relief in an odd sort of way. It couldn't all be in her imagination if Johnny thought there was something about Uncle Harry too.

'No, Johnny,' she said now, squaring her chin and looking him straight in the eye. 'Don't worry, I know.'

'You know?' Johnny jerked his head up in disbelief

and outrage. What did she know? 'He's not touched you, has he?'

'Touched me?' Ada thought fleetingly and with distaste of the feel of Uncle Harry's hands on her body. But Johnny must mean had Uncle Harry hit her and he had never done that. Eeh, no, she thought, Uncle Harry would never hit her, she was sure.

'No, no, he doesn't hurt me. I only meant I don't like him. I don't think he's a nice man, do you, Johnny?'

Johnny sighed in relief and shook his head. She really didn't know and if Harry had touched her she would do. 'Well, I mean, pet, just be careful.'

'What are you two up to? Ada! Finish your supper! It's time you were clearing the tables.' Auntie Doris had come in unnoticed by them and Johnny stood up sharply, pushing back his chair. He turned on Doris Parker defensively, more for Lorinda's sake than his own. If the old harridan said any more to Lorinda he would tell *her* a thing or two! But Ada had picked up her fork and was eating methodically; by now she was used to covering up in front of her aunt.

Doris Parker glared pointedly at Johnny and after a moment he dropped his eyes and went out into the yard. She watched him go and then turned back to Ada.

'Well, we won't be seeing much more of him, he's off to Middlesbrough at the weekend.' She studied Ada carefully for any signs of distress or surprise but Ada merely nodded and continued with her meal.

At last she was finished, and, feeling slightly sick, for she had had to force the food down, she picked up a tray and went to the dining room to clear the tables. Ada knew better than to let her aunt see she cared about Johnny leaving. If I let on, she thought bleakly, I'll be accused of daydreaming every time Auntie Doris is in a bad mood. And that was often enough these days, what with her rheumatism and all.

She piled the plates and mugs onto the tray, her thoughts dark: the future stretched ahead greyly. It was best to forget about Johnny – he wouldn't even write, he would have so much else to think about once he got home to Middlesbrough. And even if he did write, her aunt would intercept and read the letters first. And even if Ada did get to the letters first herself, she couldn't read them properly any road. She carried the tray back to the kitchen, the heavy load seeming to pull her arms out of their sockets. She was strong, though, she managed the job. As she rubbed her shoulders before starting the washing-up, she decided there was nothing she could do about the situation so she might just as well get on with it.

Chapter Four

Johnny went off to Middlesbrough with a light heart and some excitement, for he was looking forward to seeing his family again. He climbed onto the train leaving for Darlington, where he had to change for Stockton-on-Tees, and took a corner seat, where he could look out at a countryside shrouded in fog. His mind wandered, thinking about his brother, Fred. He had told no one in Bishop Auckland of his brother, Joseph Frederick Fenwick. Well, it might not have done him any good with his fellow workers in the ironworks or with the lodgers in Finkle Street.

He'd done well, had Fred. He was a partner and managing director of a sprawling steelworks on the coast, a self-made man who believed in the value of hard work.

'No brother of mine is going to walk into the works at the top,' Fred had declared when he took Johnny out of school and sent him to Bishop Auckland to serve an apprenticeship. 'You'll have to prove yourself, my lad.'

Maybe Fred is getting a bit softer, Johnny mused as he changed trains at Darlington Station. The local train to the burgeoning industrial centre on Teesside was crowded and Johnny was squeezed in between two women with large baskets who insisted on talking loudly to each other over his head.

There's nothing wrong with travelling third class,' Fred had said. 'It won't hurt you. I had to do it often enough.' Johnny grinned as he looked past the other passengers at the flying countryside. Fred didn't travel third class now, oh no. Well, it didn't fit in with his position.

Johnny breathed a sigh of relief as the train pulled into his station and he descended to the platform. He looked around him, not that he expected to be met, but he was hopeful of seeing old friends. A bit silly that, he told himself, any friends of his from his early days would be either working or away at school.

Maybe Fred *had* softened in his attitude towards him, thought Johnny, as he set off on the final walk to the imposing stone residence where Fred lived with his wife Dinah and their two boys. Though the boys would be away at school now, he remembered, the Friends' School at Great Ayton. Fred had some powerful Quaker friends and business associates.

Turning his thoughts to the question he had been asking himself ever since he had got the letter from Fred, informing him that his brother had bought him out of his indentures and was ordering him to return home, Johnny wondered yet again if Fred had had a change of heart. Well, he would soon know. Happily he climbed the steps to the front door of the mansion and lifted the heavy knocker, dropping it with a resounding bang onto the plate. This was the first time he had been allowed home since Christmas and he was very pleased to be here.

'Yes, sir?'

The girl who opened the door was dressed in a neat, black dress with a starched white cap and apron. She was new to Johnny as he was new to her. She gazed at him doubtfully, unsure what to do; his clothes weren't too bad, they could be those of a gentleman, and his bag had the initials JHF on it. Yet his hands were roughened with hard work, scarred as badly as her father's hands, and her father worked on the shop floor in the steel mill. She didn't have to decide whether to let him in, however, for he moved forward himself, into the hall, slinging his bag into a corner as he did so and smiling at her.

'Hello, you must be new here,' he said, in a pleasant voice very much like the master's. 'I'm Johnny Fenwick. Tell my brother I'm here, will you?'

'Johnny!' Dinah had heard the knocker and was making her way down the curving staircase with her hands outstretched in welcome. She was a tall, buxom woman, fair-haired and red cheeked. 'I'm so glad to see you. Come into the drawing room – there's a fire in there and you must be cold.' She took his hands and kissed him on the cheek. Johnny was delighted to see her for when he was smaller Dinah had been as a mother to him.

'Bring some tea, please, Norah. And some of those nice scones Cook baked this morning.' Dinah said over her shoulder as she swept ahead of Johnny into the drawing room, talking as she went, hardly pausing for breath.

'Fred is still at the works. We'll have a cosy chat by the fire while we drink our tea. Bye, how you've grown, Johnny!' She paused and looked him up and down, critically. 'And we'll have to do something about getting some clothes to fit you.'

Johnny smiled indulgently. Dinah never changed, she was still the same amiable chatterbox he remembered. Of course, he thought, now Stephen and Arthur were away at school, she would miss having them to talk to. And Fred spent such long hours at work that the solitude would be hard for her, Dinah was so completely involved in her home and family.

Soon they were settled beside the tea tray and johnny was polishing off scones liberally spread with strawberry jam. Dinah, quiet for once, sat back and sipped her tea, watching her husband's young brother with a deep affection. She loved Fred and everyone connected with Fred unreservedly and his brother especially. 'Oh,

Johnny, it'll be nice to have you here where I can keep an eye on you. I was so worried when you were sent away from home so young. But I comforted myself thinking that Fred knows best. And, Johnny, Fred was right, you've come through fine, haven't you?'

Johnny smiled indulgently. 'Yes, but it's good to be back, and for good at last!' He sighed and sat back in his comfortable armchair, licking jam from his fingers.

'You were all right over in Bishop, though, weren't you?' Dinah's glance was anxious as she picked up the feeling in his voice. The lad was thin and growing out of his clothes. Dinah always thought of Johnny as 'the lad'. She couldn't understand why Fred sent the family away, first Johnny and now the boys, though they were only at school at Great Ayton – just up the road really, she liked to think. She studied the thin face with its frame of fiery red hair glinting in the firelight, a glint which was reflected in the green eyes. He was so like Fred had been when they first met that her heart melted within her.

'Oh, I was happy enough and I did get enough to eat,' Johnny teased her, looking at the empty tray.

Dinah relaxed. 'You know Fred thought it was for the best.'

The best for him but not for his own boys, Johnny reflected, his eyes hardening for a second. But he didn't really begrudge the boys an education, not really, it was just that sometimes his own lack of schooling rankled.

'Yes, I know, but why has he brought me home so early? Has he got a job for me?'

'I'm worried about him, Johnny, he's so tired now when he gets home. He works too hard and worries too much. I persuaded him that he could start training you as an assistant.' Dinah saw Johnny's start of surprise. 'Oh, I know you're not out of your time but you have a good brain, love, you two should be working together for only you could give him the right help.'

Johnny's face flushed with excitement. The chance of using his brain and maybe putting into practice some of his own ideas on improvements might be near. Well, he temporised, he was a bit young and inexperienced, he knew, but some day . . .

Johnny was brought down to earth when he met his brother that evening before dinner.

'Don't read too much into this, lad,' said Fred in his usual forthright manner. 'You're still very much the apprentice, you have a lot to learn.'

Johnny faced his brother across the desk in Fred's study. He was dismayed to see how much Fred seemed to have aged since Christmas, which was the last time they had met. Fred was twenty years older than Johnny and his hair was grizzled now rather than red. His face reflected the hard work and determination which had dragged him upwards to his present position. But the rugged lines of his face were blurred now, something Johnny had never noticed before.

'You'll be no more than an office boy at first.' Fred stared squarely at his brother, challenging him to object. Johnny stared squarely back, his expression no less determined.

'I want to go in for designing,' Johnny said flatly.

'Designing, is it!' Fred looked him up and down. 'Aye well, you'll have to creep before you can walk.' And the subject was closed.

After dinner they sat in the comfortable drawing room, red plush curtains drawn against the dark November evening and the fire in the grate radiating warmth. Johnny stared at the flickering flames and couldn't help contrasting his present comfort with the rather spartan amenities of Finkle Street.

'Glad to be home, Johnny?' Dinah had been watching his happy and relaxed expression.

'I certainly am!' Johnny grinned but then a shadow crossed his face. 'There are some things I'll miss, though. You don't spend years of your life in a place without growing attached to it in some ways. There is a young girl, Ada is her name . . .'

'A girl?' Fred interrupted sharply. 'You want nowt with girls, not yet! Why, man, you're barely seventeen.'

'No, no, a little girl, a tiny little thing. She's an orphan and works all hours at the Parkers, where I lodged. Yet she's such a bonny, sunny little girl. I used to buy her pear drops.'

'Pear drops!' Fred grunted and lost interest and at that moment Norah came in with the tea tray. Dinah busied herself pouring tea and Fred began to tell Johnny what was expected of him at the works. Soon the clock was chiming ten, the old grandfather clock Johnny remembered from his parents' house in Hartlepool. It reminded him of his father and mother, dead so long ago, and he thought how proud they would have been of Fred getting on so well.

His first day home was over, he thought as he climbed the curving staircase to his old room. Tomorrow was the beginning of his new life.

Johnny thought about his old life in Bishop Auckland often in the first year he was home. But as time went on and he became more involved in his new life, the memories faded. At first he had fully intended to visit Ada but somehow, with all he had to do, every time he thought he would journey back to see her and made tentative arrangements to go, perhaps on a Saturday afternoon, something stopped him. Either Fred wanted him to stay back at work and finish something or Dinah wanted him to drive her over to Hartlepool to see old friends. What with one thing and another, he didn't manage to get back to Bishop Auckland at all and the years were going by swiftly.

One evening when for once he had no night class, he was sitting with Dinah in the drawing room, enjoying the unaccustomed leisure. The lamps were lit, for the April evening had darkened early with squally showers. He looked around the room, thinking how quickly he'd got back into the way of expecting the comforts of life – when he had time to enjoy them, that was. He was working full time at the office and the steel mills, and studying hard in the evenings at the institute, determined to show Fred what he could do if he only had the chance. Johnny was sensible enough to realise how little he did know and he had an eager thirst for knowledge.

Johnny sighed. He had done well, he knew, but Fred seemed to take it for granted – after all, Johnny was a Fenwick. Yet Fred was relying more and more on him, Johnny thought, easing his own burden onto his younger brother's shoulders. Not that Johnny objected; he was young enough to take it, he reckoned.

'Happy with life, Johnny? You're looking more contented these days, though sometimes I think you work too much.' Dinah looked up from her book. She was reading *A Christmas Carol*: Dinah loved Dickens, Fred thought his works sentimental claptrap, so Dinah read his books only when Fred was out of the house.

'Just enjoying the peace,' Johnny answered.

'Well, it's nice to have you in, especially when Fred had to go to that civic dinner. I appreciate the company. But sometimes I think you should go out and enjoy yourself once in a while. It would be lovely if you found yourself a nice girl. You're twenty-two now, maybe you should think about it.'

'Oh, Dinah, I haven't time for girls, not yet. In a year or two maybe.'

'In all the time you've been home, you've never shown any interest in a girl. Maybe I could have a little dinner party . . .'

'Dinah!' Johnny laughed, 'Don't go matchmaking now.'

As he spoke, Johnny thought suddenly of Ada: her small, white face and unusual violet eyes came vividly into his mind. He realised it was ages since he had written to her or even thought of her. He had sent her postcards once or twice in the beginning but no replies had been forthcoming. No doubt that harridan of an aunt had blocked all Ada's attempts at getting an education, he mused. How many years had it been? Five. Five years and he had not been to see if she was all right. In sudden resolve as his guilty conscience smote him, Johnny excused himself to Dinah.

'I won't be long, I've just remembered something I wanted to do.' He went up to his room and walked over to his desk. Reaching for pen and paper in the drawer, he began a letter to Ada. He had gone to the trouble of finding out the number of the house the Parkers were moving to in Tenters Street before he left, so at least he still had her address. Although, he mused, he had not had any reply from any of his cards – perhaps she had left her aunt's house?

Chapter Five

The best thing about the move to Tenters Street from Finkle Street for Ada was having a room of her own. No longer did she have to sleep in the kitchen; when work was done she could tuck herself away in the attic room and feel safe. Ada never turned the key in the lock at night without a feeling of satisfaction.

'Aye,' Auntie Doris said when the move was completed and everything put straight, 'we've come up in the world now, all right.'

'Bye, it is nice, Auntie,' Ada answered, looking round the kitchen at the new gas stove and the linoleum on the floor. Without thinking, she added, 'I like having a room of my own with a lock on the door, too. I can lock meself in.'

There was a silence for a minute.

'Well,' Auntie Doris said, not looking directly at Ada, 'You never know, lass, you never know. Not with so many strangers in the house.'

Did Auntie know about Uncle Harry? Ada wondered and backed away from the thought, it was upsetting. Johnny wasn't here to turn to now and if Auntie Doris . . . No, Auntie couldn't know.

Gradually the boarding house filled up with guests. They were called 'paying guests' now, not common lodgers. No more rough, labouring men for the Parkers. The guests they took now were on the stage at the Eden Theatre and they were a cleaner class of people altogether from the men from the works. Ada liked the guests, and she got to see a lot more of them as she grew older. Always ready to talk about their lives on the road, they brought a touch of the exotic into her life. There were magicians, conjurors and comics. Ada often paused on the landing outside the rooms and listened to them practising.

'Don't let Ma get you down.'

That was the advice offered to Ada more than once when she was caught wasting time by listening to a singer practising something from *The Chinese Honeymoon* or *Flora Dora*, and got a slap for her pains. Somehow their sympathy helped, the slap didn't hurt too much and her day was lightened. Ada would hum, 'O tell me pretty maiden, are there any more at home like you' from *Flora Dora* or some other song from a popular musical comedy as she washed and scrubbed the kitchen floor, and the work was easier for it.

Ada always remembered Johnny. He didn't fade from her thoughts even though all she had to remember him by was the occasional postcard he sent her. She was always first up and picked the letters up from the doormat just in case there was a postcard from Johnny. But they were few and far between and the intervals between them got longer and longer. One day, Ada thought, one day she would go to Middlesbrough and maybe get to see him. But really she knew it wasn't very likely to happen. Johnny would have a girl of his own now, he would have forgotten about her.

When she was downhearted, Ada would climb the attic stairs and take out the treasured hoard of cards from Johnny. Of course, she didn't know what they said, but she liked to look at the pictures and his handwriting. She didn't find anyone to read them to her until Eliza came. Then at last she had a friend she could trust.

When Eliza Maxwell came to work in the boarding house in late 1909, she was a widow of eighteen – not much older than Ada, really, but there was a world of difference between them in experience of life. Eliza was kind and friendly but unimaginative and certainly not given to moaning about the hard knocks that had been her lot up to then. The two girls became fast friends and exchanged confidences and their hopes and fears for the future.

'Eeh, I'm that glad you came to work here!' Ada said

one morning as Eliza came in the back door and hung up her shawl.

Eliza smiled her slow smile and bent over her little boy to take off his coat. 'Aye. Well, I'm glad to be here,' she said. 'I'm glad of the money, for one thing. But it's nice to know you, Ada, though I can't say the same about that other two.' She straightened up and put a hand to her back. 'But you know I won't be here much longer. I doubt if Doris Parker wants a body with two bairns trailing after her. Not when she can get somebody else, like.'

Ada glanced at the bump under Eliza's apron and quickly away again. This would be the other girl's second child and here she was having to work as a 'skivvy', as Auntie Doris called her. Beyond knowing that Liza was a widow, Ada knew very little about how the other girl had come to be in such reduced circumstances. Eliza hadn't volunteered the information and Ada was too sensitive of her feelings to ask.

'Are you finding the work too hard then, Eliza?' Ada ventured now, thinking how bleak her days would be without Eliza to talk to.

'Why, I'm all right, pet. I can carry on a bit yet.' Eliza sighed and poured herself a cup of tea out of the pot on the fender, at the same time watching the door for any signs of Doris Parker. She added a dollop of condensed milk to the tea and drank it in one swallow, hot, strong and syrupy sweet. 'Mind, that was good. I didn't have time to take anything this morning.'

Ada looked down at Bertie. He was standing by his mother, gazing gravely at her. He was a quiet, serious little boy; though only two years old, he seemed older than his age.

'Why don't you stay here with me, Bertie? It's nice and warm in the kitchen. I'll get you some paper and a pencil and you can sit up at the table and draw.' She smiled at the boy, trying to coax him. He would be no trouble sitting in the kitchen but his mother had the staircase to do and if he stayed by her side Eliza would have the extra trouble of watching him too. Bertie rarely left Eliza, though.

To her surprise, Bertie nodded his head shyly and went to Ada.

'Mind, you're honoured!' Eliza laughed. Ada found a piece of wrapping paper and a stub of pencil for the boy. 'He's pale, like, isn't he, Ada?' Eliza's face sobered and took on an anxious expression. 'I should get out with him more, mebbe a bit of fresh air would do him good.'

'I think he's all right, though, Eliza, he's not coughing or anything.' Ada studied the boy. He was pale and thin, it was true, but she didn't want to strengthen Eliza's fears. She looked at Eliza, who was filling a bucket of water at the sink. The very hunch of her shoulders looked dispirited.

'I wish I still had the little house on the railway line, though. We had a nice garden and plenty of room, it was a good place for bairns to grow up.'

'You had to leave it, then?' Ada ventured.

Eliza turned round, twisting the wash-leather in her hands, the possible entrance of Doris Parker into the kitchen forgotten. She had to speak her fears to somebody and it wasn't fair to burden her auntie in George Street, who had been good enough to put them up until the baby was born. And Ada was a friend.

'Why, aye, we had. Well, it was a railway house, you, know. When my Albert died it was needed for the man who got his job. And Albert wasn't killed on the line, though he caught pneumonia working on it. Well, that's how it is, I had to make way for the new man. I thought I would be all right but when I found out about the new babby –'

'Oh, Eliza!' Ada's heart overflowed with sympathy for the other girl. 'I'm that sorry!'

Eliza braced her shoulders and turned back to the sink for the bucket of water. 'Aye. Well, don't get me wrong, I wouldn't be without the bairn, or the new one either. I'll manage till it's born and then I suppose it'll be parish relief for a week or two. But I'm not going to the workhouse.'

'Eeh, no, Eliza!'

Ada was shocked at the thought, they shared the

same horror of the redbrick building up beyond the railway station.

'I'd better get on, then, or I'll have that one on me back.' Eliza's voice was back to normal.

'Aye. Well, don't worry about the lad, I can watch him while I do the baking.' There was nothing more Ada could say, nothing she could do. Eliza went out to the stairs and Bertie lifted his head to watch her go. For a minute Ada thought he was going after her.

'Here, Bertie,' she said quickly, 'I'm going to be making pies. If you're a good boy you can make a little one for your mam's dinner.'

Bertie was diverted and spent the rest of the morning earnestly rolling a lump of grey dough, which he never seemed to get to just the right shape so he had to do it over and over again. When Auntie Doris came in, Ada expected a caustic remark about wasting food, but she simply sniffed at the boy and otherwise ignored him.

'Do you think I look sixteen, Eliza?'

Ada's friend looked up from her rhythmic turning of the washing-machine handle and considered the slim figure of Ada standing by the set pot boiler. The steam was rising and sticking Ada's dark curls to her white forehead, and her arms and hands were red with the heat of the water. She was picking clothes out of the boiler with a pair of long, wooden tongs and winding them through the huge rollers of the mangle.

'Well, I don't know. You're only little, pet,' Eliza answered after a moment. Ada was small for her age and slight, in sharp contrast to Eliza, who was tall, fair and buxom and obviously pregnant. Eliza continued with her turning, round and back, round and back, while suds peeked up through the lid of the machine and the paddles went slap, slap in a steady rhythm, flinging the clothes this way and that.

Ada sighed and looked through the doorway of the wash-house at the blue sky. It was a bright morning in April and crocuses were making a brave splash of colour in the tiny back garden, startlingly blue and yellow against the damp earth. She and Eliza Maxwell were working together in the wash-house which stood just outside the back door of the boarding house in Tenters Street.

'Well, I think I'm sixteen next month but Auntie Doris says I'm not fifteen yet,' Ada commented as Eliza finished her turning and stood up straight with a sigh. 'She says I'm still a bairn and she has the charge of me.'

Eliza pursed her lips as she considered Doris Parker.

'Bye, she doesn't do right by you, lass, and you working all the hours God sends for no pay! Maybe you're right and the old woman thinks to keep a better hold on you by telling you you're younger than you are.' Shrugging, Eliza began wringing out clothes and throwing them into the tin bath by her side. What could she or Ada do about it?

'Don't you know? Have you not got a certificate?' she asked.

'A certificate? No. I don't think so.' Ada was puzzled. 'Where would I get a certificate?'

'Why, I think you could get one from the registers, everybody gets registered when they're born. I had to get Bertie done.'

Ada thought about this. Would she have been registered when she had no father? Once again there was this thing about her birth. Still, she mused, she didn't have the trouble that Eliza had.

'Howay now, Bertie, we'll be using those pegs now.' Eliza leaned back again with a sigh of relief and held the small of her back with both hands. Bertie looked up from his game where he had the dolly pegs ranged as soldiers along the back doorstep; his face was mutinous. But it was so only for a moment before he obediently began to replace the pegs in their bag.

'Will you help me with something, Eliza?'

The older girl looked up as Ada put her hand in her apron pocket and pulled out an envelope. Her friend's face flushed as she asked for help, but though she could make out her name on the envelope she couldn't read anything else.

'What is it? A love letter?' Eliza asked playfully but,

seeing Ada's expression, she went on quickly, 'Eeh, give it to me, love.' Wiping her hands on her apron she took the letter.

Of course Ada knew Johnny had sent the letter as soon as she saw it come through the letter box. She knew his hand even if she couldn't read, anyway, Johnny was the only one to send her anything. He has not forgotten me, she thought, happiness overcoming her embarrassment for a moment. The letter this morning had been a lovely surprise, she thought, as she gazed eagerly at Eliza, waiting to hear what Johnny had written. There had been a long interval since the last one, a card with a picture of Saltbura sands, which had reminded her of Redcar. She had been frightened he had at last forgotten her.

'My dear Lorinda,' Eliza said in the funny voice she kept for reading aloud. 'Lorinda! You know, pet, it's a pretty name.' She smiled at Ada, but Ada was impatient at the interruption.

'I hope you are well and happy and standing up for yourself. You must be quite grown-up now and I would love to see you. Now for the exciting part. I am going to be in Bishop Auckland this coming Wednesday! Please try to get away to meet me, it's been so long since I saw you. I often think about you and your life with your aunt and uncle.

'I'll be coming by the train which gets in at three o'clock. Can you be there to meet me? Do try, for if you are not there I will walk down to Tenters Street and call to see you. I'm determined about it and surely now you are old enough to see whoever you want to.'

Eliza glanced up from her laborious spelling-out of the letter. 'Eeh, Ada! He's coming here special, just to see you! You'll have to get off so you can meet him.'

Ada didn't answer. Her face was a study in conflicting emotions. Absently she picked up a dish of steaming clothes and dumped them in the tin bath of blue rinsing water. She pulled them back and forth in the water before wringing them out by hand and taking them over to the mangle.

Johnny! she thought, oh, Johnny! He was still the object of her affections even now. She had built him up in her mind, pretending he was waiting to come for her and take her away, but she knew it was all make-believe. How could she be anything to him but a child he felt sorry for? Oh yes, she would be able to get away to meet him – Auntie Doris would be having her nap at three o'clock – but would he be interested in her when he saw her? He said in his letter she would be all grown-up now, but did he realise it in his heart?

'Ada! What do you think?' Eliza had gone over to the doorway and was helping Bertie pick up the pegs. Mother and son gazed at Ada, the fair-haired girl and the thin, dark boy.

'Oh, I don't know. Johnny likely won't even recognise

me. And any road, I've nothing to wear.' Ada turned the handle of the mangle and flattened garments fell into the basket with a plop. Eliza eyed her sadly. It was true, Ada had no decent clothes. Drab serge skirts and black shirtwaisters were all that Auntie Doris thought necessary for her. And even those were bought off a second-hand stall on the market.

'I tell you what' – Eliza had an idea – 'you come back with me tonight. I have a good dress, a pretty one. I know it will be too big for you but we can alter it –'

'Oh, Eliza, I can't take your dress!' Ada protested.

'Get away, man! I'll never get into it anyway, not since I had the bairn. An' after the next one.' She glanced fondly at Bertie before going on. 'Slip down tonight after the washing-up. Bye, you'll look lovely in my blue.' Eliza took up the peg bag and walked down the yard to the clothes lines. 'Now we'd better get on or this lot will never be finished.' As far as Eliza was concerned, it was settled, Ada would wear the blue dress.

Busy as they were with the washing and ironing, the day was bright with excitement for Ada. She had never been out with a boy; she was curiously young for her age in spite of the attentions of Uncle Harry or maybe because of them. The only boy who held any interest for her was Johnny and it was so long since she had seen him that his image was blurring a little. She began to look forward to Wednesday and her meeting with

Johnny with a mixture of anticipation and trepidation.

Ada lay in bed that evening too excited to sleep. The letter from Johnny had made her think back to her life when she had first come to the house in Finkle Street. It had been so hard! And the ache for her grannie had never gone away, it was still there but now it was a sadness at the back of her mind, not the overwhelming misery it had been at first. It was Johnny who had helped her then. And now he was actually coming to see her! Ada hugged herself at the very thought, smiling secretly. She would recognise him immediately, she told herself, oh aye, she would. Even though her memory of him was slightly blurry. And even though he was a grown man now she would know his friendly grin, his bonny red hair. Funny that his colouring should be so like Uncle Harry's and yet so different, she mused. A familiar cloud descended on her mind at the thought of Uncle Harry. Had she locked the door? Maybe she hadn't, thinking about Johnny an' all. Jumping out of bed, she ran to the door. Yes, it was locked, of course it was; she always locked it, she didn't even have to think about it.

The Eden Theatre showed cine-variety now, she thought, her mind wandering. Ada was sorry she had not been allowed to go and see the shows even though she was often offered complimentary tickets. But now there was the new Hippodrome opened and besides the 'Lantern coolers' on at the Eden, there were variety acts from the Hippodrome and sometimes the Parkers got people from there. Like Professor Naughton.

'Ma's an old slave driver, so she is,' Professor Naughton had murmured to her once. 'Don't let her get you down. Why, you're pretty enough to go on the stage yourself, dearie.' Professor Naughton was billed as an 'Original Eccentric Comedian'. Auntie Doris had come into the dining room and found him showing Ada magic tricks.

The trouble was, the artistes went away after a week or sometimes two, though some of them came back 'by popular request'. And they usually came back to the boarding house in Tenters Street, for, though they weren't too fond of Auntie Doris and Uncle Harry, they did like the good food and clean beds. Even though Auntie Doris, or Ma as they all called her, charged a penny extra for salt and pepper on their dinners.

Ada turned over onto her back and laced her fingers behind her head. She peered out of the tiny window of her room at the clouds chasing across the sky. The wind was freshening. Oh, Lord, let it be fine on Wednesday, she prayed. What would she and Johnny do if it rained? She sighed and looked round the room as the moon came out from behind a cloud and filtered through the threadbare curtains. She looked over at the door as she heard footsteps on the stairs, but it was only a lodger going into the room below on the first landing.

She began thinking about Uncle Harry, now greyer

and smaller somehow, but Ada knew how strong his hands still were. She remembered the feel of his hands, hard and hot and hurting, and she shivered. Ada had become very good at leaving a room if there was no one else there and Uncle Harry came in. And she locked her door every single night, though so far she didn't think Harry had tried to get in.

Now Ada stretched luxuriously and yawned. The clock in the hall chimed distantly, two o'clock. She knew she had to get to sleep but her mind ran on, back to her favourite subject. Maybe Johnny would know whether she was sixteen or only fourteen as her aunt maintained. She would ask him, she thought. She turned over on her side and fell asleep.

Tuesday morning dawned cold but clear. In spite of missing sleep, Ada's heart was light as she ironed a mountain of shirts and sheets and tablecloths. Eliza came into the kitchen carrying the bucket she had just emptied in the yard drain and took it over to the sink to refill it. Tuesday was the day she scrubbed the front steps and polished the brasses.

'Bye, it's a wonder what a letter from a lad'll do!'

Ada looked up at her friend's joking remark. She had been smiling softly to herself and humming a tune without realising it.

'Better not let Doris see you or she's sure to think

something's up,' Eliza observed as she added a ladle of hot water from the boiler to the cold she had already run into the bucket.

Ada grinned wryly. 'Don't worry, I'm used to covering up now. I've done it all me life!'

'Never mind the old witch,' Eliza said quickly. 'You don't want to let the thoughts of her spoil your day tomorrow. I hope you have a grand time, pet, you don't get many good times.'

Doris Parker came into the kitchen from the front of the house and glared suspiciously at the two girls. 'Howay then, the pair of you, get on with your work!'

Ada bent her head over the pillowcase she was ironing and forbore to answer.

Chapter Six

Wednesday came at last and, with her aunt safely upstairs for her lie-down, Ada hurried round to Eliza's house and changed into the blue outfit. With Eliza's good wishes ringing in her ears, she sped up to the station in time to meet the three-o'clock train.

She heard the hoot of the engine and saw the smoke rising in the distance as it came slowly round the bend from Shildon. She stepped forward anxiously. The wind was biting though the day was bright, but it was not only the cold that made her shiver.

She looked down at the pretty dress which had been Eliza's wedding gown. It was the nicest thing she had ever worn. Its tight sleeves were puffed at the shoulders and its formed bodice accentuated her tiny waist and swelling breasts above the billowing, full skirt. She would never be able to thank Eliza enough for the dress and the matching light jacket.

The train was drawing into the station. Ada's breast rose and fell quickly and her pulse raced as the engine came to a halt. There was a hissing of steam and all the rowdiness of the porters shouting and doors banging as people jumped onto the platform. Ada couldn't see Johnny anywhere. She was sure she had looked at every passenger who got off the train and she stood quite still until every last one had left the platform, but nowhere could she see the gangling lad with the bright-red hair and green eyes.

The excitement died from her eyes and a great weight of disappointment settled on her. Sadly she sat down on the bench outside the station master's office and stared unseeingly at the hard concrete of the platform. Her expressive face portrayed her feelings exactly.

So it was that Johnny saw her as he climbed down from the first-class carriage. An air of authority sat on him as naturally as did his well-cut clothes; his broad shoulders were encased in Harris tweed. Ada had become a woman since last they met but there was no mistaking those strikingly beautiful violet eyes set in the rose and white face. Those eyes were now suspiciously wet.

'Lorinda.'

The sound of her name, spoken so softly in that well-remembered voice, brought her leaping to her feet, her face vitally alive in her gladness. The contrast with the moment before was striking. There he stood before her,

her Johnny, a man now, broad and dependable, his bright eyes laughing and causing a confused melting feeling in her stomach.

Involuntarily her arms went out to him. Then, suddenly shy and gauche, she dropped them again to her sides and veiled her eyes with her long lashes. Her voice was a mumble as she greeted him. What would he think of her, being so forward?

'Hello, Johnny.'

Johnny was having none of it. He took her by the shoulders and kissed her soundly on one cheek and then the other before holding her away from him and laughing down into her face.

'Is that all you have to say to me? After all this time?' he teased, grinning widely.

Ada laughed shyly. 'How are you, Johnny? You look so fine, I thought it was a gentleman, I didn't recognise you. I thought you weren't coming!'

'Not coming? I said I was coming, didn't I? And guess what I've brought for you!' Laughing he gave an exaggerated bow and held out a bag of pear drops.

'Oh, Johnny! Pear drops! Fancy you still remembering how I liked pear drops!' And it just goes to show you still think of me as a child, said a small, warning voice in the back of her mind but she quickly pushed it away.

'Well, let's not waste any time. I want to know every-thing that has happened since I saw you. There's such a lot for me to catch up on.' Johnny took her arm and turned towards the station exit.

Ada laughed, conscious only of the feel of Johnny's hand as it clasped her arm; happiness welled up in her as they joined the crowds thronging South Road. Shop folk, most of them: Wednesday being half-day closing, they were out for a stroll in the fresh air.

'Where shall we go, then?' Johnny put a comradely arm about her shoulders. 'I have the afternoon and early evening, I can catch a late train back.'

'Oh, Johnny, I've to get back to do the teas.' Suddenly the long afternoon before them seemed dreadfully short to Ada, and her tone was doleful. Though the huge dinners which had been served to the iron workers at six o'clock were not necessary with the new clientele, the artistes expected a light meal before the show and supper afterwards.

Johnny smiled down at her. 'Well, cheer up, pet. We'll go to the Bishop's Park. We can have a good old chinwag and you can tell me everything and I'll tell you about everything.' Johnny was bright and happy, and Ada's spirits soared once again from their temporary low.

They were so wrapped up in one another that they failed to notice the man standing in the doorway of Braithwaite's, the newsagent on the corner of the market-place. Uncle Harry was collecting his *Northern Echo*. He, on the other hand, did not fail to see the young couple.

He took particular notice of their closeness and stored the information away in his mind for later use.

Looking back on that magical afternoon, Ada could hardly believe it had actually happened, it was all so dreamlike. She and Johnny strolled under the arch to the long, broad path running alongside the Bishop's Castle. The sun sparkled on the new and intensely green grass of the lawns on their left while to their right the buds on the trees were bursting green at the tips. The gardens of the castle sloped down to the river bubbling away at the bottom of Durham Chare.

She felt a kinship with the other young couples who were walking along to the kissing gate leading to the natural park, where they could wander off and find little private places among the trees. Oh, the sun shone and Johnny was gallant, holding the gate open for her to sweep through nonchalantly. And she could pretend that they were real lovers planning a future together.

'Let's walk up to the deer house,' Johnny suggested. 'If we go down to the river on the other side we'll be sheltered.'

Ada readily agreed; she would have agreed to go anywhere with him. She was intoxicated with his nearness, walking on air rather than the rough gravel path. Sneaking a glance up at him, she found he was gazing down at her and they both burst out laughing in delight.

She was enchanted with everything around her – the brightness of the grass, the shape of an oak leaf.

Soon they were sitting in a grassy hollow warmed by the sun and sheltered from the still sharp breeze. The river was full with the spring rains and the water was brown and peaty as it tinkled along before them. Johnny was quiet, simply watching her, a gentle smile on his face. He was fascinated by the sparkle in her eyes and her eager chatter.

At Johnny's prompting, Ada told him about the lodging-house 'guests'. One with a funny name, Will E. Stoppit, had been on at the Hippodrome when it opened just before Christmas. Then there was Jenny, a soprano who sang in her bedroom when she came in from the theatre, no matter how late the hour. How Ada loved to hear her clear, sweet voice!

Johnny was content to watch her animated face as she talked, and a warm feeling of protectiveness and something else indefinable crept over him. When she grew quiet and sat watching the sunlight on the water, he began to tell of his own hopes and dreams.

'One day, pet, one day I'll be at the top. One day the mill will run to my ideas, my designs. We'll be more efficient, more productive. Yet we can still be fairer to the men, it will be great for them too.' He paused, visualising this Utopia.

'You must be very high up in the steelworks now,

Johnny,' Ada said humbly and looked up at him wonder-ingly. 'You dress so fine, you are a gentleman now.' The thought saddened her. Johnny was going away in more ways than one, and soon he would be out of her reach.

'Get away with you!' Johnny laughed softly. 'I'm still Johnny Fenwick who brings you pear drops and you're still my Ada-Lorinda. Unless . . . I suppose you have a boyfriend now? The lads won't leave a bonny lass like you alone; I bet you have loads of lads after you.'

'Oh no, Johnny, not a one. I don't want lads after me. Any road, you know Auntie Doris, she'd murder me!'

Johnny's face darkened. Yes indeed, he knew Auntie Doris and he knew Uncle Harry, too. Now that he was older he understood more about Harry Parker and he looked down at Ada as he remembered his suspicions of long ago. But Ada looked so innocent sitting there on the grass – surely there was nothing like that, everything must be all right. Still, he couldn't help wondering. He glanced at his wristwatch. Goodness, it was five o'clock! Scrabbling to his feet, he pulled Ada up after him.

'Come on, pet, time to go or you'll have Auntie Doris out for your blood! I was going to take you out to tea too, and now it's too late. And I may as well catch the next train.'

The afternoon was rapidly descending into evening; the sun was falling down behind the ridge of the town and Ada shivered.

'Do you live in a very grand house, Johnny?' she asked in a very small voice as she felt the gulf widening between them.

'Oh, a very grand house!' he teased, seizing her hand in his and running along the path, pulling her breathless behind him, laughing at her protests. Stopping, he put his hands around her waist and swung her off her feet, round in an arc as easily as if she was the small child he had known so long ago. Seeing the dampness in her eyes, he squeezed her hands in his and took them to his lips.

'Cheer up, love! It's all right, I promise it is. I'll be back. And one day, when you have summoned up the courage to leave that miserable house and your Auntie Doris Parker, we will fly away together on a magic carpet, clean across the world!'

It was almost dark when Ada let herself in through the back door of the house. She went straight up to her room to change, thankful that Auntie Doris was nowhere about. She was very late but Eliza had covered for her, she had the salad washed and the shoulder bacon sliced and set out on plates all ready to serve when Ada came back into the kitchen, dressed once again in her dark shirtwaister and serge skirt. They had no time to talk until after the meal was served and the dishes brought back from the dining room.

'Howay then, tell me all about it!' Eliza said as they

shared the washing-up. They were on their own apart from Bertie, who was dozing in the wooden armchair by the range.

'Tell you about what?' Ada grinned and shrank playfully away as Eliza threatened her with the dishcloth.

'Oh, you mean this afternoon. It was all right, I suppose.' Eliza pulled a disbelieving face and Ada burst out laughing. 'Oh, Eliza, it was lovely. Johnny is lovely. He's tall and handsome and he's rich, you wouldn't believe how he looked! His clothes were lovely, he's a real toff, so he is. And we walked down the park and sat on the grass – though I didn't get the dress stained or anything, Johnny put his handkerchief down – and we talked and talked and, oh, he's lovely, Eliza!' The excitement died away from her eyes and her voice was quieter as she went on, 'But Eliza, he still thinks I'm a little girl, he does.'

'Eeh, don't worry about that, man! He'll soon notice you've grown up if I know anything about lads! He's coming back, isn't he?'

'He said he'll come back . . .'

'Who said he'll come back?' Auntie Doris limped into the kitchen. She had grown stout in the last few years and her joints were painful as well as her leg ulcers. She rarely helped in the kitchen now, simply keeping an eye on the two girls; she relied heavily on Ada. Now she glared at Ada suspiciously.

'Er . . .' Ada quavered, unable to think of an answer.

'Professor Naughton, Mrs Parker,' Eliza intervened swiftly. 'He said he did so well at the theatre he'll come again next season.'

Ada let out her breath in relief: that was a bit of quick thinking! Eliza rinsed the sink and hung up the dishcloth to dry, acting normally to cover Ada's moment of confusion.

'That's that, then!' she said. Scooping up little Bertie, she wrapped him in her shawl. 'Howay, it's home time for us and up the loft to bed, pet.' She went out of the back door, winking at Ada surreptitiously as she passed.

'She hasn't long to go,' Auntie Doris observed as Eliza's bulky form retreated down the yard. 'Now we're going to have to look for someone else and we won't get anyone as cheap as Eliza, not unless we can find another widow with a bairn hanging round her.' She gazed thoughtfully at Ada. 'Unless you think you can manage on your own, like.'

'Auntie Doris!' Ada protested. 'How can I manage on my own when the house is full?'

'Well, we'll see,' said her aunt tartly. 'Girls these days have no gratitude.' She limped out of the kitchen, banging the door behind her.

Chapter Seven

Ada felt weary and defeated as she turned off the gaslight in the kitchen and climbed the stairs to her attic bedroom. A life of drudgery stretched before her in her mind's eye as her aunt's words rang in her ears. She closed the door behind her and placed the candlestick on the chest of drawers, which, apart from a battered washstand, was the only piece of furniture in the room besides the bed. Though the rest of the house was lit by gas, the system did not extend to the attics.

Sighing, Ada sat down on the bed and took off her boots. How could Auntie Doris expect her to take on Eliza's work on top of her own? She felt the whole day had been spoiled.

Rebellion began to take shape in her thoughts. She would run away – she was old enough to work for a living without the help of Auntie Doris and Uncle Harry. The workhouse couldn't get her now. All she needed was the courage to set out on her own. Blowing out the candle, Ada climbed into the narrow iron bed and lay back on the pillow, stretching out and consciously relaxing. She was too tired. Tomorrow was soon enough to worry about the future. For tonight she had the meeting with Johnny to think about, which was so much more pleasant. A smile curved her lips as she relived the lovely afternoon and her eyelids drooped slowly till at last she fell asleep, her worries forgotten.

A muffled thud intruded on her dreams. Vaguely she wondered what it was before drowsily turning over onto her side so that she was facing the door. She snuggled down further – and saw the door open to the steep attic staircase. Blinking, she stared at it. The dark hole where the door should be was visible in the moonlight which filtered through the tiny skylight.

She was suddenly wide awake as danger signals rang in her head – had she forgotten to turn the key? But she knew she had closed the door. Struggling to sit up, she felt a hand on her arm holding her down and involuntarily she opened her mouth to scream.

'Quiet now. You'll hush up, my girl, if you know what's good for you.' Ada's stomach knotted as she realised the whispering voice belonged to Uncle Harry.

'Leave me alone! Don't you touch me! I'll yell so loud the whole house will be up here and Auntie Doris with them!'

'Oh no, you won't, my high and mighty lass. I saw you today. Oh aye, I did, I saw you, you and that fancy gentleman. How long have you been sneaking out and meeting lads, eh? What do you think Doris would do about that if she knew? And don't think I don't know what you were up to, and you all prissy and prim wi' me. All the same, you lasses are. Aye, you were away down the park and you don't go down there wi' a chap for nowt. Rolling in the grass you and him no doubt, you dirty little buggers!'

'We didn't! It wasn't like that.' Ada almost choked over the words.

'No? Well, I saw you and if you want me to keep my mouth shut you'll give me a bit of what he was getting!' Harry kept his voice low but all the time he was pulling at her nightdress, his dank, bony hands fumbling at her as she tried to fight him off.

'I don't care what you saw,' Ada whispered desperately. 'You leave me alone or I'll yell the house down!' She opened her mouth wide as his fingers found the soft flesh of her breast and dug in cruelly.

The scream died in her throat, however, as Harry Parker held her by that breast and, doubling his other fist, drove it into the side of her head, knocking her back onto the pillow. As she lay there stunned he quickly closed the door and, still speaking softly, almost conversationally, he returned to her, stripping off her nightgown, squeezing and pulling till the pain brought her back to consciousness.

'Oh no, my lass, you won't scream. You'll do just as I say. You didn't have me fooled, you little whore. This is what you wanted all the time, wasn't it? Aye, it was, wiggling your little bottom at me all the time and in front of Doris an' all. Oh aye, you led me on all right.'

In the moonlight Ada's white skin glistened with sweat as she tried to throw him off, but though he was a small man he was still a man and she was tiny for her age. Almost absent-mindedly he slapped her hard across one cheek and back across the other. She moaned softly as a trickle of blood appeared at the corner of her mouth and ran down her chin. Semi-conscious again, she was barely aware of him until a great shaft of pain sprang through her whole body and a cry was wrung from her. But he was ready for it and a hand was clamped over her mouth, cutting off the cry before it began.

A minute later it was over and Uncle Harry pulled himself off her. He clambered to his feet and stood looking down on her as she sobbed quietly, shivering and in shock.

'You'd better tidy yourself up,' he remarked and fingered her chin, examining her battered little face. It's your own fault you got hurt, you know. You shouldn't have fought wi' me.' He studied her for a moment or two. 'You can say you fell down the stairs, that'll be the best.'

He nodded his head, pleased with his own idea. 'And don't try to blame me for it or you'll be right sorry. I'll tell Doris about your fancy man – it was that Johnny Fenwick, wasn't it? Aye, it's just come to me, that's who it was, I remember him from years ago. He's gone up in the world, I must say, but then he always did think he was better than us.' Uncle Harry walked to the door but as he reached for the knob he turned back to her.

'Any road, even if you did tell Doris and she believed you, she'd still turn you out of the house. And then where would you go? It would be Oaklands Workhouse for you then, my lass. So you'd better leave your door unlocked from now on. I might fancy a bit tomorrow night.' And with this parting shot Harry Parker disappeared down the stairs.

Ada lay still, her whole body throbbing with pain. 'Tomorrow night.' The words rang in her brain, she could think of nothing else. It would happen over and over, for as long as Harry Parker lived. She couldn't stand it, she couldn't live through it again. Anything was better than that, even the workhouse.

Gingerly she pulled herself up into an upright position and carefully placed her feet on the floor. The lino was blessedly cool on the hot soles of her feet as she dragged herself over to the chest of drawers. Feeling about for the matches, she found them at last, lit the stub of candle and peered at her face in the looking glass. Her left eye was closing rapidly and her upper lip was swollen and cut. Carefully she probed her aching teeth with her tongue, wincing as she caught against her bruised cheek. Not too bad, she thought, at least none of them was actually loose.

Ada moved to the washstand by the door and poured water from the battered enamel jug into the basin. She bathed her face, wincing as the water stung the cuts. Then, stripping off the remains of her nightgown, she soaped the harsh flannel and scrubbed her body, rubbing the filth of the act away, almost rejoicing in the further pain from her bruises. But when she was finished she still felt unclean. Taking a blanket, she wrapped it around her naked body and lay down on top of the bed, waiting for the dawn.

A plan began to form in her mind but she needed to rest at least for a few hours before she could put it into effect. No, no, Uncle Harry, she thought, you are wrong. I won't go to the workhouse. I can keep myself. Determination grew in her and after a while her shivering body stilled and she fell into a light sleep.

At seven o'clock next morning a slight figure clad in a black skirt and with a shawl pulled over her head could be seen hurrying down Tenters Street and turning left into George Street. Ada had packed her few belongings in the box she had brought from her grandmother's house in Durham and was now taking it to Eliza's. She had to catch Eliza before she set out with Bertie for her work in the boarding house. As Ada put the box down on the step and knocked on the door, she prayed it would be Eliza who answered, for she didn't feel at all like going into explanations with Eliza's aunt. At least not until she had seen her friend. Luckily it was Eliza who opened the door.

'Gracious, Ada, what in the world has happened to you?' Eliza stared in horror at Ada's battered face before recollecting herself and standing back from the door. 'Come on, howay into the kitchen, pet, you can tell me all about it in the warm. Howay, never mind your box – I'll get it – just go away through. Auntie's still in bed, she's feeling bad.' Eliza picked up the box easily with her strong arms and shoulders and placed it by the hall stand before hurrying Ada through a narrow passage to the kitchen. Sitting Ada down before the range, where a blazing fire supported a large, black iron kettle, Eliza gazed at the slight figure of her friend in consternation.

Ada sat beside the fire, teeth clenched to stop their chattering, purple bruises standing out against the white of her face. 'What was it? Did *they* do this to you? Just because you went out with a lad? Did they find out? Eeh, by God, I'll swing for those two! I will!' Eliza began to shake with rage and her normally placid voice rose. Bertie, who was gazing at Ada with his great, dark eyes, began to whimper. Ada couldn't speak for she knew if she tried she would break down.

'There now.' Eliza lowered her voice and put a protective arm around Ada's shoulders. 'There now, pet, you're all right here, nobody can touch you. You needn't say anything yet. I'll make some tea and dripping toast and when you've had a bite to eat we'll talk.'

Ada gave a convulsive sob as the warmth began to seep through to her bones. She hadn't realised she was so cold, though the frost had lain white on the pavement as she had walked through the streets. Bertie came to her and took hold of her hand, laying his head on her knee and gazing up at her face anxiously.

Eliza said no more but cut slices of bread and held them to the bars of the grate with a toasting fork. When the toast was ready she got a pot of beef dripping from the cupboard and spread it on the toast. She mashed the tea in a large, brown pot and poured Ada a mug, adding a dollop of condensed milk.

'Howay, Bertie.' Eliza lifted the child and sat him at the table with a slice of bread and dripping and a cup of milk before him. Once Bertie was contentedly chewing on the toast, with rivulets of fat running down his chin, she turned to Ada, waiting until her friend had sipped the tea and eaten a little toast.

'Now then, pet.' Eliza settled herself in the chair opposite Ada. 'Now, tell me what ails you.'

Ada swallowed hard. 'It wasn't Auntie Doris. Auntie Doris knows nothing about it.' She stopped speaking and took a bite of dripping toast. The warmth of the fire and the hot sweet tea were having a calming effect on her. The hollow feeling inside her stomach was fading; she chewed cautiously, using the right side of her mouth only. She realised she must have been hungry in spite of everything and finished her tea and toast with Eliza watching impatiently.

'I'm finished, Mam, can I get down now?' Bertie broke the silence as he looked over to Eliza, a rim of milk on his upper lip.

'Aye, pet.' Eliza wiped his mouth with the corner of her apron and lifted him down from the table. 'Go and play in the front room, hinny. Quietly now, Ada and me want to have a talk.'

'Yes, Mam.' Obediently the boy trotted to the door which led into the passage.

The kitchen was quiet for a few minutes, the ticking of the clock sounding loud in the silence. Ada stared into the fire, not knowing how to start. She felt so dirty and guilty somehow – maybe it was her own fault, maybe she could have done something . . .

'Well, Ada?' Eliza prompted. 'You'll have to tell me. I can't help you if I don't know what it's all about.'

'Yes.'

Ada gazed into the fire still as she began to tell her

story. She spoke in a flat, monotonous tone, rapidly. Eliza had to lean forward to catch all the words and when she finally realised what Ada was saying her heart ached with pity and a rising fury. Only a bairn! she thought indignantly, forgetting the small age difference between herself and Ada.

'We should get the polis!' she said at last when Ada had relapsed into silence, her tale told. 'That dirty old sod's not getting away with this! Bye, I'm so mad, I could knock him senseless meself!' But even as she said it she knew it would harm Ada too much if the story came out – mud would stick, as they say.

'No, Eliza, no, we can't do that. He'll put the blame on Johnny and I couldn't bear it! I couldn't bear for Johnny to know about it either! And everyone would know about me if we go to the polis, don't you think I feel dirty enough? And no one would believe me any road!'

'Eeh, I don't know. We have to do something, man! He can't just get away with it!' Eliza was at a loss; she cast about for an answer to the dilemma and found none. 'Well,' she said at last, 'what can we do? Look, wait on a minute and I'll just take Auntie some breakfast up. Then we can decide what to do.' She put the kettle on the fire and made some fresh toast. Warming the tea with boiling water, she set a mug and a plate of toast on a tin tray and went out of the kitchen.

Bertie wandered in and climbed onto Ada's lap,

causing her to wince as his head brushed against her bruised breast.

'What's the matter, Auntie Ada?' A tiny frown appeared on his brow as he felt her flinch.

'Nothing. Nothing's the matter, pet.' Ada hugged him to her in spite of the pain for she found comfort in the little body in her arms.

'Bertie! Leave Auntie Ada alone! She's feeling bad!'

Eliza spoke sharply as she came back in. Her son's lower lip quivered and pouted, ready for tears. Sighing, she picked him up and set him on her knee. 'No, no, don't cry, pet, Mammy's not cross. It's just that Ada's feeling bad.'

'I'm all right, Eliza,' Ada suddenly said resolutely. 'And I think I know what I'm going to do, an' all. That is, if you'll help me?' Ada faltered on these last words and the appeal was not lost on Eliza.

'Course I will, hinny! You know I will! Just you tell me what to do and I'll do it.'

'Well, I thought, if you go to work as if you hadn't seen me, do you think? I know you're going to be late but you can say your auntie kept you or something. She was bad or something. If I can stay here until about eleven I can catch the train to Durham. I'll be able to get a place there.'

'Without money and wearing a black eye like you've got? Don't be so daft! Nobody's going to take you on looking like that. No, it'll be best if you stay here a few days, that's what I think. And Auntie won't mind, I'll ask her.'

Eliza's face puckered with anger as she thought about Ada's battered face. 'Eeh, mind, I'll have a job keeping me mouth shut, though, if I see Harry Parker, that is. Though I don't see a lot of him usually. But if I do –' She glanced up at the clock on the wall. 'Look, pet, I'd better be off or I'm going to be really late. And Doris Parker might guess the reason, realise where you are. Aye, she'll likely tumble to it.'

'What about Bertie?'

'No, no, Bertie won't let on. He doesn't talk much and never to those two.' Liza tied Bertie's muffler across his chest and fastened it at the back before taking his hand and leading him out of the kitchen. I'll nip back after dinner when Doris Parker's taking her nap,' she called over her shoulder.

Ada was left in the quiet kitchen. She felt decidedly less threatened now; having a friend she could rely on made all the difference. She stared into the fire and thought about the future. Eliza was right, with her face all bruised she would be noticed as soon as she left the house. Someone would tell Auntie Doris where she was. And even if she got to Durham, who would take her on? They would think she was trouble and there were plenty of other girls looking for work. No one wanted a girl who carried trouble with her.

At least I have money, she mused. She had enough to get by on for a short while if she was very careful. She fingered the two sovereigns in her pocket. They had been on the back-room mantelpiece, hidden away in a pot. Auntie Doris kept the housekeeping money there and Ada didn't feel a bit guilty about taking it. She reckoned she was due some back wages for her years of work. And then she had ten shillings of her own, money saved from tips. Sometimes, if the houses had been good during the week, the theatre folk could be generous. Oh, aye, she could manage for a few weeks.

Why she wanted to go to Durham she didn't know, it was so long since she had been there. But she'd been happy there with her grannie. As she remembered it, Durham was lovely. Her mind returned to her aches and pains as she moved in the chair. Oh, if only she could have gone to Middlesbrough and poured out the whole story to Johnny! She longed for that, but of course she couldn't. If Johnny knew what had happened, he wouldn't want her any more. Not that he had really wanted her before, she thought dismally. She felt so low and worthless, she sank down in the chair and closed her eyes. At last nature took a hand and she fell asleep by the fire, her dark head drooping over her arm.

*

A hand on Ada's arm made her start up in alarm, shrinking away and turning to face whoever it was.

'Leave me be!' she shouted, her chin up, her fists raised and her eyes dark with horror.

'Nay, nay, lass!' Mrs Rutherford, Eliza's aunt, stepped back and fluttered her hands in concern. 'Nay, lass, it's only me and I'm not going to hurt you. Eeh, that must have been an awful dream.'

Ada dropped her hands and shook her head slightly to clear it. She felt befuddled and weary, heavy with sleep. 'I'm sorry, Mrs Rutherford,' she mumbled and brushed a dark curl from her forehead with the back of her hand.

The old woman came nearer and inspected Ada's bruised face. Eliza must have given her aunt her own version of what had happened for she stepped back tut-tutting.

'Eeh, if those two did that to a bit of a lass they want laying in! There's no call for it, even if you had been out wi' a lad!'

'Oh, Mrs Rutherford!' Ada said helplessly. Of course everyone would think she'd done something bad to deserve such a hiding.

'I didn't do anything, nothing at all!'

'Aye, well, hinny, mebbe you didn't. The Lord knows they're a rum pair up at that boarding house! Never mind, when Eliza comes in we'll have a talk and decide what's to be done. But for the minute you'd better sit down afore you fall down. We'll have a nice cup of tea and a bite.'

Ada smiled gratefully at the old lady. She was a plump, motherly-looking woman but her face betrayed the hard life she had led. Eliza might have had some hard blows in her life but at least she had an auntie worth ten of Doris Parker! She remembered the story Eliza had told her in snippets as they were working together in the boarding house.

'Auntie was a widow early in life, just like me,' Eliza had said. 'She worked in the fields on a farm out Bolam way. Then she lost the bairn she was carrying. She was hoeing turnips when it happened and she had a bad time with it. Then there was the diphtheria, that took her other two.'

Ada watched her as she moved about the kitchen. She had a calm, placid air about her, obviously she was not surprised by any disaster life showed her.

'I'll make the toast then, eh?' Ada made to rise but the old lady shooed her back into her chair.

'Nay, lass, I know where everything is.'

She moved heavily from table to cupboard to range, placing the iron frying pan on the glowing coals in the grate and cutting two slices of fatty belly bacon. The pot of tea she made was so strong you could stand the spoon up in it. Even though it wasn't long since she had eaten with Eliza, Ada tucked into her share of the food and drank the hot, sweet tea. For the simple meal was delicious and she felt at home and safe in the bare little kitchen. Yet she knew she couldn't stay for long. Mrs Rutherford hardly had enough to feed herself and Eliza was the same. No, she would have to carry on with her plan to go to Durham as soon as her face returned to normal.

'Bye, what a carry-on there was up there! There's war on right enough!' Eliza bustled in by the back door with Bertie holding onto her skirt. 'Your Auntie Doris is ranting and raving about thieving lasses with bad blood in them who turn on the only family they've got and have ever tried to help them. And Harry Parker, he's skulking out of the road, hiding upstairs. Which is a good thing really, for I swear, I'd have a job not riving him to bits with me bare hands! If I got hold of him, like.' Eliza paused for breath and smiled at Ada.

'You all right, pet? Feel a bit better now, do you?'

'Eeh, Eliza!' Ada had only heard the bit about thieving and suddenly felt guilty about the two pounds. 'She didn't guess where I was, did she? Is she going to fetch the polis?' Her eyes widened in alarm.

'Why, no, man, she's all talk!' Eliza was dismissive. 'She wouldn't dare any road – if she did, it would all come out about her keeping you as a skivvy. Don't worry, pet! I tell you what, though, it wasn't easy to slip out the day! That one's been in and out of the kitchen all morning. Not that she got any work done before she had to have a sit-down again. Any road, she had to go for a lie-down in the end.' Eliza struck a pose with her hands on her hips and an expression on her face remarkably like Doris Parker's.

' "That lass'll be the death of me! I'll have to have a lie-down or else I'll be laid up and then what'll we do?" And off she went, so I slipped out with the bairn and here we are.' Eliza plumped down on a chair by the fire and stretched out her hands to the blaze.

'Bye, but my back is giving me gyp! I tell you what, it'll be a relief when the babby comes and I can have a few days' rest. Aye, and it'll serve her right, that one, she'll have to get someone else and pay them right, that's what!' She shook her head in satisfaction as Mrs Rutherford gave her a pot of tea.

'Aye, well, get that down you. And what's going to happen when the babby comes? That's what I want to know. We're just going to have to have a proper talk about it. It's no use putting it off,' she said.

Eliza sighed heavily. It was true, the baby was well down now, she could have it any time. And there would be no parish relief in Bishop, she'd have to go back to her own parish in West Auckland. There'd be a place to find and Bertie to see to as well as any new baby, and at the minute, there was Ada.

*

That night, Eliza's baby slipped into the world easily and swiftly. Ada, who was sleeping on a shake-down bed on the floor of Eliza's bedroom, hardly had time to fetch the midwife before it was all over.

The new baby was a tiny version of Bertie and Eliza named him Miles, after her own father. Bertie, who had been bundled out of the bedroom still asleep, was bewildered to wake up wrapped in a blanket and lying on the settle in the front room.

'Mam?'

His frightened cry was heard by Ada as she came downstairs and she rushed in to the boy. He was sitting up on the settle, still with the blanket round him, his hair tousled and his sleep-filled eyes staring round him.

'It's all right, pet,' she hastened to reassure him. 'Come on now, I'll take you to your mam and then won't you be surprised!'

Ada carried him, complete with blanket, up the stairs and in to see his baby brother. He gazed wide-eyed, thumb in mouth for a moment, then suddenly struggled out of Ada's arms and climbed into the bed with his mother.

'Bertie!' Ada made to take him back but Eliza would have none of it.

'Let him be,' she commanded, lying back on the pillows with a son on each arm.

'I'll send the lad next door up to the Parkers, eh?' Mrs

Rutherford came in behind Ada. 'Bye,' she continued with a rare smile, 'I can just see her face when she finds out she has it all to do herself until she gets somebody.'

'I don't care, I'm not going back.' Ada was guiltily defiant.

''deed no, pet!' the old lady exclaimed.

'Aw, she'll soon find someone else, don't worry about it,' Eliza asserted. 'You've got away now, it would be daft going back.'

Ada had been working out how to avoid doing just that. She would spend a few days in George Street, she thought, helping out until Eliza got over her lying-in period, but she would insist on giving Mrs Rutherford five shillings for her food.

The problem would be how to get out of the town without the Parkers seeing her. She was sure they would be watching the railway station. Now, contemplating Eliza and her children, she came to a decision.

'I'll go on Tuesday morning, Eliza – that is, if you're well enough by then. I'll get off early, about five in the morning when nobody's about. I'll walk to Spennymoor, I can get a train to Durham there.'

A shadow crossed Eliza's face. 'You will be all right now? I mean, when you get to Durham?'

'I think so. There's plenty of work there, especially during term time, if you don't mind scrubbing and such. Yes, I'll be all right.'

Mrs Rutherford listened to the conversation in silence. Poor lass, she thought, but what can we do? We need all we've got for our own. For Eliza and her children were her whole family now.

Chapter Eight

Ada's face was only a slight yellowy brown on one side the morning she set off on her journey to Durham City. She stood at the door of the house in George Street saying her goodbyes to Eliza, whispering so as not to wake up Mrs Rutherford or the children.

'Eeh, pet, I do hope you're going to be all right,' Eliza murmured anxiously. 'You'll let us know, won't you? I mean, about getting a place to stay and work and everything. If you don't manage, come back here now, promise?'

'I'll be all right, really I will.' Ada wrapped her shawl around her head, shivering in the chill of the pre-dawn darkness. 'I'll be getting on now, Eliza. Thank you for everything, you've been a true friend to me. I will let you know, I'll find a way.' She hugged her friend and kissed her on the cheek. Indeed, now the time had come she did have misgivings about going. But she couldn't stay here, she told herself. Picking up her box she set off down the street, turning to wave to Eliza as she reached the corner. She had to fight the impulse to turn back as she saw Eliza's arm waving vigorously in reply.

Down Durham Chare she went and out on the road to Spennymoor, passing no one on her journey but the farmers' milk carts with their churns and measuring cans, on their way to deliver milk in Bishop Auckland. She had eight miles to walk to Spennymoor and as she trudged along her natural optimism began to surface once more.

I'm not frightened of hard work, she told herself, and living anywhere will be better than living in the same house as Uncle Harry. She could still remember the name of the street in Gilesgate where she had lived with her grannie, Thomas Street it was. She would go there first and see if she could get lodgings with one of Grannie's neighbours. Most of the women in the street took in lodgers, it all helped to pay the rent.

Ada had to pause once or twice on the road to have a rest; though her basket-work box had not seemed heavy as she set out on her journey, it got progressively heavier as time went on. Yet as the day lightened and the sun came up, so did her spirits. She breathed heavily of the fresh, country air and began to look about her at the hilly countryside. The pastures were bright with new green and the grass sparkled in the morning sun. Lambs were skipping and jumping beside their mothers and birds were singing. New life was everywhere.

Just like me, she thought as she picked up her box once again and headed for the village she could see in the distance, Middlestone Moor. My new life starts today.

Passing through Middlestone Moor she saw more people about, miners coming off night shift and others on their way to work. Most of them said, 'Good morning' as they passed Ada, attracted by her bright, young face. She had let her shawl slip from her shoulders as the sun became warmer and even her black shirtwaister and serge skirt could not disguise her lovely figure and springing vitality.

By mid-morning she had reached the small but growing town of Spennymoor. She had to wait half an hour on the platform for the train to arrive and she stood beside her box, trying to look unobtrusive. She began to be fearful that somehow her aunt had found out where she was and sent someone after her, or perhaps had notified the police. A policeman came onto the platform and walked its length, whistling softly to himself as he eyed the few people waiting for the train. Ada shrank back behind a luggage trolley – was he looking at her suspiciously? But no, he passed on, he was simply waiting for the train the same as she was herself.

'Daftie!' she chided herself, but nevertheless she was very glad when the train puffed into the station and she was able to climb aboard. She found a seat in a third-class carriage and stowed her box on the rack. All the while her heart was beating rapidly. This was the first time Ada had left Bishop Auckland since she was a very small girl. In spite of her optimism, she knew she faced an uncertain future. Determinedly, she gazed out of the window at the fields, woods and rolling hills in the distance.

The journey was quite short and before she knew it the familiar shape of the cathedral appeared on the skyline. It had an immediate calming effect on Ada. She swallowed the sudden lump in her throat and took down her box, gravely refusing the offer of a young workman to help her with it.

'Thank you. I can manage,' she said and, taking her box, stepped down from the train. She handed her ticket in at the barrier and paused a moment before walking down the hill from the station. The sun was shining on the roofs below, the great cathedral towered over them like a guardian and Ada's sense of homecoming was almost overwhelming. Here she could begin to rebuild her life.

'Eeh, you mean to tell me you're Ada Leigh's little lass? Well! Who would have thought it? But mind, you have a bit of a look like her. The same lovely hair and skin. Have you been living with your mam? Bye, me and your grandma were good friends. I didn't half miss her when she died, poor thing. No, that's right, you went to live with your auntie, didn't you, I remember.' Mrs Dunne paused for breath before standing aside and motioning Ada forward into the front room which the front door opened directly into. 'Well, don't just stand there on the doorstep, hinny. It may be spring but the wind's still enough to cut you like a knife.'

Ada looked around her with interest as she went in. The room was furnished with a heavy mahogany sideboard and chiffonier, a whatnot on the wall crowded with knick-knacks, a pottery cottage emblazoned with 'A souvenir from Whitley Bay' and a rather fine Linthorpe pottery vase crowded among them. On the wall hung a pair of Sunderland plates with religious texts and a looking glass over the mantelpiece was framed in a dark oak. The walls themselves were covered in a light-brown paper patterned with sprays of faded flowers. The horsehair sofa and armchairs looked hard and uncomfortable and were devoid of cushions. But then, Ada reflected, front rooms weren't meant to be lived in, they were for show and Sundays.

Mrs Dunne herself was a sprightly woman of around sixty with birdlike blue eyes and faded, greying hair fastened back in a knot like Auntie Doris's, but there the likeness ended. Her smile was kindly as she studied Ada with interest.

'Bye, it's nice to see you again after all this time, mind!' Mrs Dunne's eyes sparkled with curiosity. 'Looking for a place to stay, you said? Left your auntie's, then?'

Ada stood awkwardly; she hadn't yet been invited to sit down.

'Yes, I have,' she said, then realised Mrs Dunne wanted her reasons. 'I fancied coming back to Durham,' she said lamely.

'Aye, well, I dare say it's nicer than Bishop.' Mrs Dunne was obviously waiting for more but Ada wasn't about to satisfy her.

'Yes. Well, I thought I'd get a room first and I thought I'd likely get one along here. I remembered the street, you see.'

'Fancy that! You were only a bairn when your grandma died, bless her soul!'

'I was seven,' Ada stated. 'Well, as I said, I thought I'd get a room and then I could look for work. I've a bit of money, I can afford to pay rent in advance.' Ada added the last bit hastily, having noticed the slight frown on Mrs Dunne's face, and that lady looked suddenly relieved.

'Well, as it happens – and mind, you're lucky, because I'm usually suited – I could let you have the back bedroom. I had a gentleman in it but he's gone to work in Darlington. You could give it a try if you like – two and sixpence for the room and no food, or five shillings with your breakfast. What do you think?'

Ada nodded eagerly, pleased to be settled. This was the third house she had tried in the street and the terms were no more than she had expected to pay.

'Mind, I want it in advance.' Mrs Dunne had become strictly businesslike.

Ada delved into her pocket and took out the money. 'I'll have breakfast, I think, Mrs Dunne,' she said. 'At least at first, till I've found my feet.'

Mrs Dunne took the money with a satisfied air. 'Howay into the kitchen, pet, I'll make a cup of tea. Then I'll show you the room.' Now that the business part was over, she had reverted to the kindly, gossipy woman who had opened the door. She sat Ada down at the kitchen table and pushed the kettle which had been simmering on the hob, back onto the coals. 'Mind,' she said as she worked, 'no men in the house.'

Ada looked suitably scandalised at the very idea and Mrs Dunne went on, 'What was your name, pet? Something fancy, I seem to remember?'

'Oh no, just Ada, I'm called Ada now.'

I don't have to be called Ada now, she realised suddenly. If she liked, she could call herself Lorinda. But only Johnny called her Lorinda now, it had become a special name. She wasn't sure she could bear to hear it from anyone else. A shadow crossed her face; bleakly she thought she had to put all thoughts of Johnny out of her mind, because he was way above her now.

Mrs Dunne glanced at her in surprise but offered no comment. It was no business of hers, so long as the lass could pay for the room she cared little about the name. She looked up at the mantelpiece where she had put Ada's money.

'Lucky that you've come just now, after the last lodger's gone,' she commented. 'Last month I would have turned you away and then where would we be?'

Ada said nothing. Hungry after her long walk of the morning, she was just glad of the bread and butter Mrs Dunne put out to have with their tea. Still, she was careful to eat no more than one piece, being sensible of the fact that it was an 'extra' and not included in her board.

Afterwards, Mrs Dunne showed her the bedroom. It was much as she had expected: a single iron bed, a chest of drawers and a washstand on one wall with an enamel jug and bowl standing on the marble top. It was cold and smelled slightly of damp but that was normal too. And the bed had two blankets on it with a Durham quilt on top so it would be snug enough. To Ada it was a haven and she was glad of it. She didn't even mind the damp-stained wallpaper, its dark blue relieved by the heavy red roses printed on it.

Ada wasted no time in looking for work. As soon as she had unpacked her box and laid her meagre possessions in the chest of drawers she put on her shawl and went out on the quest for employment. She knew it would be a waste of time asking at the university: the academic year would be drawing to a close in a few months and they would be unlikely to be taking on more servants now. But in the better part of the city, on the banks overlooking the Wear, there were many prosperous-looking houses. She decided she would try as many as she could before dark.

At three o'clock, her bright hopes were dimmed a little and she felt discouraged and dispirited. She had tried a number of would-be employers, to no avail.

'What do you want, girl? There's no free hand-outs here!'

'I'm not looking for a hand-out, I'm looking for work!' Ada was stung to reply to the red-faced cook who answered at one back door. 'I'm willing to do anything, washing, ironing, housework –'

'There's no work here either!' the cook snapped. 'We're well suited with what we've got! Now be off with you and stop wasting my time!'

Ada trudged down the drive and out into the roadway again. Her stomach rumbled and she remembered that she hadn't had anything to eat since breakfast, apart from that one piece of bread and butter at Mrs Dunne's house. Maybe if she found something she could make it do for the rest of the day. It was beginning to look as if her two sovereigns were going to have to last a long time. Abandoning the hunt for work, she turned for Silver

Street and a butcher's shop she had noticed on her way into Durham.

Once standing outside the shop, breathing in the heavenly smells from the hot pies and pasties, she hesitated. Her mouth watered at the thought of a pie, but she knew it wasn't sensible to buy one; if she went on at that rate she would soon run out of money. Pushing the temptation out of her mind, she went in.

'Two penny dips, please. And a quarter of hot pease pudding.' That should fill her empty stomach and last until breakfast-time at Mrs Dunne's, she thought.

'Mind, you are going to have a feast.' The butcher was disgruntled; the day was fast turning into evening and he hadn't sold anything like the number of pies he should have done.

Ada ignored him. All she was interested in was the small parcel he handed over to her in exchange for her threepence. It might not be a meat pie but it still smelled lovely. She found a sheltered spot down by the Wear and sat down to eat. The pease pudding she put between the two penny dips to make a sandwich; breaking about a quarter of it off to eat later in the evening, she tucked into the rest. Contentedly she gazed out over the river as she chewed, savouring every mouthful. Trout were rising to the evening flies and she watched a lone fisherman on the other side casting his line. With delight she saw a bedraggled water rat scuttling along within feet of her and going 'plop' into the water, where he quickly disappeared.

Bye, it was nice! Ada sighed with pleasure. Now she had eaten she felt more optimistic. She would be all right, she would, someone would take her on! Standing up, she brushed the few crumbs from her skirt and patted her hair tidy. There was time to try again before dark. Only this time, she thought, she would try houses a little less prosperous-looking, where they might have only one live-in servant. It would be people like that who might use a girl like her to do the washing and ironing and maybe the hard scrubbing.

Ada was right. Within a day or two she found enough work to keep her going. Hard unremitting work, washing and ironing at other people's houses, but paid work nevertheless. She still had a lot of disappointments, of course – some would-be employers looked dubiously at her slight figure and turned her away – but there were those who were willing to give her a trial, and they found her willingness and capacity for hard work made her well worth the small wage.

Every weekday morning, she rose early, breakfasted with Mrs Dunne on a good filling breakfast of oatmeal followed by bacon and fried bread, and set out for work. It involved a great deal of walking about the town in between the various houses, but the year was turning into summer and she enjoyed being out in the fresh air.

For half-a-crown a time Ada would pound clothes in a poss tub in back yards. lifting the heavy stick with the three-branched paddle at the bottom and driving it down again, forcing the soapy water through the clothes. She puffed and panted as she turned the wooden rollers of the great iron mangles and hung out the washing to dry, returning the next day to set flatirons on the hobs of kitchen fires to iron the clothes. She occupied her mind with dreaming about Johnny or sometimes imagining what sort of lives the owners of the house led or what the other rooms looked like. For she never got further than the kitchen in any of the houses she worked in. She bought a postcard and stamp and was going to ask Mrs Dunne to write a message on it for Eliza, but in the end she was too ashamed of letting her landlady know of her inability to read and write. Maybe some day soon she would manage to go to see her friend.

Happy was the night she returned to her lodging and a tiny worry at the back of her mind disappeared as she undressed for bed. Her monthly had come: she was not carrying Uncle Harry's bastard.

'I'll be all right now,' she said aloud in her relief. She stared into the small fly-spotted mirror of the washstand. 'And I won't be a washerwoman all my life, either. You'll see I won't.' Ada smiled at her reflection in the mirror and jumped into bed, snuggling down under the bedclothes, her eyelids drooping at once. For every night she was physically exhausted, but she was managing. Oh yes, she was managing fine.

Hanging out clothes one morning, a fine summery morning which made Ada feel glad to be alive, she paused for a minute, struck by the beauty of the garden beyond the kitchen enclosure. It was the first time she had worked at this house, she had been recommended to it. It was a square, stone-built house standing on the bank above the river, and belonged to a doctor she knew, Dr Gray.

A small breeze sprang up and Ada breathed deeply, delighting in the smell of roses and honeysuckle intermingled with that of freshly mown grass and the slightly soapy smell of the clean laundry fluttering on the line. Bye, it was grand! Ada hugged herself and unconsciously moved nearer the garden for a better look.

A girl of about her own age, fair-haired and delicate-seeming, a bit 'femmer' as Auntie Doris would say, was sitting on an ornate garden seat, a cushion at her back, reading a book. Ada watched her quietly. Bye, she was pretty, she thought. Sensing Ada's eyes on her, the girl looked up from her book and smiled.

'Good morning!' she called. 'Lovely day, isn't it?'

Ada was so surprised to be noticed by the girl that she

blushed heavily. Mumbling a reply, she turned at a rush and went back to her work. The girl, however, had laid down her book and sauntered over to the fence, where she watched Ada's activities with interest.

'Do you like doing the laundry?' she asked.

Ada paused again and looked across at the girl. She had friendly blue eyes and a wide, likeable smile despite her apparent frailty.

'Well, it has to be done,' Ada answered after a moment. Work was work, she thought, liking or not liking did not come into it.

'Oh, I'm sorry – I'm Virginia Gray, what's your name?'

'Ada, Miss.'

'Hello, Ada. Nice to meet you. I was getting bored by myself. I'm supposed to be getting some fresh air and sunshine, sitting here in the garden. But it is so boring with no one to talk to, don't you agree?'

Ada thought about it, considering the question gravely. Boredom was a strange concept to her. It was very, very rarely she had nothing to do, and then she was only too pleased for the tiny respites in her working day. Still, the lady must know what she was talking about, so best agree.

'Yes, Miss Gray,' she said shyly.

'Oh, Virginia, please. My name's Virginia, not stuffy old Miss Gray.'

'Yes, Miss Virginia.'

'No, not Miss Virginia, just Virginia,' she insisted. 'Well, Ada, let's have a talk, shall we? You can take a little break, can't you? Cook won't eat you! And I've been so ill with this wretched pneumonia, I can't go to school this term. I'm so lonely for most of the day!'

'Well, I don't know, I'll have to hang out the washing or it won't be dry by this afternoon.' Ada gazed at Virginia, flummoxed at the idea of anyone as old as this girl still going to school. She turned to the line and hung out a fine white linen shirt, watching it catch the breeze and lift in the air.

'Well, go on then, we'll talk while you work.' Virginia came through the gate which connected the two parts of the garden and leaned against the fence.

'But what would we talk about, miss?'

'Oh, I don't know. Do you like to read? What books do you like? What else do you do when you're not doing laundry?'

Ada paused, her mouth full of pegs. Here it was again, always her lack of reading embarrassed her. Why was this girl asking her such questions? She noticed the grass stains on the hem of Virginia's white broderie anglaise dress and sighed – that was more work for her, getting out the stains. The pay was the same whether the clothes were lightly or heavily soiled. Ada turned away and stretched a sheet along the line before replying; she pegged it firmly against the breeze, giving herself time to get over the upset she had no right at all to be feeling.

'I can't read, miss,' she said at last, 'and this is what I do, washing and ironing. When I'm not washing I'm ironing and when I'm doing neither I'm sleeping.'

Virginia didn't notice the shortness of Ada's tone, she was so astounded by the revelation. 'You can't read at all?' she gasped.

Ada kept her face averted. She didn't know why she had let out her secret to this girl whom she didn't even know. But it was done now.

'Not at all. Well, only a tiny bit.' Ada remembered the lessons long ago with Johnny.

'But didn't you go to school? Everyone goes to school, it's the law.' Virginia still couldn't understand.

'Well, I didn't, miss. I was too busy.'

'Busy? When you were a little girl? How could that be?'

Ada considered the question but decided that she wasn't going to answer it. She turned again to the basket of clothes, bending over it and taking out a bolster case. In the momentary silence, Virginia remembered her manners.

'Oh, I'm sorry, it's none of my business, is it? I was just interested, that's all.'

'That's all right, miss.'

'Oh, do call me Virginia.' A thought had just occurred

to her and impulsively she came straight out with it. 'I know! I'll teach you.'

Ada thought about it, picking up her empty basket and holding it against one hip. Girls like Virginia never saw any problems, she realised, not even the basic one of having to use all your time and energy in earning a living. But it would be lovely to learn to read and write.

'I haven't the time,' she replied at last, her voice dismal. 'I have to work.'

'No, no, you must have breaks. Just half an hour a day at least? Oh, come on, Ada, why not?' Virginia was all enthusiasm, she quite fancied herself as a teacher.

'Because I have to live, that's why not!' Ada burst out, then immediately regretted it, for she couldn't afford to lose a customer. 'I'm sorry, miss, I didn't mean to be disrespectful. But I do have to go now. I'll be back tomorrow to do the ironing.'

Ada turned to the kitchen door. It was time for her to go on to her next customer in Elvet, where a pile of ironing awaited her.

'They know nowt,' she said hopelessly under her breath, feeling the world on her shoulders. A world altogether different from that of Virginia Gray.

'Ada! Wait a minute,' Virginia called after her. 'Look, I'm sorry if I offended you. But do try and come.'

Ada stopped walking. Bye, she desperately wanted to read and write. If she could write she could send Johnny a letter. There would be no harm in writing to him. Maybe if she started a little earlier every morning and hurried between houses, and maybe if it didn't rain too often, so that the clothes dried on time . . . This might be the only chance she got, should she throw it away? Ada turned in her tracks and lifted her chin. She *would do it*, she determined.

'All right, miss.' Resolutely she looked at Virginia's triumphant smile before faltering. 'But are you sure? I mean, is it allowed? Your family might not like it.'

Virginia laughed. 'They won't mind. They'll be only too happy I have something to interest me. I'll see you tomorrow then? What time do you think?'

Ada considered, working out her day. 'I'll be doing the ironing here in the afternoon. I'll try to get here early, maybe by half past eleven. I can bring a sandwich if that's all right. Is that all right, miss?' Ada felt presumptuous, stating a time.

'Lovely. Well, I'll see you then, Ada. And don't forget, it's Virginia, not miss.'

As Ada went indoors, Virginia returned to her seat on the garden bench, pleased with herself. She was tiring already – she soon tired after her illness earlier in the year – but she felt a warm glow: she was doing something for someone else, it was a lovely feeling. It must be how Daddy feels when he cures people, she thought, relaxing against a cushion. That was why he didn't mind being called out during the night or in the middle of a meal. And wouldn't he be pleased with her for being so unselfish?

Ada went on to her next job with hope springing within her. She bought a penny dip in the market for her lunch and sat in the sun munching happily, savouring the taste of beef fat and gravy. The dip was especially nice today, she mused, the bread bun was soaked in gravy.

She leaned back against the wall, licking her fingers clean, and smiled softly to herself. She was happy, and it was a lovely day. The sun warmed her and shone off the bronze statue of the man on horseback in the middle of the marketplace. The stallholder glanced more than once at her small face so full of vitality and her huge violet eyes. She looked no more than fourteen, sitting there on a stone jutting out of the Town Hall wall. Her snowy white shirtwaister was open slightly at the neck, revealing the smooth, white skin of her throat.

Ada was oblivious of him. She was dreaming about the lovely letter she would write to Johnny, telling him she was seeking her fortune in Durham City. He would come to see her and they would walk along the river path by the racecourse and they would have a grand time –

Ada stopped dreaming with a jolt. She'd been away with the mixer there, she thought, Johnny wouldn't come to see her here. What did a fine gentleman like Johnny

Fenwick want with a washerwoman, and one who had been taken down at that? She stood up, the dreams fading from her eyes. Here she was wasting time when there was so much to do. She hurried away down the hill to Elvet. There was still that mountain of ironing to do before she got her two and sixpence to pay the rent.

Chapter Nine

That July, Johnny wrote again to Ada. He had recently acquired a spanking new car and was enormously proud of it. It was a Lanchester open tourer, very useful to him in his work, for Fred relied more and more on him to do business which in earlier days he had always done himself. Johnny had grown assured and knowledgeable about the business in the last few years; he had all the information he needed at his fingertips.

'You need a car,' Fred had said one day when Johnny missed his last train home and had to stay the night at Coventry. Johnny travelled around the country a lot now that Fred himself stayed at home more. So now there was the Lanchester for medium to short journeys. Of course, Johnny still had his heart set on designing but for the moment he was fully employed as a sales manager.

He thought about Ada when the car was delivered. How she would love it! He often thought about Ada now, his little Lorinda, and the things she had said that spring afternoon in the Bishop's Park. Even a simple pleasure like that walk in the park had made her eyes sparkle as brightly as the sun on the water of the stream. He could hear her happy laughter now. How she would love to ride in the Lanchester! I'll write and tell her I have to visit the forge in Auckland next week, he decided. If he got his business done early he could meet Ada and take her out to lunch.

'What is it making you smile like that?' Dinah asked, her voice arch. The family were gathered in the drawing room after dinner one evening. The air was filled with the fragrance of night-scented stock, for the windows were open to the garden which was ablaze with July flowers.

'Eh? What do you mean?' Johnny came back to the present, wrenching his thoughts away from Ada and how delighted she would be when she saw the car. 'Oh, nothing, I was just thinking of something.' He turned back to his letter.

'Someone, more like!' Dinah laughed and winked at Fred. 'Only a lass can make a lad smile like that. Now, who is it? Aren't you going to tell us all about her? Someone you've met on your travels, is it?'

'Leave the lad alone, Dinah! He's entitled to some privacy.' Fred defended his brother idly but he too had noticed Johnny's glowing face as he wrote the letter.

'It's all right, Fred,' said Johnny. 'It's nothing like you think either, Dinah. I'm just dropping a line or two to Ada. You know, the little girl I told you about, the one I got to know in Bishop Auckland. I thought I might see her when I go to the forge next week. I can give her a spin in the Lanchester, she'll like that.'

'That car! You think everyone will love it the way you do yourself. Nasty noisy thing. You wouldn't get me in it, I can tell you, not for anything.' Dinah was thoughtful for a minute as she returned to embroidering an ornate 'F' on a lace-trimmed pillowcase.

'Surely, though, Johnny, this girl must have grown up by now? It's almost six years since you left Bishop Auckland, nineteen hundred and four, wasn't it?'

'Yes, that's true, of course.' It was Johnny's turn to look thoughtful. Ada was growing up, even if she was still only five foot nothing. He pictured the trim little figure in the blue dress she had worn that afternoon: she was definitely rounded in all the right places.

'Johnny? She is grown-up, isn't she?' Dinah had that speculative look in her eyes and Johnny hastened to scotch any idea she might have about any romance between him and Ada.

'Yes, Dinah, I suppose she is. But I still think of her as a vulnerable little girl in need of a friend. Well, I've told you about her dragon of an aunt.'

'Hmm.' Dinah sounded sceptical. Johnny was going

to argue the point but he saw she had returned her attention to her needle. Oh, well, he thought, it doesn't really matter.

Leaning against the side of the Lanchester which he had parked at the end of George Street where it formed a corner with Tenters Street, Johnny frowned and checked his watch for the third time. It was two thirty. In his letter he had said he would meet Ada at two. Had something happened? Maybe he was simply being impatient, maybe she couldn't get away on time. Or perhaps she couldn't get anyone to read the letter to her? No, he decided, that couldn't be it, she would have found someone. There was that friend she talked about, the young widow whom she worked with.

He looked round the corner and up the hill of Tenters Street. There was no sign of Ada, in fact the street was deserted. He wrinkled his brow in puzzlement as he climbed back into the car. Impatiently he tapped his fingers on the steering wheel.

'Hey, mister!' A dirty, freckled face crowned with a stiff thatch of straw-coloured hair appeared at his elbow. 'Hey, mister, can I have a look at your motor?' The apparition grinned, revealing uneven little teeth. Gathered around him were half a dozen similar urchins and they were all gazing at the car, reverently touching the gleaming paintwork.

'Tell you what,' Johnny said, 'if you take a message for me I'll give you a ride round to the marketplace and back. How would you like that?'

The boy's eyes glowed but he was suspicious, there had to be a catch. 'Take a message where, mister?'

'Tenters Street.'

There was a chorus of 'I'll do it' from the gang but a firm glance from their leader quickly quelled it. He waited until they were quiet, and then turned back to Johnny.

'Righto, mister, what do you want me to do?'

'Go to the back door of number 21 and ask for Ada. Just say Johnny is waiting.'

'You her sweetheart, mister?' The cheeky face broke into a wide grin. 'Righto! Righto!' He ducked Johnny's threatening hand and ran off round the corner. Johnny waited impatiently.

'Ada doesn't live there any more.' The boy was soon back, panting after his run up the hill and back down. 'Can I still have a ride?'

'Doesn't live there?' Disbelievingly Johnny stared at the boy. 'You sure you went to number 21?'

'Aye. I did, honest, mister.' He was earnest, looking longingly at the Lanchester. 'The lass said that Ada doesn't live there any more.'

The lass said? That must have been Eliza, she was the only other lass there. Well, he would just have to go and find out for himself what was going on. Johnny opened the car door.

'Hey, mister, what about the ride?' Freckle-face was self-righteous; after all, a bargain was a bargain. 'It isn't my fault Ada doesn't live there now.'

Johnny hesitated, he was anxious about Ada. Still he had promised and a few minutes wouldn't make much difference. He leaned over and opened the rear door.

'Climb in then, and it's just to the market and back, mind.'

'I'll sit in the front, mister.' The whole gang climbed into the car and Johnny realised his bargain had included all the boys. How had he fallen for that? Well, better make the best of it.

There was a twitter of excitement, a 'Sit still now' warning from Johnny, the Lanchester shuddered into life and away they went – along George Street, turning into Bondgate and back along Newgate Street, completing the circular tour. The boys gasped, chattered and waved grandly at passers-by. Johnny thought that if Ada had been in the car she would have been worried by all the attention they were attracting. He had to blow the horn often at people who were not yet used to the speed of cars or indeed any motor traffic at all.

Back in George Street the children reluctantly trooped out onto the pavement. 'Thanks, mister.' They echoed each other excitedly. Their grins threatened to split their faces and their eyes shone; the treat had been all the more glorious for being unexpected.

Johnny climbed out, too. 'Watch the car for me, will you?' he enquired of Freckle-face, who immediately took up a position of importance by the bonnet, warning off any boy who came near. Johnny smiled, confident the car was in safe hands. He glanced at his watch, it was almost three o'clock. Probably a good time to catch the Parkers at home. He set off up Tenters Street and into the tiny front garden of number 21.

'Is Ada in?' he asked the young girl who answered his knock. He might as well make sure that the boy's story was true.

The girl shook her head surlily. 'I told the lad,' she said, 'Ada doesn't live here any more.'

'Are you Eliza, then? Do you know where Ada went?'

'No. I've just worked here a month. I don't know where Eliza went, either. You'd better go, mister, or you'll lose me my place.'

'What is it, lass, what is it?'

Johnny would have recognised Harry Parker's quavering voice anywhere as he appeared beside the girl, shouldering her aside. His braces dangled down from his grease-spotted trousers and his old slippers were worn away altogether at the heel. Recognition dawned as he saw Johnny.

'What do you want?' he said truculently, rubbing the

end of his nose with the back of his hand. 'Ada's not here,' he added, proving he knew quite well what Johnny was after.

'Where did she go then? Did she get my letter?' Johnny demanded, the old contempt for this man welling up in him.

'No, she didn't. Doris found it. How long have you been writing to Ada on the sly? Doris was fair frothing! She reckoned Ada had run away with you, the dirty slut!' The last words were venomous, almost spat out from under his quivering, wet moustache. His pale eyes gleamed with malice.

'Don't you call her a dirty slut, you – you mangy cur!' Johnny was suddenly worried stiff, his thoughts whirled. Ada had nowhere else to go! 'When did she go? What did you do to her to make her go?' he demanded.

'What do you mean? I bet it was your fault. I saw you out with her that day, you must have put ideas into her head, that's what!'

'You did do something to her, didn't you?' Johnny stepped forward angrily, catching hold of Harry by his shirt front.

'I'll call the polis!' Harry shouted, while the maid, who had been standing behind him with her mouth hanging open, shrieked and ducked back into the house.

'What's all this racket?' Doris came along the hallway, her face suffused with rage. 'You leave my man alone! Ivy, go and get the polis.' She stopped and looked narrowly at Johnny. 'I know you, don't I? Aye, I do. It's Johnny Fenwick, isn't it? Righto then, what's all this about?'

'You'd better ask your man! What has happened to Ada? That's what I want to know. And if anyone calls the police it will be me!'

'You get away in – clean up the dining room,' Doris said sharply to the maid who had crept up behind her, her face alive with interest. Then she turned back to Johnny.

'Now then, *Mister* Fenwick, I'll tell you what happened to Ada, the thieving, ungrateful little bitch. She ran away! Pinched the housekeeping money and ran, that's what, not so much as a word to me, who brought her up all those years, who took her in and fed her –' The tirade stopped for want of breath while Doris's face got redder and angrier.

'You mean you treated her like a slave!' Johnny burst out. 'A kitchen skivvy! Oh yes, I remember, the poor girl was not even allowed to go to school.'

'You mind your own bloody business!' Doris gasped, shaking with rage.

'Aye,' Harry butted in maliciously. Johnny had released his shirt front when Doris came on the scene and he had made a strategic retreat behind his wife's back. 'And do you want to know when she went? That day I saw you out with her! What did *you* do to her, that's what I want to know.'

'What did I do? Why, you little toad! If anyone did anything to her it would be you, you with your hot little eyes following the lass about. Don't think I didn't see you, even though I was a youngster myself! And Ada just a child. Why, I'll –'

'Get out! Don't you come here threatening us! She's gone, and good riddance to her. I knew she'd turn out like her mother.' Doris caught hold of Harry by the shoulder and glared at him too. 'You get in there, do you hear?' There was an indefinable something in her voice as she spoke to her husband but she was a true virago as she turned back to Johnny.

'Have you not gone yet? I'll take the broom to you, coming here creating! Bloody well get and don't come back here!'

Johnny stared at her with a set face but in the end he turned on his heel and stalked up the yard. His blood was boiling as he strode down the street. On reaching the car he slammed into the driving seat, his thoughts in turmoil as he tried to think what to do. What was the name of that girl? A minute ago he'd remembered, but now it was gone. She had a little boy, he remembered that.

'I looked after the car, mister.' Freckle-face was watching him gravely. Something was up with the toff.

'What? Oh yes, thanks.' Johnny reached absent-mindedly into his pocket and found a penny. He looked thoughtfully at the boy before handing it over.

'Do you know the girl who used to work at the Parkers', the one with the little boy? What was her name? Eliza! That's right!' The name popped into his mind. 'She used to live in George Street, I think.'

'Eliza Maxwell? Aye, she used to live with Mrs Rutherford, number 4, that is. But she's gone now, her and Bertie an' the new babby.' Freckle-face grinned, pleased to be of service to Johnny and even more pleased to earn a penny.

'Thanks, son. Number 4, you said? Righto. Watch the car a minute more, will you?' Johnny got out of the car and walked along the street until he came to number 4, where he knocked on the door.

'Eliza? My niece, Eliza? Nay lad, she doesn't live with me any more. No, she had to move to West Auckland, you know. Well, that's her parish, she had to go to get the parish relief – well, she had the bairns, you know. What did you want her for?' Mrs Rutherford paused long enough in her explanations to enquire.

'I'm looking for Ada really, Ada Leigh. Did you know her? She told me that Eliza was a good friend of hers. They used to work together.'

'Oh, aye, of course I know Ada.' Mrs Rutherford gave Johnny an appraising glance before deciding to let him in. 'I tell you what, come away in for a minute and I'll tell you.' She led the way into the front room. Johnny was not the sort you took into the kitchen, she thought.

140

Anyone could see he was a gentleman. She motioned him to sit down on the settle and sat down in the wooden rocker opposite him.

'Aye, poor lass, she was in a real state. I don't care what she'd done, they had no right to knock her about like they did. No right at all. Maybe she had been out with a lad – it wasn't you, was it?' She looked suspiciously at him. 'If you earned her that good hiding you ought to be ashamed of yourself, her poor face was all bruised.'

'She did nothing wrong!' Johnny was getting angry again. 'We went for a walk, that's all. A walk in the park. I knew her when I lodged with her aunt in Finkle Street, she was only a child. That vicious woman, I'll have the law on her!'

'Nay, lad, they are her legal guardians, the Parkers. They'll say she was running wild. I don't think the law would do any good.'

'Hmm. Well, I intend to get to the bottom of this, find out what happened. Where did she go? I'll have to find her, make sure she's come to no harm.'

'Well, she told Eliza she was going to Durham. That's where she lived when she was a bairn, I think.'

Johnny bit his lip, considering what to do. He could go to West Auckland to see if Eliza knew any more, but it was already getting late. He could go to Durham and look for Ada, see what he could find out there, but he couldn't go today, he had to get home. He felt helpless but it would have to wait – until the weekend, at least, he thought, then he would have more time. Johnny stood and held out his hand to the old lady.

'At any rate, thank you for your help. If you give me Eliza's address I'll try to see her and find out if she knows any more. Or maybe you could ask her to write to me? If I leave my address and the postage?'

Driving back to Middlesbrough, he could think of nothing but Ada and the trouble he seemed to have caused for her. The sooner he found her the better. He resolved to further his enquiries in Durham at the weekend.

Chapter Ten

In Durham, Ada was catching glimpses of a very different life to the one she was used to: it was another world. Virginia and her family were so kind and friendly.

'That's one thing about the doctor and the missus too,' Cook remarked to Ada while she was having a cup of tea with her feet up by the range and Ada was ironing on the kitchen table. They treat servants as people, not like most folks. There's no side to them, none at all. But don't you go taking advantage, like,' she added.

Dr Gray, who had leanings towards the Fabian Society, had no objections at all to Virginia bringing Ada to the front of the house and teaching her her letters, so Ada need not have worried about that.

'A very nice thing for you to do,' he said to Virginia approvingly. 'It will give you an interest, too, until you're well enough to go back to school. But be careful not to overtire yourself.'

Ada had never been in such fine surroundings as the day she was taken in to see Dr and Mrs Gray, and at first she was nervous and hesitant about sitting on the grand upholstered furniture. But Virginia and her parents acted so naturally that Ada just had to relax. Even so, she was a little tongue-tied in the presence of the doctor and she was glad when she and Virginia were alone together.

When the weather was fine, as it was for most of the summer, a picnic lunch was served to the girls in the garden. It was a far cry from the penny dips Ada usually bought. There was often chicken and salad or even fresh salmon, for Virginia had been ill and her appetite needed tempting. It was almost as nice for Ada when it rained, for the two girls sat in the conservatory in wicker easy chairs with plump cushions.

Bye, it's really grand, Ada was thinking one day as she finished the exercise Virginia had given her and looked up and out over the garden. She handed the paper over to the other girl, smiling hesitantly.

'My goodness, you are doing well.' Virginia was truly surprised and proud of her pupil. 'You're learning quickly.'

Ada smiled, gratified. The daily lessons and laborious study in the privacy of her bedroom during the long, light summer evenings were having their desired effect, she thought. It was worth the hard work.

'Anyone would think you'd had some lessons before,' Virginia continued, smiling at her pupil. Virginia looked a picture in her white muslin dress decorated with blue ribbons which set off her fair hair and complexion. The fresh air and sunshine were beginning to have a beneficial effect on her and her cheeks showed a hint of rose. The contrast with Ada in her workaday black serge was striking. Ada's wealth of black, curly hair looked even darker against Virginia's blonde looks but if anything her skin was even whiter than her friend's, for no amount of sun seemed to affect it.

'I did have someone teach me once but it was years ago and not very much,' Ada confided. 'I thought I'd forgotten all of it but it has helped.' She bent her head, thinking of Johnny.

'Someone else gave you lessons?' Virginia was curious, not least because she had noticed Ada's softened expression and air of sadness when she spoke of it. 'Ada! I do believe it was a boy. Who was it? Oh, go on, tell me all about him.' Virginia's eyes danced with mischief as she saw Ada's embarrassment.

Ada blushed and bit her lip. 'It was a boy, someone I knew years ago. He went to live in Middlesbrough so the lessons stopped.'

'Oh, what a shame! Didn't you see him again?'

'Yes. Yes, I did. I saw him this year.' Ada allowed herself the luxury of dwelling on Johnny. 'Eeh, he's lovely, Virginia, tall and handsome with auburn hair and smiling, green eyes.' She sighed. 'But I don't suppose I'll see him again. Since I moved to Durham he won't even know where I am.'

'You could write to him. Oh, come on,' Virginia said impulsively, 'we'll write to him now, how's that?'

Ada stood up abruptly, her face set. Formally she thanked Virginia for the lunch and picked up her sacking apron. 'No,' she said, 'No, thank you. I've got to get back to work now, thank you very much, Miss Virginia.'

'I thought we'd agreed it would be plain Virginia,' the other girl pouted.

'Plain Virginia, eh? Well, if that's what you want to be called it's all right with me.' Both girls started and turned to where the teasing voice came from. A dark-haired young man was lounging against the doorway of the house.

'Tom!' Virginia sprang up, holding out her arms to him. 'Tom! We weren't expecting you till next week.' She ran lightly over to him and kissed him soundly on the cheek.

'Hey, steady on there, plain Virginia!' He laughed and glanced across at Ada, intrigued by the slim figure and dark beauty which the rough working clothes couldn't hide.

'Oh, Ada. This is my brother, Tom. I've told you about him, haven't I? He's learning to be a doctor in Newcastle. Tom, this is Ada and I'm teaching her to read and write.'

Ada blushed yet again as Virginia let out her secret.

She hated anyone to know of her lack of literacy. Virginia noticed and was immediately contrite.

'Well, it isn't her fault, Tom,' she said lamely. 'She didn't get a chance to go to school.'

Tom raised his eyebrows at this – surely everyone went to school now? But he smiled and nodded to Ada, who began backing towards the kitchen garden. 'I hope I'm not driving you away?' he asked.

'Oh no, I have to go.' Ada was suddenly conscious of her local accent, such a contrast to the cultured speech of brother and sister. She hurried away, feeling sad, shabby and confused. The closeness of the pair was something she could only look on and wonder about. Indeed, they inhabited a different world. Suddenly her heart longed for Eliza, the only friend she had who came from the same world as she did herself. Eliza understood her, she would understand her diffidence about writing to Johnny.

I'll try to get through to see Eliza, Ada decided as she came to Elvet Bridge and stood for a moment, watching the students rowing their boats in the water below. They looked so serious, heaving away, with the cox calling, 'Pull! Pull!' through his megaphone and the boats gliding swiftly over the surface. Ada wondered if that was all they had to worry about, winning some boat race. Sighing, she went on her way, her mind made up. She would try to visit Eliza. She should be able to avoid going anywhere near Tenters Street now that Eliza lived in West Auckland. She was pleased that she had asked Virginia to help her with the card giving her friend Mrs Dunne's address. Eliza had written back, telling of her move back to her own parish. Oh, what a pity it was that Eliza didn't live somewhere near! She would have loved to talk things over with her. Eliza was so full of down-to-earth common sense.

At that moment Eliza Maxwell looked flushed and harassed, wisps of hair falling over her forehead as she clutched a screaming Miles to her breast and paced up and down the kitchen. Bertie, his eyes large and anxious in his pale face, was standing by the back door of the house in Front Street, West Auckland, his fists clenched by his sides.

'Go away!' The yell burst out of him. 'Leave my mam alone!'

Eliza rushed over to him and pulled him away from the door, pushing him before her into the front room. 'Eeh, Bertie, don't take on like that, pet. The nasty man will go away in a minute, just so long as we take no notice of him, man.'

Though it was early afternoon, the pub next door to Eliza was full of men off shift or simply taking the day off. The smell of pipe smoke and beer drifted through the door to the yard and in through the badly fitting door to Eliza's cottage, for the yard was common to both properties. Eliza held Bertie to her and, on her shoulder, Miles hiccuped softly and fell into an exhausted sleep. The noise from the yard continued unabated.

'Howay, lass, let us in! You won't be sorry, we'll make it worth your while. We got the brass.' The hammering on the door which had wakened Miles and set him crying in fright stopped for a minute. Bertie lifted his head and looked up at his mother.

'Have they gone, Mam?'

Eliza patted his head. Bye, she thought, the poor lad was getting in a right state. Anger welled up in her as she shook her head. She could hear the whispered consultation going on in the yard; there must be two or three of them this time.

'Will I go for the polis?' Bertie whispered. She shook her head as another man started trying to wheedle her to open the back door, in a voice she recognised.

'Eliza? Howay, hinny, let us in. Nobody will know, and we know you could use the money.' The slurred voice broke off as one of his drinking mates burst into a fit of sniggering. As Eliza walked to the back door, Bertie still clinging to her side, she heard the drunken giggling.

'Not just the brass you could be doing with, eh, Eliza Maxwell? How long is it since you had a man? Let us in and we'll show –'

'Get away from my door! I'll call the polis, I will! And you, don't think I don't know who you are, I'll let on to your missuses. Do you hear me, Albert Jones? And you –'

Eliza had no idea who the others were so she stopped in mid-sentence and listened. But her words had already had their effect on their fuddled minds.

'Aw, gan on then, dirty hoor! Howay, lads, we'll have another pint. There's more to beer than a hoor any road!' Eliza listened, holding her breath as the men retreated down the yard to the pub. The hush was disturbed only by Miles, who whimpered in his sleep and moved restlessly. Maybe he's teething, Eliza thought listlessly. She felt utterly drained by the incident. What would happen if men actually got into the house? Eeh, it was awful! Even going out to the yard was taking a chance with that lot in the pub.

'Will I go for the polis now?' Bertie loosed his hold on her skirt and stared earnestly at her.

'No, no, pet.' Eliza smiled gently at him. 'I tell you what, we'll all go out, eh? We'll go across to the chemist's and get some gripe water for Miles. Then we might go for a walk down by the beck, you like to do that.' Going out of the front door which led directly onto the green was safe at least, she thought bitterly. Those men might be drunk but they still had enough sense not to be seen openly chasing after a widow woman. Carrying the baby and with Bertie trotting by her side, Eliza walked over the green to the chemist's shop.

'Why, hello, Eliza!'

Eliza turned at the sound of the familiar voice, her feeling of depression lifting as she saw her old neighbour from the railway cottages up the line.

'Hannah! Eeh, it's grand to see you!'

'And you an' all. And I see you've got the new babby. Is it a lad or a lass?'

'A lad.' Proudly Eliza showed Miles off to Hannah. 'I'm that glad to see you, I am. I don't know many people in the village, what with living up there on the line.'

'You went to Bishop Auckland, though, didn't you? Didn't you go to your auntie's? Bye, that woman who's come next door now isn't half as nice as you were. Eeh, this is Bertie an' all? He's grown a bit since I saw him, mind.' Hannah bent down to the boy, who was gazing gravely up at her.

'Do you remember your Auntie Hannah, pet?'

Bertie shook his head.

Hannah laughed. 'Shy, are you, pet? Bye, but he's like his da, isn't he, Eliza? Such a good bairn an' all, different to that tribe next door now – cheeky, why, they're brassent fond. I was just saying –' Hannah broke off, forgetting what she was going to say completely, her mouth dropping open in shock, for Bertie had turned to his mother and in a loud, piping voice asked her a question.

'Mam, what's a hoor?'

'It's bad to say that!' Eliza said sharply. 'What will Auntie Hannah think if you say naughty words?' Bertie's lip quivered and he stuck his finger in his mouth, but for once Eliza was not sensitive to his feelings. She looked at her old neighbour's shocked face. Hannah was a chapel woman, wasn't she?

'Eeh, I don't know where he heard that, Hannah,' she said, her face red with embarrassment.

'It was that man in the yard, Mam.' Bertie was being helpful.

'Bertie! Hold your tongue.' Eliza was fairly shouting now and Bertie burst into tears. 'We share the yard with the Rose and Crown, you know.' She looked anxiously at Hannah, who stepped back as though distancing herself from the little family.

'Aye,' said Hannah. 'Aye, well, I've to be getting back now, it's a fair walk back home.' She hesitated for a moment and Eliza knew she was in two minds about asking her up. 'It's been nice seeing you any road, Eliza, mebbe I'll see you again . . .' she finished lamely.

'Aye. Yes.' Eliza watched her as she crossed over the green and hurried up the road which led to Spring Gardens. Then she bent down and dried Bertie's tears. It wasn't the bairn's fault, she thought, it was living in that house that did it.

'Howay then, Bertie, never mind now. We'll go down

152

by the beck for that walk. Be a good lad now and I'll get you a stick of liquorice. You like that, don't you?'

Straightening up, she stared over at the Rose and Crown and her cottage beside it. When she had first come back to West Auckland she had thought the rent was low because the locals believed the cottage was haunted. It had been rented by a murderess, Mary Anne Cotton. Most of her family had died of arsenic poisoning before she was arrested and carted off to Durham Gaol, eventually to be hung. Eliza wasn't afraid of ghosts, but she was afraid of the drunken men in the yard. No wonder no one wanted to live there. If only she could afford another place!

They walked along by the side of the beck, the same beck which ran near the railway cottages up the line, the Gaunless. And after a while Eliza regained her normal outlook on life. She chuckled; it had been funny really, Bertie saying that in front of Hannah. It was a lovely day and she found a sheltered spot hidden from the path by a large oak tree. There she fed baby Miles while Bertie ran about picking daisies and dandelions and bringing them to her.

'Eeh, they're lovely, Bertie!' she said, smiling at him as he proffered the flowers, heads mostly – he hadn't yet realised it was better to pick them with stalks. 'We'll take them home and put them on the windowsill in a jar.' Her heart filled with love for him; she shouldn't have shouted at him. Who cared about friends, any road? It was the bairns that mattered. And Ada, of course, Ada was more than a friend.

Chapter Eleven

Lying on top of her bed that night, weary but wakeful, Ada was unusually restive. The night was hot and oppressive and the room seemed airless even though she had pushed the sash window open as far as it would go. Sighing, she rose and went over to the washstand. Pouring water into the bowl, she soaked the piece of flannel and held it against her forehead and cheeks, enjoying the coolness of it. She squeezed the cloth out again in the cold water and carried it to the window. Drawing the thin curtains aside, she perched on the ledge and looked down onto the moonlit yard. She moistened the nape of her neck and the top of her breasts. Why did she feel so unsettled? she thought.

She remembered Virginia's suggestion that she should write to Johnny. Her instinct was to wait until she could write herself, properly, without even Ginny knowing what she had written. It should be private. Her thoughts wandered to Ginny and her brother, Tommy. How lovely it would be to have a family like Ginny's! But they soon strayed back to Johnny, her idol.

I will wait until I can write the letter myself, then I'll go to Middlesbrough, she decided. That'll be best. I'll work and work at it until I can do it.

Ada had all the cards and letters Johnny had ever written to her and now she ran over to the chest of drawers and got out the bundle from under her one good petticoat. The petticoat had been passed on to her by Virginia; the hem had been torn when Virginia caught it on a bush but Ada had mended it so that you could hardly see the repair.

'I'll wear my blue dress,' Ada said aloud as she carried her precious bundle of postcards over to the window. 'The dress Eliza gave me.' Planning made her feel better already, it gave her something to look forward to. Taking a card from the bundle, she strained to make out Johnny's address. She could read it now, albeit laboriously, for her reading had improved much faster than her writing. 'Stockton Road', she spelled out and smiled secretly. Letting the curtain fall back into place, Ada took the bundle of postcards back to bed with her and fell asleep almost at once.

Next day was Tuesday and Ada started her morning's washing early at Mr Johnson's cottage. She wanted to be in good time for her lesson with Virginia. Mr Johnson was an old man who lived down by the racecourse. Ada enjoyed working for him; the work wasn't too hard and besides, he always had a friendly word with her. Sometimes no one spoke to her the whole time she was working for them, but Mr Johnson was different. This morning he sought her out as she was filling the tub with hot water, ready to start the wash.

'Hello, Ada,' he said.

Ada paused in her work and smiled at him. She liked Mr Johnson, he was tall and distinguished-looking with a mass of snowy hair and well-kept hands and nails. She understood he was retired from the university. He was usually immersed in a book, his house was full of books, but Ada thought he must be a bit lonely. He didn't even have a housekeeper. The back door was always open for Ada when she came and she usually got straight on with her work.

'Morning, Mr Johnson,' she answered.

'Would you like a cup of tea, Ada?' Mr Johnson lifted the kettle from the hob and placed it on the fire.

Ada was pleased, it wasn't very often she was offered any refreshment. She had to get on if she was going to have time for her lesson but she would make time for a cup of tea.

'Yes please, Mr Johnson,' she said. 'I'll make it if you like.'

'Oh, I'm quite used to doing for myself.'

He spooned tea into the pot and got out cups and saucers. Ada looked at the book he had carried with him into the kitchen; it was open and showed solid chunks of text. He must be very learned, she thought. Mr Johnson saw her interest.

'Do you like books on history, Ada?'

Ada blushed. 'I don't know much about it,' she mumbled.

'Didn't you learn any history at school?'

'I didn't go to school.' She looked up defensively. 'I can read, though.' Well, she was learning, she told herself.

'You didn't go to school and yet you can read? You must be quick to pick it up without going to school.' Mr Johnson brought a tin of biscuits over to the table and sat down. 'Come on, dear, sit down and have your tea. Milk and sugar?'

'Yes please.' Ada accepted the delicate bone-china cup and saucer, holding it carefully. Wouldn't it be awful if she dropped it? Carefully she took a sip. It had a different taste somehow, not like any tea she had had before. But then, she didn't very often drink tea with fresh milk, it must be that.

'Hmm. Earl Grey is nice, isn't it, Ada? Refreshing.' Mr Johnson offered her the biscuits and she took a piece of shortbread. That was good, too, she thought, nice and buttery.

Ada looked up to find Mr Johnson gazing thoughtfully at her.

'I've just thought of something,' he said when he saw she had noticed his look. 'If you like, my dear, I can lend you books. If you're interested in history, that is.'

'Oh! I don't know, Mr Johnson –'

'But why not? I've got lots of books, you must have noticed.'

'Yes. Well.' Ada finished her tea quickly and stood up. 'Thank you for the tea and the shortbread, Mr Johnson, but I must get on now.'

'Yes, of course, my dear.' He nodded absently and Ada turned to her work – the water would be getting cold if she didn't hurry up. And then she wanted to get over to the Grays' house in good time.

Soon she was thumping the possing stick up and down, up and down. It was a lovely day, and if she got the clothes out on the line by eleven she could take them in when she left the Grays'. Mr Johnson sometimes forgot so that they were still there when she went back on Wednesday afternoons, and if it had rained they would have sooty marks on them.

By half past eleven Ada was ready to go. The washtub and stick were washed out and upended in the yard to dry and the clothes were fluttering in the wind. As she went to the back door to collect her shawl, Mr Johnson came into the kitchen again, carrying a slim volume.

'I've got just the thing for you,' he said, handing it to her so that she could hardly refuse to take it. 'It's folk tales of the county. You might try it first and if you like it you can borrow some more documented history. I do hope you find time to read it.'

'Thank you, Mr Johnson,' she said awkwardly. She felt terrible for telling him she could read. Well, she could read a bit, but she would have a hard time spelling this book out, she knew, slim though it was. 'I'll see you tomorrow, then.'

I will read it though, she determined as she rushed over Elvet Bridge. I'll have a try every single night, so I will.

She had thought that Virginia would have forgotten about Johnny but she certainly had not. No, Virginia greeted her eagerly, drawing her into the garden where she had the books, writing paper and pens laid out on the ironwork table.

'Shall I help you write a letter to your boyfriend, then?' she said before Ada had time to take off her shawl.

'He's not my boy! He's a friend, that's all. And I don't want to write to him any road.'

'Oh, come on, I'm sure he'd be pleased to get a letter from you.'

'Oh, Virginia, I'd rather wait until I can write better. Really I would. I want to be able to do it myself. Why, we didn't even see each other for so long. I'm sure he doesn't even think of me very often. I don't want to make myself look a fool.'

Virginia pouted. 'But I wanted to help you write the letter today,' she said.

'Well, maybe you can help me write a letter to Eliza? That's my friend in West Auckland.' Ada tried to be conciliatory.

'Well, all right. But it's not so good as writing to a boy.'

Ada breathed a sigh of relief. For a moment there she had thought Virginia was going into a huff and would refuse to teach her any more.

'What do you want to say?'

Ada thought about it. There was so much to say to Eliza, so much had happened since she last saw her. Much more than she could say in a letter, even with Virginia's help.

'Well?' Virginia was getting impatient.

'Er, just that I am all right here, I've got plenty of work and I'm managing fine. And ask her how she is, and if Bertie and Miles are well, and does she like living in West Auckland.'

'Hmm. You'd better put it differently. First you ask after Eliza and the children, then you say how you are and then you tell her any news. That's the way to write a proper letter.'

Virginia had taken on the air and voice of a

school-marm, as she pursed her lips and tilted her head on one side. 'I think you should write it out on scrap paper first, then you can copy it onto a sheet of my good writing paper.'

Ada thought she could write it on a postcard, for the postage on a postcard was only one penny while a letter cost more. But she didn't argue with Virginia. Obediently she took her pencil and a piece of scrap paper and tried to follow the other girl's instructions. They ate dainty chicken and salad sandwiches as they worked, with homemade lemonade which tasted like nectar to Ada.

By the time the letter was finished, Ada was running late. Hurriedly she picked up the envelope and her shawl.

'Eeh, thank you, Virginia, thank you for the lunch and everything. I have to go now, though, I'm late.'

'Leave the letter, I'll put it with Daddy's post on the hall table. And do stop saying "Eeh", Ada, it's so common.'

'I can post it myself.' After all, she had had a free meal, she didn't want to sponge so much on the Grays.

'Nonsense. It can perfectly well go with Daddy's. All my letters do.' Firmly, Virginia took the letter from Ada, who gave in to her immediately.

Ironing that afternoon in the kitchen of a house in Crossgate, Ada remembered Virginia's remark about her speech, feeling a bit hurt. Everyone said things like 'eeh', 'bye' or 'mind', it was just a way of making what you said sound natural. Still, she had to admit that people like Virginia or Tom or the doctor didn't say them. They said things like 'oh' or 'I say'. They must think it sounded better. Ada was confused, she didn't know whether she wanted to be loyal to the speech of her own people or not. 'Common', Virginia had called it.

Well, Ada reflected as she folded a shirt and hung it on the clotheshorse to air, she wanted to get on and if she had to change her way of talking, she would. After all, Johnny talked the way the Grays did. She would like to talk like Johnny; if he ever came to see her he would be impressed. Of course they could only ever be friends now, after what had happened to her, but wouldn't it be lovely . . .? Ada was lost in her favourite daydream.

In Middlesbrough, the subject of her loving thoughts was lost in grief. For a while, any thought Johnny had of visiting Durham had to be put out of his mind. He had fully intended to seek Ada out as soon as he got the letter from Eliza giving her address in Gilesgate. But shortly after his return to Middlesbrough the lives of all the Fenwicks were thrown into chaos.

Fred died. Fred, who had been like a father to him, the man he had always looked up to and whose success he strove to emulate, had a seizure and died at his office desk. The office staff went to pieces and it was Johnny who had to pull himself together, send for a doctor and hurry home so that he would get to Dinah before the news reached her.

'Johnny! What are you doing home so early? What a surprise! We can have tea together. I'll ring for Norah.' Dinah crossed to the bell rope before turning back to him. Her face changed, alarm swiftly taking hold of her.

'Johnny? What is it? Is something wrong? It's not Fred? No, no, of course it's not Fred, I saw him this morning, he was fine.'

'Oh, Dinah . . .' Johnny paused. 'Dinah, sit down. I have something to tell you.'

'Tell me then, tell me, I can't stand it! It's not Fred, is it? Has there been an accident with the men? For God's sake, Johnny –'

Johnny crossed to her swiftly and put his arm around her. 'Come on, Dinah, sit down, dear. It is Fred, I'm afraid. A seizure, I think.'

'He's not dead, though, I would know if he was dead.' Dinah shook her head vigorously.

'I'm sorry, Dinah. But I'm sure it was sudden, he died without any pain.'

Dinah dissolved into hysterics, sobs racking her shoulders, and Johnny tried to comfort her, knowing there was really nothing he could say.

'Sir?'

He looked up to see Norah in the doorway, staring at Dinah in fear and alarm. He would have to alert the household staff at once, he thought. There were things to do, arrangements to make.

'Stay with your mistress, please, Norah,' he said, gently disengaging himself from Dinah, who hardly seemed to be aware of his going.

In the hall he found Pierce, the butler, hovering; Cook had her head round the door to the kitchen, and the footman was at the bottom of the stairs. They had been drawn to the hall by the sound of Dinah's cries. Quietly he told them of Fred's death and then, before they could go to pieces as the staff in the office had done, he turned to the butler.

'Pierce, the doctor will be here shortly. I want him taken in to Mrs Fenwick at once. I'm sure you can organise the staff to prepare the house, there will be things to do. I must go to Great Ayton, I want to tell the boys myself.'

It was not until after the funeral that Johnny even had time to think about his own future. Fred had always given him to understand it was secure. There was the business and Johnny was the only one of the family who had the experience to run it. When the will was read he found that the bulk of Fred's assets were left to Stephen, his eldest son, with provision for Arthur and Dinah. There were small bequests to the servants and a thousand pounds for Johnny but Stephen had control of the business. Johnny received no shares in it whatsoever.

Well, fair enough, he reflected, Fred had his own sons to consider first. Stephen was old enough to leave school and no doubt he felt responsible for his mother and brother now. Johnny himself was content enough to work as managing director. He was very busy for the next few weeks sorting out the business, introducing Stephen to it and starting the task of showing his nephew how things worked. He thought of Ada sometimes, promising himself he would go to see her as soon as he could.

Ada was working hard at her reading and writing. Two or three times a week she spent her lunch hour with Virginia, spelling out the letters in the children's books both Tom and his sister had used when they were small, and gradually she began to make sense of them. Tom had taken to dropping in on the lessons. At first Ada was embarrassed, but after a while she didn't mind. She got so absorbed she would forget he was there until she looked up and found his eyes on her.

'I think Tom is taken with you, Ada,' Virginia commented once. 'He's always watching you.'

'Eeh – I mean, oh, Virginia,' Ada swiftly corrected herself, 'that's silly.'

They were sitting on the lawn one warm summer's day. Tom had come out and sat with them for a while but he had gone back into the house now. Ada glanced behind her at the door. If he heard Virginia's nonsense

166

she would be shamed to death, she thought. Tom wasn't the sort for her and she wasn't going to marry anyone, she was quite determined.

'Hmm.' Virginia tried to look wise and succeeded only in looking remarkably like her mother. 'We'll see.'

Ada much preferred reading from Mr Johnson's book of folk tales to the children's stories. Slowly, she was beginning to get through it, often sitting late into the August evenings at the window of her bedroom, straining to catch the last of the light.

There was the tale she had heard of a wild boar in the Bishop's Park at Auckland. She could picture it as she read, thinking she knew the very oak tree where Pollard the hunter had hidden to trap the boar by heaping the ground beneath with oak and beech mast he had collected. The boar, which had terrorised the neighbourhood, had eaten until it fell asleep under the tree and Pollard had jumped on it and killed it. She remembered Pollard's Inn in the town and marvelled that it should still bear the hunter's name. The story of the Lambton worm was in the book, the one about the Stanhope fairies and other familiar tales. They were much more interesting than reading nursery rhymes.

At last the time came when Ada thought she could write a letter to Johnny without making too many mistakes. Virginia kept mentioning it whenever Ada was with her.

'Are you going to write to your young man today? Oh, come on Ada, you can do it now. I'll help you,' she would say, until eventually Ada agreed.

'I want to write it on my own, though.'

Virginia pouted. 'You might make a mistake. I should at least look it over for you.'

Tom, who was sitting by them, had frowned when Virginia brought it up and now he said sharply, 'Virginia, letters like that are private.'

'He's not my young man,' Ada put in. 'Just someone I know. All right, Virginia, you can look it over.'

'I'm off.' Tom stood up and disappeared into the house. Ada looked after him in surprise at his abrupt departure, but told herself that he must have things to do.

'I'm only writing a short note. Just to say where I am and what I'm doing. I'll ask him first how he is, of course.' Ada remembered her first lesson from Virginia.

The letter duly written and then approved by her friend, Ada spelled out the address on the envelope. Mr J. Fenwick, The Beeches, Stockton Road, Middlesbrough. She knew the address by heart.

Virginia snatched up the envelope. 'I'll put it with Daddy's post, it'll go today.'

'No, no, I'll take it.' Ada held out her hand and Virginia gave it back after a second's hesitation.

'You will post it, though?'

Ada picked up her shawl. The letter had taken a while

to write and she had to go. 'Yes, of course I will,' she said. But she wasn't sure what she would do, she would like to take it herself. She would think about it while she did her afternoon's ironing. Maybe she would go to Middlesbrough on Saturday, she thought, she could hand it in. She would like to see where Johnny lived.

On reaching her lodgings that evening, Mrs Dunne popped her head round the kitchen door.

'There's a letter for you, Ada.' She held out the envelope and looked expectantly at Ada, hoping to hear about it.

'Thank you, Mrs Dunne.' Ada took the letter and to Mrs Dunne's disappointment went upstairs to her room. Slitting the envelope, she took out the single sheet and, with some difficulty, read it out aloud to herself. She still found it easier to read that way.

'Dear Ada.' (Then it wasn't from Johnny, Johnny would have called her Lorinda. And Johnny didn't have her address anyway. She looked at the signature. Eliza, it was from Eliza, that was grand.)

'I was so glad to hear you were all right, managing like. We are too, though Bertie does have a bit of a cough. West Auckland is all right, but I haven't made many friends yet. Do you think you could get away and come to see us? It would be so nice if you could.'

The letter was short and didn't exactly say Eliza was

unhappy but Ada, reading between the lines, thought she was. She sat down on the bed and thought about it. She would go to see Eliza, she would, but not this week. This Saturday she was going to Middlesbrough.

For a moment she wondered if she should go to West Auckland instead. But, after all, she could go to see Eliza the Saturday after. She had saved some money by having so many meals with Virginia. If she didn't go to Middlesbrough soon, she would lose her courage to do so. And Eliza hadn't *said* she was unhappy.

Chapter Twelve

That Saturday afternoon, Ada stood across the road from the Beeches, feeling very much overawed and also dismayed. If Johnny lived in this house he must be a bigger toff than she had thought – this house was even grander than Dr Gray's house in Durham. Its square solidity was set well back from the road on higher ground so that it seemed to impose its presence on the neighbourhood. A handsome marble portico had been added recently, the marble columns gleamed with newness. Ada looked nervously at the heavy oak door with its shining brass knocker which the portico shielded.

Indecision fluttered through her. Should she go to the front door or the back? Or should she go straight home and forget all about it? She clutched the letter tightly, for she had decided she would hand it in if Johnny was not at home. Now she thought she would hand it in in any case and not ask for Johnny. But then she noticed that the house had a closed look, with heavy curtains drawn at the windows and no one about. It looked unapproachable and Ada dithered.

The sky darkened and a few spots of rain fell, making damp spots on Ada's blue dress. A cold wind sprang from nowhere and Ada shivered, feeling a damp cold on her shoulders through the thin material. She had to do it now or she was going to be soaked. Lifting her chin, she walked up the drive to the front door. Lifting the heavy knocker and letting it fall, she bit her lip when she heard the sound reverberating through the house. She had almost decided that there was nobody there when a girl answered the knock, a girl who looked at Ada as if she definitely thought her place was at the back door rather than the front. The girl was damp-eyed and querulous and had other things on her mind.

'Yes?'

Norah stared at Ada. Who on earth was this girl in the cheap cotton dress with her chapped, red hands in sharp contrast to her pale face? And what was she doing coming to the front door at such a time?

Ada quailed. When it came to it she found it too much to ask for Johnny. She decided the best plan was to simply hand in the letter.

'Please,' she stammered and her accent broadened in her embarrassment. 'Please, this is for Mr Fenwick.'

Before Norah could answer, a man came into the hall

behind her, a man who seemed to have some authority for he surveyed the two girls at the door and frowned heavily.

'What is it, Norah? This is neither the time nor the place for gossiping,' he said sharply.

Norah's already damp eyes filled with tears at this injustice and she could hardly speak, so she backed away and left the butler to handle this intruder on the family's grief.

'Well, my girl? What is it?'

'A note, sir,' Ada said and held out the letter. He took it in a white-gloved hand, glancing only briefly at the name on the envelope.

'I . . . I thought I could wait for a reply, sir.' For Ada had suddenly realised she could not go without speaking to Johnny.

The butler drew himself up. 'Well, girl, you cannot. Mr Fenwick is unable to reply for he died a short time ago.' Firmly he closed the door.

'Who was that, Pierce?' Johnny, crossing the hall, stopped in surprise at the butler's tone – he was a normally courteous man.

'Just a messenger, sir.'

Pierce offered the letter to Johnny, who waved it aside, thinking it a message of condolence.

'Put it with the others, Pierce.'

As Johnny went into the drawing room, Pierce took the letter into the study and placed it with the others addressed to Mr J. F. Fenwick, the ones Stephen and Johnny would get around to eventually.

Ada never remembered how she managed to get to the railway station. When she heard the words 'Mr Fenwick died' it took away her breath. She hung on to a marble column for support as the world darkened for her.

'Johnny is dead! Johnny is dead!'

The words rang in an insane refrain in her head. Turning blindly, she ran through the streets as the rain became a downpour. She found the station at last and stumbled onto the right platform more by accident than anything. Her blue dress was soaked through and clinging to her thin shoulders. Her tears were indistinguishable from the rain on her face. Numbly she waited for the train and, when it came, climbed into a third-class compartment and shrank into a corner seat. If she got some curious glances from the other passengers, she didn't notice. She didn't even notice when a concerned woman caught hold of her as she stumbled getting off the train in Durham.

Somehow Ada got to Gilesgate from the train and managed to get into her lodging house without Mrs Dunne seeing her. She climbed the stairs to her room and collapsed on the bed, lying there, thinking of nothing, in a kind of stupor. Later her mind returned to it. Johnny was dead. He had been her only friend for so long, apart from Eliza, and her love-starved soul ached for the one person who had embodied all her hopes and dreams. There would be no more letters to cherish, no more meetings.

Ada lay there until past suppertime, eating nothing. The room grew darker and rain splashed against the window, but she didn't even remove her wet clothes. When she fell asleep it was heavily, her mind taking its own respite against her despair.

Waking with a start from a dream in which she and Johnny were playing tag in the Bishop's Park, darting from tree to tree laughing and calling softly to each other, she was hit again by the shock of the truth. The sun was shining on her eyelids and her eyes began to throb. Warmth and light were filtering past the thin curtains. It was broad daylight.

She tried to swallow but her mouth was too dry, her throat hurt and she ached all over her body. Trying to sit up in bed, she found it impossible and fell back, moaning softly, the room whirling around her. Vaguely she worried. It was Monday, wasn't it? She had to get up and go to the Grays' house, she had the weekly wash to do. Was it Monday? Or Sunday? The effort of thinking was too much for her.

I'll give myself five more minutes, then I'll get up. Just five minutes more, that's all I need, she thought wearily and closed her eyes. She dreamed that Johnny was in the room. Somehow he had found out where she was – had he got her note? She knew he was there just out of sight.

In a minute she would turn her head and he would be there, smiling at her. And Eliza, Eliza was holding her up and helping her to drink, a long, cool drink of water. Ada drank thirstily and lay back. No, it wasn't Eliza, was it? She tried to make out the face but it wouldn't stay still. She thought it was Eliza but whoever it was smelled sweetly, whereas Eliza smelled of breast milk, babies and soap. She knew the smell, though, she did, she wished she could remember, then she could go back to sleep. Virginia's scent, that's what it was. What was Virginia doing here in her bedroom? It was a puzzle, a puzzle which was beyond her.

Ada gave up the effort and drifted off into sleep, a sleep penetrated by voices. Mrs Dunne, was it? And Dr Gray? She tried to move her arm but it hurt so she lay still.

Johnny had gone, he wasn't there any more. Desolation hit her. She submitted to hands holding her, cool fingers on her wrist, she saw a stethoscope. She fell asleep.

Virginia burst into her father's consulting room as he was busy writing up notes after his evening surgery. Her blonde curls were falling down over her shoulders where they had escaped her hair ribbon and she was panting.

'Virginia! What on earth have you been doing? Come over here and sit down this instance. You're quite out of breath,' Dr Gray exclaimed, his voice sharp with concern, for she had only recently recovered from pneumonia.

'Please, Daddy, you must come. You have to see Ada!'

'Never mind that, you stupid girl. You have been exerting yourself, I can see. If I can't trust you to be sensible we will have to confine you to the house and garden.' He walked over to the washbasin in the corner and drew a tumbler of water. 'Now, sip this slowly and calm down.'

Virginia took the glass and sipped obediently, for in truth her rush up from Gilesgate had made her feel decidedly unwell. Perhaps she wasn't as strong as she had thought. Dr Gray watched her with concern as slowly her pulse settled down and her high colour faded.

'Now,' he said at last, 'what is this all about? Ada, did you say? Isn't that the girl you've been helping to read and write?'

Virginia nodded. 'Oh, Daddy, she didn't come today and I knew something must be wrong and I got her address from Cook and I thought I'd just walk down there –'

'I said calm down,' Dr Gray cut in. 'Take it slowly. Now, what was the matter, then?'

'Oh, she's ill, Daddy, really ill and her landlady didn't even know, she thought Ada had gone out to work.' Virginia looked up at her father with appeal in her eyes. 'You will come and see her, Daddy, won't you?'

'I'll come.' Dr Gray moved briskly now he knew the

trouble, picking up his bag and hat, he moved to the door. 'You'd better come and show me the way.'

It took less than ten minutes to get to Gilesgate in the pony trap. The arrival of the doctor caused a stir in the street; women came to their front doors and stood watching curiously and urchins gathered round. Once he was inside, Dr Gray quickly assessed the situation. Ada had a fever, her throat was inflamed and her joints stiff and painful. He looked around the shabby room and then at Mrs Dunne, who was standing anxiously in the doorway.

'Are you any relation to the girl?' he asked.

'No, I'm just the landlady. I didn't know she was bad. I didn't even know she was still in the house.'

Mrs Dunne was on the defensive. She hardly knew the girl any road, she thought to herself. She simply could not afford to keep her and nurse her. 'I haven't time to look after her properly, she's just the lodger, you know.'

'It's all right, Mrs Dunne.' The doctor had realised what was going through her mind and came to a decision quickly. This was no place for anyone seriously ill. 'She will be better off in the hospital. If you will allow me I'll borrow a blanket to wrap her in and take her myself,' he said.

The landlady couldn't help showing her relief, but then, worried that she should appear uncaring, she wrung her hands.

'I would have seen to her if things had been different. But I'm a widow, I can't manage as it is . . .' Her voice tailed off.

'No, of course not. It's all right, really it is. If you could change her into a proper nightgown? Then I'll manage.' He gazed thoughtfully at the slight figure on the bed. She would be light enough to carry. Still, though she was too small and thin for her age, these small women sometimes had iron constitutions. He only hoped Ada was one of them, for Virginia's sake as well as her own. Virginia seemed to be fond of the girl.

He carried Ada downstairs and out to the trap, where he put her half lying, half sitting along the side seat. Virginia clambered in beside her, holding her carefully as Dr Gray turned the trap round and set off through the crowd of children which had gathered. The journey to the workhouse hospital was not long but there were cobbles to negotiate in places and Ada was rocked about at times, making her moan with pain.

'Hold her, for goodness' sake, Virginia,' he said impatiently. 'Try to shield her from the bumping of the wheels.'

Virginia blushed, feeling she should have thought of that herself.

Soon Ada was ensconced in the women's medical ward, where she was given the quietest corner through the influence of Dr Gray. He was well known there through his work in the poorer districts of the city. As he left the nursing staff carrying out his instructions for her welfare, he knew she would be looked after to the best of their ability. He drove Virginia home before going on with his rounds. She was very subdued; it had been her first glimpse of the bare, dingy wards of a workhouse hospital.

'Don't worry, Virginia,' he said softly as he lifted her down from the trap. 'I know the wards are pretty spartan but the nursing staff are efficient and well used to the careful nursing required for acute rheumatism, which is what ails your friend. Goodness knows, they see plenty of it in varying degrees of seriousness.' He sighed and dropped a kiss on his daughter's solemn face. 'Rheumatic fever is only too common among the poor of this great land of ours. Now, you must rest for what's left of the afternoon or we will be worrying about you next.'

'Yes, Daddy. Thank you for what you did.' She gave him a small smile before she went indoors. For the first time she was really beginning to appreciate how fortunate she was to have been born with a father and mother who cared what happened to her. Poor Ada!

Ada was oblivious to everything but the warm bed and blessed relief from her consuming thirst. But as she gradually came back to life and reality, as she began to lift her head to see where she was, she realised that yet another calamity had befallen her. Her childhood nightmares were coming true. She was in the dreaded workhouse, the one place she had sworn she would never go. She must have done something really, really bad. She cried a lot, for she felt too weak to help herself, too weak ever to be able to work again. She had reached rock bottom. Now she felt vulnerable, at the mercy of others, she who had always been healthy and hard-working. Since that awful night with Uncle Harry, she had lost Johnny, her health and her independence. Depression settled on her and she lay unseeing and uncaring. All her ambitions had come to nothing. Even her lessons with Virginia would stop if she wasn't strong enough to do the family's washing. Virginia might not want to know her anyway, because to be tainted with the workhouse was worse than being a washerwoman.

At home, Virginia was glowing with the new image of herself as Ada's saviour. Why, if she hadn't sought the poor girl out, Ada could have died before the landlady thought to look into her room. It was nice to bask in Daddy's approval, too; Virginia liked the feeling and an idea began to form in her mind. Seeking out her parents, she put it to them.

'Have Ada here when she comes out of hospital?'

Mrs Gray's eyes widened in surprise at Virginia's

request. She didn't know what to say; she looked across the breakfast table at her husband for guidance.

'Ada will have to take things easy at first, Virginia. I'm not sure, she would only be able to take on light duties. I don't really think your mother needs more help in the house in any case and I can't afford to pay more for staff.'

'I mean as a companion to me. Oh, come on, Daddy, Ada wouldn't want any wages. There's Nanny's old room, she could sleep there.'

Dr Gray still looked dubious and Virginia played her trump card.

'Oh, Daddy, you know where she was living, it's not the right place for a convalescent. And she wouldn't get fed properly, you know she wouldn't.' Virginia put just the right note of sympathy for Ada into her voice and knew she was winning when her father gave her mother a questioning glance. She pressed her point home. 'Good food and fresh air are the best things to help one recover from an illness. That's what you said to me.'

'You will have to help get the room ready.' Mrs Gray spoke for the first time. She smiled at her husband. Virginia always could get him to do what she wanted him to, she thought fondly. Fathers and daughters!

Virginia felt sure that her offer of a home to Ada would be welcome. Surely Ada didn't want to go back to that horrible room in Gilesgate? No, she assured herself, Ada would come. She would be a fool not to. Virginia felt confident enough to start sorting out the room for Ada, her thoughts running happily on as she did so. Daddy would be really pleased with her for being so kind to a poor girl like Ada, and Mummy would get some help with light household tasks – Ada would want to do something. It was a very good thing to have thought of all round.

'Hello, Ada! Feeling better?'

At the cheery call Ada turned her head to see her friend smiling down at her so infectiously that she had to smile back, lifting her head and fluttering her hands in greeting.

'Oh, do lie still. Daddy says I have to keep you quiet or I won't be able to come again. Look what I've brought you! I pilfered the garden, I thought they would remind you of it.' Virginia laid an enormous bunch of flowers on the locker. There were phlox and delphiniums, candytuft and sweet peas, filling the ward with the scent of summer.

'And grapes, one always brings grapes to invalids.' She broke a gleaming black grape from the bunch she was taking out of her bag and popped it into her mouth. 'Scrumptious!' she declared.

'Miss Leigh is not yet allowed fruit.' An officious-sounding nurse happened to be passing the end of the bed and she looked over disapprovingly. Virginia was crestfallen for a moment but she soon brightened up again.

'Oh, well, someone will like them,' she said and perched on the side of the bed, ignoring the nurse's outraged look. 'Oh, Ada, wait till I tell you! I've had a lovely idea. I talked it over with the parents and they said it was all right.'

'What is?' Ada asked weakly. Virginia's exuberance was almost too much for her.

'Why, for you to come and live with us. As soon as you're well enough, of course. There, now, what do you think of that?'

'Come and live with you?' Ada gazed at Virginia, sure she hadn't heard her aright. 'How can I come and live with you? I'm not strong enough to work.' To Ada's way of thinking the only way she could live at the Grays' house was as a servant, for she would have to earn her keep.

Virginia was impatient. 'No, no, I mean come and *live* with us, you don't have to do much. You can be my companion. And you will get stronger, you'll see, and everything will be lovely.'

Ada was flabbergasted. It just couldn't be true! She demurred weakly but the thought of having a home at the Grays' house and being safe for a while was very tempting in spite of her independent outlook on life. Weak tears ran down her cheeks and Virginia jumped up in concern.

'Oh, dear, I've made you too tired. And I promised Daddy I wouldn't.' She leaned over and patted Ada on the cheek. 'Never mind, dear, it will be all right. It's just too soon for you to have to make decisions, that's what it is. Look, you go to sleep and I'll go now. I just had to tell you about it but if you don't want to – no, never mind, I'll go.'

Left to think about it in the intervals between her frequent naps, Ada worried about the reaction of Mrs Gray, a quiet, soft-spoken woman she hardly knew. Did she really not care if her daughter mixed with a girl of the servant class and, what was worse, the lowest rank of the servant class? A girl with no family? That was one of the many questions running around in Ada's head, but in her weakened state the thought that she could have somewhere to go when she left hospital was a tonic in itself. It was an offer of escape from the workhouse sooner than expected, a chance to begin again. In the end these were the considerations that weighed the most and Ada gratefully decided to accept the Grays' kind offer. She even began to look forward to the future a little, once again.

There had been no reason to worry about Mrs Gray not wanting her, Ada found when she finally arrived at the Grays'. Mrs Gray adored her husband and thought that everything he said was right must be so. Once he had agreed to having Ada as a companion for their daughter, it was for his wife to support him, and she did so wholeheartedly. She welcomed Ada to her house one late August afternoon with a kindly smile and warm words.

Dr Gray had called for Ada at the hospital after he had finished his rounds. He helped her down from the trap and gave her his arm to lean on as they walked to the front door where his wife was waiting.

'How are you, my dear?' Mrs Gray stepped forward. 'Better, I hope? I'm sure you will want to go straight to your room, you must still feel weak. Virginia will show you, won't you, Virginia?'

Virginia had heard the sound of the wheels on the gravel of the drive and was coming up from the garden, her face split into a wide grin. She slipped her arm through Ada's.

'You're here at last. I've been waiting for ages. Come on then, we'll go up. I have heaps to talk to you about.'

'Don't tire her, Virginia,' Dr Gray called. 'And while you're about it, don't forget you're still convalescent yourself.'

Virginia pulled a face at him and led Ada up the stairs to a small bedroom at the back of the house. 'It was Nanny's room,' she said as they stood in the doorway. 'I asked if you could have this room because it is close to mine. I know it's only small but . . .'

'It's lovely,' breathed Ada, gazing round at the bowl of flowers on the dresser, the chintz curtains at the window. The walls were distempered a very pale magnolia so that the general effect was bright, cheerful and airy. Her box must have been collected from Mrs Dunne's for her clothes were laid out on the patchwork counterpane. This, thought Ada, was by far the grandest bedroom she had ever been in. There was even a proper wardrobe of light mahogany. She wandered in and touched the smooth polished wood, unable to say more.

'You do like it, don't you?' Virginia faltered as Ada stood without speaking.

'Eeh, I do, I love it!' Ada showed it in the enthusiastic face she turned to Virginia and the way she completely forgot her resolution never to say 'Eeh' again. 'I'm so grateful, I promise I'll do my best to pay you back – as soon as I'm strong enough, that is. I'll work.' Work, Ada thought, was all she had to give. She was overwhelmed by the kindness of the Gray family. It was all completely new to her, though, this feeling of obligation to other people, and a spark of her former independent spirit was flickering to life inside her.

The two girls smiled at each other, and Mrs Gray, coming along the corridor just then, was struck by the contrast between them. Ada had become painfully thin during her illness and she had a melancholy air. Virginia, on the other hand, was getting quite plump and pink-cheeked; she had recovered almost completely from her illness earlier in the year.

'Come down when you're ready, girls,' Mrs Gray said as she passed them. 'There's tea in the conservatory.'

'Yes, Mum,' Virginia answered and waited until they were alone again before asking Ada, 'Did you hear from your friend in Middlesbrough, then?'

'I heard he died,' Ada said bleakly, turning her head away and staring out of the window to the kitchen garden.

'Oh, Ada, how sad!' Virginia put her arms around the thin shoulders and hugged her.

'It's all right,' said Ada. 'After all, he wasn't really my lad.' She felt awkward, she wasn't used to people being so demonstrative. Virginia gave her a puzzled look but said no more; unpleasant things were best forgotten in her philosophy.

Gradually, during the remainder of the summer and early autumn, Ada began to recover her normal good health. Dr Gray had reassured her that the attack had not been such a serious one; her heart was not affected so there was no reason to suppose she would not make a full recovery.

'You have a good constitution,' he told her. 'You must have been well-nourished as a child.' Ada thought about the enormous plates of dinner which Auntie Doris had served in the boarding house. At least some good had come from her childhood there.

Living with the family but not of the family, Ada had to remind herself frequently that she would soon have to leave and make her own way again. But time enough to think of that when she was well. Meanwhile, she sat in the garden with Virginia when it was fine, or took slow walks by the River Wear. She took on small jobs of sewing she noticed needed doing, repairing household linen or sewing on buttons. She tried hard to make herself useful as far as she could.

Still, the bouts of depression brought on by her illness kept recurring. At times she felt lower than she had ever felt before and found it very difficult to hide from Virginia, who didn't understand. Virginia liked everyone to be bright and smiling all the time.

If only Eliza lived nearby, she thought, longing to talk to her. Virginia wasn't the same and at the back of Ada's mind was the realisation that Virginia would go back to school in a short time. Then there would be no reason to stay with the Grays, imposing on a family which had always been kind to her.

Ada tried to keep her mind occupied by watching the family and patterning her behaviour and speech on theirs. She had almost succeeded in eliminating the scorned 'Eeh', substituting 'Oh'. Books were becoming her great delight for her reading and writing had improved at a tremendous rate, and she had discovered a great capacity for knowledge. Somehow, Mr Johnson had found out about her illness and he visited her one day as she sat in the garden alone, Virginia having gone with her mother on a call.

'Mr Johnson! How did you know I was here?'

Ada remembered her manners as the old man came across the lawn, a box of chocolates in his hand. 'How are you, Mr Johnson? I do hope you found someone else to do your washing.'

'Never mind that, how are you, my dear? I was worried about you when you didn't turn up for work.' He looked around for a seat and took a garden chair, bringing it beside Ada. 'You don't mind if I sit down, do you?' He handed Ada the chocolates, the first chocolates she had ever had in her life. 'I hope you like chocolates, my dear.'

Ada didn't know whether she did or not, but she was overwhelmed by the gift. She took the box, which had a picture of a lady in a great hat covered with roses and a bright red ribbon on the corner.

'Oh yes, I do, Mr Johnson, it's ever so kind of you.'

'Nonsense, Ada. I saw Dr Gray in Silver Street yesterday and asked if he knew what had happened to you, I remembered you mentioned his daughter to me once. I was so sorry to hear you'd been so ill. I hope you're getting better now – coming along, are you?'

'I'm almost back to normal, thank you, Mr Johnson.'

Ada made to rise from her chair. 'I've got your book of folk tales in my room, I'm sorry I kept it so long. I'll go and get it, it won't take a minute.'

'No, no, you keep it, my dear.' Mr Johnson put out his hand to stop her. He glanced at the book she had put on the table when he had come. 'What's this you're reading now? May I?' He picked up the book and scanned it briefly. 'A life of Florence Nightingale? Do you have ambitions to be a nurse?'

'Well, I had thought . . .'

'You'll need to know some elementary mathematics for that. I have just the right textbook for you. I'll bring it over.'

'Well, I haven't really thought of nursing, I don't think – with not going to school and all –'

'It doesn't matter, not if you're determined, Ada. If you are prepared to work, that is.'

Ada lay back on her cushion. Suddenly she felt tired, doubtful of herself and her abilities. Mr Johnson was well-meaning, but there was the business of earning a living, which had to come before any future ambitions. He saw she had wearied at once.

'I'll go now, Ada,' he said. 'I don't want to tire you too much. But I'll come back to see you if I may?'

'Yes, of course, Mr Johnson.'

Ada picked up the box of chocolates after he had gone. It did look lovely, it was a shame to open it, she thought listlessly. And anyway, chocolate didn't taste like pear drops. But the ribbon reminded her of the ones Johnny had bought her, long ago, on her birthday. Was it her eighth birthday or tenth? Auntie Doris had confused her. Maybe she would seek out her birth certificate.

Chapter Thirteen

'Only three more weeks and I go back to school,' Virginia said one day as they were standing in the conservatory looking out on a rain-sodden garden.

'Three weeks!' It came as a shock to Ada. Oh, she knew it had to come, but now it loomed so near she felt suddenly insecure.

'And I'll be back at university working for my finals.' Tom came up behind them and grinned at the girls as they turned to greet him. 'Then won't I be grand? Dr Thomas Gray! I sometimes think it will never happen.'

'Oh, course it will.' Virginia was stout in her support of Tom's flagging confidence. As far as she was concerned her brother could do anything.

Tom laughed at her but his eyes were on Ada. She looked up, caught his eye and was a little disturbed at the interest she saw there. Her composure slipped and she turned away, fiddling with the belt of her skirt.

'Come on.' Tom smiled and linked an arm with both girls. 'Let's not just stand here being as gloomy as the weather. We'll have a game of cards, shall we?' He marched them both, laughing, into the dining room, where they proceeded for a hilarious couple of hours to play pontoon for matchstick money. Ada was completely new to the game, there had been no time in her past life for such pastimes, and she concentrated seriously on it.

Tom cheated outrageously, acquiring a huge pile of matches and bankrupting Virginia to her squeals of protest. But he was watching the sparkle of fun in Ada's eyes as she saw what he was up to and the way she threw herself into the game with evident enjoyment as soon as she was sure of the rules.

'Let's have a stroll, shall we?' Virginia suggested at last. The sun had come out and the thought of getting out and about was inviting. So the girls brought wraps and the three of them walked down Elvet to the racecourse by the Wear. Somehow it was Ada's side Tom was by for most of the time, with Virginia in front or bringing up the rear. Virginia, never slow to spot a budding romance, ended up trailing behind wearing a knowing smile.

The sun gleamed on the Wear, which was rain-swollen and peaty brown from the fells. In the distance Pelaw Wood was becoming tinged with the colours of autumn, copper, red and gold. The grass still sparkled with rain. Tom watched the two girls. Ada's white shirtwaister was the perfect foil for her dark curls and pink cheeks, providing the complete contrast to Virginia's fair prettiness. The warmth of the sun and the warmth of Tom's smile, for he was putting himself out to charm, combined to give Ada the happiest time she had had since that spring day in the Bishop's Park, a lifetime ago or so it seemed to her.

'I think my brother has a pash on you,' Virginia said wickedly as she sat at her dressing table that evening. Ada was brushing the thick, fair hair with a silver-backed hairbrush, something Virginia loved.

'What?' Ada paused in mid-stroke, she was so surprised. She looked over Virginia's shoulder into the looking glass and saw the other girl's grin. 'Oh, Virginia, you're being daft!'

'I'm not. And I do believe you are blushing.' Virginia grinned mischievously again as Ada picked up a green ribbon the exact shade of Virginia's dress and tied it in a big bow at the nape of her neck.

'Well, *I* believe we will be late down if we don't get a move on.' Ada was brisk, the best way to cope with Virginia's nonsense was simply to ignore it. Tom was just being nice to his sister's friend because he was that sort of a lad, she told herself, that was all there was to it. But she remembered the look in his eyes earlier in the day.

'Oh, I know my own brother!' Virginia gave her appearance a cursory glance in the looking glass and grimaced at her reflection as she moved to the door. Ada followed with mixed feelings. She would be self-conscious now around Tom, she thought vexedly. But the main result of the conversation was that it had made her think again about Johnny. The picture rose again in her mind, the laughing green eyes and vivid hair, even the light, clean smell of him. She became very quiet with a faraway look in her lovely eyes as they sat down to dinner.

'Penny for your thoughts!' said Tom in the time-honoured way. He had been watching her from his seat across the table from her. She had finished her meal and was gazing out of the window at the fading sunset which lit the trees with a rosy glow. The usual family small talk flowed around her and she had been letting her mind drift. She looked up at Tom with a start.

'I wasn't really thinking of anything.'

'Perhaps this would be a good time to discuss your future,' the doctor broke in from his place at the head of the table. He too had been watching Ada and it occurred to him that she could be worrying about it. 'We thought,' he went on, 'Mrs Gray and I, that you might stay on here after Virginia goes back to school.' He turned to his wife. 'Ada could help you round the house, we thought, didn't we, dear?' Mrs Gray nodded her agreement.

'Oh, that would be lovely!' Virginia clapped her hands and grinned widely at Ada. 'Then you would be here when I come home for Christmas.'

'I don't know.' Ada faltered. 'You are all so kind to me, the kindest people I have ever met. But I must get back to standing on my own feet. I must not be a burden to you.'

'Nonsense,' Mrs Gray put in crisply. 'You will be a help, not a burden. We only have Cook living in and you can help me with the light housework. It will be nice to have you when the children go back, it's rather lonely here with the doctor out all hours. That's all settled then, at least for the present. Until you are much stronger than you are now.'

Ada had her reservations, though, and by Mrs Gray's last remark she realised it was not a permanent offer. But she hadn't been thinking about her future; her thoughts had been in the past for the whole of the evening. She thought now about the one friend she had left behind in Bishop Auckland and reproached herself for not getting in touch with Eliza before now. As soon as she could she would go to her room and write to West Auckland, she could write quite a good letter now.

A week later a reply to her letter came back. She opened the letter while sitting at breakfast one morning and read it with Virginia waiting impatiently to hear what it was all about. This was the first post Ada had received during her stay with them and Virginia was curious.

'Well, what is it? Who is it from?' Virginia could contain herself no longer.

'Virginia! Don't pry into Ada's private affairs,' said Mrs Gray sharply.

'It's all right, Mrs Gray.' Ada looked up and smiled at Virginia. 'It's from a friend of mine, I used to work with her in Bishop Auckland. Now she lives in West Auckland and she wants me to go to see her on Saturday if I can manage it.'

'Oh, yes. I remember you writing to her, ages ago,' Virginia commented. 'Do you mean to say she has only just replied?'

'No.' Ada had a pang of conscience as she remembered the appeal in Eliza's last letter, the one she had received just before she was ill. She should have gone to see her friend as soon as she was fit enough. Looking at the letter again, Ada saw that Eliza didn't seem quite so unhappy; perhaps she was getting used to living in West Auckland. 'She would like me to go to see her.'

'Why not?' Virginia blithely ignored her mother's quelling glance and looked hopefully at Ada. 'May I go with you? I've never been to West Auckland.' Virginia was always ready for an outing of any kind.

'Well . . .' Ada was a little taken aback; Eliza would not

be prepared for a lady visitor. It could be embarrassing for her, being so poor.

'Virginia!' Mrs Gray had noticed Ada's hesitation and guessed the reason for it. 'Will you behave yourself?' This time the note in her voice got through to Virginia and she subsided with a pout.

'I tell you what,' Tom chipped in, seeing his sister's disappointment. 'We will all three go to Bishop Auckland. I can take the trap and we can have a picnic in the park while Ada goes to see her friend. How about that?'

Virginia agreed with enthusiasm. 'Tom! What a good idea! I've never been to Bishop Auckland either and it will be such a nice ride out. You're the best brother anyone ever had!' she declared, rather extravagantly.

Ada smiled gratefully at Tom. She hadn't wanted to disappoint Virginia but she had been in a difficult position.

'I don't remember saying you could use the trap.' Dr Gray spoke for the first time. Virginia looked at him in consternation and he twinkled at her expression. 'Well,' he said grudgingly, 'I don't usually need it on Saturdays. I suppose you can have it.' He ducked behind his newspaper and smiled broadly at his wife.

'Oh, you!' Virginia relaxed.

'But only if the weather is fine, mind,' her father added as an afterthought before changing the subject and speaking to Tom. 'I was thinking of buying a motorcar.

Maybe next week, before you go back to university, we'll begin to look around for one.'

Tom gasped with pleasure and the rest of the conversation was dedicated to the relative merits of the various makes of car. Ada went to her room to write a postcard to Eliza confirming her visit for Saturday.

Saturday, when it came round, was a fine September day with just a hint of frost in the morning which soon burned off as the sun rose. The little party setting out in the pony trap were full of high spirits. There was enough food packed by Cook to last them for the whole weekend rather than one day. Mrs Gray came to the front door to wave them off and they set off down the drive and up the hill towards Neville's Cross sedately enough.

Turning south onto the Great North Road, however, Tom drove down the hill at a spanking pace. The valley lay spread out before them with golden fields of corn interspersed with green pastureland and the even darker green of the woods. Smoke from a colliery chimney in the distance added a soft haze to the view.

The two girls chatted together happily, looking around them and pointing out anything of interest. It seemed barely a few minutes before they were going through Spennymoor, the little town busy with morning shoppers. Ada couldn't help contrasting her situation now with that when she had last come through the town, and she was quiet for a moment as she thought how lucky she had been to meet Virginia.

'Is something wrong?' Virginia asked, having noticed Ada's solemn expression.

'No, nothing's wrong, nothing at all.' Ada smiled at her. 'Oh, look at that, isn't it pretty?' She indicated a tiny front garden ablaze with late-summer flowers, thus successfully turning Virginia's attention away from herself. Today was going to be a happy day with no time for thinking serious thoughts. As they neared the old market town of Bishop Auckland and climbed slowly up Durham Chare, turning into the marketplace by the arched entrance to the castle, the clock above the gate struck eleven.

'I'll run you into West Auckland, Ada,' said Tom. 'There's still plenty of time before lunch. It's not far and I can drop you at your friend's house, then I will know exactly where to pick you up.'

'No,' said Ada swiftly. 'There's no need. I'd rather go on the horse bus. They run quite often on Saturdays.'

Tom was about to argue the point but he saw that Ada was determined and held his peace. He was becoming sensitive to her feelings and realised that she had a good reason for wanting to go alone.

'Well, if you're sure.' He frowned slightly as he looked down at her. 'Shall I pick you up then?'

'No. The pony will have had quite enough by the time

we get home. No, the horse bus will be quite all right.'

Tom bit his lip; he was reluctant to leave her but it was obvious that was what she wanted. 'Righto,' he said at last. 'We'll meet by the castle gates then. At five o'clock? Is that long enough for you?'

'Five o'clock. Lovely.' Ada took his hand in hers and squeezed it gently. 'Oh, Tom, you're so good to me,' she said softly.

Virginia gave them both a meaningful look. 'Well, he would be, wouldn't he?' she asked archly. Ada shook her head and laughed; Virginia was incorrigible. Raising a hand in farewell, she took her basket from Tom and went off to catch the horse bus.

Front Street, West Auckland, next to the Rose and Crown public house; Ada repeated the directions in her mind as she stepped down onto the cobbles with her basket. She had small presents for the children and a fruitcake which Mrs Gray had pressed upon her in the basket, and she moved it from one hand to another as she looked around, searching for the inn sign. She wasn't long in seeing the inn board swaying in the breeze and she was soon knocking on Eliza's open front door.

'Eeh, Ada! It's grand to see you.' Eliza came bustling through from the kitchen, looking slimmer than when Ada last saw her. Nevertheless she looked blooming with health. Her fair hair was pinned in a bun at the back of her head, her black dress was covered with a snowy white apron and her sleeves were rolled up to the elbows. She kissed Ada soundly on the cheek and led her into the room, turning to look her over critically.

'I was just making a batch of teacakes. Bertie loves a teacake fresh from the oven, he's just like his da in that. And you look as though you could do with a bite of something good to eat. Have you been all right, lass? Eeh, many's the time I've thought about you. You do look a bit peaky, like.'

'I'm all right, Eliza. I was poorly for a while, I was in the hospital. But I'm fine now and living with a lovely family. Oh, Eliza, I've so much to tell you, there's so much to talk about. And I want to hear all your news.'

'Well, we'll have a cup of tea and a bite of dinner, then we'll sit down and tell each other everything. Eeh, the hospital, though. You must have been bad for that. You'll have to tell me all about it.' Eliza was so obviously concerned for her and delighted to see her that Ada's heart warmed.

She sat by the gleaming, black-leaded range where in spite of the heat of the day a fire blazed, stoked up to keep the oven hot enough for the teacakes. She watched Eliza as she brought in the baking tray with the teacakes and put it on the steel fender before the fire to prove. The heat from the fire matched the warmth in her heart as she watched her friend.

Eliza set the table with new bread, pease pudding and a ham shank which she proceeded to strip of its meat, carefully cutting away every scrap and placing it on a plate. Finally she lifted the kettle which was singing on the hob and made a big pot of tea. Satisfied with her preparations, she wiped her hands on her pinny and smiled across the table at Ada.

'I'll just bring in the bairns,' she said. 'Bertie doesn't know you're here yet. He's in the back yard watching the cradle.'

'Watching the cradle?'

'Aye. Well, you know, we share the back yard with the pub and I don't like to leave the babby out there on his own, though this early in the day there's not many of them drunk. Later on they'll be satless. But the babby does need the fresh air.' Eliza sighed. 'I wish I could afford a little house with its own yard and netty and everything.'

'But this seems such a nice little house, Eliza, facing onto the green and all.' Ada was surprised. It wasn't like Eliza to be discontented, she was the kind who accepted things philosophically.

'Aye.' Eliza glanced out of the window pensively. 'But wait until I've seen to the bairns and I'll tell you all about it.' She went off through the kitchen, leaving Ada mystified.

Soon she was back, carrying the cradle which she placed near the door, away from the heat of the oven.

Bertie followed her and climbed up to sit at the table, staring gravely at the visitor. Obviously he felt strange with Ada, not quite sure if he knew her.

'You remember Ada, don't you, Bertie?' Ada coaxed. 'Haven't you got a kiss for me, then?' But Bertie bent his head shyly and looked at his plate.

'He'll come round. Howay and sit down at the table, Ada,' said Eliza. 'It would be nice to have my dinner before the bairn wakes and starts yelling for his.' She smiled fondly at Bertie as he stolidly ate his meal; the visitor had evidently not put him off his food. After the ham and pease pudding Ada brought out the fruitcake and they sampled it.

'Bye, it's lovely and rich, isn't it, Ada? Who did you say made it?'

'The cook who works for Mrs Gray. She's a grand cook.'

Eliza nodded her agreement as she damped her finger and picked up the crumbs on her plate with it. Ada watched. Not so long ago she would have done the same, she mused. How quickly you got used to good food.

Finally, as the baby started stirring restlessly, Eliza picked him up and put him to her breast, where he sucked contentedly. She watched Bertie's face glow as Ada brought out the wooden engine Tom had given her for the boy. Tom had had it since his own childhood. There was also a tiny cap she had knitted for Miles, and Eliza tried it on him as he fed.

'It's lovely, Ada, just his fit,' she said.

'Too hot for him this weather,' said Ada deprecatingly. 'By the time he needs it it will be too small.'

'Get away! It could be blowing cold tomorrow, the weather's so changeable.' Eliza took off the cap and put it on the table. 'Any road, now we can have a proper gossip. Tell me everything that's happened since you went away to Durham.' She appraised Ada's dress, which was of fine linen. Ada had made it over from an outgrown one of Virginia's. 'I can see you must be getting along grand,' she added.

'No, you first, I'm curious. Why do you not like living here in this house? It seems quite nice.'

Eliza sighed and looked into the fire. 'Eeh, I'm that glad to have you to talk to, Ada. I can talk to you and I know you'll understand.'

Gradually the story came out. Eliza was uneasy living in the house next to the pub for more than one reason and she told Ada all about it as she sat nursing the baby and with her little boy playing happily with the engine on the clippie mat at her feet.

'I'm not frightened of ghosts or anything, it's not that. Poor Mary Anne Cotton is surely at peace now, and her bairns an' all. No, it's the pub, I wish we didn't share a yard with the pub. An' me being a widow woman an' all.'

Ada's quick sympathy was aroused as she looked at her friend's unhappy face. She stretched out a hand to her almost involuntarily, then let it fall to her side.

'It's not safe to go out there,' Eliza confided. 'Drunks fighting and brawling on Saturday nights and sometimes on week nights. There's always someone carted off to the police cells to cool off overnight. The noise wakes the bairns.'

'Oh, Eliza, that's awful!' Ada hadn't thought of the drawbacks of having a pub next door.

Eliza nodded. 'Then there's them that think a widow must be dying for it. They come knocking at the back door, shouting for me.' Eliza's voice was calm but Ada could see that she was deeply disturbed.

'Can't you find anywhere else?' she asked, concern edging her voice.

'Nothing I can afford.' Eliza paused. 'But there is one thing. Now the babby's older I could maybe get a housekeeper's job. My Albert's brother, him that lives up by Hummerbeck, he's got a little farm. He has offered me a home in return for working there.'

'Oh, that sounds like the best answer!' Ada exclaimed. Then she saw Eliza's doubtful expression and continued, 'It is, isn't it?'

'I don't know. There's things for it and things against. Albert never got on with him really, he thought he was too grasping.'

'Well . . . surely you'll still be better off than here, Eliza? It'll be better for the bairns.'

'Mebbe I will.'

Eliza fell into a thoughtful silence before shaking off her mood. Getting to her feet, she took the now sleeping baby and laid him in the cradle.

'Now,' she said, 'what about you? Here I've been going on about my troubles and just made us both miserable. Did you hear from your Johnny? Auntie said he came looking for you a while back. Then I got a letter from him asking for your address. Did he get in touch?'

Ada whitened visibly, unable to answer for the sudden distress the question had caused her.

'Oh, whatever's the matter, pet? Did I say something wrong?' asked Eliza.

'He – he wrote to you?'

'Yes, I told you. I thought it would be a lovely surprise for you when he came to see you. Wasn't it?'

'No. I mean he didn't – I'm all right. It was just the shock of you mentioning him like that. No, he didn't come to see me.' And the story of Ada's visit to Middlesbrough, of how she heard the news of Johnny's death, came tumbling out.

'Ada! I'm that sorry.'

'Yes,' Ada said simply. She went on to tell Eliza about what had happened afterwards, her illness and how she came to be with the Gray family.

'They're so good, Eliza, you wouldn't believe. And Tom and Virginia Gray came with me to the town, to Auckland. I'm to meet them by the castle gates at five o'clock.'

Eliza glanced up at the clock on the wall. It was showing half past three. 'Eeh, well, I'll put the kettle on and we'll have another cup of tea before you go,' she said and began to bustle about buttering teacakes and making tea, talking all the time as she worked.

'I'm that sorry about the lad, Ada, you were always that fond of him even though you didn't see him for so long. But you'll get over it, pet, believe me, I know.'

'Yes, of course you do, Eliza.' Ada remembered Eliza's widowhood and all the troubles which had followed on it. 'I know, it was awful for you.' Truly awful, she knew now. There were just not the words to express it.

'Aye, well, that's gone now. And I'm that pleased you've got such good friends, Ada, they sound grand, really, and I'm that pleased for you pet.'

Eventually, after mutual assurances of keeping in touch, Ada said goodbye to Eliza and the children and set off to walk the three miles to Bishop Auckland. She wanted the time to herself, she would still be in time to meet Virginia and Tom. The afternoon was warm and sunny so she took the short cut through the fields, past the Townhead colliery yard and up the hill to the hamlet of Woodhouses. The path ran through golden cornfields and green pastures and she enjoyed the walk immensely, though she did feel very tired by the time she reached the outskirts of the town. There was no doubt that she was still not perfectly fit, she thought ruefully.

Ada decided to avoid Tenters Street, just in case she should bump into her aunt and uncle, so she approached the market square by Bondgate. As she entered the square she saw it was ten to five by the Town Hall clock, she was in good time. Her pace slowed and she relaxed.

'Where've you been, my girl?' A hand clamped round her arm from behind and, as she was swung roughly round to face her assailant, her heart dropped to her boots. There stood Harry Parker, his eyes glistening with malice, his face triumphant, and beside him stood her Auntie Doris. After the first shock of seeing them, Ada struggled in his grip, but though he was a small man he held onto her with an iron fist.

'Now, my lass!' Auntie Doris moved forward and grabbed her other arm.

'Leave me alone!' Ada yelled desperately. 'Let me go I tell you!' People walking by turned their heads to see what was up and in seconds a small crowd had gathered to enjoy the commotion, but the Parkers didn't care. Auntie Doris smacked Ada's face with all the strength she could get into her free hand and hostile murmuring ran through the crowd.

'Leave her be!'

''Ere, what d'you think you're doing? Let the lass alone!'

Doris Parker turned on them. 'Aye, I'll let her alone

when she behaves hersel'. She ran away from home, she's only fifteen. She's brazent fond, she is. She's been going with lads!' Auntie Doris was self-righteous, drawing herself up in defence.

'I didn't! I didn't!' Ada cried, her face already beginning to turn colour from the blow. Her dark curls tumbled down from their fastening as Harry Parker shook her viciously. The crowd looked at each other uncertainly. Lasses sometimes took some looking after and if they went wild . . .

'Aye, well, if you didn't, now's your chance, I'm just the lad for you!' One burly young miner winked and grinned at her suggestively.

'Here! Make way there. What are you doing with Miss Leigh?' The educated voice came from the back and the onlookers automatically gave way to it.

'Tom! Thank God, Tom!' Ada strained to break away as Tom strode up.

'There! Do you see now?' Auntie Doris said passionately to the crowd. 'That's what she's like! I don't mind telling you we have the devil of a time with her. You'd think she'd never had a decent bringing-up.'

They looked at the well-dressed young man and back at the couple struggling with the girl.

'For shame, lass,' a middle-aged woman said and folded her arms across her vast chest. 'Putting a decent family to shame, get away and behave yourself.'

Harry and Doris Parker began moving away with Ada between them as Tom tried to get through to help her but the men in the crowd, mostly short, stocky miners with muscles hardened by years of underground labour, held him off. They had their own code of ethics and a toff messing about with a young working lass was not to be tolerated, not for a minute. Tom was manhandled roughly against the wall and the mood was getting uglier by the minute.

'The polis!'

The warning cry came over the heads of the men and suddenly Tom was winded by an almighty blow to the stomach before the mob scattered into the alleys which went through to Back Bondgate and beyond. He bent over double, retching into the gutter, gasping for air.

'Tom! What is it, Tom? I saw the commotion but I couldn't see what it was. Oh, Tom, you're hurt!' Virginia climbed down from the trap where she had been holding the reins. Waiting for him by the castle gates, she had finally decided to drive to the opposite side of the market-place to look for him. She hurried over to him but when she got there she was unsure what to do, so she hopped from foot to foot, watching him anxiously.

Tom straightened up at last and took hold of her arm. 'Hurry! They've got Ada,' he managed to find enough breath to pant. He rushed her back to the trap and climbed onto the driver's bench. Picking up the reins he set off up Bondgate, deaf to Virginia's anxious questions about who had got Ada. The best he could get out of the pony was a trot, but he could see the couple with Ada between them turning into Tenters Street as he rounded the corner. Too late to stop them, he saw, as she was dragged into a house and the door firmly closed. He even heard the key turned in the lock as he flung himself down from the trap and raced up to the door. He banged on the knocker and rapped on the window, beside himself with anger. Virginia sat, her hand on her mouth, unable to believe this was actually happening.

'Go away! I'll call the polis, mind!' Doris Parker shouted through the letterbox.

'Let Ada out then! You've got no right to keep her when she doesn't want to stay! Let her go, I say!'

'Why, you impittent beggar, we've every right. We're her legal guardians and she's under age. You'd better be off with you or it will be the worse for you and the worse for her.'

'Don't you touch her! Don't you dare –' Tom burst out in fury, but his only answer was a jeering laugh as Doris went away from the door. He stood, frustrated and fuming, irresolute. He banged again on the door to no response. Should he call the police, he pondered, would it do any good? Maybe the woman was within her rights.

'Come on, Tom,' Virginia said at last. 'We'll go and tell Father. He'll know what to do.' In the end it was

Virginia who had to think for them both and decide on a course of action. 'It's no good going to the police if they really are her legal guardians. No, Father is the best person to deal with this. He'll know exactly what to do.'

Reluctantly Tom had to return to the trap and set off on the journey back to Durham – a journey which seemed a great deal longer than the one in the opposite direction that morning.

Ada heard Tom banging on the door as she was thrust into her room and the door banged shut behind her. She heard him shouting through the front door as the key turned in hers and Auntie Doris answering him, her voice raised as high as his. And she heard the shouting die down as Tom went away. He wouldn't just give up, would he? She sat on the bed in the little room in the attic and stared at the locked door in disbelief. This had to be a nightmare, surely it was? But she knew that what was happening was something she had feared all summer long. She moved restlessly and felt her cheek, gingerly touched her bruised eye, frantically wondering what to do.

They couldn't keep her here a prisoner, it just wasn't possible, she would get away. What good would it do Auntie Doris to keep her a prisoner in this room? And if she let her out to work, she would surely run away. She walked over to the skylight, which was a couple of panes set in the roof, and stood on a chair to look out. She could only see the tops of the houses opposite, no one she could call to. There was no way of getting out through the skylight and even if she could, how would she get down from the roof? Disconsolately rubbing her bruised arms, she sat back down on the bed.

The initial shock and fright were beginning to wear off and in their place came a rising anger. She *would* get away. She would refuse to work for Auntie Doris ever again. Why do they want to keep me? she reasoned. Her thoughts were repeating themselves over and over. Auntie Doris wants an unpaid skivvy. As soon as I'm loose in the house, I'll tell the boarders. No, it won't work, she must be doing it out of spite.

And Uncle Harry? The shutters closed down on her thoughts of why Uncle Harry might want her. Swiftly she took the lone chair and propped it hard under the doorknob. If she couldn't get out, Uncle Harry would not get in, either.

'Ada?' It was Auntie Doris banging on the door that roused her. Ada had dropped into a light doze on the bed. The room was in half darkness for the days were getting shorter. Jumping up as she heard the voice, she was instantly on the defensive.

'Ada, do you hear me?' Auntie Doris tried the door again, then there was a thumping sound as Uncle Harry put his shoulder against it but the door held. Ada, who had been watching it with bated breath, breathed her relief.

'Ada! Let me in, I've brought you some supper!'

'You let me out! I'll open the door all right when I go free and not till then!'

There was a whispered conversation outside the door which Ada couldn't quite make out. Then the key turned again, locking the door.

'Right then, madam!' said Auntie Doris. 'We'll see who tires first and it won't be me!'

'You can't keep me here! And if I hear Harry Parker on the landing again I'll scream the house down! Don't you let him near me! He can keep his filthy hands to himself.' Ada was beside herself with rage. The thought of that man being so close to her made her flesh creep.

'What? What did you say?' Auntie Doris's tone altered, she sounded uncertain of what Ada meant.

'You heard what I said! You keep him away from me or by God I'll swing for him!'

There was the sound of furious whispering outside the door, intensifying, then dying away, accompanied by retreating footsteps. Ada sat down on the bed, shaking uncontrollably. After a while, as the darkness deepened, she rose and went to the door, making sure the chair was firmly in place. She lay down on the bed and tried to relax. She needed all her strength for what lay ahead.

*

The sun was streaming in through the skylight when Ada awoke. She must have slept for the whole night, and she was incredulous that she could do so in her present predicament. She felt stiff and uncomfortable after sleeping in her clothes and she badly needed to pass water. She found a chamber pot under the bed and so was able to relieve herself, but when she looked in the jug on the washstand there was no water.

A glance in the looking glass showed her hair was tousled about her ears; she took out the hairpins and tried as best she could to comb it with her fingers before pinning it back into place. Sitting down, she considered her position.

She was no longer frightened of Harry Parker, she decided. Not in the daylight. Somehow or other she would make her escape and she would never come near Bishop Auckland again. She walked over to the door and took away the chair. Next time they came to open it she would be ready to get out.

Ada had not long to wait. Her straining ears caught the sound of footsteps on the stairs and she moved to the door and put her hand on the knob. She was all ready to fling open the door as soon as the key was turned and dive past whoever it was. The key did turn in the lock and she was away, pushing past Auntie Doris and taking both flights of stairs two at a time till she reached the hall. The front door was open but there was someone standing in the way of her headlong rush. She thrust out her hands to push whoever it was out of her path.

'Ada!' Strong arms grabbed her and she struggled frantically. 'Ada, it's all right, it's me! Ada . . .' Ada looked up into the smiling face of Dr Gray. All her nervous energy drained from her and she collapsed against his chest.

Travelling back to Durham, Ada felt as though a great shadow had been removed from her life. She sat in the trap beside Tom, who held a protective arm around her, his face full of concern. She was light-hearted, almost dizzy with relief. The scene around her was unreal to her eyes for she couldn't believe she was out of that room.

'How?' she asked at last as they turned the corner at Neville's Cross. 'How did you do it?' And Tom told her.

'We went straight home, Virginia and I. Oh, I'm so sorry we couldn't do anything yesterday – we thought about the police but we didn't really know if they could do anything, if that pair were your legal guardians. We told Father everything, all about those awful people – we knew we had to get you away but we didn't know how and Father said we knew you were older than fifteen and how could they keep you if you didn't want to stay? And I said we'd come straight away in the new motorcar – oh, Ada, Father's bought a spanking new Riley, but he said it was too late and anyway he had to practise driving first and me too, I'm going to learn – then in the end we waited until today and brought the trap. It was the safest.'

'Tom, if you don't pause for breath you'll die from lack of oxygen.' Dr Gray laughed, for Tom was going on as he had done as a boy when presented with an unexpected treat. Tom blushed and fell silent; he realised his words had been falling over themselves in his eagerness to tell Ada. Ada took his hand and squeezed it encouragingly.

'Oh, do go on! How was it that Auntie Doris gave in so easily?' For this was the question which had been puzzling Ada the most. Why take her at all just to give her up without a fight?

'It was strange, very strange,' Dr Gray remarked, nodding thoughtfully. 'Why did they give you up so easily? I simply knocked on the door and said that I wished to see you. I said if I didn't see you I intended to get legal advice on their right to hold you and also that if you were hurt in any way I would bring in the police. The woman looked an absolute fright, her hair was all over the place and her eyes were red with weeping. She just stood there, listening to me, then she stumped off up the stairs.

'"Take her! Take her!" she cried over her shoulder and the next thing you were flying down the stairs and nearly knocked me off my feet, and that was that. It's a wonder you didn't break your neck.'

'Oh!' Ada said quietly. She remembered the previous night, how she had shouted about getting the police to

Uncle Harry, telling Auntie to keep him away from her, she had been beside herself. And so, when she thought about it, she had a fair idea now of the reason for her aunt's sudden change of heart. Whatever had passed between her aunt and uncle, she would have liked to have been there to hear. She felt a rush of happiness: she was free now, both mentally and physically. It could never happen to her again.

'Never mind why the old harridan let Ada go, it's just a jolly good thing it's all over and done with,' said Dr Gray.

'Yes, indeed.' Tom was emphatic in his reply. He took Ada's hand and held it firmly in his own for the rest of the journey. He never wanted to spend another night like the one he had just gone through.

Chapter Fourteen

The house was very quiet when Tom went back to medical school and Virginia to her boarding school. Ada helped Mrs Gray around the house but still found she had time on her hands, something that was a completely new experience to her. She spent a lot of time reading books, some which Mr Johnson lent her and some from the Grays' library. She was also doing mathematical exercises which Mr Johnson set her each week and she really enjoyed doing them. Mr Johnson seemed to enjoy teaching her, too, he was always waiting for her when she paid him her once-a-week visit.

'It's a pleasure to teach such a quick mind, my dear,' he said when she thanked him for his help one day. Ada supposed he just liked to keep his hand in with teaching; after all, it had been his life's work.

One morning, as she dusted the furniture in the hall, she caught sight of her hands in the looking glass above the hallstand. They were so white, almost like a lady's hands, she thought, with a start of surprise. What a difference it made not having to immerse them in hot soapy water every day! The skin was white and soft, the nails no longer brittle and broken but a smooth oval like Virginia's. Despite all the years of hard work in Auntie Doris's boarding house, they had not been spoiled altogether.

Absent-mindedly Ada rubbed the already shining hall table. Why had Auntie Doris been so determined to keep her in the house in Auckland? she wondered. She must have known it couldn't last for ever, that she could not get away with telling Ada she was younger than she was when Ada knew it was a lie. But then, she decided, Auntie Doris was like that. A lot of folk were, it was just putting off the day, as they say. Eliza had said she could get her birth certificate from the register office, she remembered now. She glanced at the clock: it was almost noon. She would ask Dr Gray about that when he came home for lunch, it would be best to have it anyway.

'Why, yes, Ada,' Dr Gray replied to her query. 'The register office is in Old Elvet. If you go down there you can get a copy of your birth certificate.' Dr Gray paused for a moment before going on. 'There is a small fee, sixpence I believe. Do you have it?'

Ada blushed. She did have a small amount of money,

but she didn't actually get a wage from the Grays; after all, she didn't really do enough work to pay for her keep in her own estimation. She had thought she could begin doing the washing and ironing again for the household, but Mrs Gray wouldn't hear of it.

'No, no, Ada,' she had said when Ada suggested it. 'I'm perfectly satisfied now I send it out to that new laundry in the marketplace. The work was too hard for you in any case. It's better for me too, no clothes about the place on wet days or lines cluttering up the garden.'

Ada knew she would have to find a way of making some money, even though, for the time being, she had her home and food with the Grays. She needed extras, and she wanted Christmas presents for Virginia and the others . . . And shortly she would have to find a home elsewhere, and for that she had to earn. Still, she could manage sixpence for her birth certificate.

'Oh, yes, I'm all right, doctor,' she answered now. When she first came to the house Ada had thought that the Grays must be very rich to live the way they did, but now she knew they had to be careful with their money. There was rich and rich and it all depended on whether you were looking at it from a labourer's point of view or someone's further up the scale.

Ada was given the idea for a solution the very next time she went to see Mr Johnson, a visit she meant to combine with going to the register office. They sat in the deep leather armchairs in his study, a fire blazing in the hearth for the day was cold and dark. Mr Johnson was opposite Ada, the firelight glinting on his snowy hair, his face animated as he talked of his favourite subject, history, in particular, local history. Today he was telling her of the battles against the Scots.

'A warrior race, the people of Durham,' he said. 'Independent and brave. You can be proud of your ancestors, Ada.'

Ancestors, thought Ada. If only she knew her immediate family, let alone those who lived centuries ago, the ones Mr Johnson was talking about. He fell silent, staring into the fire, and Ada looked around the room. It was obviously a man's room, with its leather chairs, dark wooden furniture bought for utility rather than elegance, and a faded carpet on the floor. Books were everywhere and she noticed most of them were covered in a film of dust. Mr Johnson had a woman coming in a couple of times a week, Ada knew, but the house had an air of neglect. Ada had an idea; she put it to Mr Johnson before she could think twice about it.

'Mr Johnson, couldn't you do with someone to help out in the house?'

He looked up in astonishment, his thoughts had been elsewhere. He glanced around him. It seemed all right to him.

'I don't know, Ada. I have someone coming in. I don't want a stranger disturbing my things.'

Ada saw his surprise and realised she might have sounded a bit cheeky. 'I'm sorry, Mr Johnson, I just thought, if you needed someone I could –'

'Oh! You mean yourself?' He bit his lip as he thought about it. 'I couldn't afford to pay you, Ada. And I couldn't expect you to do it for nothing.'

'I didn't mean I wanted paying, Mr Johnson,' Ada replied quickly, though in truth she had been hoping. 'I could come anyway. I wouldn't disturb your things but I could come over a little earlier than I do now and maybe just do a few jobs.' After all, she thought, he was so good to her, helping her to educate herself.

'That would be very kind of you, Ada,' he said. 'But I do think you should give some thought to your future. Have you thought any more of becoming a nurse?'

'Not really, I don't think I know enough yet.'

'Nonsense, Ada, you have a fine mind and you're learning fast. I'm sure you could pass an entrance examination. Of course, it would mean you would have to leave the Grays: probationer nurses have to live in, I understand. Would you mind that?'

Mind it? Ada saw this was just the solution to her problems. She could be independent again. 'No, I wouldn't mind at all, Mr Johnson.'

'I think you should ask Dr Gray to find out for you

when you should apply and what it will entail,' Mr Johnson was saying.

'Yes, of course, he'll know, won't he?' Ada was getting excited at the thought. 'Bye, Mr Johnson, wouldn't it be grand if I could be a nurse?'

'I don't know about grand,' he said and laughed. 'It will be hard work. But of course you can do it, Ada, if you set your mind to it.'

Ada left his house feeling quite hopeful: she would have a career, she would be independent. She would ask Dr Gray to look into it for her as soon as she saw him that evening. Now, however, she had to go to the register office before it closed.

Ada sat on a bench by the river and stared at the envelope containing her birth certificate. As the doctor had foreseen, she had had no trouble, all she had needed to do was give her mother's name and the house where she was born, her grannie's house in Gilesgate. And now she had it, here in her hand. Slowly she drew it out of the envelope and opened it up. She was born on 20 May 1894. She had been right about her age and Auntie Doris must have known it. She read on: 'Child's name, Lorinda, Mother's name, Ada Leigh, spinster.' The place which should have contained her father's name was blank. Well, of course she had known it would be, but still, seeing it like this . . . Ada stared out at the river,

226

running high now, grey and icy-looking. She shivered and stood up, carefully putting the birth certificate back in the envelope. She walked back along the riverbank, feeling the shame which Auntie Doris had instilled into her as a small girl because she had no father.

As she walked she wondered about her mother. Why had she not come back for her? Was she dead? Or was she married now with a new family? Ada resolved to try to trace her mother. Perhaps the doctor could help her with that too.

Ada knocked on the door of Dr Gray's study after supper that evening. At least, Ada still called it supper in her mind though the Grays called the evening meal dinner; to Ada's mind, dinner was eaten at midday. Whatever the meal was named, Dr Gray usually retired to his study afterwards to catch up on paperwork.

'Hello, dear, have you something on your mind? Do sit down and tell me what it is.' Dr Gray leaned back in his chair, glad of the break. He had been working on the household bills.

'I was wondering, doctor . . .' Ada hesitated. Perhaps he would think she was aiming too high; after all, it was a long jump from an illiterate washerwoman to a probationer nurse.

'Yes?' he prompted.

'I was wondering, do you think I could train as a nurse?' It came out in a rush in the end.

Dr Gray considered the question. Ada was going to have to do something, he hadn't thought of nursing but now he realised it was perhaps just the thing for her. He was quite pleased: it showed she had been influenced by the caring image of his own profession. Then, too, it would mean she would live in at a hospital. Not that he was sorry he had asked her to stay, but it would be nice to have just the family at home again.

'Why not? You're intelligent, you've proved that this last year, and you have worked very hard. No one would now believe you had no schooling. You have recovered your health and I think you must have a strong constitution. I tell you what I'll do, I'll find out all I can for you. How old are you, Ada?'

For the first time Ada was able to say exactly how old she was.

'I will be seventeen in May, doctor,' she answered.

'Hmm. You'll have to be eighteen to begin training under the Nightingale Fund. But I can have a word with Matron at St Margaret's and see if she'll take you on as an undernurse, then, when you're eighteen, if you work hard and pass your entrance examination, you will begin training.' He sighed and glanced down at his desk. 'Now, I suppose I'd better get on with this, if you don't mind, Ada.'

Ada rose to her feet. 'Oh, no, doctor,' she said, 'and thank you, thank you for everything.' Then she remembered the other thing she had been going to ask him about. 'There was something else, though. I thought I might try to trace my mother. She went to London when I was a baby, and I wondered –'

Dr Gray was already shuffling papers and he looked up with a trace of impatience. 'I'm busy now, Ada.' As he saw her crestfallen look, he added, 'Why don't you write to the Salvation Army in London? They trace people, I think.'

The Salvation Army, of course, Ada thought, she would do it straight away. Going up to her room, she took paper and pen and composed a letter to the Salvation Army, discarding her first two attempts before she was satisfied with what she had written. She hesitated over the address, in the end deciding to simply send it to the Salvation Army, London. She didn't want to bother the doctor again and she felt sure it would reach its destination.

Next morning Ada slipped out to the pillar box on the corner and posted the letter before she could change her mind.

Two weeks later, Tom and Virginia arrived home for the Christmas holidays. Ada had never known such preparations for Christmas; Cook and Mrs Gray were busy for hours in the kitchen every single day. Puddings had been boiled and put away on the larder shelf in

October, the Christmas cake too had been baked for weeks, and now it was brought out to decorate. The smell of spices and cooking haunted the whole house.

Ada went in the trap with Dr Gray to meet Virginia from the train, looking forward to seeing her and talking over with her her decision to go nursing. For Dr Gray had indeed seen Matron for her and she was to start at the hospital in the new year.

Virginia climbed down from the train and eagerly looked up and down the platform. Seeing her father, she ran into his arms, flinging her arms around his neck and kissing him soundly. Ada stood back, feeling a little out of it.

'Daddy!' Virginia cried, tucking her arm in his. 'I'm so glad to see you. Just think, I've a whole three weeks at home, isn't it lovely?'

Dr Gray gently disengaged himself. 'Hold on, Virginia, I'm glad to see you too, but I have to get your luggage.' Only then did Virginia notice Ada.

'Oh, hello, Ada, how nice of you to come and meet me,' she said, but her eyes held only a faint interest and Ada felt chilled.

'Hello, Virginia. It's lovely to see you again,' she answered, feeling slightly hurt. Anyone would think Virginia had forgotten all about her while she'd been at school, she seemed almost surprised to see her.

Tom was quite different when he saw Ada. He lifted

her off her feet and swung her round in an arc, putting the bowl of holly on the hall table in grave danger of being knocked to the floor.

'Ada!' he cried. 'You look lovelier than ever, you'd turn any lad's head.'

'Don't talk daft, Tom,' she mumbled, flushing a rosy red, and he laughed.

'But you are, Ada, the loveliest girl in the world.'

'And what about me?' Virginia pouted. 'You always said *I* was.'

'That was before,' Tom said.

'Before what?' she demanded.

'Before you got fat and grew a pimple on your nose,' Tom answered wickedly.

'I have not!' Virginia rushed to the looking glass on the wall and examined her nose anxiously. 'Tom Gray, you're a liar. There's no pimple on my nose and I'm not fat either.'

'Aren't you?' Tom teased and she rushed at him, pummelling him in the chest. 'All right, all right, I give in!'

Ada watched them, once again feeling slightly envious of their closeness. She would have loved a brother like Tom, she thought. He saw her wistful expression and put an arm around both girls, leading them into the dining room where the huge tree was waiting to be decorated.

'And what have you been doing while we were away, Ada? Did you miss me?'

Ada took the question seriously. 'Yes' – she nodded her head – 'the house has been quiet without you. But I've got some news: I'm going to be a nurse after Christmas.'

'A nurse! Can you do that?' Virginia was very surprised. 'I always thought a good education was needed for a nurse.'

Ada bit her lip. Virginia sounded as though she thought she was aiming too high.

'Your father says I can do it. Of course, I'll just be an undernurse at first, but when I'm eighteen I can become a probationer.'

Virginia still looked sceptical but Tom smiled warmly at Ada, squeezing her arm. 'Well, I think you can do it, Ada,' he said, frowning at Virginia. 'Of course you can.'

Virginia shrugged. Now she was back at school she was not so interested in Ada as she had been, the novelty of helping an unfortunate had worn off. 'Oh, well, I'm sure you'll make a good undernurse,' she said.

Ada was determined she wasn't going to be upset by Virginia's cavalier attitude. Naturally, she told herself, Virginia was more interested in her own friends. She watched the other girl's vivacious face as she chatted about them to Tom. It didn't matter; Virginia would always be dear to her, she would always be grateful for what Virginia had made possible for her.

*

Christmas 1910 was a magical holiday for Ada. Never before had she had such a good time, not since the one Christmas she could remember before her grannie died. At Auntie Doris's house, Christmas had gone by almost unremarked, Auntie didn't believe in wasting money on festivities. Johnny had always gone home for Christmas, so Ada had been miserable until he came back.

As they did every year, the Gray family attended the midnight service in the cathedral on Christmas Eve and Ada was enthralled with it all: the majestic old church, the singing of the choir, everything. Tom couldn't keep from watching her eager, upturned face; she felt his eyes on her constantly. When she looked up from her hymnal he would catch her eye; when she sought for her wrap at the end of the service, he was there, handing it to her. She saw Tom's mother and father looking at them and knew they had noticed too. How could anybody not notice? The Grays were a nice couple, they had taken her in when she had nowhere, but would they be pleased if Tom chose her?

To be honest, Ada wasn't sure about it herself. Of course she was flattered, as any girl would be – Tom was handsome, he had a nice nature, he had prospects. But he wasn't Johnny. There now, she thought, she had determined she wasn't going to think about Johnny. She had to forget him, she told herself, Johnny was dead. If Tom asked her, she would have him, for nothing was going to bring Johnny back. But not until she had proved to herself she could make a success of her life on her own.

Ada had puzzled over what to give the Grays for Christmas presents; in the end she saved the box of chocolates given her by Mr Johnson and gave them to Virginia. For Mrs Gray and her husband and Tom she spent hours in her room sewing handkerchiefs from scraps of linen she had bought from a market stall. When the family gathered round the tree after dinner on Christmas Day and handed over presents, she was filled with anxiety. The handkerchiefs which she had laboured over seemed so poor in comparison with what the others were giving.

She got a pretty string of crystal beads from Virginia but was more delighted when Dr and Mrs Gray presented her with a textbook, *Nursing, its Theory and Practice* by Percy Lewis. Tom had also thought of her future career; he gave her *The Nurse's Pronouncing Dictionary of Medical Terms and Nursing Treatment*, by Honor Morten.

'We thought it would come in handy,' the doctor said. 'You'll find it useful, I'm sure.'

'Oh yes, thank you, doctor, and you, Mrs Gray. Oh, thank you all, you are so very, very kind to me.' Ada embraced them all with her smile.

'Do you think you'll need them if you're just an undernurse?' Virginia put in. 'I mean,' she added as her family stared at her in astonishment, 'Ada might not pass the entrance examination, she might –'

'Virginia, of course she will,' Tom said sharply.

Ada looked down at the books in her hand; perhaps Virginia was right and she didn't have it in her to succeed. For a moment self-doubt clouded her thoughts.

'Come on, Ada, let's go for a walk before tea, we'll walk off the effects of that enormous meal.' Tom jumped to his feet and pulled Ada with him, Virginia following as a matter of course.

'Oh, Virginia –' Mrs Gray stopped her – 'I want you to come with me, I promised to look in on Alice.' Alice was a friend of Mrs Gray's who had been recently widowed. Virginia looked mutinous for a moment but a quelling glance from her mother, who supposed Tom wanted Ada to himself on the walk, caused her to subside.

'Oh, all right,' she muttered.

'And I'm going to have a nap, just in case I get called out later,' said her father. 'Someone always overeats on Christmas Day.'

Tom and Ada walked along the riverbank under the shadow of the castle and cathedral. There were few people about, the city was taking its Christmas afternoon's rest. Frost sparkled on the grass, a freezing fog obscured the battlements above them and the river was dull and lifeless. On the water's edge a jackdaw pecked at something unmentionable, then flew off with a melancholy 'chack, chack, chack', low over the water to the other side.

In contrast, Ada and Tom were well wrapped up and warm, and Tom in particular was in good spirits. He was telling her of the exploits he and his fellow students got up to in rag week. Ada laughed in delight as he told her of dressing up as a nurse and wheeling his friend Christopher round the streets of Newcastle in a pram.

'All for charity, of course,' he added.

'Bye, I'd have loved to see you!' Ada cried, and then he said it.

'Ada, my love, you are my love, really you are.'

Ada stopped walking and turned a suddenly solemn face to him. 'What?'

'I want you to marry me, Ada, say you will, please say you will.'

'But how can we? I mean, I've not even started my nurse's training, and you, you've not finished your training either.'

'No, no, that's true, I don't mean now, this minute, though I would dearly love that; no, I mean later – we can look forward to it. Say you will, Ada.'

'I don't know, Tom.' Ada had known this was coming, but somehow, hearing the words was very different from expecting them. 'Are you sure, Tom? Are you really sure, have you thought it all out? I'm not good enough for you, you want someone of your own class, someone with an education who can help you in your work. You don't really want me, a penniless working girl.' All the pitfalls such a marriage could bring were becoming apparent to Ada.

'It's you I want. Please say yes, Ada, I can't live without you!' Tom pleaded. Taking hold of her arms, he brought her closer to him, and she could see the entreaty in his eyes.

'Are you sure your parents won't mind? They have been good to me, I don't want them to think I repay them by stealing their son. Tom, think about it, I was a washerwoman, before that I was a kitchen skivvy.'

'Oh, Ada, that's rubbish. Father doesn't believe in class differences, he's a socialist, they both are. And they like you, Ada, they do. And if you train as a nurse, you will be able to help me in my work, won't you?' He caught hold of her hand and pressed it to his lips.

Fleetingly the image of Johnny came into her mind, but Johnny was gone now, along with her childhood dreams. For that was all they had been – Johnny had thought of her as a little sister, not a lover. It was best to try and forget him. She was fond enough of Tom and she knew he loved her. Surely it was the sensible thing for a girl in her position to do? She would be secure for life. Ada dismissed this last consideration from her thoughts, Tom deserved more than that.

'Well . . . If you think . . .' she faltered.

Tom clasped her in his arms, shouting in triumph so that a duck which had been pecking about at the bank of the river swam hurriedly off, quacking loudly. A few flakes of snow fell onto his upturned face, heralding the storm the dark clouds in the sky promised.

That Christmas was very different to the ones he had known for Johnny, too. On Christmas Eve, as Johnny returned to his office from the shop floor where he had been overlooking a rather tricky order, he met Stephen at the door. He smiled at the youthful businessman, Stephen was really taking his position seriously, donning a slightly pompous air as he did so. Johnny's smile disappeared fairly fast at his nephew's tone.

'I think we should have a talk, Uncle John. Will you step into my office?'

Nonplussed, Johnny followed Stephen into what had been Fred's office, where his nephew took the chair behind the desk and gestured Johnny to sit down facing him.

'What is this all about, Stephen? There's things I have to do before we close for Christmas this afternoon –'

'Don't worry about that, Uncle John,' Stephen said smoothly. 'What I wanted to know is, what you intend to do now?'

'Do now? What do you mean exactly?'

'Well, now that Father has gone and I am head of the family firm, I really think you can no longer expect us to keep you and provide you with a position in the business. After all, my father was good to you, you were his brother and he gave you everything, but it is different now.'

'Stephen, listen to me.' Johnny was getting nettled at the young man's tone but he strove to keep his temper. 'I worked hard for this business, I earned every penny I got.'

'Come now.' Stephen took a cigar out of the box on the desk and cut the end before going on. Distractedly Johnny wondered if Dinah knew her son had started smoking.

'Let's not argue about it, Uncle John. I simply believe it would be best for us all if the break was made now. It couldn't go on, you know, you are just an employee. This is my firm and I will run it. I am perfectly capable of it.'

'You are very young, Stephen.'

'But I need no help from you,' Stephen answered in a voice which brooked no argument.

The young pup! Johnny thought, as they faced one another across the desk in silence. The ticking of the marble clock on the mantelpiece sounded loud and inexorable – ticking away the seconds of my life, he mused bitterly.

'What does your mother think of this? Does she agree?' Surely Dinah had not turned against him too?

'My mother is not to be bothered with business

matters.' Stephen rose and moved around the desk. 'Now, I consider the matter closed. You will, of course, receive three months' salary in lieu of notice in which to make other arrangements, but I would thank you not to trouble my mother about it.' He paused and turned back to the desk. 'By the way, I found this note among my father's correspondence. I think it must be for you.' His nod of dismissal was a parody of his father's attitude to troublesome employees.

A little dazed, Johnny took the note and walked out. He was beginning to realise that Stephen must have resented him for a long time. Why, Johnny was at a loss to understand. Was he jealous of his parents' affection for him? But Fred had given his own boys a much better education than his brother. Not for them the rigours of starting from the bottom, whereas Johnny had had to make his own way up ever since he was a young boy.

Well, he thought, as he emptied his desk, he would show Stephen that he was not simply a dead weight in the business. He was good at his job, Johnny told himself, he knew he was, he would get on in the world of steelmaking. There were other opportunities. He stared at the note he had put down on his desk without really seeing it for a moment, then, shrugging, he picked it up and opened it.

Ada! It was from Ada, there was the signature at the bottom of the letter: 'from your ever loving friend, Ada

(Lorinda) Leigh.' Dear little Ada! His heart warmed at the memory of her, his friend from so long ago. She at least was steadfast in her affections. She had got out of the clutches of the Parkers and managed to stay out, then. And she had written the letter herself, she must have worked hard. But he always knew she was a determined little thing, and if she wanted something badly enough she would strive for it.

I'm so glad for her, he said to himself. She seems happier now than she ever was in Auckland. I'll go to see her, I will, there's nothing to stop me now. He sighed. First it was imperative for him to secure a position, either at home or abroad, he didn't care which, not now.

The next few weeks he spent all his time investigating the prospects of a suitable position, so when he finally got round to planning a visit to Durham to see Ada he was considering an offer from Canada. The opportunities were boundless there, or so he was assured.

Chapter Fifteen

Ada was a little apprehensive when they faced Dr Gray that evening, but Dr Gray reacted exactly as Tom had said he would, giving his consent to the match without hesitation.

'I'm very happy for you both,' he said, stepping forward and kissing Ada on the forehead. 'However, I'm sure you are both sensible enough to know it is a betrothal only for a while. Long engagements are a good thing at any time, they give the young couple a proper chance to get to know each other, and in this case Tom has to qualify and be in a position to support a wife and family if need be.'

'Oh yes, Father, we both know that.' Tom took Ada's hand and held it to him. Feeling her slight tremble, he smiled tenderly at her.

'What a good thing Ada decided to train as a nurse,' his father went on. 'She will be specially helpful to you.

And in the meantime you will both be busy and have enough to occupy yourselves, the time will fly by. Now, let's go and tell the family.'

Mrs Gray congratulated them quietly. 'I'm so happy for you both, my dears,' she said. Virginia said little; although she had encouraged them in the summer, she had not really thought the romance would go so far. From her face, Ada knew she wasn't sure about it.

'Aren't you glad for us, Virginia?' Tom had seen her doubts and as usual came straight to the point.

'Oh, Tom, if you're happy, then I'm happy,' she answered, but Ada noticed that she didn't actually offer felicitations to her.

'Come on, dear,' Dr Gray said to his wife. We'll have a glass of that rather fine sherry to toast the betrothed couple.'

Tom had dismissed Virginia's hesitation at once, so Ada decided to forget about it too. Virginia loved her brother; perhaps she was a little jealous of someone else taking first place in his affections. But that inevitably had to come some time. Virginia would come round.

They had a party to celebrate the engagement on the evening before Virginia was to go back to school and Tom to Newcastle, where the medical faculty of Durham University was situated.

Ada had a few qualms about it when it was first

suggested, but Tom and Virginia were keen on the idea. Enthusiastically, Virginia began to plan what she would wear. She also thought she should have a say in arranging the guest list.

'I think that is up to Tom and Ada, Virginia, it is after all their party,' Mrs Gray said firmly when Virginia began suggesting her school friends.

'Oh, but surely I can ask my friends too?' Virginia protested. 'Ada has no one she wants to ask, and we'll need some girls. Tom's friends are all boys.'

Ada thought about Eliza, the only friend she would have liked to invite. But even if Eliza were able to leave her children, she would be so much out of her own environment that she would be embarrassed, she knew. Ada would be uncomfortable herself, she thought, out of her depth, despite what she had learned in the last few months. And what on earth was she going to wear? She had a good home with the Grays, but until she was actually working at the hospital and earning, no matter how small the sum, she had no money for clothes, not the sort she would need. How could she compare with Virginia's friends?

'Ada? What do you think, can I invite a couple of friends from school? They can stay here overnight and we'll travel back together.'

'Of course, Virginia, it'll be fun for you. And it's true, I have no one to ask.'

Virginia jumped up. 'I'll write to them now,' she said. 'It'll be grand. Oh, thank you, Ada, I knew you'd back me up.' She smiled brilliantly at Ada and rushed from the room.

Ada watched her go. Sometimes she found it hard to understand Virginia – was she pleased about the engagement or not? Tom came up behind her and put a proprietorial arm around her shoulders.

'You're not sad, are you, Ada? You look a little sad.'

Ada shook off her mood and smiled warmly at him. 'No, of course not,' she said. 'Why should I be sad? I'm the happiest girl in the world.' And Tom was satisfied.

In the event, Ada need not have worried about clothes. On the evening of the party, as she gazed at her reflection in her dressing-table mirror, she looked very fine indeed, she thought happily. The dress was a deep blue, almost violet, the colour of her eyes, and had snowy, white lace at the collar and cuffs. The narrow sash was low on her hips in the new fashion and tied at the back in a bow. It was a betrothal gift from Mrs Gray and the finest dress she had ever seen, never mind owned. Mrs Gray, quiet though she was, had guessed immediately what Ada's dilemma was and she came up with the ideal present.

Ada's eyes glowed excitement. She felt so good in the dress that she could hardly wait to show it off – to Tom, of course, she reminded herself. For a moment there her thoughts had slipped to someone else. Firmly she set her mind on Tom. It was him she wanted to impress. Oh, she would make him a good wife, she would. But that was ages away. Picking up her crystal beads which had been Virginia's Christmas present, she clasped them round her neck and went downstairs feeling, as her grannie would have said, grand enough to invite the queen to tea.

Virginia was dressed in pink, which set off her fair curls to perfection. In the end, she had invited two school friends. The noise from her bedroom as they dressed for the party together resounded all over the house.

'Are you sure there's no one, dear, that you would like to ask?' Mrs Gray had said when they were alone together one day.

'No, no one,' Ada had replied, silently sending another longing thought to Eliza. When the time came for the wedding, Eliza and the two boys would be invited, she was determined on that. Meanwhile, she would go to West Auckland to see her friend, the day after the party, perhaps, when Tom and Virginia had gone. Ada was to begin work at the hospital at the start of the next week, so there might not be another chance for a while.

The party was a great success. Virginia's two friends sat together and giggled a lot, and at first Christopher and Gerald, Tom's fellow students, were very correct, addressing the doctor as 'sir' and answering his questions politely. Virginia was not inhibited at all, she was happy and excited and flirted outrageously with Christopher, who slowly began to rise to her bait.

Ada watched, feeling years older than the giggling schoolgirls, though in fact there was little difference in their ages. Dr Gray looked amused and Mrs Gray slightly disapproving, though she didn't say anything. After dinner, the party livened up considerably. They removed to the drawing room, where the phonograph was brought out, the carpet rolled up and Tom played his collection of ragtime. After a few moments, the older Grays left for the comparative quiet of the small sitting room.

'You look adorable tonight,' Tom whispered, bending his head to Ada's, his eyes full of love. Tightening his hold on her waist, he drew her to him as they danced. Ada had not danced before but after a few wrong moves her natural sense of rhythm took over and she found she was fitting her steps to his easily. The tune ended and Tom reluctantly loosed his hold on her as the distant sound of the doorbell rang through the house.

'I'll get it!' Virginia, full of bouncy life, flew into the hall and called to her parents, 'It's probably a call-out, Daddy, poor you.' Her pink skirts rustled as she passed the hall mirror. Glancing in it, she was satisfied with the pretty picture she made. She was still wearing a pleased smile when she opened the door.

'Good evening. I'm looking for Miss Leigh. Miss Ada

Leigh?' A tall, well-dressed stranger, auburn-haired and handsome, smiled down at her courteously, his hat in his hand. Virginia's cheeks dimpled; he was *so* good-looking, she thought. The glass of champagne she had drunk to toast her brother's engagement added to the sparkle in her eyes as she looked at him. For a moment she didn't answer.

'I was told I would find her here? Miss Leigh? Oh, I'm sorry, my name is Fenwick, John Fenwick, here's my card.' He offered her the thin piece of card and she took it, staring at it, her mind racing.

'But – you can't be! Ada said Johnny Fenwick was dead.' She stared up at him in consternation and the sparkle left her eyes.

'Ada said what? Oh, look here, there must be some mistake. She must have meant someone else.' His brow creased in perplexity as Virginia made no move to invite him inside. 'She's here then? May I speak to her?'

There was an awkward moment. The tinny strains of Scott Joplin came from the direction of the drawing room, accompanied by happy, laughing voices. Johnny tried again.

'Look, I have a note here from Ada. I know it was written a long time ago but there was some delay in my receiving it. I went to Gilesgate but Mrs Dunne told me she was here. Er, you are Miss Gray, are you not?'

'Yes. Virginia Gray. I remember the letter, she told me

about it, but that was ages ago. She went to Middlesbrough and they told her you were dead.'

Johnny frowned. 'I can't think how that happened. Unless . . . It was about the time my brother died, there must have been some misunderstanding. Oh, poor Ada, what a shock she must have had! Will you tell her I'm here? I must explain to her.'

Virginia's thoughts were in a turmoil. She hadn't been too happy at the idea of Tom marrying Ada, but on the other hand, if she should jilt him, it didn't bear thinking about. Tom did love Ada, and she must protect him from this man.

'No!' she said firmly and closed the vestibule door behind her, cutting them off from the rest of the house. 'You can't see her tonight, not now. You'll spoil everything.'

'What on earth are you talking about?' Johnny was becoming impatient with this girl.

'Well . . .' Virginia searched for a reason desperately. It had to be a good reason, a reason which would stop Johnny ever coming back again. He was a threat to her brother's happiness, she couldn't allow it.

'Well?' Johnny's expression was determined, he took a step forward and raised an eyebrow enquiringly.

'She's engaged to be married!' Virginia could think of nothing better than the truth. And, after all, it was a good reason. 'This is her engagement party.' Laughter could be heard from the house as the phonograph fell silent, the sound of young people enjoying themselves. 'You can hear how happy they are. Ada's going to marry my brother, they love each other. And I don't want you coming in upsetting things.'

Johnny stepped back, his eyes suddenly bleak. 'Oh. Oh, well, then,' he murmured and stood biting his lower lip, unsure whether to insist on seeing Ada or take Virginia at her word and go away.

'Virginia! Who is it?' Mrs Gray called from the hall. 'Is everything all right?'

'Go on!' Virginia hissed. 'You don't want to cause any trouble, do you? Trouble for Ada?'

'No, no, of course not. If Ada is happy . . .' Johnny turned on his heel and strode away, jamming his hat on his head as he went.

'Who was that, Virginia?' The vestibule door opened behind her just as Johnny disappeared around the corner at the entrance to the drive.

'Oh, no one. Well, only a salesman and I got rid of him.'

'A salesman, on a Saturday evening! Really,' her mother said crossly. 'Well, do come in now, I don't want you to catch cold in that flimsy dress.'

Virginia watched Tom's face as she entered the drawing room. It was so close to Ada's, so adoring, he was wrapped up in her. She knew she had done the right thing and dismissed Johnny from her thoughts along with the slight feeling of guilt. Soon she was flirting with Christopher again and he was gazing into her face with an open admiration which she found very exciting.

Johnny climbed into his car and hurried away from the house and from Durham City. He felt very despondent and couldn't understand why. He should be glad that Ada had found happiness, God knew she deserved it. But ever since Fred had died, in the back of his mind there had been this small longing to see Ada. It was always there, like an aching tooth. He had told himself that it was because he had to reassure himself she was all right, and now he knew she was. In fact she was more than all right, her future was rosier than it had ever been. So why did he feel as he did?

She's still a child, a young girl, he told himself. How could she be in love and engaged to be married? Sixteen, not seventeen until May, that was how old she was. He remembered that birthday in Finkle Street when he had brought her ribbons, how pleased she had been. Johnny sighed. Sixteen, he realised, was old enough. He remembered that day in the park, was it last April? How sweet she had been that afternoon! He could remember the feel of her tiny waist as he swung her up in the air, and the way she had laughed. There was a vitality about Ada when she was happy, enhanced by the piquant expression she had had even as a small girl. Johnny smiled fondly.

Dear little Ada! If she loved young Gray, then he was happy for her. So why did he feel so bereft?

Like a shaft of light on his shattered thoughts, the reason came to him. He loved her himself! He didn't want her to marry anyone else, he wanted to marry her himself. Even though he had seen so little of her since he left Bishop Auckland, he loved her.

Johnny stopped the car and sat in the quiet dark, thinking. He would turn back, he would insist on seeing her, he wasn't going to give in without a fight. She couldn't love this Gray, he knew she loved him. But did she? Ada must have grown up a lot in this past year. She might see things differently now. Groaning, he laid his head against the cool windshield.

He had nothing to offer Ada. She would be better off with young Gray. Since Fred died, Johnny was on his own, he had to make his own way. His bright future was in ruins.

Reluctantly, Johnny started the car again, savagely turning the handle until the engine burst into life. If only he had come sooner! What a fool he had been! He continued on to Middlesbrough, regretting lost opportunities. He had been blind to his own true feelings. Well, he would go to Canada, he decided. Best to get right away – away from Middlesbrough and his lost hopes, away from the temptation of trying to seek out Ada.

Arriving home at last, Johnny drove the car round the

back of the house and parked it in what had been the stables. He climbed out and looked down at the car. He had been so pleased when he had first got it, but now it too had to go. Really, it belonged to the business, not to him.

Well, regrets would get him nowhere, he mused. He had to put it all behind him and start a new life. Without knowing it, Johnny began whistling a tune Ada used to sing as she worked, 'O, tell me pretty maiden, are there any more at home like you,' as he walked to the house. His new life, he vowed, would be every bit as successful as his brother's had been, at least with regard to business. He was young and strong and he had a good working knowledge of all aspects of the iron and steel industry, thanks to his hard grounding at the ironworks in Auckland and later in the family steelworks. He had experience of management and some great ideas in designing. He would succeed, there were plenty of opportunities in the New World for a determined young man such as he. Realising what he was whistling, he stopped abruptly. Goodness, he hadn't thought he would remember that tune, it was so old now.

Johnny took the stairs two at a time and immediately got out his trunk and began packing. He would sail next evening on the boat leaving Liverpool for New York, journeying on to Canada from there. But first he had to break the news to Dinah.

'But why, Johnny?' Dinah was distressed after dinner that night, she couldn't understand why he was deserting the family. 'Why now, surely you could be of great help to Stephen? Don't you owe him something? And me, aren't you sorry to be leaving me?'

'Yes, of course I am,' Johnny answered. Dinah had been so kind to him ever since he was a young boy, but how could he tell her it was her own son who was pushing him out? Best to let her think it was his own decision. He knew Dinah loved him as she would have loved any brother of Fred's, and that she was unhappy at his going, hurt at the betrayal, as she saw it.

'Oh, Dinah, I will always remember you with love and affection,' he said tenderly, 'but I have to make my own way now. I'll write to you and let you know where I am. Please don't fret, Dinah. You have Stephen and Arthur, you'll be all right.'

And with this, Dinah had to be content. She still had her illusions about the boys, at least, Johnny thought, as he drove away to the station next morning, waved off by a tearful Dinah and a triumphant Stephen, who was hard put to it to keep the satisfaction from his face.

Chapter Sixteen

This time Ada took the train directly to West Auckland and followed the directions Eliza had given her in her last letter. There was a mile to walk out to Hummerbeck and up the bank after the hamlet; though the weather was cold, it was dry, so she quite enjoyed her walk out. When she at last reached the little farmhouse she had some misgivings about knocking. There was no smoke coming from the chimney and all she could hear was a pig squealing from the pigsty attached to the nearest end of the house. Maybe she should have written to Eliza and told her she was coming, but it had been a spur-of-the-moment decision, there had been no time. And in two days' time she had to report to the hospital for her new job.

Hesitantly, Ada walked up the dirt path which skirted the long, low building and knocked at the door, but there was no response. Undecided what to do, she walked round the side of the house to see if anyone was there.

'Here, what do you want?'

The truculent voice came from a man in filth-encrusted overalls who was tipping pigswill over the half-gate of the sty into a trough.

Ada wrinkled her nose at the smell and his scowl deepened. He put the bucket down and strode towards her, eyeing her up and down.

'Well?'

'I'm looking for Eliza Maxwell, she lives here, doesn't she?'

'Oh, aye, she lives here, what do you want with her?'

This must be Eliza's brother-in-law, Ada surmised. She wasn't surprised now that Eliza had hesitated before taking up his offer. He didn't seem too friendly.

'I'm her friend, her friend from Durham. Eliza wrote and told me she had moved up here. Is she about the place?'

'No, she's not.' He seemed to think that the conversation was ended. Turning on his heel, he went to the back door.

'But where is she?' Ada demanded. What a surly, horrible man, she thought.

'She's working, out selling the milk. Where else would she be? Some people haven't time to go gallivanting all over the country.' He regarded her sourly.

'But when will she be back?'

'How the hell do I know? She gets gossiping down there in the village with her cronies and takes twice as long as she should. By the time she gets back it will be time for milking again.' He spat across the dirt path outside the door and went inside, closing it behind him.

Ada was seething. The man had no more manners than the pigs he kept. She set off walking back to West Auckland, her mind frothing with what she would like to have said to him if only she had thought of it at the time.

Halfway there, Ada saw Eliza coming towards her. She was pulling a handcart with a milk can in it and Miles, wrapped in a blanket, beside it. Bertie was trotting by her side, a large muffler crossed over his chest and his nose red with the cold.

'Ada! Eeh, I am glad to see you.' Eliza's tired face brightened as she saw her friend, then took on an anxious expression. 'There's nowt wrong, is there? You're all right, pet?'

Ada hastened to reassure her. 'I'm in fine fettle, really I am, Eliza. I know I shouldn't have come without letting you know, but it was the only chance –'

'Why, man, that doesn't matter. I'm that set up to see you. It was a right miserable day, me fingers are fair numbed. Howay, we'll get in and I'll build the fire, we'll have a warm. Eeh, I'm over the moon to see you, pet.'

'Me too, Eliza,' Ada answered and smiled down at Bertie, who was standing quietly with his thumb in his mouth. His nose was running and she took her hankie out of her pocket and bent down to wipe it; it was red and sore with the cold. 'Hello, Bertie, love, would you like me to give you a carry?'

Bertie's eyes brightened. 'Piggyback?' he asked.

'Piggyback it is,' she agreed and bent down so that he could climb on her back. 'Hold on tight then.'

'Did you see Albert's brother, then?' Eliza asked as they walked up to the house.

'I did.'

Something in Ada's tone made Eliza look quickly at her. 'He wasn't rude to you, was he?'

'Well . . .'

'He's not so bad as you think, not when you get to know him.'

Ada was saved from answering as they had reached the house. Eliza led the way round the back, where she left the cart outside the door and picked up Miles, who was sound asleep.

'Howay in, Ada, it's warmer inside.'

Inside, there was no sign of Ralph Maxwell, Ada was glad to see. She slid Bertie from her back and untied his muffler for him while Eliza stirred the fire in the range with a poker, added coal from the bucket and put a tin blazer in front of it. The chimney must have had a good draught for the fire quickly burst into life, roaring behind the blazer, which Eliza then took down and outside, away from the children. The heat from the fire soon warmed the room.

'I'll put the kettle on, pet, I won't be a tick –' Eliza bustled about – 'then we can have a good chat and you can tell me everything that has happened. Bye, I was as mad as hell when you told me about those Parkers getting hold of you. Still, it came out all right, didn't it?'

A dish of bread dough covered with a white cloth was already rising on the hearth, and Eliza took a lump and rolled it out on the table. 'I'll put a stotty cake in, it'll do nicely for our teas while the loaves are proving.' Swiftly and efficiently, Eliza cut the rest of the dough and put it into tins, placing them on the fender to prove.

As she worked, Ada looked around her with interest. Beside the fireplace there was a door and from the lowing behind it she guessed that it led directly into a cow byre. The walls were dingy brown with smoke and the windows uncurtained. The chairs were all odd, rickety and comfortless, Ada saw, except for the rocking chair by the hearth where Eliza had gestured her to sit. But a new clippie mat lay before the fire on the flagged floor and mat frames in the corner held another half-finished. Eliza was obviously trying to cheer the place up.

'That one'll be in bed.' Eliza nodded to a doorway at the other end of the kitchen, at right angles to the front door. 'He likes his bed of an afternoon. We'll have a while to ourselves.'

'Are you happy here, Eliza?' Ada ventured. Bertie had climbed up on her lap and she sat back with him leaning against her breast. He had grown since she saw him in the summer, she thought. 'Bye, what a big boy you are, Bertie,' she said admiringly and he snuggled into her, content.

'Happy enough.' Eliza said after a while. 'It's hard, like – the cows to milk and the house to see to and the bairns. The worst is having to sell the milk, it takes a bite out of the day.'

'Couldn't Mr Maxwell do that?'

'He works at the pit, you know, he hasn't the time.' Eliza opened the oven door and a heavenly smell of baking bread rushed out. Expertly she turned the stotty cake on the oven floor as the kettle began to sing. Ada was silent; he still shouldn't expect Eliza to do so much, she thought.

Eliza finished setting out the table and sat down opposite Ada. Sighing, she looked into the flames. 'You know, Bertie's better since we came up here. Better than he was in the village.' She looked fondly at her elder son, who had fallen asleep on Ada's lap. 'Don't you think he looks better, Ada?'

Ada watched the sleeping boy. Indeed, he had grown and there was some colour in his cheeks. He had lost that anxious look he had about him the last time she had seen him, too.

'I think you're right, Eliza,' she said.

The kettle boiled and soon they were drinking tea and eating hot stotty cake smothered in golden syrup. It tasted heavenly, thought Ada. Bertie woke up and demanded his share, then got down onto the mat and played with his wooden engine. Ada told Eliza everything that had happened to her: her engagement to Tom and her new job at the hospital. Eliza's pleasure for her good fortune was very satisfying to her. Bye, she thought, there was no one she could talk to like Eliza. Before they knew it, the afternoon was getting darker. Eliza fed little Miles and changed him and he settled back into his cradle, a cradle which was getting too small for him, Ada saw. They had a lovely, cosy time, brought to an end by the appearance of Eliza's brother-in-law.

He came through the door into the kitchen, yawning hugely and scratching his chest through his shirt. His face was unshaven, his hair stood on end and his braces dangled about his thighs. Without speaking, he went over to the mantelpiece and picked up a cigarette end, lighting it from the fire before turning round to toast his backside.

'Isn't it time you were out milking?' He scowled at Eliza, ignoring Ada.

'Aye. I'll be doing it directly. Do you want some tea, Ralph?'

'Aye. I was thinking I wasn't going to be asked, when

you have your fine friend here. In my house too, think on.'

Ada rose to her feet. If she stayed any longer she would give this cretin a piece of her mind, she thought. 'I have to go any road, Eliza,' she said. 'I have the train to catch.' Bending, she kissed Bertie, still playing quietly on the mat, and went over to the cradle for a last look at Miles.

Eliza went with her to the door, her face red with embarrassment. 'It's just his way,' she whispered.

'Yes,' said Ada, and turned to Mr Maxwell. 'Thank you for your hospitality.' But the derisive note in her voice didn't penetrate his skin; he merely grunted and spat into the fire.

Later that evening, Ada lay in bed and opened her textbook of nursing, reading by the light of her candle. Her bag was packed all ready for the short journey to St Margaret's Hospital next day. She was becoming excited at the prospect of starting her new life, though a little apprehensive: she thought she would be unable to sleep, but perhaps a few minutes' reading would settle her down. Ada turned to the page where the requirements for probationer nurses were set out.

'You are required to be sober, honest, truthful, trustworthy, punctual, quiet and orderly, cleanly and neat, patient and cheerful and kindly,' she read. An angel, she thought wryly, that was what they wanted. This Florence Nightingale had certainly been a martinet.

'You are expected to become skilful in –' There followed a long list of skills necessary to a nurse. When Ada got to the one about the application of leeches, she stopped reading. Better leave that particular bridge until she came to it. She turned the page.

'Now that nurses are drawn from a better class with more brains,' she read. Oh, dear, was she of a better class with more brains? Would she get in? Restlessly, Ada closed the book and blew out her candle. The words of the good doctor Percy Lewis were adding to her inability to sleep, not settling her down.

She thought of Tom, who had gone off to Newcastle early that morning. He would be back for Easter, he had called from the train as they parted on the station platform.

'I'll be counting the days, my love,' he had said. And Ada had watched him disappear along the bend in the track and then crossed over the line for her train to West Auckland. Tom believed she could do it, and so did his father.

Ada turned over on her side and closed her eyes, willing herself to sleep. This was no time for doubting. She could become a nurse and she was damn well going to; failure was definitely not part of her future. She would pass her entrance examination, she would go to the County Hospital and complete her training, she would do very well indeed, maybe even one day becoming a matron. And she would marry Tom. But that particular bit was far in the future, she didn't have to worry about it yet.

Being an undernurse at St Margaret's was not much different from being a skivvy in a boarding house, Ada found. In fact, the boarding house had been good practice for it. She scrubbed floors, emptied bedpans, scoured the sluice and helped change the beds of incontinent patients.

'Have you not finished that yet?'

The voice of the ward sister coming up behind her twenty times a day sounded remarkably like that of Auntie Doris and their sour expressions were very similar too. Ada learned to confine her answers to 'No, Sister' or 'Sorry Sister', while she carried on scrubbing. For six and a half days a week, ten hours a day, she had no time to think of anything but the next task, collapsing on her bed in the tiny cell allocated to her at the end of a shift to even dream about the ward, the poor old women in their regimented beds, the uncomfortable feel of the stiff uniform collar on her neck, which was now permanently reddened from the contact.

Gradually, Ada found she got used to the work. Her hands returned to a callus-hardened state, her nails became brittle and she was required to keep them cut as short as possible. She studied when she could and looked forward to her half-days when she could walk over to see Mrs Gray, calling on her way at Mr Johnson's cottage.

Mr Johnson was always happy to see her. His face would light up when he opened the door to her and he always had a supply of cream cakes for them to have with their tea. Ada found the cream cakes too rich and sweet but every week she ate one with apparent enjoyment while they discussed the latest book she had been reading, or her chances of getting into the County Hospital to train.

'You'll have no problem, no problem at all, Ada,' he would say to her often. 'You have a good brain and you like to use it.'

Ada would leave the cottage feeling buoyed up and sure of herself. As she walked by the Wear week by week and saw the snowdrops fade and the crocuses spring up, followed by the primroses and daffodils, she was filled with hopeful expectancy for what the future would bring.

Tom came home at Easter but Ada saw little of him, she had to work that weekend as she did every weekend. They did snatch an hour together and he too was full of the future. His finals were only weeks away, and things were about to happen.

'I miss you, Ada,' Mrs Gray admitted one afternoon in May, just before Ada's seventeenth birthday. 'Virginia leaves school this summer but she won't be home for long. She and Christopher are announcing their engagement as soon as he qualifies. They want to be married in the summer. Christopher's father has a big practice in

Jesmond and, in any case, Christopher has money of his own. So Virginia's future is assured.'

Ada was surprised. Of course she had known Virginia and Christopher were interested in one another, but she hadn't realised the romance had gone so far. But then, she thought, it was weeks since she had seen Virginia, most of her time having been spent at the hospital.

She was even more surprised to receive a letter from Virginia at the beginning of June, inviting her to be bridesmaid at the wedding, which was to be in the cathedral. It was going to be a very grand affair, Ada saw, and wondered why Virginia hadn't asked her friends from school. The letter was very brief and Ada wondered a little sadly at how Virginia had changed since she first met her. She could have been writing to a stranger.

Visiting the Grays the following week, Ada listened to Mrs Gray chattering happily about the great event.

'There's to be three bridesmaids: Virginia's friends from school and you. Virginia was only having the two but Tom suggested you might like –' Mrs Gray broke off as she saw Ada's expression. 'Oh, Ada, it was just that Virginia didn't think of you, but when Tom pointed out that he was best man and it would be nice . . . Well, I'm sure you understand. Don't worry, everything will be provided, you'll have no expense.'

'Hmm.' Ada grinned as she thought of her meagre salary. 'Just as well. I dare say the dresses will be very expensive. I only hope I can get the day off from the hospital.'

'Oh yes, dear, it will be all right, the doctor will have a word with Matron.'

And, of course, given Dr Gray's position at the hospital, Ada got time off, though she didn't get away until the patients' breakfast dishes were all cleared away and washed.

The wedding day dawned bright and clear with the promise of a hot day to come. The marquee on the lawn was up and ready and the caterers installed when Ada arrived at the Grays' house from the hospital two hours before the ceremony. Ada went straight up to Virginia's bedroom, where she found the other two bridesmaids already dressed and busy helping the bride. Virginia saw Ada come in through her dressing-table glass and frowned.

'Ada! Where on earth have you been? You're supposed to be helping me and here you are not even dressed yourself yet.'

'I'm sorry, Virginia, I got away as soon as I could,' Ada answered mildly. 'I had to –'

'Oh, never mind what you were doing. Go and get dressed, I want you to help me with my hair,' Virginia snapped.

Naturally Virginia was nervous, that was the trouble,

Ada said to herself as she changed into the dusty-pink silk dress and pink satin slippers. She gazed at herself in the looking glass, and thought she looked completely different. The dress was the latest fashion, shorter than usual; it reached only to her ankles and clung to her hips, making her look even slimmer than she was. The skirt was decorated with two fringes which danced as she moved, shimmering in the sunlight. Ada twisted this way and that to see her back. The neckline went down in a V almost to her waist and the dress was sleeveless, leaving her upper arms bare even when she drew on the silken gloves.

'Ada!'

At the imperious call, Ada picked up her beaded bag and hurried back to Virginia who was waiting, hairbrush in hand.

'Oh, for goodness' sake, Ada, what a mess your hands are! You'd better keep your gloves on all day.'

'I'm sorry, Virginia,' Ada said for the umpteenth time as she finished piling the thick, fair hair on top of Virginia's head and put in the last securing hairpin. 'It's the ward work, you know.'

'Well, you'd better go and do something with your own hair.' Virginia dismissed her and turned to chat to her friends, who were sitting on the bed dressed in replicas of Ada's gown.

*

The wedding in the cathedral was like any fairy tale. Christopher, handsome as a prince in his morning suit, waited proudly as Virginia walked down the aisle, the bad temper of the morning forgotten. Her face was wreathed in angelic smiles, and the white satin of her gown gleamed as it clung to her curves.

Later, at the reception in the marquee, Tom sat next to Ada, holding her hand. 'Our turn next,' he whispered and she nodded.

'Plenty of time yet, though,' she whispered back.

Tom thought she sounded wistful but in reality Ada was becoming apprehensive about her own marriage, even though it was a year or two away. Listening to Virginia make her vows in the cathedral, she had been struck by the solemnity of the marriage service. Was she doing the right thing? Evidently Tom had no such doubts, he was very sure he wanted to marry her.

Ada sighed. It was still a long time off. Tom had only just qualified and he was going to stay on at Newcastle as a surgical houseman.

'I want all the experience I can get, my love,' he told Ada. 'But with you carrying on with your training, you won't have time to miss me. And before you know it, we'll be together again. We'll have our whole lives to be together. It only wants a little patience, a little vision for the future.'

Yes, thought Ada, she would be going to train at

the County Hospital in the new year. Oh, she hadn't passed her entrance yet, that was not until October, but she would, she knew she would. She had worked hard enough for it.

The bride and groom went off to Paris in a flurry of laughter, excitement and good-natured bantering, driving to the station in the Rolls-Royce belonging to Christopher's father, all gleaming white paintwork and well-stuffed leather. Following tradition, Virginia threw her bouquet to the waiting bridesmaids. Instinctively, Ada hung back so that it was someone else who caught it.

'Don't worry, Ada,' said Tom. 'You don't need any good-luck signs, you've already got me.'

'Yes, Tom.' Ada shook herself mentally – what on earth was the matter with her?

Ada passed her entrance examination with flying colours and in February 1912 entered the nursing school at the County Hospital. She was still a few months short of being eighteen, younger than most of the other probationers. She had thought she would have to wait until later in the year to commence her training, so she was very pleased when she got the letter telling her to report in February.

Before Ada began her training, she took a day off and went to visit Eliza once again. She was still worried about Eliza, remembering what the smallholding had been like and the instant dislike she had felt for Ralph

Maxwell. When she got to Hummerbeck she realised that she had underestimated Eliza's willpower and her ability to make a home of wherever she was. That was Eliza's great strength, Ada mused, she would always do her best with what she had. Ralph was at the pit, she was thankful to learn, she didn't have to meet him this time.

'But he's not so bad, Ada,' Eliza reassured her. 'He's good with the bairns, Bertie's quite fond of him. He likes to help him see to the pigs and things.' Eliza paused thoughtfully. 'I suppose the bairn likes having a man about the place; he follows Ralph around all the time.'

Ada fervently hoped Bertie was not modelling himself on his uncle. She shuddered to think it but tactfully didn't let Eliza see that.

'And they are both blooming with health. They're grand, Ada, not a cold so far this winter.'

'I'm glad of that,' Ada said warmly. She watched Miles as he played with an enormous tom cat – a very patient tom cat, she thought, as Miles pulled himself up by the poor animal's fur, then tugged and strained to pick up the animal, which was almost as big as he was. She thought the cat might scratch, but instead it simply moved away to the other end of the room and stared at Miles with unblinking eyes as the child tottered uncertainly after it, his fat little legs, with the feet encased in tall boots to strengthen his ankles, plodding across the flagstones until with a grunt of satisfaction he reached the cat.

Whereupon the animal rose and stalked regally back to the other side.

'Leave Timmy alone, Miles,' Eliza said gently, picking her son up and hugging him. Miles struggled to get down again but Eliza held him firmly. 'He doesn't like having his fur pulled, pet.'

Ada looked round the kitchen, which had changed a great deal since the last time she was there a year ago. There were cheap but pretty curtains at the sparkling window and cushions on the chairs. Eliza had been busy.

'You've made it nice, Eliza,' she said.

Eliza glanced round herself. 'It is nice, isn't it? Well, you need a bit of comfort, don't you?' Her tone turned pensive as she went on. 'It's not going to last, though, I don't think so, any road. Ralph's courting, and if he gets married, well, they won't want me and the bairns, will they?'

'Getting married?' Ada was astounded that anyone would marry Ralph. She thought about his appearance that day the year before – how could someone want to marry him?

'Aye.' Eliza wrinkled her brow, thoughtfully. 'Still, come September, Bertie will be at school and I'll only have the babby during the day. Why, man, something will turn up. We've not starved yet.'

Ada didn't know what to say. It seemed to her that

every time Eliza seemed to be getting somewhere, something happened. Eliza saw her concern.

'Never mind now, I'll make out. Let's have a walk out and find Bertie, he's playing somewhere down the field. The fresh air will give us an appetite for our teas.'

Bertie was soon found. He was busy turning over the muck heap and he stank to high heaven. His uncle had put him a small handle into a blunt pitchfork but he wasn't supposed to be using it without his uncle there.

'Bertie!' Eliza said sharply. 'Put that down, you'll stick yourself with it.'

'No, I won't,' Bertie said stoutly. Nevertheless he pushed the fork into the pile and turned to Ada. 'Hello, Auntie Ada.' He smiled his slow smile and went to kiss her.

'You'll have to have a wash first, Bertie. Auntie Ada doesn't want you touching her like that, you'll make her smell of muck. Go on, do as I say.'

'Never mind, pet.' Ada saw his crestfallen face. 'I can kiss you without touching you, can't I?' She bent down and pecked his cheek. 'Bye, Bertie, what a big lad you're going to be!'

'I'm big now, Auntie Ada,' Bertie said proudly. 'Uncle Ralph says I'm a big lad.'

Ada smiled at the boy. He certainly looked much healthier than he had been before they came to live on the farm, she thought. It would be a pity if Eliza had to leave it. And then where would she go? Ada, in spite of her dislike of Ralph Maxwell, fervently hoped the little family would be allowed to stay on the farm for a year or two, perhaps, until the boys were older.

'Come back as soon as you can,' Eliza said as Ada took her leave. 'You know how we love to see you.'

Ada went down the road, turning at the bend where a new sign had been erected, warning of 'Land subsidence due to pitfalls', to wave before she went out of view. Pitfalls, she thought ironically – there was more than one kind of pitfall and Eliza's life seemed strewn with them.

Chapter Seventeen

The County was not far away from St Margaret's on the outskirts of the city. Ada knew it was funded by voluntary subscription and took patients from the whole of the county apart from the large conurbations on the coast, and it pleased her sense of justice that this was somewhere ordinary people were treated without the stigma of the workhouse hospitals.

She found the actual work of a junior probationer was not so different from that which she had been used to as an undernurse. All the same, it was another step up for her; she was on her way. Everything was a challenge to her, and she enjoyed it all despite the hard work.

By the time Ada had been at the hospital for a couple of months, it was fast becoming her whole world. There was so much to do and so much to learn that everything else in her life was fading into the background, even her future husband.

Tom wrote to her with unfailing regularity, his letters loving and full of their plans for the future, but Ada had to admit to herself that she forgot all about him until his letters arrived. Her world was work, study, the writing-up of her ward book and sleep. Every night she went to bed as soon as she could and slept soundly until Night Sister's call woke her at half past five next morning.

Walking to the wards after breakfast one morning, Ada was accompanied by a fellow probationer who was on the same ward. Meg Morton came from Bishop Auckland, her father was a master at the grammar school there. She was homesick and when she found out one day as they talked casually over tea that Ada had lived there, she liked to talk to her about the town. This morning as they passed the office they saw by the small group of nurses around it that the post was in. Meg, ever eager for news from home, paused.

'Let's see if there are any letters for us, Ada. We have the time,' she said, joining the queue without waiting for a reply.

Ada consulted the watch pinned to her apron, a present from Tom for her eighteenth birthday, which had been the week before. The watch was not an expensive one but it had a second hand so it was easy to time pulse rates and it was the envy of her fellow probationers. She saw it was true, they had a few minutes before they were due on the wards. She wasn't expecting a letter herself, Tom's had arrived the day before but she waited patiently with the other girl.

In fact there was a letter for her: it was from Eliza. That was nice, she thought, with a little thrill of pleasure; tucking it under her apron bib she decided she would read it at lunchtime. It was something pleasant to look forward to besides the fish pie and cabbage which she knew would be the fare that day, for the menus varied not at all week by week. As the two undernurses reached the ward and were plunged into the usual hectic round of cleaning and bedmaking in preparation for the rounds of the 'Great One', the head physician, she forgot about the letter and everything else not to do with her work.

It was not until Ada was back in her tiny room that night, preparing for bed, that she took off her apron and the letter fell to the floor. Lovely, she thought, her tiredness lifting a little, now she could read it in bed in comfort. Quickly she finished getting ready and slipped between the sheets.

She lay against her pillow to read but within seconds she was sitting bolt upright, her pulse quickening with a turmoil of emotion. A cutting from the *Auckland Chronicle* had fallen from the envelope when she opened it and idly, she picked it up and read it. Eliza sometimes sent her little items of news about people they knew in the district, but this particular cutting was not just about an acquaintance or a town notable.

It was headed, 'Bishop Auckland man sent for trial at the next Quarter Sessions', and what followed was like a door opening on Ada's past.

'Appearing before Bishop Auckland magistrates this Thursday last, Harold Parker of Tenters Street, charged with gross indecency towards two small girls in the Bishop's Park on Sunday last. Police Constable Albert Smith happened to be walking with his family by the deer house in the park when he heard the children crying. Deciding to investigate, he found the said Harold Parker with the girls. A further serious charge of a sexual nature is being considered. Parker is remanded to Durham Gaol until the next Quarter Sessions.'

Ada's first feeling was one of relief. She dropped the cutting and stared unseeingly at it. Harry Parker was locked away, he would not be molesting little girls again. No other child would ever have to suffer what she had suffered at the hands of her uncle. Her stomach churned at the thought of those times when he caught her in the kitchen or on the upstairs landing – the feel of his hands and worse. He had hurt her, oh aye, how he had hurt her. Sighing, she lay down and picked up Eliza's letter.

'So you see, he got caught at last,' Eliza had written and Ada could almost hear the satisfaction in her friend's words. 'I feel a bit guilty that we didn't tell the bobbies before, Ada. Those poor little lasses, you feel for them don't you, though why they were there by themselves I don't know. I bet their mams look after them better now. But who would think anything could happen in the Bishop's Park? On a Sunday like when there are a lot of people about, too. There was even a rally there further along, the Primitives I think. Mind, I don't know what your auntie will do now, she won't be able to hold her head up in the town. The bairns' fathers were pitmen, they work at Newton Cap Colliery, they look after their own, the colliers, don't they? Doris Parker had her windows broken last night and now she's trying to sell up. Bye, if they got a hold of her man they'd lynch him.'

Ada put the letter down with a sigh. How would Auntie Doris earn her living now? Nothing was ever straightforward, there were always more things than one to think about. Looking back on it now, Ada realised this was what her aunt had feared for years. The bitter thought that Doris Parker could have shielded her own niece from her husband occurred to her: oh aye, she could. Why did some women let it happen to bairns? The question was unanswerable. She turned over on her side, restlessly. Well, she mused, both her own mother and her mother's sister had been unlucky with men.

She began to think about her own mother. Nothing had come of the letter to the Salvation Army, there had been no response at all. Perhaps she would try again; maybe if she put an advertisement in the London papers her mother would see it.

Ada turned out her light and settled down in the bed. She *would* try again, she thought. Maybe her mother hadn't come back in the beginning through no fault of her own and now thought it was too late.

As usually happened when Ada was reminded of her time in Auckland, her thoughts turned to Johnny and the familiar sadness flooded through her. Why could she not forget him? Despite all her efforts to focus her mind on Tom and their bright future together, the future they were both striving for, the image of Johnny remained, stubbornly there in the recesses of her mind, waiting to pop out again to torture her with memories of her lost dreams. Ah, Johnny! she cried deep down inside. Johnny, I loved you, Johnny.

John Fenwick, head of the Fenwick Steelworking Company of Toronto, was sitting at his desk, feeling very pleased with himself. He had been in Canada for a little over a year and already the small firm he had founded with the money left to him by his brother Fred was burgeoning and he was contemplating taking on extra workers. Fortunately there was a large pool of men who had emigrated to Canada in the last year or two and a lot of them had experience of the industry.

Johnny had just landed a fat contract with a company in Ontario. His designs had reached a lot of the right men in this country and caught hold of their imaginations. Chary though they could be of innovations, some of them were beginning to appreciate Johnny's work. The prospects for the small company were very good indeed and getting brighter by the day. A discreet knock at the door of his office caught his attention.

'Come in, Frances,' he called and the door opened on the girl who had been with him from the inception of the business, Frances Holden.

She was a pretty girl, with dark hair swept up severely in a knot on top of her head in the way commended at the business school where she had trained as a stenographer. She was dressed in a severe white shirtwaister and black skirt with a black bow tied under her collar. Holding her notebook and pencil and with a spare pencil stuck in her hair, she was the epitome of the New Woman, the efficient secretary.

'Sit down, Frances.' He smiled at her triumphantly, wanting to share this new success with her. 'I want you to take a letter.'

As he dictated his acceptance of the contract on his desk, Frances grinned in delight. He had worked long and hard at this one, and she had been behind him throughout. Dropping her notebook on the desk, she ran round to him and flung herself in his arms, the New Woman forgotten.

'Johnny! Isn't it great? Oh, let's go out and celebrate! Forget work for the day, this calls for champagne and caviar.'

'Miss Holden, please, remember where you are,' Johnny said primly, but he couldn't keep it up and, laughing uproariously, he kissed her soundly. Her breath tasted of peppermint, another of the maxims of her business college, 'Always make sure you do not annoy your employer with the smell of stale breath.' Her lips were soft and inviting; Johnny kissed her again, lingeringly this time. Then reluctantly he put her firmly away from him.

'Time to celebrate later, Frances. First of all we have this letter to send, I want it off today. Also I want you to place an advertisement in the paper for workers.'

'Yes, sir.' Frances picked up her notebook and returned to her seat, but as her pencil squiggled over the paper the dimples in her cheeks kept deepening. Johnny was a lovely man, she thought. She couldn't help it, she was quite besotted with him.

They ate in an intimate French restaurant conveniently close to the office. In the rosy glow from small lamps above each table, Frances's hair gleamed darker, almost black, and she had loosed the severe topknot so that it hung down on her shoulders, secured only by a loose red ribbon. Johnny ordered a bottle of champagne to celebrate his success of the afternoon. His mind was full of hope and determination; he was on his way now, he thought jubilantly.

'Here's to you, Johnny,' Frances said softly, holding her glass out to him, and he clinked his own against hers.

'No, no, Frances, here's to us. Where would I be without your help? You organise the office for me, you know every customer and handle them perfectly. Here's to us, I say.'

They sipped the champagne, savouring the delicate taste and the feel of tiny bubbles bursting against the roof of the mouth. Johnny smiled across the table at Frances – dear Frances, where would he be without her?

Frances, seeing the affection in his expression, dropped her eyes in momentary confusion. When she looked up again her cheeks were rosy and she was gazing at him mistily, the very picture of a girl in love. For a split second Johnny had misgivings he didn't mean – No, he thought, he had been reading more into her gaze than was actually there. Frances was simply pleased about his willingness to share the credit for his success. He picked up his soup spoon and began eating his bouillabaisse enthusiastically.

'Tuck in,' he advised Frances, 'it's delicious.'

After a moment Frances picked up her spoon and followed his example.

They talked companionably over the meal, discussing the extra problems which would come with enlarging the business. Johnny ordered another bottle of champagne over the *noisettes de boeuf aux champignons*, and afterwards they finished off with a Napoleon brandy to drink with their coffee. So it was already after eleven when they left the restaurant.

Laughing together over something that had been terribly funny though they couldn't remember what it was, they went out into the cold, frosty air of a Canadian spring. Johnny grabbed hold of Frances as she swayed suddenly, almost falling.

'Whoa, there, Miss Holden,' he joked, drawing her to him, and his arms slid round her waist. 'Anyone would think you had had too much to drink. Shame on you, how will you get up for work in the morning? I warn you, as your employer I cannot countenance such goings-on.'

The mock severity in his tone gave way to chuckles as he tightened his hold: she was looking up at him, her great dark eyes gleaming in the light from the streetlamp outside the restaurant, her lips parted and inviting. Johnny bent his head and kissed her. The kiss was gentle at first but as her lips opened to him and her arms stole round his neck it became hard and demanding.

At last, shaking a little at his own feelings, Johnny gently disengaged himself. 'I'll get you a cab,' he said.

'Yes.' Her whisper was barely audible. She still clung to his arm and he could feel the trembling heat of her body close to his despite the cold night.

The street was deserted, not a cab in sight. Frances lived about two miles away from the restaurant, in a hostel for women run very strictly by an immigrant Presbyterian family from Scotland; the guests were expected to be safely tucked up in bed by midnight. Even in her slightly dazed state of euphoria, she began to worry about getting home on time.

'Let's walk to the corner of the block,' Johnny suggested, 'maybe there'll be a taxi there.' Holding her firmly to his side, for she needed his support, he walked her to the end of the street, but it was to no avail. The whole town appeared to have closed down for the night, the streets were deserted.

'What am I going to do? If I get caught going in late I'll be asked to leave, then what will my parents have to say? They might make me go home to the farm.' Frances sounded as though having to go home to the farm and give up her idea of being a New Woman was the equivalent of being consigned to a nunnery.

Johnny thought quickly. They were both shivering as the night air penetrated through their clothing, and they had to get indoors. His own apartment was only a block away by this time, for they had been walking in its direction. He could go and get his car, which was parked there, and run Frances home himself.

'Don't worry, Frances,' he said. 'I'll have you home in two shakes of a lamb's tail.' And they set off.

By the time they reached his apartment block, he was beginning to think that the plan was not a very good one after all. He was woozy himself and in no fit state to drive through the city. There was no help for it.

'You'd better come in with me. You can take my bed and I'll sleep on the sofa in the living room.' Johnny hesitated. 'Will they know you're not in at the hostel, do you think?'

'It'll be fine, Johnny, really.' Frances was beginning to lose all her inhibitions: she was cold, she wanted to get back into the warm, but most of all she wanted the evening with Johnny to go on and on, never to end.

It was a small block of apartments without a night porter, so Johnny had his own keys to the main door and they got into the flat unseen by anyone. Woozy though he was, Johnny still held onto the idea that he had to protect her reputation. Though the apartment was lovely and warm from the central heating, he felt her shivering when he took her coat.

'I'll make some coffee,' he whispered, taking her in his arms and holding her close, feeling the shuddering in her body and waiting for it to subside a little. Her arms crept round his waist and she laid her head on his chest, closing her eyes. Her shivering gradually lessened as the warmth of the room seeped into her. She felt deadly tired but didn't want to say so, she wanted him to hold her like this for ever.

Johnny looked down at her. Her hair had tumbled over her face and her white skin was tinged with rose. With her slight frame and her eyes closed she could almost have been . . . No, it was an illusion, it was the wine, he told himself.

'Come along, dear, I'll get you to bed. You're dead on your feet,' he said and took her with him into the bedroom. Her arms were, by this time, around his neck and she refused to let go, drawing him down onto the bed with her. He could feel her yearning reaching out to him. Before he knew what was happening they were in the bed together, clasped heart to heart.

He buried his head in the curve of her neck, feeling the soft swell of her breasts against him and breathing in the clean, fragrant smell of her hair. Frances gave herself to him joyously. She had loved him so long, ever since she had walked into his office, fresh from the business college, and taken the post he offered.

'Lorinda!' Johnny sighed into her hair. 'My lovely Ada-Lorinda.'

But Frances didn't hear what it was he was saying, only the love in his voice as he said it. Exhilaration flooded through her: he was hers now, all her dreams were being realised.

Chapter Eighteen

Tom and Ada were married on August Bank Holiday Saturday, 1914. Ada had at last completed the two years of her training and received the certificate saying so. Tom was back in Durham, his time as a houseman finished; he was going into practice with his father.

On the morning of the wedding, Ada sat before the dressing-table looking glass in the spare bedroom in Mr Johnson's cottage, gazing at her reflection. She was on her own; Virginia, who was to be matron of honour, had not yet appeared.

'You must be married from my house, my dear,' Mr Johnson had declared. 'You can't possibly go to the church from the Grays' place, it would be a bad omen for your future life. No, I insist. You'll have left the hospital by then and in any case it would not be suitable for you to marry from there.'

Ada was persuaded. 'You're very good to me, Mr

Johnson,' she had replied. 'Why are you so good to me?'

Mr Johnson had looked flustered for a moment before recovering his poise. 'Nonsense! I'm a lonely old man and you have been good to me, visiting me and telling me all your news. You're like a breath of fresh air in the place. You're sure you don't mind me giving you away? I only suggested it because I thought –'

'No, no, Mr Johnson, indeed, it's very good of you to bother. And you're right, having Dr Gray giving me away was perhaps not the best thing.'

'Well, I'm proud to do it. I'm fond of you, you know. And proud, too, after all, you are a product of my teaching.'

And a little effort on my part, thought Ada, but she merely smiled wryly.

Now, on the morning of her wedding, Ada sat and pulled her hairbrush through her hair, little flutterings of apprehension coursing through her veins. The doorbell rang and she heard Mr Johnson's voice as he opened the door to whoever it was – Virginia, probably. There was a soft knock on the bedroom door.

'Come in,' she called.

'Ada! Howay, man! Aren't you getting ready? You don't want to be late for your own wedding.'

It was not Virginia who walked in but Eliza and her two boys. Bertie was now a solemn seven-year-old, thin and ill at ease in his new tweed suit and high collar,

Miles, a sturdy four-year-old, still had the plump cheeks of babyhood.

Ada jumped up in welcome. 'Eliza! Oh, it's lovely to see you, it is that.' She hugged her friend and gazed critically at her, it was a few months since she had seen her. Eliza looked tired and careworn, she thought, a trifle anxiously. 'Bye, I'm glad to see you, Eliza, and the bairns too. Haven't they grown?'

'Auntie Ada, Auntie Ada.' Bertie and Miles were tugging at her skirt, trying to get her attention. She bent and put an arm around each of them, kissing them soundly. 'Aren't you big, both of you?' she cried, and the boys puffed up with pride, both standing as tall as they could.

Eliza laughed. 'They've been looking forward to coming all week,' she said. 'They couldn't sit still on the train, they were so excited. I thought I might have a bit of trouble finding the right house, but it wasn't so hard. I –'

They were interrupted by a perfunctory knock on the door and Virginia swept in, plumply pretty in pink tulle. She briefly acknowledged Ada's words of introduction to Eliza and the boys.

'Pleased to meet you,' Eliza mumbled, holding out her work-stained hand, which Virginia barely touched. Eliza stood back, looking decidedly uncomfortable, with the two boys by her side, watching Virginia with wondering eyes.

'Oh, come on, Ada,' Virginia said crossly. 'For goodness' sake! It's time you were dressed. Why you wanted to go to the church from here I can't imagine, it would have been so much more convenient if you had been at Daddy's. I had to trail all the way down here, everything's been such a rash, with us having to come from Jesmond.'

'Sorry, Virginia,' Ada murmured, more interested in putting Eliza at ease than in what her future sister-in-law was saying. 'Eliza, take the boys into the kitchen. I made some lemonade this morning specially for them.'

Eliza looked relieved and even Bertie brightened up. His lower lip had begun to stick out as he heard the lady scold his Auntie Ada.

'Yes, yes, I will, thank you, Ada.' Eliza took the boys and crossed to the door, turning as she got there. 'I'll go on then, as soon as they've had a drink,' she said, looking nervously at Virginia.

'Yes, you know where it is, don't you, Eliza? Go up to the marketplace, it's on the right there, you can't miss it.' Ada ignored Virginia's impatient frown and went to her friend, pressing her arm. 'I'll have a word with you afterwards at the reception,' she said softly. 'You won't go before I do, will you?'

'No, no, I won't,' Eliza agreed slowly, showing Ada she had guessed her feelings aright: Eliza was obviously hoping the rest of Ada's new friends were not so intimidating as Virginia.

*

Ada, dressed in cream-coloured lace with shoes to match and carrying a nosegay of fragrant rosebuds, was a vision of petite loveliness. She was not twenty-one years old and still possessed the air of delicate innocence that had first attracted Tom, now emphasised by the creamy veil covering the dark curls piled on top of her head.

She was escorted down the aisle of St Nicholas's Church by an obviously proud Mr Johnson, distinguished-looking in morning dress and followed by Virginia, her matron of honour, smiling now, the bad temper of the morning forgotten. With the organ ringing out 'Here Comes the Bride', everyone standing and all eyes on her, Ada felt suddenly sick. All she wanted to do was turn and run; she couldn't possibly go through with it, she knew she could not. She faltered and Mr Johnson took a firmer grip on her arm. Then she saw Eliza standing near the back of the church, the two boys peeping round her skirts. The three of them, even little Miles, were smiling at her so proudly that her momentary panic subsided and she gave them a tiny wink.

As Ada approached Tom, standing by Christopher, his best man, she saw he was watching her, his eyes full of love, pride and tenderness. She looked up at him. Over the last few years, Tom had outgrown his boyishness; this was a mature man, calm and confident, a rock to depend on. But was it what she really wanted? Ada's doubts returned in full force.

Why was she doing this? She knew she was not really in love with Tom – oh aye, she loved him all right, she did. But *in love* with him? As she had been in love with Johnny? Her heart beat faster and faster. What was she doing? I'm not being fair to Tom, she told herself, no, I'm not. She panicked. Why had she not told him the truth during all those years of engagement? Her thoughts raced in the few seconds it took for him to step forward. Virginia took her nosegay but Ada hardly noticed it, her vision blurring.

Mr Johnson was well aware of her panic, but he put it down to the nervous reaction common to most brides. Firmly he took her in hand, leading her to Tom's side and placing her hand in her bridegroom's. Tom held it firmly, proudly, and the ceremony began.

Ada made her responses in a dream. Everything was unreal to her, what was she doing? Yet she carried on doing it, not knowing what else she could do. And at last it was over and they came out into the sunlight with well-wishers crowding round them. She was married now, she thought, for better or worse. She had to put aside her doubts, it was too late to change her mind. With quick resolve she told herself she would make Tom the best wife she could.

*

The reception was held at the Grays' home but, in contrast to Virginia's wedding, there were not many guests and they fitted easily into the house with no need for a marquee. It was informal, a buffet with plates of cold chicken and salad, and the guests, mostly friends of the Grays with a few colleagues of Ada's from the hospital, who had managed to get the time off from the wards, chatted happily among themselves. All but Eliza, Ada noticed; Eliza was standing in a corner with her children.

Ada's heart smote her: Eliza looked middle-aged already. Her fair hair, drawn back into a bun at the nape of her neck, was lustreless and had threads of grey running through it. The skin beneath her eyes was already lined and she had a general air of weariness. She wore a cheap print dress which must have looked pretty to her this morning, but now, contrasted with the dresses of the girls around her, it looked what it was, a dress from an Auckland market stall. Yet Eliza was only in her early twenties, and only a short time ago she would have looked pretty in anything.

Ada started to make her way towards her friend but was stopped by Meg Morton. Meg too had gained her certificate of nursing and was about to take up a position at the Lady Eden Cottage Hospital in Bishop Auckland.

Meg was very excited at going back to Auckland at

last. 'I'm looking forward to it, Ada, and you must be too, starting a new life – won't your nursing come in handy as a doctor's wife? I hope you'll both be very happy.'

'Thank you, Meg, and you too, good luck in your new post,' Ada echoed. 'I don't know if you know my friend Eliza Maxwell? Come over and I'll introduce you. Eliza lives near West Auckland.'

Introductions over, the three women chatted together for a few minutes until Eliza, hearing the clock in the hall chiming three, declared she had to get back.

'There's the milking to do, Ada,' she explained and looked around for her two boys. They were quite close, sitting together on a sofa and watching the people around them with large, solemn eyes. 'Howay, pets, time to go to the station,' she called, and the two little boys scrambled down and came to her side.

'Oh, are you going by train? I am too, we might as well go together. I was going to catch a later train but it will be nice to have company. What lovely boys you have, aren't you lucky? Whereabouts do you say you live? On a farm it must be – that's grand for them.'

Meg, being the friendly soul she always was, chatted away as they walked to the door with Ada and Tom, who had joined her, slipping his arm through hers with a proprietorial air.

'I'll get through to see you as soon as I can after we come back,' Ada promised Eliza. 'We'll have a chat, just like old times. And when Miles starts school maybe you'll be able to visit me.'

Eliza bit her lip. 'We'll see, pet, we'll see. You know, love, I'm so pleased for you. Tom's a grand man, he is. Eeh, fancy, little Ada Leigh, a doctor's wife. Who'd have thought it a few years ago?'

Tom didn't hear this, he was walking on down the drive to the entrance with Meg. Ada watched him as he reached the gate and paused, half turning, as he made polite conversation to her colleague. Who would have thought it indeed, she mused. He was so handsome, so decent, so dependable. She would make him a good wife, she would make up to him for not loving him as she should, she vowed. But Eliza was saying something.

'I might be getting married myself, later on.'

'What?' Ada was startled.

'Well, I'll tell you about it when I write, Ada. I've got your new address. We'd better be off now.'

Ada kissed the boys goodbye and then she and Tom were walking back to the house. It was almost time for them to leave themselves and they had to change for the journey. Most of the wedding party accompanied them to the station, laughing and joking, noisy with the unaccustomed champagne drunk in the middle of the day.

Ada threw her bouquet from the window of the train and the girls in the crowd scrambled to catch the nosegay of Gloire de Dijon roses. She didn't see who got them for at last they were off.

'Seven whole days, darling.'

Tom picked confetti out of Ada's hair before gathering her in his arms. Elation shone in his eyes as he bent to kiss her, pleased he had had the forethought to reserve the whole carriage. He looked quite squiffy with the champagne and excitement. He had waited so long and patiently for this, Ada thought as his lips met hers, gentle at first and then with a new, demanding desire.

A memory which had lurked at the back of her mind for years came to the forefront, causing her instant disquiet: the thought of Uncle Harry and what he had done to her. She sat quietly in Tom's arms, dread creeping over her. All during their long courtship Tom had behaved with admirable restraint on the occasions they had been able to meet on their own. With Tom in Newcastle and Ada working long hours at the hospital, those occasions had been few and far between, and Ada had been able to forget the thought of what this night would bring.

Men could tell when a woman wasn't a virgin, couldn't they? she thought. Especially when they were doctors. She had been violated and Tom would think she was a loose woman. He was looking at her with adoring eyes now but would he do so tomorrow?

Tom dropped a kiss on top of her head and picked

up the hand which bore his ring. She smiled a tired, tremulous smile at him.

'Tired, Ada? The wedding was a bit of a strain, wasn't it? Don't worry, you'll soon recover your spirits. I know my girl: you may be little but you're tough, tough and resilient,' he said fondly. Lifting her hand, he rubbed the ring between finger and thumb, his face reflecting his inner contentment.

They took a cab to their hotel, which overlooked the Spa on Scarborough's south beach, and later, as they sat through dinner, Ada became more and more distracted and withdrawn. She barely touched her meal, her appetite deserting her completely. She couldn't seem to pull herself out of her depression, the depths of it dismayed her.

Oh, she thought, I'm not in love with Tom, no, I'm not. And that is going to make things ten times worse. I'm not in love with him and I'm going to hurt him and I don't want to, no, he's a lovely man. He doesn't deserve getting someone like me. Why didn't he pick someone his own kind?

'Gosh, you do look tired, my love,' Tom's concerned voice broke into her chaotic thoughts. 'Shall we go up?'

Ada looked at his kind, loving face, knowing he thought she was quiet because she was shy now the time had come. She managed a small smile before she nodded wordlessly to him and allowed him to take her arm and lead her out of the dining room and up the staircase.

'Men don't like damaged goods.' How many times had she heard that expression when she lived with her aunt and uncle in Bishop Auckland? Usually it was her aunt who was using it, and usually when she was pointing out what a no-good, unmarried mother Ada had. Or when she was railing at Ada, telling her it wasn't going to happen to any lass in her house, no, not if she, Doris Parker, had anything to say about it. Ironical, really, Ada thought, after what had happened in her house. Her thoughts returned to the present as they reached their rooms.

The bridal suite at the Grand Hotel had a separate sitting room with windows overlooking the sea. Ada walked over to them, exclaiming in simulated delight. Tom could only spare seven days from the practice, which had been expanded, since he joined his father, so he had felt he could afford the best for the short time they were there.

'Oh, look! Isn't it lovely?' She gazed out at the twinkling lights of the promenade below. She was trembling uncontrollably now.

'Darling! You're shivering.' Tom came up behind her and took her in his arms. 'You're not frightened of me, are you? Surely not. Don't be a little goose, Ada.' He lifted her chin and kissed her tenderly on the mouth. 'I won't hurt you, I promise I won't. Go on now, change and hop into bed. I'll just smoke a cigar on the balcony before I join you.'

Ada turned obediently and as she turned he patted her bottom, playfully. 'Go on, now,' he said.

Immediately a spectre rose up before Ada. She could still feel the touch of his hand on her bottom, just as she could always feel the touch of Uncle Harry's hands for hours afterwards; it sent shivers up her spine.

'My God!' Ada breathed under her breath as she undressed and slipped into a fine lawn nightgown. 'It's going to be Uncle Harry all over again!'

All thoughts of damaged goods were driven from her mind. She climbed into bed and lay there, rigid. All she could think of was that night when Uncle Harry had come into her bedroom in the attic in Tenters Street, and it was all going to happen again, just as it did then. Ada closed her eyes and fought for self-control, struggling against the images racing across her eyelids: Uncle Harry's leering face, the wet hair of his moustache, the hand descending to slap her. Gradually, the images began to fade; she gained a tenuous hold on herself and concentrated on her racing heartbeat, willing it to slow down, and it did. Ada relaxed a little.

So that when Tom slid into bed beside her she was thinking only that this was Tom, Tom, repeating it over and over in her mind. Tom, who loved her, Tom, who would never, never do anything to hurt her. And at last she could lift her face up to his kiss. Everything was going to be all right.

But as soon as she felt his hands on her body, cupping her breasts, they tensed against the hurt they had known. As his hands slid down over her hips and stomach, to the mound of thick, dark hair, lingering, she stiffened. There was nothing at all she could do to control it now.

Her mouth opened in a soundless scream of horror; taking Tom completely by surprise, she fought him, silently, as she had tried to fight Uncle Harry so long ago. She fought Tom mindlessly too, with nails out to tear and scratch, her teeth bared in a grimace as he released her abruptly, shaken to his core. Ada scrambled from his embrace to crouch at the furthest end of the bed, glaring her hatred.

'Ada,' he cried, 'for God's sake, Ada! Whatever is the matter?' He sprang out of bed, his cheek bleeding from where she had managed to catch him with her nails. Eyes wide, he looked at her, stretched out his arms to her.

'Don't! Don't touch me.' Ada shrank further onto the pillow, pressing herself against the ornately carved, wooden bedhead. Losing her balance with the instinctive gesture, she almost fell out of bed and had to catch hold of the bedpost to regain her balance.

Tom stood, frozen, staring at her; he didn't know what to do or say. Gradually the wild look faded from her eyes and as she returned to normal she began to realise what had happened. Her grip on the bedpost slackened and she bent her head as the tears came. Covering her face with her hands, she wept bitterly.

Tom was even more bewildered – nothing in his life had prepared him for this. Oh, he knew girls were often shy and ignorant of the sexual act, but usually they were girls from a sheltered background, whereas Ada was a girl of the people and a nurse at that. Where was the efficient, self-reliant, happy girl he knew and had grown to love? This was a new Ada altogether. Now she was reduced to a shivering bundle of misery, her thin shoulders shaking with the force of her sobbing. His heart turned over as he saw it.

'Don't, Ada, please don't, Ada. I'll not touch you if you don't want me to,' he said at last, hesitating to go to her. 'Not like that, I won't. Just let me comfort you, please, let me comfort you.' Tom opened his arms and after a long moment, Ada crept into them.

'I'm sorry,' she wept. 'I am, Tom, I am. I can't seem to help it. I should have told you.'

'Sh . . .' Tom rocked her in his arms, his face puzzled. He opened his mouth to frame a question but Ada was still talking.

'Don't ask me, Tom, not now. Later maybe, but not now, I couldn't stand it.'

Tom continued rocking her back and forth, back and forth, as he would a baby, feeling the sobs racking her slender body. And after a time the sobs lessened and she was quiet, her shoulders stilled. He waited, his thoughts turning bitter now he was getting over the shock. Now, when it seemed that all his plans, all his dreams were coming to fruition, they came crashing down on him. All through their long engagement he had been patient with her. He had respected that 'touch me not' air of innocence about her but he had never thought it would be carried over into marriage.

'Oh, Ada,' he said helplessly. How could she have nursed, seen life on the wards of a general hospital and yet know so little of human nature, of human sexuality? He tried again. 'Tell me, Ada, tell me what it is. You can't be so frightened of me, really you can't.'

Dumbly Ada looked back at him, the tears still beading her lashes; her violet eyes were enormous in her white face. What could she say? she wondered dumbly. She found herself altogether unable to tell him about Uncle Harry – the years of sly touching and squeezing, the years of feeling dirty and worthless, and the night of the rape, which had been the culmination of those years. Her mind shied away from it all; no, she did not have the words to speak of it.

Tom saw the conflict in her face, the torment in the shadowed pools of her eyes. The white skin round them was red with weeping. And Ada, he knew, did not weep easily; there was more to this than he could see now, there surely was. Wearily she brushed a tear away with the back of her hand, like a child. Indeed, she felt like a child to him as he held her slight body, his child not his wife. What had reduced his tough little Ada to this? he wondered again.

'Never mind, petal,' he said softly. 'It's been a long day, we're both exhausted. Let's go to sleep now, eh? You'll see, everything will look better in the morning, everything will work out fine.'

Ada smiled gratefully at him: dear Tom, how had she got them both into this mess? But she couldn't disguise the fact that she was relieved that tonight at least she could sleep in peace.

'I'll sleep on the sofa in the sitting room, dear,' he said, putting her gently from him and covering her with the sheet.

'Thank you, Tom,' she whispered. What else was there to say? she thought. It was hopeless and she should have known it. Though why she should have foreseen it she wasn't quite sure.

Tom settled down to a wedding night which was very different from the one he had looked forward to so eagerly only that morning. Only that morning, he mused as he lay sleepless, but a lifetime ago.

Chapter Nineteen

Breakfast on the first morning after their wedding was a sombre meal for Tom and Ada even though the weather was near perfect. The sun shone through the windows of the dining room, and Ada looked out at a sparkling sea, calm and blue, in complete contrast to her troubled spirits.

They both picked at their food. Tom picked up his coffee cup and stared moodily into the murky brown liquid. Ada grimaced as she sipped hers. Why on earth, she wondered distractedly, had she not asked for tea? She hated coffee. Was her self-confidence shattered even to the extent that she was nervous of saying what she would like to drink? She regarded Tom covertly; he looked so unhappy, poor man.

I *will* control myself tonight, she resolved. It's only an aversion. If I can drink coffee and appear to like it, I can make myself be a proper wife to Tom. She'd tell him so.

'Tom –'

'Ada –'

They both began to talk at once and stopped abruptly. Somehow the tiny coincidence broke the ice and they smiled at each other.

'You first,' said Tom.

'I was just going to say I'm so sorry –'

'No, don't say it. We'll forget about it today, we were both tired last night. Today we'll go out and enjoy ourselves, take a carriage ride to the North Shore, maybe even walk back. What do you say?'

Ada assented. She could see that Tom was determined to put the night behind him. He couldn't really believe her behaviour was anything but an aberration, so he had decided it was all due to wedding fatigue. There was no point in talking about it, he was right about that. And in any case, it was going to be all right that night, it was, really it was, she told herself.

They rode along at a spanking pace in an open carriage drawn by a dapple-grey horse. Ada shaded her complexion with a parasol on the insistence of Tom, though she giggled inwardly as she thought of the picture she made; Eliza would have laughed at her. They paid what Ada considered to be an exorbitant amount for the privilege and afterwards walked back to the south pier and listened to the band. Then they sat on deck chairs on the sand watching the waves roll in and breathing in the fresh, salty air. They watched the children riding on the donkeys and smiled at one little girl who stood with hands on hips and glared her outrage at her parents for their supposed desertion when she at last saw them. Ada had noticed the child's momentary panic after thinking they had left while she took her trip on a donkey wearing a straw hat with 'Daisy' on it.

'You moved!' the child insisted, stamping her little foot.

Her parents, who had not moved an inch from the chairs where they had been sitting watching her, laughed and the child got angrier and angrier. But when the mother gathered her up and hugged her and the father vowed he would never have lost his little treasure, she was mollified.

'Just wait, in a year or two it could be us sitting here, an old married couple, watching our children on the donkeys,' Tom said.

'Oh, yes! Wouldn't it be grand?' Ada replied. Tom gathered her hand in his and his love for her shone from his eyes. Everything is going to be fine, Ada told herself as she returned the pressure of his fingers.

As the lovely day wore on, both Tom and Ada began to recover their spirits and their appetites, so that by the time they eventually arrived back at the hotel to dress for dinner they were laughing at the antics of Punch and Judy and marvelling at the hydraulic lift which had brought them up the cliffs to the hotel.

'A great feat of Victorian engineering,' Tom declared, 'which only proves the power of water.'

They dined to the sound of a string quartet playing romantic melodies and this time they both ate well, the sun and the sea air had done their work. And afterwards, Ada felt happy and confident as she went upstairs on her husband's arm. This time it was going to be fine, she would be able to control herself and Tom would be happy and pleased with her.

It was not fine, it was a disaster to equal the disaster of the night before. There seemed to be nothing she could do about it, nothing at all, she simply couldn't face the act of making love. The episode ended once again with Tom sleeping in the sitting room and Ada, exhausted with emotional turmoil, falling asleep in the small hours to dream endlessly of Uncle Harry, his watery eyes close to hers; his face somehow turned into the face of Tom but when she relaxed with the relief of it, it was Uncle Harry once more.

She must have talked in her sleep, shouted even, for the next morning Tom entered the bedroom and sat down on the end of the bed.

'What was it that Uncle Harry did to you?' He came straight to the point.

Ada was bereft of words for a while, she had no idea what to say. 'Did I talk in my sleep?' she asked, biting her bottom lip as she looked at his grave young face.

'You did. Now tell me, Ada, what was it that your uncle did to you?'

Ada couldn't tell him – how could she? What would he think of her?

'Ada, tell me, I have a right to know.' As Ada continued staring at him, her violet eyes dark-rimmed with lack of proper sleep, he tried a little persuasion.

'Ada, it might surprise you to hear it, but I am a doctor and I've worked in a hospital in a big city. Believe me, I don't think there's anything you can say that will be new to me or shock me. I've seen it all, things which are not mentioned in polite society. Did your Uncle Harry beat you? Is that why you're so frightened?'

At Ada's expression he moved closer to her, taking her in his arms and holding her to him. 'Tell me,' he repeated.

Ada couldn't hold out any longer. 'My Uncle Harry . . .' she said and paused.

'Yes?'

'My Uncle Harry is in prison,' she said at last, her voice low. 'He is in prison for molesting little girls.'

'But Ada, you can't be blamed for that, surely – My God! Do you mean to say that he interfered with you?'

Tom sat back and Ada could see that he was desperately wanting her to say it wasn't true. But Ada nodded, dumbly. He looked as though a great blow had knocked all the wind out of him. His hold on her slackened, she felt his physical recoil from her. Oh, she knew she shouldn't have told him!

'Er, I'll just get a glass of water, dear,' he mumbled, fled back into the sitting room and poured a glass of water from the jug standing on the table. He took it over to the window and drank, giving himself a minute or two to think.

He had seen quite a lot of the seamier side of life; the slums of Newcastle were teeming with every kind of vice and the victims frequently ended up in the Infirmary. But that was Newcastle, that wasn't home, not his own family – they were distanced from all that. Such things were never even mentioned in his home world, never. That his wife should even know that it happened, let alone experience it – his mind shied away from the thought. He pictured Ada, her anxious little face as he walked out of the room, his feelings mixed. Of course he still loved her, it wasn't her fault, how could it be? It was the fault of that uncle of hers. Such things were common among the labouring poor, he thought, overcrowding and all that. It bred such beasts. For the first time, Tom began to doubt the socialist principles of his father; he couldn't help the thought sneaking into his mind that this would never have happened if he had married someone from his own level of society.

He sat down on the sofa, suddenly feeling his legs couldn't bear his weight. He had married Ada because he loved her, she was all he ever wanted. And no doubt she was lying in bed on the other side of the bedroom door, wondering if he was going to cast her off because she had told him the truth. Pulling himself together, he went in to her.

Ada was not lying in bed. She was up and dressed and facing the door with a pale, determined face. She lifted her chin as the door opened, resolved that if his face still showed the signs of revulsion she had seen earlier, she would offer him his freedom. It was only fair.

Tom crossed the room and took her hands in his, kissing her lightly on the forehead. 'We will never talk of this again,' he said. 'Now, let's go down to breakfast.'

The outbreak of war on 4 August gave Tom the perfect excuse to cut short his honeymoon in Scarborough. The situation was becoming intolerable to him, Ada could see it in his face. He smiled much less and laughed not at all, not even at the comic on the end of the pier.

Every day Ada resolved that if Tom still wanted her she would give herself to him, she would not panic again. Every evening Tom would come to her bed, trying desperately to turn his marriage into a normal one. Every evening they both failed miserably. Ada watched his unhappiness, feeling guiltier all the time.

'We must pack immediately.' Tom left his meal and rose from the table when the announcement was made in the dining room. 'We'll take the first available train back to Durham.'

There was an excited hubbub among the diners as people left their meals untouched and forgotten. Action seemed to be called for, though what particular action wasn't clear at first. They stood around in small groups, talking the news over with one another, most of them exhilarated and only the odd few looking gravely solemn.

Ada was oblivious of all this; she was staring at Tom in surprise. How would going back to Durham help? she wondered. Somehow, outside troubles, even the enormous one of war with Germany, seemed insignificant to her against her own, just now.

'Must we?' she asked, but even as she uttered the question she felt a great sense of relief. The forlorn hope she had nurtured that they might be able to put things right before they went home to their little house in Hallgarth Street died.

'I think so,' Tom was saying as he moved round behind her chair to pull it out for her. She rose obediently.

'Yes, of course, Tom.'

As they came downstairs to the lobby of the hotel, followed by a porter with their bags, Ada saw that the place was bursting with activity. She waited beside the luggage while Tom paid his bill, looking round at the hustle and bustle. The general air was one of heady anticipation rather than dismay at the thought of war. Tom had to wait in line to settle his account, for a number of other people had also felt the need to cut short their holiday and rush home. Ada still couldn't understand why.

They had to wait for a cab to the station, too, and the journey home was very different from the one they had taken only a few days before at the start of their honeymoon. This time they sat opposite each other in a crowded carriage. The train was so full that Ada had thought they would have to stand, but Tom, with his usual efficiency, secured them seats at the last minute.

The other occupants of the carriage were discussing the probability of a quick war which would be over in a few weeks, but Tom and Ada spoke little. Both of them stared out of the window at the passing scenery.

'I will enlist tomorrow,' Tom said abruptly, sounding as though he had come to a decision and was going to stick to it.

'But what about your father, the practice?' Ada turned startled eyes upon him. 'Won't it be too much for him?'

Tom made a dismissive gesture. 'Father will manage.'

Ada stared at him miserably. If it hadn't been for her and the unhappiness she caused him he wouldn't be going, she knew. She felt even guiltier than she had before. She gazed out of the window again, unseeingly. Because of her, Tom was going to war and could very well be killed. Ada had read the books Mr Johnson had lent her about the Napoleonic Wars and the one about

Florence Nightingale in the Crimea. Soldiers got killed and injured in wartime, war meant battles and battles meant casualties. She was not blind to this fact as so many of the people around her seemed to be.

When the train reached Durham, Ada and Tom went straight to the little house in New Elvet which Tom had bought for their new home. Tom lit the sitting-room fire while she went upstairs to unpack. What a homecoming, she mused as she hung his shirts in the mahogany wardrobe and put a stone hot-water bottle in the bed to warm it. She hesitated for a moment or two – should she put one in the bed in the spare bedroom? She decided she would, she could always take it out again if the bed wasn't used. The weather was warm but the house had not been lived in and could be damp.

Downstairs, Tom was waiting for her. He rose to his feet as she entered the room. He stood before the fire, absently drumming his fingers on the mantelpiece.

'I must go up and see Father,' he said. 'You'll be all right on your own? It's only fair to let him know I'm going as soon as possible.'

'Yes, of course, Tom, if you're sure. Will you be back for dinner? I left the pantry well stocked with tins and dry goods, I'm sure I can soon get something together.'

Tom hesitated. 'I'm not sure. We may have to discuss arrangements, we'll have a lot to talk about. I will probably have to leave fairly quickly.'

They were talking to each other like polite strangers, Ada reflected. 'Well, don't worry about me, I shall be all right,' she said evenly. Without further ado, he left. She heard the front door bang shut after him and sat down in an armchair, looking round the room. They had spent all their spare time furnishing the house. She had thought she could make a home there, her very first real home, but now, as she looked round, it seemed like a stranger's place to her. She settled down to wait for her husband's return, feeling friendless and alone. Oh, if only she had had a mother she could confide in! she thought. But nothing had ever come of her attempts to find her. Eliza, now, she could have confided in Eliza but she was too far away and it was not the sort of thing Ada could put in a letter.

In the weeks that followed, everything began to move at what seemed a frightening pace to Ada. The city was in the grip of war fever: wherever she went it was being discussed. Many young men enlisted right at the very beginning and Tom's departure went unremarked by anyone but his close friends and family, who were very upset by it.

Ada pondered what she herself was going to do now. She couldn't stay in the house on her own with nothing to do, not for any length of time. For Ada was not one of those who believed the war would be over by Christmas;

perhaps not even next Christmas, she thought sadly as she crossed over Elvet Bridge and turned to walk up New Elvet one day, after shopping.

She would return to nursing, that was what she was trained for, and nurses would be needed now, more than ever. She had read in the *Northern Echo* only that morning that many nurses straight out of their training were leaving for army hospitals in France and England, so she would go back to the County Hospital. Even though she was married now, her husband was away and she was sure she would be welcomed back.

At home there was a letter waiting for her from Tom. With the now familiar feeling of sadness, she opened the envelope and read the terse note within. Tom was coming home on embarkation leave, he would soon be going to France. Well, she would tell him of her plans when he arrived. Apprehensively, she wondered if he would think they were a good idea. Ada looked at the date and saw that he would arrive the next day.

When Tom arrived, resplendent in his uniform of an army captain, he was enthusiastic about the war, full of talk of his fellow officers and eager to get over to France and start taking part.

'Just think, Ada,' he said, 'I'll have a much greater chance to gain experience in surgery, it will stand me in great stead. I'm going to a field hospital, I'll be in charge

– well, of course there will be a regular army surgeon in overall charge, but that will be of several field hospitals. In effect, it means I will be in charge.' He grinned at her and she remembered how engaging his grin could be, how infectious his enthusiasm. He seemed to have forgotten about their differences.

They were sitting in the small sitting room drinking afternoon tea and Tom picked up his cup and saucer and strode over to the window, looking out on Hallgarth Street. He had a restlessness about him which kept him from being still for long.

'Are you going over to see your parents tonight, or waiting until tomorrow?' asked Ada.

'Oh, tomorrow, I think, let's have the evening to ourselves,' Tom answered. Nervously, Ada felt small flutters of apprehension run up her spine. Quickly she changed the subject.

'Tom, I was thinking of going back to the County. A lot of nurses are leaving now and I'm sure I can be of use, after all I don't want to waste my training and with you away, well, it will give me something to do.'

'Back to nursing? But you're a married woman. What about me when I come home on leave, what about the house?' Tom had turned to face her, a quick frown on his face.

'But they are taking married women, especially those who are married to men in the forces. After all,' Ada tried to put the reasonable case to him, 'after all, we all have to do what we can and it is what I'm trained for.'

'You could help Father in the practice, I'm sure he could use your help.'

'But I'd rather go back to hospital nursing, it's something I know I can do. Really, Tom, you must realise that nurses will be in short supply, there will be a great demand for them. And I can close the house down until you get back, I'll have to stay at the hospital. And I'm sure Matron will be understanding about leave when husbands come home.'

Tom sighed. 'Oh, well, I suppose you're right,' he said, confounding Ada, who had marshalled even more arguments to bolster her case. They spent the evening sitting companionably by the fire and went up to bed together, for Ada was determined that this time she would command her own behaviour.

She did manage not to scream, shout or cry when Tom drew her into his arms and caressed her breast. Encouraged, he went further; he was prepared to forget her past as he expected her to do. But Ada stiffened up too much in her attempts not to give way to her feelings, biting her lip until it bled.

'Relax, darling,' Tom whispered. 'You wouldn't send a man off to war without giving him –' He broke off what he was saying as he looked her full in the face and saw her white, strained expression. Abruptly, he let her go. Turning over onto his back, he stared into the dark, his breathing ragged, until eventually he gained control of himself.

'Don't worry, I'm not going to bother you any more,' he said flatly. Both Ada and Tom lay a long, long time before getting to sleep.

Next morning Tom was up before Ada woke. She came downstairs at nine o'clock, heavy-eyed and head aching, to find an empty house. She cleaned the house, more to pass the time than because it needed it, and when Tom still did not appear by twelve she cooked and ate a solitary meal. Just as she was thinking of going up to his parents' house to see if he was there, she heard a knock at the door.

Tom! He must have come back, was her first thought as she hurried to answer it, but even as she opened the door she knew it couldn't be. Tom had his key, he wouldn't knock.

'Hello, Ada.'

Virginia stood there, her face set in an angry frown. Before Ada could answer her greeting, she pushed past and walked into the sitting room, turning to face Ada, who had followed her.

'Have you seen Tom?' Ada asked, knowing full well Virginia had. What had Tom said to her to make her so angry? Surely he hadn't told the family their private business? Ada quailed at the thought.

'Indeed, I have seen Tom. I came down from Newcastle to see Tom this evening, I travelled yesterday so as to have the weekend with my parents. Now, what I want to know is, what happened between you and Tom to make him so unhappy? What have you done to him?'

'Done to him?' Ada echoed, her stomach doing a quick somersault.

'You know what I mean. Why did Tom come up for breakfast at our house looking so strained? Oh, he told us there was nothing wrong, he'd woken early and thought the walk would be nice, but I know Tom, I can tell what he's feeling.'

'I didn't do anything. He went out before I woke this morning,' Ada said lamely. 'Er . . .' She cast around for something to say, something to calm her sister-in-law. 'Would you like a cup of tea, Virginia?'

Virginia snorted. 'No, I would not. I'm very angry with you, Ada, we all are. I'm sure if it hadn't been for you Tom would never have joined the army, he would never have been going to the front.'

'But he's not going to the front, he'll be working in a hospital,' Ada answered reasonably.

Impatiently, Virginia pulled on the gloves which she had just taken off while she was speaking. 'Don't be silly, Ada. Where do you think field hospitals are if not close to the front? No, if anything happens to Tom it will be your fault entirely. There was no need for him to go, he was doing essential work here, and now Daddy has to take all the strain of the practice on his own shoulders. I tell you, Ada, I will never forget this.' Virginia swept past Ada and out of the house, leaving Ada feeling more miserable than ever.

What had happened to the Virginia she had first met? Ada wondered sadly. She had changed so much as she grew older. Though it was true, brother and sister had always had a very close, loving relationship; Ada remembered how she had envied their closeness when she first saw it. Virginia would never forgive anyone who hurt Tom.

Tom didn't come back, and by two o'clock Ada thought she had to get out of the house or go mad. She decided to go to see Matron at the County and offer her services, at least that would be something constructive. Changing into a dark-blue costume, she brushed her hair and drew it back into a severe bun at the nape of her neck. The more businesslike she looked, the better, she thought. Leaving a note for Tom, she left the house.

The interview with Matron was entirely satisfactory. Ada had been right in supposing that a lot of nurses were leaving for army hospitals in England and France.

'You can start as soon as it suits you, Nurse,' Matron told her when Ada put her request.

'Will the beginning of the month be all right, Matron?' Ada asked. 'I have the house to close up and other things to see to first.'

Matron sighed. 'Well, I could have used you sooner but the beginning of the month will do.'

Ada thanked her dutifully. Matron had been the terror of the probationers during her training, but now the older woman – who had herself trained in the Nightingale Training School of St Thomas's Hospital in London and was a firm believer in Florence Nightingale's ideas on discipline – looked tired and strained. Ada guessed she was working seven days a week in the effort to keep the hospital going despite the shortage of nurses.

As Ada left the hospital, her attention was drawn to a poster for nurses and other hospital workers under the Voluntary Aid Detachment scheme. She paused and read it.

'VAD' it read in large letters. 'Nursing members, cooks, kitchen maids, clerks, housemaids, ward maids, laundresses, motor-drivers, etc. urgently needed.'

If it hadn't been for the Gray family I might have been applying for a post as laundress, she mused as she walked home to New Elvet. She owed everything to them, it was true. Her conscience was causing her a great deal of discomfort by the time she arrived at the little house in Hallgarth Street.

Tom was home; as Ada opened the front door she saw

his army cap on the hallstand and smelled the strong tobacco he had begun smoking since he joined the army. Relief flooded through her: for a while that morning she had worried that he was not going to come back to her at all. Quickly she looked at herself in the mirror over the hallstand; loosing her hair from its knot, she threaded her fingers through it and patted it into place. She was very pale, she noticed, and pinched her cheeks between finger and thumb to bring some colour into them.

'Is that you, Ada?' Tom called from the sitting room.

'Yes, I'm coming, Tom,' she said.

Chapter Twenty

The last few days of Tom's leave were days of great strain for Ada. Dutifully, she went with him to his parents' house for dinner and sat through a very uncomfortable meal. Both Mrs Gray and Virginia were barely civil to her and she was glad when the time came round for her and Tom to return home.

'I'm staying a few days, Tom,' Virginia said as they said their goodbyes in the hall. 'I'll see you before you go.' She kissed him on the cheek, hugging him to her. 'I can't let you go without saying goodbye properly.' She pointedly ignored Ada, who was just glad that the evening had at last come to an end.

As their own front door closed behind them, Tom grasped Ada's arm firmly. She looked at him in surprise, seeing the new air of determination about him.

'What are you doing, Tom?'

'I'm doing what I should have done in the beginning,'

Tom declared. 'Now, no protests, no hysterics, I am going to make you see reason. It's past time you became my wife in more than name.'

Dragging her up the stairs, he threw her on the bed and began ripping off his clothes. Ada sat up, fear creeping up her throat and threatening to choke her.

'Tom, Tom –'

'Never mind Tom,' he barked. 'Get your clothes off now, or I'll tear them off for you.'

Dumbly, as she saw the resolve in his eyes, Ada began to take off her dress, her shoes and stockings. She tried again.

'Tom, not like this,' she begged. 'Please, Tom –'

For answer, Tom threw himself on her, knocking her back on the bed and taking the breath from her body. Pulling the strap of her underbodice roughly down so that it tore, he caught hold of her breast, smothering her cry of pain with his mouth. He took her quickly, forcing her legs apart to accommodate him, till at last he pulled himself off her and lay on his back, panting.

Ada lay as one stunned, aching all over, feeling indescribably dirty. All men were the same then, she thought dully. Tom was as bad as Uncle Harry, or nearly as bad, when it came to gratifying his sexual urges. After a moment she sat up and pulled her torn bodice together.

'Where are you going, Ada?' Tom asked, but she couldn't even look at him. Without answering, she went into the bathroom; locking the door behind her, she ran the bath and, not caring that it was barely lukewarm, climbed in and began soaping herself all over. Tom knocked at the door but she ignored him. He called to her and knocked again, but in the end he went away.

Methodically, Ada cleaned herself and towelled herself dry. When, wrapped in towels, she opened the bathroom door, Tom was standing there in his pyjamas waiting for her.

'Ada,' he said, 'I had to do it, it was the only way. I thought it would make you love me.'

Ada didn't even look at him. She walked past him and into the spare bedroom, where she locked the door behind her and crawled into bed.

Next morning she was out of bed early after a sleepless night. She went downstairs, made a pot of tea and sat drinking it as she watched a watery sun rise over the houses behind the garden. Oh, God, she thought, what am I going to do? It was obvious to her that she would never be any good to a man, never be able to get over her revulsion for the sexual act. She had to let Tom go. She didn't know anyone who had actually divorced, but there must be a way to do it. This was no good to Tom and it was no good to her. She would make nursing her life, that was the only thing to do.

Tom came into the kitchen dressed for the day and sat

down opposite her at the table.

'How do you feel?' he said, hesitantly.

Ada ignored the question and got straight to the point. 'Tom, I think we should get a divorce,' she said. 'I'm no good to you, you want someone –'

'A divorce?' Tom interrupted. 'Don't be a fool, Ada. What do you think that would do to my career? A divorced doctor – why, it wouldn't do at all, men wouldn't tolerate their wives seeing a divorced doctor. No, I have the practice to think of even though I'm in the army for the present.'

'I thought, if I take the blame, you can divorce me, or seek an annulment or something.'

'It's out of the question, Ada. I won't have our private affairs bruited about in public and that's what would happen, believe me.'

Ada was silenced. She picked up the teapot and poured another cup of tea, stirring sugar into it, absently. Tom rose to his feet.

'Don't worry, Ada. I won't trouble you again. I'm going back to my unit today. I've already packed.'

'Oh!' Ada lifted startled eyes to him. 'What about your family?'

'I'll go up to see them this morning, say I was called back, I think. That would be best.'

By nine o'clock, Tom had left and the house settled back into its now familiar silence. Ada washed the cups and saucers and tidied up the kitchen, feeling deathly tired. Walking into the sitting room, she looked around; in the grey light filtering in through the lace curtains it seemed cheerless and depressing to her. Her body ached and her right breast was as sore as a boil. She sat down on the sofa and put her feet up, dropping off to sleep after a few minutes.

She was awakened by a loud knocking on the front door. Sitting up, she rubbed her heavy eyes, trying to collect her thoughts. The knocking sounded again. Wearily, Ada went to the door. Who on earth was it now? Her stomach began to churn as she opened the door and saw Virginia once again.

'You ungrateful little bitch!' Virginia greeted her, barging into the hall. Sighing, Ada closed the door and turned to face her. Now what was it? she wondered wearily.

'Don't look at me as though you don't know what I mean. I heard the whole story from Tom. Why did you marry my brother? Did you see a nice secure life ahead of you as the wife of a doctor? Not bad for a grubby little washerwoman, was it? You knew what you were doing, all right, but that wouldn't be so bad if you made him happy, but you're not prepared even to do that. A cold, calculating, frigid little guttersnipe, that's what you are. I should have left you to die in that miserable hovel in Gilesgate. I rue the day I got Daddy to let you come and live with us.' Virginia paused to get her breath. Ada just stood there, seeing no point in answering or defending herself.

'After all we did for you!' Virginia had got her second wind and started again. 'You never loved my brother, your head was too full of nonsense about that chap from Middlesbrough, that Johnny what's his name. It's not because of him, is it? Have you been seeing him? Did he come back to see you? I told him that day you got engaged when he came sniffing round –'

'You told him?'

'I did. I told him you were in love with Tom, may God forgive me – this might not have happened if I hadn't done that. I should have followed my first instinct –'

'You mean he was alive when I got engaged to Tom? Johnny, Johnny Fenwick?'

'Well' – Virginia's voice was heavy with sarcasm – 'how else could he have come to see you if he wasn't alive? I wasn't saying I saw his ghost. Don't pretend to be stupid, Ada, that's one thing I know you're not. No, you were cleverer than any of us, weren't you?'

Ada finally took charge of the situation. With a new air of determination she walked up to her sister-in-law.

'Shut up, Virginia! And get out of my house, now.'

'Your house! Why, my brother –'

'Get out, I said, or I'll put you out. How would you like people in the street seeing that, Virginia? It doesn't matter to me, guttersnipe that I am, but you, Virginia Gray?' Ada made to take hold of Virginia's arm.

'Don't touch me! Don't you dare! I'm going in any case, I wouldn't stay another minute. I've said what I wanted to say.' She turned with her hand on the doorknob. 'But if you have any decency at all –'

'Just go, Virginia,' Ada said calmly.

When the door finally closed after her sister-in-law, Ada stood with her back to it, leaning against it. Slowly, the import of what Virginia had said seeped into her mind. Johnny was not dead, Johnny was alive. Suddenly filled with a wild gladness, Ada clasped her arms about herself and danced around the tiny hall, singing aloud, 'Johnny's alive, Johnny's alive,' over and over again. She could go to Middlesbrough and see him, she could tell him her marriage to Tom was all a mistake, she could –

Ada stopped whirling about, and her arms fell to her sides. How stupid she had been! she thought. Everything that had happened had been all her fault. A terrible sadness filled her for what might have been. But it was too late now, of course it was. Even if Johnny wanted her she was still tied to the man she had married, she was bound by her debt to Tom.

Mechanically, Ada climbed the stairs and began to pack her bags. It gave her something to do, though she wasn't due to start at the hospital until the following week. Vaguely she looked around; there were other things to do, too, she thought dully, if she was going to close up the house. She felt very alone, and the silent house seemed to emphasise it.

Maybe she was destined to be alone all her life, unlucky in love, just like her mother. Had her mother suffered as much as she did? she wondered. But maybe she was not alone, that mother of hers, maybe she had not answered Ada's advertisements because she was married now and had a new family to love and care for.

Ada fastened the straps on her bags and sat down on the chair by the bedside. Tom now, she thought, Tom would never be completely alone for the Grays were a close, loving family. And now, estranged from them, she had no one to talk to in Durham except for Mr Johnson, and he wouldn't understand, he was too old. Ada caught a glimpse of herself in the dressing-table looking glass, she looked thoroughly miserable. Absent-mindedly she picked up her hair brush and tidied her hair, tying it back off her shoulders. Mentally she shook herself; being dismal never got anyone anywhere.

'Pull yourself together, woman!' she said aloud, squaring her shoulders and pinned a determined expression on her face, and an idea popped into her mind. She would go for a walk in the fresh air, that was what she would do. If she didn't get out of this house immediately, she would smother in its stifling atmosphere.

*

Captain John Fenwick stood at the rail of the troopship *The Duchess of Cornwall* and peered ahead at the coastline emerging from the morning mist of a bitterly cold winter's day. His feelings were all mixed up as he watched the line of wharfs and docks become clearer and clearer. In truth, he didn't know what he felt about coming back to England after the years in Canada, though there was an undeniable feeling of coming home. The last time he had seen Liverpool, he mused, was the day he had caught the emigrant ship to Canada; on that occasion too the man by his side had been with him.

'Hasn't changed much, has it, captain?' Norman said now in a thick Scouse accent that the years in Toronto had failed to soften. 'Not since we left it, eh?' He gazed at the shoreline with pride and affection and Johnny smiled at him.

'A view of great scenic beauty, yes,' he ragged. Norman twisted his face into a conceding grin.

'Aw, hey, man, I know it's not that, like,' he answered, forgetting he was now a sergeant and Johnny the officer of his platoon. He looked again at the busy but scruffy docks, the water oily and smelly. 'But it's home, like. It hasn't changed, though.'

'Not that I can see,' Johnny agreed. He regarded Norman with affection; they had become firm friends over the last few years. Norman had worked for Johnny ever since he came to Toronto and started the small steel plant there. He had seen his own fortunes rise as Johnny's ideas became profitable and a steady demand for his products grew. Without Johnny he would have been nowhere, as he was always willing to tell anybody who showed the least bit interest. When Johnny had joined the army, Norman followed him without hesitation, for wasn't Johnny Fenwick his luck and his fortune? So now they were both part of the Twenty-Ninth Canadian Division, on their way to help out the old country.

The corner of Johnny's mouth turned up in a lopsided smile as he looked at the brawny figure of Norman. 'Sure it's safe for you to come back to Liverpool, Norman?' he joked. 'I seem to remember something you said about being chased out of there. Do you think plenty of time has gone by for them to forget?'

'Aw, well, you know how it is, they knew they couldn't win this war without me. No, they'll be that glad to see me back, they'll be dancing in the streets, you'll see.'

The two men grinned at each other in perfect harmony. He couldn't have done better than have dependable old Norman as his sergeant, Johnny thought, he was a man to rely on. His attention was drawn inexorably back to the shore, looming ever closer. Now it was possible to make out individual buildings.

'Wonder how long we'll have in England,' Norman mused as he too gazed over the intervening water to his home town. His voice was dreamy and his eyes full of memories.

'Not long, I think,' said Johnny. 'Before we know it we'll be on another boat bound for somewhere in Belgium or France. I don't think we'll be stopping off here for long.'

Johnny was right in his surmise. Norman had no time to look up old friends or take a look at his native city; he saw nothing of it except for the dock where the ship berthed. The Canadians were promptly hustled aboard a train bound for London amid a great deal of noise and seeming confusion. The train was packed with troops and hot and uncomfortable; even for the officers in the first-class carriages the air was thick and sour. Johnny managed to open a window only to have an inrush of black, sooty air to a chorus of protests from his fellow officers. At least, he thought, the train appeared to be going direct to Euston without stopping, so the journey would soon be over.

The crowds were even thicker at Euston Station. The Canadian soldiers piling out onto the platform joined a sea of khaki, everywhere men were milling around. Noncommissioned officers shouted orders and somehow order came out of chaos and men marched off, kitbags on shoulders. Engines hissed and roared and railway guards whistled, adding to the hubbub.

'Cup of tea, soldier? Sandwich?'

Women at long makeshift tables were handing out refreshments to the passing soldiers, pouring tea from tall copper tea urns into enamel mugs and offering them to the Canadians. But Johnny's platoon had no time to drink tea. Norman had them sorted out and formed into lines with the brisk efficiency he used to organise the steel workers in the mill in Toronto. He marched his charges out to the waiting omnibuses which were to take them to the church hall in the suburbs where they were to be billeted for the night.

'See you tomorrow, sir!'

'Yes, tomorrow, sergeant.'

Norman saluted Johnny formally now the platoon was with them. Climbing onto a bus, he was off. Johnny followed his fellow officers to the nearby hotel which had been commandeered for their use. Looking about him at the crowds, he hoped to hear an accent from the northeast, but in this he was unlucky.

Johnny felt curiously melancholy as he washed and shaved in preparation for the evening. Inevitably, being in England made him think of his home in the northeast, of Middlesbrough and Dinah. He wondered how she was faring; they had written to each other and she had sounded contented enough, but still, he would have liked to have seen her.

Although he was only 250 miles away from Middlesbrough, nearer than he had been for years, he felt homesick, more homesick than he had ever been. Thoughtfully, he wiped his cut-throat razor on the towel over his shoulder. And Ada, he mused, sweet little Ada-Lorinda, what was she doing now? A reminiscent glow came into his eyes as he thought of her, his little love. What a fool he had been! he thought. He should have insisted on seeing her that time he went to Durham; at least he should have written to her. Was she happy with the doctor husband she had married? Happier than he had been with Frances?

Sighing, Johnny thought of his own brief marriage. If he had paid more attention to Frances instead of putting all his time and energy into the business, maybe she would not have left him.

'You don't love me,' Frances had written in the note she left for him one evening when he had returned to an empty house. 'I was fooling myself that you did. Now I've found someone who really wants me.'

There had been others besides Frances, short-lived affairs which never came to anything. There was always something missing with them. Johnny finished shaving and cleaned his razor. He would have liked to go north, but even if there had been time to go and get back before the embarkation for France, there was no point, he mused sadly. With Ada married and Stephen in control at Middlesbrough, there was no place for him.

On impulse, Johnny decided to go to King's Cross

Station where the trains came in from Scotland and the northeast. Perhaps he would hear the familiar tones of Durham or the North Riding, even the burr of Northumberland. It was the next best thing to getting on a train and going there, he reckoned. Having decided, he placed his cap firmly on his head and shrugged into his greatcoat.

'Aren't you coming in to dinner?' one of his fellow Canadian officers called out to him as he went through the lobby of the hotel.

'No, I'm not really hungry. I thought I'd go out and have a look around,' Johnny answered over his shoulder. The other man shrugged and continued on his way to the dining room.

Out in the night the cold air struck damp and Johnny shivered, glad of his greatcoat. He looked about him for a passing cab and when one came along he hailed it and climbed aboard, thankful for its protection against the wind.

'Where to, guv?'

'King's Cross Station.'

After instructing the driver, Johnny leaned back against the cushioned seat and lit a cigar. The Napier taxi hooted and chugged its way through the traffic while Johnny watched the people on the pavement, old memories crowding in on him.

''Ere we are, guv. King's Cross.' The driver's cheery

voice broke into his thoughts as they pulled up. Johnny got out and paid his fare before hurrying into the warmth of the station.

As he had thought, the place was milling with troops from the north of England and Scotland, broad Scots and Geordie accents mixed with the flatter tones of Yorkshire and over all came the shrill twang of the local cockney. Coming fresh from the vast area of Canada, where the accent variations were mainly between French and English speakers, Johnny wondered at the difference a few miles could make to the speech of England. He stood quietly for a while and listened for the particular local accent of Auckland, Durham or Middlesbrough, but without success.

'I'm a sentimental fool!' Johnny murmured as he stood aside for a bevy of nurses. In their navy-blue caps and cloaks they stood out distinctively in the sea of khaki. They walked past so quietly that Johnny couldn't even hear their accent.

'I must have been mad to think I might meet someone I know coming down at this particular time of the evening on this particular day,' he added to himself and turned to go back to the hotel.

'Nurse! Howay, man, we haven't got all night. Don't just stand there, we'll miss the bus.' The voice was sharp and exasperated and pure Auckland.

'Ada!'

Johnny rushed over to the slight woman wrapped round in a heavy blue cloak and with her nurse's cap pulled down almost to her eyes. Grabbing her arm, he swung her round. 'Ada!' he cried, then dropped his hand. The woman was fair-haired and brown-eyed, and resembled Ada not at all except for her accent. Now she was staring at him indignantly, backing away from him.

'What do you think you're doing?'

'I'm sorry, I thought you were someone I knew,' Johnny mumbled. Turning, he walked rapidly out of the station, his heart pounding with the sharp disappointment which was flooding him.

Meg Morton looked after him, the need to get her nurses on the bus forgotten for a moment. Ada, had he said? The only Ada she knew was her friend from the hospital in Durham. But he couldn't have meant her. What could a Canadian officer want with Ada Gray? Dismissing it from her mind, Meg looked round at the nurses waiting for her.

'Come on, then, let's away. I want my bed the night even if you don't.'

Chapter Twenty-One

Ada went to see Eliza the first chance she got. Eliza was just about to go round the henhouses collecting eggs, so Ada walked with her.

'We can have a bit of gossip as we go, Ada,' Eliza commented as she delved her hand under a protesting hen and brought out a large brown egg. She looked sideways at Ada. 'I haven't seen you since the wedding and letters aren't the same, are they? How's being wed suit you? I must say you don't look over the moon with it. Is it because Tom's away in the army? Are you worried about him, like?'

'Well, there's always a worry, though I think he'll be all right. He'll be in a hospital, you know, not in the front line.' Ada wondered whether to confide in her friend. Goodness knew, Eliza had enough troubles of her own, so perhaps she shouldn't. But Eliza was not satisfied, she knew there was something.

'Were you not getting on, then?' she probed.

'No, we weren't,' Ada admitted. 'Eeh, Eliza, I tried, but after Uncle Harry –'

Eliza was not slow to realise what Ada was talking about. 'You mean in bed, like? Eeh, that bloody man, he had a lot to answer for, God rot his soul.'

'Had?' Ada looked up at Eliza, her brow creasing in a small frown of puzzlement, and Eliza bit her lip.

'Aye,' she said, 'I wasn't going to tell you. He died, you know, in prison. When you didn't say anything I thought I wouldn't bring it up.' She looked across at Ada, who was standing in the middle of the henhouse, bucket in hand and eggs forgotten.

'Died?'

'Aye.'

'I never knew. I haven't heard from Auntie Doris since that time years ago, in Auckland.'

'She's in the workhouse now, poor soul, couldn't make a go of it in Blackpool so she's back. Her arthritis, you know.'

'In the workhouse?' Ada was stricken with shock. Despite everything she had gone through with her aunt and uncle, she wouldn't have wished the workhouse on either one of them. Eliza saw how she felt and knew why; all the folk she knew would feel guilty and in some way responsible if a member of their family ended up in the workhouse, no matter how poor they were themselves.

'There now, that's just why I didn't tell you,' she declared. 'I knew you would feel you should do something about it and what can you do?'

Ada thought about it. It was true, there was nothing she could do at present, she had to go into the Nurses' Home the next week. The house would be closed down and even if it wasn't she could hardly ask Tom if she could bring a destitute relative to live in it, not when things were so bad between them. But maybe in time to come, she would be in a position to help Auntie Doris, she thought. During the rest of her short visit she was distracted, only half listening to Eliza as she told her of Emmerson Peart, a widower who wanted to marry her.

Ada went in to see Auntie Doris on her way home. Visiting hours were strictly weekends only, but once she had convinced the Sister in charge that she was a nurse herself, she was allowed in.

There were the usual long rows of beds in the women's ward, bleak, cheerless and regimented exactly in line, with the counterpanes pulled tight and straight over the frail bodies of the old women and the bedside cabinets in their regulation places beside each bed, just like St Margaret's in Durham, she thought. But a ward maid was dispensing thick mugs of cocoa from tall enamel jugs and the nurses looked kindly enough. Doris Parker, in the third bed from the end, turned to watch as Ada walked up the ward. Her niece was shocked at the change in her. Auntie Doris had shrunk in on herself; she had lost the last of her teeth so that her lips seemed to disappear into her mouth and her grey hair was scantier than ever. But it was the hopeless look in her eyes that shook Ada the most. Doris Parker had always been a fighter but now she looked as though she had just given up altogether.

'Oh aye, so you've come to see me at last,' she greeted Ada. 'After all I did for you an' all.'

'Hello, Auntie,' said Ada, ignoring the old woman's querulous tone. When she had worked in St Margaret's she had got used to old ladies and their bad tempers. Though when she thought about it, Auntie Doris had been little different when she lived in Finkle Street. Ada forced herself to smile.

'I've brought you some flowers, Auntie,' she said, 'do you want to smell them? Violets are lovely.' Auntie Doris curled her nose and shook her head.

'I can't abide them nasty smelly things.'

Not put out, Ada laid them on the bedside cabinet top, the only flowers in the ward. She'd see about something to put them in when she went out, she thought.

'How are you, Auntie?' she asked brightly.

'How do you expect me to be, lying here? Eeh, look what I've come to, me, who's worked hard all me life.' She looked hard at Ada, taking in the nice costume and the warm woollen coat, her gaze lingering on the fur collar.

'Mind, you seem to have done all right for yourself. Married a toff, did you?'

I did, Ada thought wryly, a little surprised at it; she hadn't thought of it that way before.

'Aye, well, you would fall on your feet, just like our Ada, no matter what she did she fell on her feet. I suppose that's why she didn't come back,' Auntie Doris said sourly. A speculative gleam came to her eye. 'Have you come to take me out? It would be only right, after all I took you and I didn't have to, you had no claim on me.'

'Oh, Auntie, I can't. I'm a nurse now, I'm going to live at the hospital. I couldn't have you living with me even if –' She stopped, realising what she was going to say.

'Even if you wanted to, you mean, don't you? Bye, you always were an ungrateful little bitch. I should have knocked it out of you when I had the chance.'

Ada took little notice as Auntie Doris went into a tirade of abuse. There was a time when it would have had its desired effect on her but now she took it for what it was, an old woman releasing her pent-up rage for the situation she found herself in. But Auntie Doris was getting too excited, she'd better leave.

'I'll come back to see you, Auntie, first chance I get,' she said and hurried off down the ward.

She travelled back to Durham in a reflective frame

of mind. The events of the last few days had been momentous for her. Once again she thought of her mother – had she really fallen on her feet as Auntie Doris had said she would? She would try again to find her, she thought suddenly.

Arriving back in New Elvet, the first thing Ada did was write an advertisement and send it off to the London papers.

'A letter for you, Sister Gray!'

Ada was hurrying from the nurses' dining room to the men's medical ward one morning after breakfast. She was in a hurry, for she was now Sister in charge of the ward and liked to be punctual for the report from the night staff. She paused impatiently as the porter called her from the hospital entrance, and retraced her steps. It was from Tom, she saw as she recognised the familiar handwriting on the buff-coloured envelope. The usual twinge of guilt assailed her as she tucked it into the bib of her apron.

'Thank you, Geordie!' She smiled at the cheery little man with the blue-black scars on his hands and face from a lifetime spent down the pits. Geordie beamed at her, he was glad Sister had got word from her husband. He knew it was her husband because of the army envelope.

'I hope he's in good fettle, Sister!' Geordie stumped off back to his post.

'Thank you,' Ada answered as she went on her way. Most of her patients were miners as Geordie had been before his accident, which had given him a permanent limp. Some of them were ex-miners or their wives who had fallen ill. They kept their cheery spirits, though, she thought as she shed her cloak and straightened her apron before taking the report from the night staff nurse. She shivered slightly; there was an early morning mist which was damp and cold, a penetrating cold. Perhaps it was a sea fret rolling in from the coast, that sometimes happened.

Nice to think it was Wednesday and her half-day. She would get right away from the hospital and do a little shopping if she could manage it. It was 16 December already, time was getting on.

By a quarter past eight the beds were all freshly made and breakfast dishes cleared away. The ward became quiet as the men dozed after all the early-morning activity. Ada was preparing the treatment trolley, watching the patients as she did so, reminding herself which patient needed which treatment and putting the appropriate articles ready for use. There was a pleasant hum of conversation among the patients who were recovering and well enough to start taking an interest in life again.

And then, quite out of the blue, the very walls shook and the windows rattled as distant but loud thuds and booms resounded in the air.

Ada froze, astonished. A particularly loud bang caused the enamel kidney dishes to dance on the trolley. Patients started up in alarm and Ada collected herself swiftly.

'Nurse Brown!' she called urgently as an old man attempted to get out of bed. 'Quickly, now!'

Ada's young probationer rushed out of the sluice, where she had been cleaning bedpans, her eyes wide and frightened. The ward had erupted noisily, there were raised voices and panic-stricken cries.

'An explosion! A pit explosion!' one of the men shouted.

'No, man, it's the Hun. They're here, we'll all be murdered in our beds!' cried another and tried to climb out of bed. Ada walked over to him, pushed him firmly back between the sheets and tucked him in, looking round for signs of panic among the others as she did so.

'Nonsense! Of course the Germans aren't here,' she said, though in truth she wondered about it herself. The nurses had their hands full trying to calm the patients and keep them from attempting to flee their beds while the strange thuds and booms continued.

Had there been a pit explosion? Dear God, please not, Ada prayed. In her time as a probationer she had had to help with some of the injured men from a pit explosion and she never wanted to see it again. The hospital had been flooded with men crushed and broken when the roof of the tunnel where they had been working caved in. No, it couldn't be a pit explosion, the booming was going on too long for that. Apprehension flooded through her as she wondered what it *could* be.

As suddenly as it started, the noise faded away and the ward quietened down. The old men lay back on their pillows, looking at one another, and the younger ones began to talk excitedly. Whatever it was, perhaps they were not going to be murdered that day.

'What do you think it was, Sister?' Nurse Brown was still pale and shaken as they began the treatment round with the trolley. 'Do you think the Germans have landed?'

'Oh no, I don't think so. I hardly think they would land up here in the northeast. No, I'm sure we'll soon find out what it was. In the meantime try to keep your feelings to yourself. We are not here to alarm the patients.' Ada spoke severely. It was for the nursing staff to keep their heads no matter what, that was the teaching of the great Florence Nightingale and it still held true today. Nurse Brown looked suitably chastened at the reprimand, blushing furiously. She carried on with the work without saying any more.

Ada discovered the reason for the disturbance later in the morning when she found herself summoned to Matron's office.

'Ah, Sister Gray.' Matron looked up from her desk where she was studying the off-duty chart. 'It's your afternoon off, isn't it?'

'Yes, Matron,' Ada admitted. Was she going to be asked to work through her free time yet again? Inwardly she sighed; it was getting to be the usual thing.

Matron's reply came as a complete surprise but the thuds and booms of the morning were explained, though the explanation brought Ada's heart to her mouth.

'I have some bad news, Sister. Word has come through by telephone that all off-duty staff, medical and nursing, are needed at Hartlepool,' she said. 'German warships have bombarded the coast and there is a great deal of destruction in the town. We don't know yet how many are injured. Are you willing to go?'

'Of course, Matron,' Ada had no hesitation in replying. All thoughts of her afternoon shopping were abandoned. She wondered how many had been injured; she had only a hazy idea of what damage the guns of a warship could do to a town but guessed it might be extensive.

'Good.' Matron smiled her approval. 'You can leave on the twelve-thirty train, you'd better go now and get ready. Report to the Cameron Hospital.' Matron looked down at her chart. I'm hoping to send at least six nurses. By the way, you'd better pack an overnight bag. Goodness knows what you'll find when you get there.'

She shook her head sadly as Ada left the office. Now she had the task of reorganising the nursing staff left to her to cover the wards.

*

349

Back in the Nurses' Home, Ada briskly set about preparing to leave. Taking out her small travelling bag, she put in a couple of clean aprons and caps alongside a change of underwear and her night things. It wasn't until she undid the bib of the apron she was wearing before changing into her outdoor bonnet and cloak that Tom's letter fell to the floor.

Picking it up she gazed at it guiltily, she had forgotten all about it. Well, she thought, she could read it on the train. She barely had time to get to the station on time as it was. Swiftly she donned the distinctive outdoor bonnet and cloak and hurried out of the door.

Once safely on the train, Ada was lucky enough to find a seat, albeit squashed in with four other nurses on a bench in a third-class compartment which was meant to take only four in the first place. But she was in the corner and was able to read the letter as the others chatted among themselves, speculating what they would find when they got to Hartlepool. The letter was brief, almost curt, and Ada couldn't help thinking about the happy, chatty letters he used to send her in his university days.

Dear Ada, I hope you are well as I am. I thought I would let you know that I am going off to xxx. [Here the words had been erased by the censor but Ada knew that he meant he was embarking for the continent.] I am back in England for a few days but have decided not to come home but spend the leave I have due to me here in London. I will write to you when I can.

Regards,

Tom.

Guilt once again struck Ada. Because of her he would not be coming home to see his family before he went out again to France or Belgium or wherever it was he was going. She had been an ungrateful fool or worse, for she had hurt the family which had befriended her. She thought about Virginia's reaction if she ever found out that Tom was back in England and not coming home. It didn't bear thinking about. Folding the note, she replaced it in her bag. This was no time for personal thoughts and emotions. The train was pulling into Hartlepool Station and the nurses were about to face they knew not what; none of them had had to deal with the victims of shelling before. Already they could hear some of the pandemonium outside.

Getting down from the train with four of her colleagues from Durham, Ada saw immediately some of the results of the shelling. The station yard had been hit and workmen were busy trying to clear a way for wheeled traffic, that was the shouting she had heard.

'Can you get us a cab to the Cameron Hospital?' she enquired of a porter with a wheelbarrow full of rubble rather than the luggage which was his usual load. 'Or at least tell us where we can get one?' she amended, for it had been silly of her to ask. He released the handles of the barrow to rub a grimy hand down the side of his face, leaving sooty marks on his sweat-stained cheek.

'I dunno, Sister,' he replied. 'All the cabs are busy like, with those injured, you know.'

'It's not far to walk,' one of the nurses broke in. 'I know the way. We'll be better off walking in any case.'

The small party of nurses picked their way out of the station yard and set off for the hospital. When they arrived, the Cameron was a hive of activity. Injured men, women and children were being brought in even now, so many hours after the shelling had happened, and the steady flow of people seemed endless. The nurses from Durham were welcomed with open arms by the hard-pressed staff and were soon hard at work helping to calm both the injured and their families, helping to strap up broken limbs, clean and bandage wounds and prepare patients who needed surgery.

In fact they were doing the work of any casualty department but on a much larger scale. There seemed to be a never-ending supply of patients for them to treat before sending them on to where porters were putting up extra beds on the wards.

'There now,' said Ada as she straightened up after bandaging a splint into place on a young boy's broken arm. 'You'll be all right now, fine and dandy. John, isn't it? You'll see, you'll be as right as rain in a week or two, John.' She paused for a moment before going on to her next case and smiled down at the thin face of the boy who was scratched and bruised from his encounter with a falling wall. He was white with the shock and pain, his eyes ringed with tear-sparkling lashes.

'Bloody Hun!'

The boy's father, a burly fisherman, put his arm around him protectively. 'Aye, but never you mind, lad, we'll get our own back, aye and more besides!' He looked up at Ada. 'Did you see how the patrol boats chased them off, Sister? Bye, I'd bloody well like to see them blown out of the sea, begging your pardon, Sister, for me swearing, but it's enough to make a saint swear, it is that, shelling and killing innocent bairns!'

His wife shushed him uncomfortably. She too had her arm in a sling but her eyes were on her son, anxious and dark with shock.

'Don't you shush me, woman!' The father gave vent to his feelings. 'I'm telling ye, they won't get the better of us, by hell they won't. I'll be volunteering for the navy the day. And by God, we'll chase them to hell and back, we'll show them not to fight their war against little bairns and women.'

'Eeh, no, Harry, don't say that!' his wife cried. 'How will we manage without you if anything happens to you? And what about the boat? Who'll go after the fish?'

'Please try to be quiet,' Ada intervened softly. 'You're not helping things here, these people need peace and quiet.'

'Aye, sorry, Sister, you're right.' The seaman lowered his tone. 'But you'll see, everybody will want to go now. Did you hear they'd hit St Hilda's? And the gasometer's alight. Why, I heard a whole family in Dean Street got wiped out. Bloody –'

'Yes, yes, it's terrible, but think of the boy now, you have to get him home and keep him quiet.'

Ada finally managed to usher the family out, still arguing about who would do the fishing if the man went to war.

'I tell you, woman, there's bigger things to catch now than fish!' he exploded as he reached the door.

Ada sighed and turned to her next patient.

She worked steadily on through the afternoon and evening, for the dead and injured were much more numerous than was thought in the beginning, and were still being dug out of the rubble. This was by far the largest disaster she had had to help with, although she had often tended to injured miners after small explosions or falls of stone. That experience stood all the doctors and nurses here today in good stead, she thought wryly. The injuries were pretty similar, though it was heart-rending when it involved women and children too.

A similar attitude to that of the vociferous fisherman

was beginning to surface among all the people around. There was a general outrage and desire to fight back, give as good as they got. Now the initial shock had passed, the desire for revenge took hold of them. Ada was beginning to think that she might go herself, perhaps answer the advertisements in the *Northern Echo* for nurses to join the Duchess of Westminster's teams to go out to France. But it was only a thought really, she knew she was needed just as much here at home.

As the numbers killed and wounded in the bombardment rose and the full extent of the damage became known, more and more men enlisted in the army; war fever was at its height and Ada could understand why it was so. Not only Hartlepool but Scarborough and Seaham had been shelled and the people of the northeast were up in arms.

Chapter Twenty-Two

It was a warm afternoon in June 1915 and Ada was off duty. She felt strangely restless as she changed out of her uniform in the bare little room of the Nurses' Home, not sure how she wanted to spend her precious few hours of freedom. She stood at the window and looked out at the fresh green leaves on the trees, bright against the pale-blue sky with its white shreds of cloud.

There was Mr Johnson. She hadn't seen him for a good while, she ought to visit him. Sighing, she turned to the small looking glass on the wall and combed through the curls which had fallen to her shoulders when she let it down from the tight bun she wore under her 'Sister Dora' cap on the wards. It was only two o'clock, she thought dreamily; she would take her time, stroll by the river and enjoy the warm, fresh air. It would be a nice change from the acidic smell of carbolic solution, which did not always eliminate that of septic wounds.

Picking up her hat, Ada left the hospital and turned towards the old city, walking slowly and looking around her as she went, noting with pleasure the slowly opening buds of roses in the tiny front gardens, the boughs laden with May blossom leaning from the hedges and beginning to shed flakes of white on the paths. Spring was late this year as it so often was in the northeast, but when it came it was the more welcome for that.

She came to a newsboy and bought a *Northern Echo*, thinking she would read it later, when she got back to her room in the evening. The war news was usually depressing but there were sometimes articles of local interest. Tucking it under her arm, Ada went down to the river and strolled slowly along, delighting in seeing a small family of ducks – father, mother and half a dozen chicks – sailing along like a miniature fleet of ships, quacking softly as they went and leaving a shiny wake in the quiet waters of the Wear.

Bye, it was good to be alive! Ada's spirits bubbled up happily and she lifted her face to the sun. Lately her life had been full of work and worry. Tom seldom wrote to her and when he did it was just a note, curt and businesslike. In some ways Ada dreaded the end of the war, when he would be home for good. She had become used to living as a single person again. She never even touched the allowance she was allotted through Tom's position in the army, no, she liked being her own woman, she earned enough to live on herself. Her marriage was more and more unreal to her, and sometimes she wondered, had it really happened?

Ada stopped walking and gazed at the river, watching the sluggish movement of the water, hearing the 'plop' of the occasional fish rising. The sun was warm on her back through the thin cotton of her simple beige dress, and it was pleasant just to dawdle for a change. Well, she thought at last, best get on; she would go to see Mr Johnson first, in his cottage down by the racecourse.

The cottage, when she finally got there, looked strangely empty: no smoke curled from the kitchen chimney, and the bedroom curtains were drawn even though the hour was late. Ada frowned a little as she pushed open the garden gate and walked up the path. Mr Johnson was usually pottering around the place but now there was no sign of him. She knocked on the front door and waited to hear the shuffling of his footsteps, but the house was silent. Perhaps he was in the back garden, she thought, or he could be out, though he didn't go far these days.

Ada walked round the side of the house, looking round the garden for any signs of the old man; she knocked on the back door and tried the handle but it was locked.

'Mr Johnson!' she called. 'Are you there?'

Sooty, the black cat, emerged from the toolshed at

the bottom of the garden and came up to Ada, rubbing against her legs and mewing plaintively.

'Hello, Sooty, where's your master?' Ada asked; she was beginning to get really worried about Mr Johnson. Something must have happened to him, she thought, stepping over a flowerbed to peer in through the kitchen window. There was nothing to see but a solitary cup and saucer on the draining board beside a half-bottle of milk. She went back round to the front of the house and peered in through the letterbox. At first she could see nothing but as she screwed her head round to the right she could make out what looked like a heap of clothes in the doorway to the sitting room. It didn't look at all as if there was a person in the clothes, just a pile of laundry, but then the pile moved, slowly.

'Mr Johnson?'

It was the old man; she could make him out better now as he moved a little more in response to her voice. Ada straightened up and considered what to do. She had to get into the house one way or another. She ran out into the road but there wasn't anyone about, and no one answered the bell of the house next door. There was no help for it, she decided, she had to break the window. She found a large stone and threw it hard at the bottom panel and the sound of breaking glass sounded loudly in the afternoon hush. In a few minutes she had the window open and had climbed in.

Mr Johnson had had a stroke, she saw immediately as she turned him over onto his back, one eye was half closed and one side of his face all twisted. Clutched in his hand he held a telegram.

'Ad – A – A-A –' he mumbled, his mouth slack and saliva dribbling down onto his chin.

'Don't talk, Mr Johnson,' Ada said to him. 'Save your strength. I'll make you comfortable now and then I'll get the doctor.'

Swiftly and efficiently she dragged him further onto the sitting-room carpet, but didn't waste time trying to get him on the sofa. She found a cushion for his head and a rug to cover him. Feeling for his pulse, she found it was rapid but steady, so she didn't think he was in any immediate danger. He couldn't have been there long, she surmised, he wasn't dehydrated at all.

'I'll go for Dr Gray,' she said. 'I won't be long. You'll be all right there until I get back.' Ada looked at the telegram in his hand, but thought it best not to try to take it from him.

'Ada!' The doctor rose to his feet as she entered and gestured her to a chair, a polite smile on his face, though his voice was distant rather than welcoming. But Ada hadn't time to take notice of that.

'Oh, doctor, I'm so glad you're still here. It's Mr Johnson, I'm afraid he's had a seizure.'

Dr Gray, ever the professional, lost no time in asking for details. It seemed only a few minutes before he and Ada were lifting the old man onto the sofa and the doctor was examining him.

'You're right, I'm sorry to say,' he said. Gently he prised the note from Mr Johnson's hand. 'And here's the reason: bad news, I'm afraid. This damn war!' He glanced at Ada. 'Come into the hall for a moment, Sister?'

Once out of the room, the doctor handed Ada the telegram. It was brief and to the point. 'REGRET TO INFORM YOU MAJOR WALTER JOHNSON HAS BEEN KILLED IN ACTION.' That was all. Even the regrets sounded perfunctory, thought Ada.

'He'll have to go to the County. I'll arrange for an ambulance,' Dr Gray said. He paused as though he was going to say something else but changed his mind and turned to the door. He was almost like a stranger now, she thought. 'Well, I'll be on my way. Things to do. I'll ring the hospital and arrange for the ambulance.'

'Yes, of course.' She went to the door with him, feeling she was growing further and further away from the family. Sooty came in – through the broken window, she supposed – and curled round her legs.

'Howay then,' she said briskly, 'let's find you something to eat. Then you'll have to go out again.' She found some scraps in the pantry, gave them to the cat and poured out a saucer of milk.

Ada hurried back in to Mr Johnson after Sooty was banished into the garden again and the window secured by fastening a tin tray over the hole. He was still lying helplessly in the same position they had left him in, but his head had slipped from the cushion a little and was lying at an awkward angle. Gently she took out his handkerchief, wiped his face and positioned the cushion more comfortably.

'I'm so sorry,' she said gently. 'Was he your son?'

His voice was low and his speech very thick so that she had to lean close to catch what it was he was trying to say in answer.

'Br – br –' he struggled, and Ada was puzzled.

'Brother?' Surely not, she thought; any brother of Mr Johnson would be too old to fight in France, wouldn't he? But she dismissed it from her mind. The old man was getting too agitated.

'Never mind now,' she said. 'The ambulance will be here shortly and we'll take you to hospital. I'm sure you'll be more comfortable there.' But he was still trying to tell her something and she couldn't make head or tail of it.

'I'm coming with you in the ambulance. Tell me later, save your strength for now,' she urged him and was glad when she heard the ambulance in the street outside. Quickly she scribbled a note of explanation to the neighbour and asked him to feed the cat, slipping it through the letterbox. She secured the house and made sure the door of the garden shed was ajar for Sooty, then, with a last look round to make sure she hadn't forgotten anything, she climbed into the ambulance beside the old man. At least he had someone to go with him, she thought, even if he had no relatives left.

One cold and blustery day that autumn, Ada was in the throes of moving from the Nurses' Home; she was busy packing her box when she heard a knock at the door of her room.

'Yes? Come in,' she called, a little surprised – who on earth could it be?

Home Sister entered the room.

'There's a visitor for you, I've left him in the sitting room.' Sister gave Ada a disapproving look; visitors were definitely not encouraged at the Home, especially not male visitors, not even husbands. But this one was an army doctor and sometimes exceptions had to be made, she conceded.

Ada looked at her in surprise. 'A visitor? For me? Who is it?'

'Why don't you go and find out,' Home Sister said shortly and went on her way, though Ada glimpsed a smile as she closed the door. A little impatient at the delay, Ada left her packing and went downstairs to the sitting room.

It was Tom. He was standing by the window, staring

out at the garden, and as she entered the sitting room he turned to her, looking quite resplendent in his major's uniform.

'Hello, Ada,' he said coldly.

'Tom! How nice to see you.' Ada wasn't sure how to greet him, he seemed like such a stranger in her life now. 'How are you?' She moved over to him, leaving the door open as rules demanded when there were male visitors, and he kissed her on the cheek. His lips were warm and dry and he smelled of polished leather and bay rum.

'Matron told me you were leaving,' he said evenly. 'I rang her up this morning to find out what duty you were on. She told me I was lucky to catch you, you were leaving for Crossgate Hall.' Tom paused and gazed at her for a moment, his face expressionless. 'Do you think we can go somewhere and discuss it?'

'Yes, of course, I'll just get my coat and hat. I'll be with you in a tick.' Ada hurried upstairs and took her coat from the bed where she had laid it while emptying the wardrobe. He was annoyed because he had found out about her new post from Matron, she thought. Pulling her hat over her head and wrapping a scarf round her neck, she hurried back down to Tom, wondering how she was going to tell him she only had a few hours before taking up her new post. That wasn't going to help matters between them at all. But if she had waited to make up her mind until she'd written to Tom and got his consent, she would have lost the job.

Ada had secured the post of Matron at a nursing home just outside Durham, for wounded soldiers. Her ambitions had been fired when she saw in the *Northern Echo* that Crossmoor Hall was to be turned into an army convalescent home and she had applied for the post and got it. But she had not written and told Tom – oh, she knew she should have done, even if she didn't wait for his reply, but she hadn't. She felt the usual flutterings of apprehension now as they left the building and walked over to his car.

Tom said nothing until he had negotiated the turn out of the drive and set off for the centre of Durham. Then he glanced down at her, his expression hard and cynical.

'Of course, you couldn't be bothered to tell me you had changed your job, I had to find out from Matron. What sort of a fool do you think that makes me?'

'I was going to write to you, Tom, but everything happened in a rush. Besides, I wasn't expecting you home just yet, I didn't know there was any hurry.'

'Don't lie to me, Ada, don't make excuses. Father said he had told you I was coming. He also says you didn't even tell the family of your move.'

Ada bit her lip. It was true that Dr Gray had mentioned Tom was coming home, one day when she had bumped into him at the hospital. 'Well, after all, you haven't written to me for a good while,' she said, on the defensive. She gazed out at the passing streets, realising they were going to the Grays' family home.

'Oh,' she cried, panicking, 'let's go somewhere else, somewhere where we'll be on our own.'

'We can be on our own here,' Tom answered as he pulled into the drive. 'There's only Mother at home and she'll understand we want to talk privately. After all, now you've closed our own home, where do you expect us to go?'

He stopped the car and went round it to open her door, formally polite. Ada hesitated, but she really had no choice but get out and follow him into the house.

'Is that you, dear?' Mrs Gray came out of the dining room smiling, the smile fading a little as she saw Ada. 'Hello, Ada.'

'Good afternoon, Mrs Gray. How are you?'

'I'm well, thank you.' Mrs Gray turned to Tom. 'Would you like tea, Tom? I'll get Cook to bring you in a tray.'

'Not now, Mother, later perhaps,' Tom replied, and Ada realised Mrs Gray was not expecting to join them. Had the family been discussing what to do about her? Ada wondered. Tom led the way into the sitting room.

'Sit down, Ada,' he said, though he himself did not take a seat. Instead he stood before the fireplace with his hands clasped behind his back and looked down at her, making her feel at a disadvantage.

'Now, tell me all about it,' he said. 'You owe me a proper explanation.'

So Ada told him about seeing the notice in the *Northern Echo* and applying for the post of Matron. 'After all, Tom,' she said earnestly, 'it is a good move for me with regard to my career. The experience will be good for me and the salary is high. It will help the war effort, too.'

Tom's face took on an expression of distaste. 'What do you mean, the salary? Don't you have enough money for your needs? The salary shouldn't come into it. You are a Gray, my wife, what do you want with a career? It was one thing you nursing at the hospital while I'm away, but let's have no nonsense about a career. Your career is as my wife.'

Ada stared at him. His face red with anger, he began walking up and down in agitation, his fists clenched by his side. She sighed, depression settling on her. These last few months she had fooled herself into thinking of her life as her own, her future to be in nursing. But, of course, Tom saw it differently.

'Oh, Tom,' she said helplessly, 'it really isn't any good. We'll never be happy together. Can't you see –'

'I can see that you are determined to have your own way in everything, that's what I can see. But you wait, my girl, you wait!'

Tom had paused in front of her. His voice rose to a

shout and he was towering over her, she thought for a minute he was going to strike her. Nervously she moved over on the sofa so that she could stand up, edging away from him.

'Tom,' she said, 'Tom, please, don't let's fight now. I'm taking the job, I have to be there tonight, really, it's too late now. And anyway, what difference does it make whether I'm at the County or Crossmoor Hall?'

Tom began to rage and shout at her. She walked backwards to the door, she had to get away; nothing could make her stay, nothing.

'Tom! Tom, get a hold of yourself, old chap.'

The door had opened behind her and Dr Gray came into the room. He went swiftly over to Tom, putting a restraining hand on his shoulder. 'Tom! Tom! Calm down, please,' he said.

Tom's fists unclenched and he struggled for a moment to contain his anger. 'It's all right, Father, I'm sorry I shouted,' he said more quietly. 'I apologise if I upset you.'

'Don't worry about that, Tom, I understand. It was your mother who was worried. Now, let's all sit down, I think we should discuss this situation calmly and quietly.' He glanced across the room to Ada, unsmiling. 'Come and sit down, Ada.'

'I . . . I have to go,' Ada stammered, 'I have to be at the Hall this evening.' She felt she couldn't possibly face a family discussion with herself cast as the errant wife.

She simply had to get away. She turned and took hold of the doorknob.

'But Ada, what about –' Dr Gray began, but he was interrupted by his son.

'Oh, let her go, Father. It's no use.' Tom shook his head and sank into an armchair, his head in his hands. Ada looked at him – what could she say?

'I have to go,' she repeated in the end; opening the door she fled from the house, her eyes blinded with tears. Oh, she thought, it was all her fault! She knew that by all the conventions she should give in to Tom, do what he said and strive to make him a good wife. But she also knew she couldn't; it was no good, she had to be her own woman. Why couldn't Tom accept it? After all, he would be going back to his unit and she would be left on her own, so why shouldn't she pursue her career?

She walked all the way back to the County Hospital; going up to her room she finished packing her belongings and hurried away. Her goodbyes to the rest of the staff had all been said that morning, and she had even found time to visit Mr Johnson, who showed a slight improvement. Now, she was in no fit state to talk to anyone.

Ada took a cab to Mr Johnson's cottage before she left. She wanted time to recover her equilibrium before she went to the Hall. In any case, she wanted to check on Sooty for the old man. The neighbour was looking after the cat but Mr Johnson had asked her about him the last time she had been to see him. She could always get a bus out to the Hall.

Sooty was there, still living in the shed despite the fact that summer was over and the nights were getting colder. He came out to greet her when she called, purring loudly in satisfaction, his tail straight up in the air.

'I would take the cat in to live with me, but he likes the shed,' the neighbour called. He had come out to investigate when he heard noises in the next-door garden and he saw her over the fence. 'Maybe in the winter he'll think better of it. But I see he gets fed, he takes no harm. How is Mr Johnson, then?'

'He's improving. Thank you for seeing to Sooty,' Ada replied, hoping she didn't seem too rude as she kept her tear-ravaged face averted from him. She had splashed her face with cold water before leaving the County but fresh tears had sprung to her eyes since then. She opened the door of the cottage and went in. The place felt damp and cold, and she shivered a little as the dankness hit her. Perhaps she could ask the neighbour to light a fire in it occasionally, she thought distractedly. But for the moment she couldn't even remember what his name was.

She went upstairs and into the bathroom. In the glass over the basin she saw her eyes were red and puffy. She splashed them with cold water once again, patting them dry with a towel. Well, she thought, she might as well check on the rest of the house before she went.

Nothing had been disturbed, she saw as she went from room to room. The cushion in the sitting room still bore the imprint of Mr Johnson's head; she plumped it up and put it back in position on the sofa. As she noticed the undisturbed layer of dust, she remembered she hadn't asked Mr Johnson about his daily woman, but she was old, and perhaps she had just got too old for the work.

Ada deliberately kept her mind on the cottage as she waited for the horrible lump of chaotic feeling to go, willing the sickness in her stomach to settle. She went into the kitchen and looked around. Everything seemed all right, though there was a newspaper on the floor. Mechanically she picked it up and glanced at it, realising it was the paper she had bought on her way over to see Mr Johnson that day in the summer. She pulled a chair out, sat down at the kitchen table and opened out the newspaper.

The war news was old, of course; Ada only skimmed the headlines before turning the page, looking for anything to distract her thoughts and something did, immediately. It was the name Fenwick that caught her attention and she paused to read the article properly.

'Fenwick Steelworks to step up production,' it read. Fenwick Steelworks? That must be Johnny's firm, Ada thought. She read on eagerly. 'Mr Stephen Fenwick announced today that since the mill turned over to munitions they were now running at full capacity and were hoping to expand even further in the near future.

"It behoves us all to play our part in bringing this war to a successful conclusion," Mr Fenwick stated.'

Stephen Fenwick. Not Johnny, then. Ada stopped reading and sat back in the chair. But she was sure Johnny was probably still working in Middlesbrough. In the emotional state she was in after the confrontation with Tom, she yearned for Johnny, crying inside. Rising to her feet, she left the house, locking up after her and leaving the key with Mr Johnson's neighbour. She walked up to the marketplace, carrying her bag, and caught a bus to Crossgate Hall.

I'll write to Johnny, she decided, as she sat on the bus staring out of the window. Even if he's not in Middlesbrough any more, surely his family will forward the letter. She felt quite cheered at the thought and began composing the letter in her head. She could remember the address, The Beeches, in Stockton Road, that was it. By the time she climbed down from the bus, Tom had been pushed into the background of her mind. She was going to start a new job in charge of this convalescent home and she was going to make a great success of it, she was determined she would. And she would write the letter to Johnny the same night, before she could change her mind.

As it happened, Johnny returned to Middlesbrough only a couple of days later; he was back in England on a week's leave from the front. Riding up from King's Cross on the train, he couldn't help wondering what his reception would be when he got there. Oh, he didn't doubt that Dinah would be glad to see him but he had mixed feelings about his nephews, Stephen and Arthur.

Still, he thought, as he changed trains at Darlington and crossed over to the Middlesbrough line, it was Dinah he wanted to see and if the boys didn't like him coming they could lump it. He dismissed his nephews from his mind.

'Johnny! How lovely to see you.' His welcome from Dinah was all he could have hoped for: she flung her arms around him and sobbed with happiness.

'Dinah, Dinah! Tears? What sort of a greeting is that after all this time?'

Dinah laughed shakily. 'Oh, Johnny, I'm so happy. I was just thinking about you only this morning. I was just saying to Stephen – Oh, but come in, come into the drawing room, we'll have some tea. There's a good fire, you can have a warm, you must be cold.'

She led the way into the drawing room. 'I'll go and make the tea, I won't be a tick. Just you make yourself comfortable, Johnny.'

Johnny raised his eyebrows. 'But where's Norah? Can't she get the tea?'

'Oh, Norah left ages ago, at the beginning of the war, it was.'

'But can't you get someone else?'

'What, with girls able to earn so much more in the factories? Why, some of them are even on the buses. No, I'm all right, I've still got Cook, thank goodness. And between us, we manage. It probably won't be for long, this dreadful war can't go on for ever. Now, I won't be long.'

Johnny stood before the fire while he waited for her, looking round at the familiar room with interest. It hadn't changed a lot since he lived there himself, he noticed. But his brow furrowed as he considered Dinah: when he first saw her as she opened the door, he had hardly recognised her. She looked old and careworn, not at all like the old light-hearted Dinah he had known. He wondered about the cause. Surely, with the extra demand the war brought for steel, it couldn't be the business? Well, he would do his best to find out before he went back to France, he decided as he heard Dinah returning.

'Here I am. There now, that wasn't long, was it?'

Johnny hurried to take the tray from her and put it down on a small occasional table by the side of his chair.

'Such a lovely surprise, Johnny! Why didn't you let me know you were coming? I would have got Cook to bake some fresh scones – these are yesterday's. Still, they'll still be nice with the strawberry jam. We can't waste food nowadays, can we?'

Dinah sat back in her chair with her cup of tea in hand

and beamed at him. 'Now, tell me everything that has happened to you. Bye, lad, you're a sight for sore eyes. I was so pleased to hear you were so successful in Canada. But what's happening now, while you're in the army? Surely you haven't had to let it go?'

Johnny smiled fondly at her. 'No, Dinah, it's in capable hands. Very capable hands. I have a good manager. But tell me what's been happening here. How is Stephen? And Arthur, has he joined the firm now?'

'Stephen's doing all right, the business too, though he doesn't tell me much.' Dinah sighed, looking into the fire. 'I miss the old days, you know, when Fred would tell me all about his days at the mill. I felt I knew everyone there myself, he talked about them so much. But Stephen doesn't; he doesn't want to bother me, I suppose. There was a time, just before the war, when I thought the business wasn't doing too well, and Stephen asked me to invest some of my capital in it. Which I was glad to do, of course, I knew it would be safe enough. And it's doing well now, I know.'

It would be, Johnny thought grimly. Any steel mill which did badly in wartime deserved to go under. Still, he was glad, for Dinah's sake if nothing else.

'And Arthur?' he probed gently.

'Oh, Arthur, poor boy.' Dinah smiled fondly, thinking of Arthur. 'He's not really cut out for business, though he joined Stephen in the office when the war came.'

Dinah glanced swiftly at Johnny in his Canadian Army uniform and added defensively, 'Arthur's better off in the business, some boys are too sensitive to make good soldiers. And the work at home is just as important. Stephen says so.'

'Yes, of course.' Johnny smiled at her and she relaxed. 'And Pierce? Has Pierce left too?' he went on.

'Yes. Well, he and Stephen didn't get on . . .' Dinah didn't finish the sentence and Johnny felt a flush of anger, for Pierce had been with the family for years. He must have had a serious disagreement with Stephen if it had forced him to leave. Johnny asked no more questions, thinking that perhaps it was best not to. But he was beginning to see the reasons for Dinah's air of unhappiness. Things had indeed changed around here and the changes were not for the best. Instead he began to reminisce about Fred, and Dinah joined in eagerly; there was nothing and no one she would rather talk about than her beloved Fred. They passed a pleasant hour or two in this way and before they knew it, Stephen and Arthur were back from the office. Even before they came into the room, they could be heard bickering loudly as they entered the house, and Dinah looked apprehensively at the door.

Stephen came into the sitting room, scowling fiercely. 'Mother,' he began, then noticed his uncle sitting there. 'Oh, hello, Uncle John,' he said.

'Hello, Stephen, Arthur,' Johnny answered quietly. He watched his younger nephew as he followed Stephen into the room with a feeling of dismay. Though he was hardly into his twenties, Arthur had a dissipated air about him: his eyes were bloodshot, his cheeks blotchy, and his lower lip stuck out petulantly as he crossed to his mother and gave her a perfunctory kiss on the cheek.

'How are you, Arthur?' she asked him anxiously. 'You seem a little pale, I hope you're not sickening for anything.'

Stephen snorted. 'A monumental hangover, more likely. Do you know it was eleven o'clock before he condescended to come in to work this morning? How on earth I'm supposed to run the business with him messing up everything he does, do you know what –'

'Don't listen to him, Mother. I can't help it if I suffer from these confounded migraines. How can I be expected to work when I'm ill?'

'Oh, Stephen, perhaps you're too hard on him,' Dinah put in anxiously. 'He's still only a boy, he's still growing, I'm sure he is.' She looked from one to the other, helplessly. 'Please don't argue, boys, you know how it upsets me. Look, isn't it lovely to have Johnny for a visit? I thought we could have a grand time together. He's only got a few days, we should make the most of it before he has to go back to the front.'

Stephen looked sourly at his uncle. 'You're going

back to war, are you? You'll be one of the glory boys, I suppose, a hero for going over to France and sitting about most of the time. That's what it's like, I've heard all about it. While we at home are working all the hours God sends, doing without things, having all the worry and getting white feathers for our pains. Where would you be without us? That's what I'd like to know.'

Johnny was so surprised he grinned in disbelief. Briefly his thoughts went back to the last few weeks in the trenches, the mud and the stink, the sheer horror of going over the top. He looked across at Dinah to see what she thought of Stephen's outburst, but his sister-in-law was biting her lip, looking distressed.

'You haven't got a white feather, Stephen? Surely not, after all you are doing –'

'No, of course not, Mother!' Stephen interrupted her. 'But I've heard of men getting them, good men too.'

Johnny decided not to argue with Stephen, it wouldn't do any good. Instead he changed the subject for he was interested in hearing about the business.

'I hear the works are doing well, Stephen,' he said.

'Did you think they wouldn't? I suppose you thought I wouldn't be able to manage without you. Well, I proved you wrong, didn't I?'

Johnny thought fleetingly of Dinah saying she had had to put money into the business before the war. 'I'm pleased for you, Stephen, very pleased,' he said mildly. For the moment he had had all he could take of his nephews, Stephen in particular. He was glad they would be out of the house for most of the time he was in Middlesbrough.

'If you don't mind, Dinah,' he said, rising to his feet, 'I think I'll just go up to my room. The same one, is it?'

'The spare room, do you mean?' There was a slight sneer in Stephen's voice.

'Yes, of course, it won't be my room now, not after all this time,' Johnny answered evenly.

'Yes, it is, Johnny.' Dinah gave Stephen a reproachful glance before answering Johnny. 'I will always think of it as your room. The bed is made up, I always leave it made up, all ready for you. I'll put a hot-water bottle in it later.'

'Oh, don't bother, it'll be fine. Heaven, in fact, after the trenches,' he couldn't help adding to Stephen as he left the room.

He sighed as he unpacked his bag in the large square bedroom he had had since he was a boy. If every evening was going to be like this, he thought, his leave was going to be very trying indeed. No wonder Dinah was so unhappy.

Johnny's views were reinforced later in the evening when he was about to leave his room to go down to dinner. He started to open his door when he heard Arthur's voice close by and hurriedly he closed it again.

'Mother,' Arthur was saying plaintively, 'I'm a bit short and I'm going out for the evening. Could you let me have a tenner?'

And I thought Arthur was unwell, Johnny thought grimly. Oh, Fred, perhaps it's just as well you died when you did. If you were to come back now, what would you think?

Dinah was the only one who joined Johnny in the dining room at eight o'clock that evening. Stephen was off somewhere on business, or so his mother said. And no doubt Arthur had got his tenner, Johnny surmised.

'Oh, Johnny, I forgot to tell you in all the excitement when you came,' Dinah greeted him, 'this came for you.' She handed him a letter and he looked at it in surprise – who would be writing to him here? And then he saw the handwriting and a wave of nostalgia hit him; he stared at the Durham postmark, remembering. Dinah was talking but he hardly heard what she was saying.

'It came yesterday, I was saying to Stephen he should post it on to you. But he said he was too busy to bother – poor boy, he does have a lot of work. And it's just as well, isn't it?' She looked up at him in surprise as he didn't answer. He was staring at the envelope with a stricken look on his face.

'Johnny?' she persisted. 'Johnny, aren't you going to open it? You look as though you've seen a ghost.'

'What?' Her anxious voice drew Johnny's attention

at last. 'Oh yes, of course. I'll open it after dinner.'

Johnny put the letter away in the pocket of his jacket. All through dinner he was conscious of its presence there and as soon as possible made an excuse to go up to his room to open it. Somehow, he couldn't bear to open it in front of anyone, not even Dinah.

Chapter Twenty-Three

Ada soon settled into her new position at the Hall. She delighted in her tiny flat at the very top of the house, which had a small sitting room and a separate bedroom. There was even a tiny kitchen where she could boil her own kettle on a gas ring and cook simple meals if she didn't want to eat with the rest of the staff. She felt she could retire to the flat in her off-duty hours and get completely away from the wards, though in fact she was usually on call in case of emergencies. And she found she liked being in charge. The doctors were visiting ones from the hospital, as the patients were convalescents, so she was in complete control.

One evening early in 1916, Ada went upstairs with a feeling of great relief. The day had been quite hectic for even though they only had beds for twenty-five patients, she had been working all day with the help of only two young VADs and was exhausted. She had been glad when her undernurse, Nurse Simpson had returned from her off-duty and taken over from her. There were still the rounds to do at ten o'clock, but until then she was free.

Ada took off her cap and apron and loosened her hair from its hairpins, letting it fall over her shoulders. She ran her fingers through it and rubbed her forehead just between her eyes, where a pulse throbbed painfully. She was tired, that was all, she thought and went to put the kettle on the gas ring. A cup of tea was what she needed, and then she would have a rest for a couple of hours.

She was carrying her cup of tea back into the sitting room when there was a knock at her door, disturbing her blessed quiet. Ada sighed, what was it now? she wondered.

'Come in!'

Millie, the housemaid, opened the door and came in. 'There's a gentleman to see you, Matron, a soldier,' she said.

Ada's heart dropped. Not Tom, let it not be Tom, she prayed, not now, she was too tired to deal with Tom. She hadn't seen him or heard from him since that traumatic time in the autumn and had presumed he had gone back to France. Putting down her cup, she looked in the glass above the fireplace. Pulling her hair into some sort of shape at the back of her head, she secured it with dolly grips.

'Tell him to come up, please, Millie,' she said.

'He's here, Matron,' the girl answered.

Ada turned quickly to see a tall man in khaki step through the door. Her eyes opened wide with shock, she couldn't believe what she was seeing. She stood there, mouth open; Millie went out and closed the door and still she felt unable to move.

Johnny! It was Johnny! He took off his cap and gave her the same lopsided smile that she remembered so well from long ago, his red hair glinting in the light from the lamps almost as brightly as the buttons on his uniform.

'Aren't you pleased to see me, Lorinda?'

The sound of his voice speaking her given name, an echo from the past, galvanised her into action. Forgetting everything – her tiredness, everything – she stepped forward to throw herself into his arms, hesitating at the last minute and gazing up at his face. Oh yes, she wasn't dreaming, it was Johnny's face; the same green-flecked eyes, the same freckled forehead, slightly marked where he had removed his cap.

'Oh, Johnny. Oh, Johnny!' Ada was incapable of saying anything else.

Johnny took her in his arms, holding her close. Lifting her off her feet he buried his face in her hair, breathing in the fragrance of her. His lips moved to her cheek and found it wet with tears. Groaning, he found her lips and both he and Ada were lost to everything but each other, here, in a room at the top of an old house in the Durham countryside. Rain spattered on the windowpanes and there were muffled noises from the lower regions of the Hall but neither Johnny nor Ada was aware of them.

He picked her up and carried her to the sofa and they sat there, arms wrapped round each other, murmuring softly to one another. Talking and explanations could come later; now was the time for giving themselves up to the pure joy of being alone together.

It seemed to Ada like only an instant later when another knock at the door penetrated through the haze of happiness which enveloped her.

'Yes, what is it?' she called.

'Time for your rounds, Matron,' Nurse Simpson reminded her.

'I'll be there in a minute.'

Ada disengaged herself from Johnny's arms and, rising, tidied herself up and put on her cap and apron. Johnny lay back against the cushions and watched her, a gentle smile hovering around his lips.

'You won't be long?'

Ada bent and dropped a kiss on his cheek. His arms went up to her again but she swiftly evaded them, backing away from him towards the door, chuckling as she did so.

'I'll only be half an hour, I promise.'

She flew down the three flights of stairs, her heart singing, Johnny's here, Johnny's back. Nothing and no one could possibly spoil the sheer happiness she felt at the thought of him waiting for her upstairs.

In the main ward, which was actually the drawing room of the Hall converted to hold twelve beds, Ada found the men settled down for the night. She walked round the beds, checking that everything was in order. There were unlikely to be any problems that night, she knew, for most of the patients had been there for a while and were well on the way to recovery. Some of them were still awake and soft calls of 'Good night, Matron' followed her on her way.

The second ward was quiet too. There was a young boy in a small room at the end of the hall, which had once been the master's study, she supposed. He was moving restlessly in his bed, grunting incoherently.

Ada went in and laid her hand on his forehead, murmuring soothing words of comfort to him and he relaxed into sleep. He was fresh from a field hospital in France and still plagued by nightmares. A cradle in the bed kept the bedclothes from irritating the now healing wound at the end of his thigh where his left leg should have been.

'He's had his sedative, Nurse?'

'Yes, at nine thirty, Matron, as Doctor ordered,' Nurse Simpson whispered.

'He should sleep till morning then.'

They left the door ajar so that Nurse Simpson could hear him if he woke, and went to the desk in the hall where she would sit between duties during the night.

'I'll leave you then, Nurse, I don't think you'll need me again tonight.'

Ada noticed that Nurse Simpson had left an unemptied bedpan in the makeshift sluice – a patient had called and no doubt she had forgotten to go back to it – but Ada was too happy to mention it. Nurse Simpson emptied and cleaned it now and put it in the rack before going out again to check on the patients, thankful that for once Matron's all-seeing eyes had missed it.

'Mind, she's in a good mood tonight,' she said to her junior with a sniff.

Upstairs, Ada found Johnny still sitting by the fire, his long legs stretched out before him and his hands behind his head.

'You look comfortable,' she said, unable to stop smiling, for coming up that last flight of stairs she had had a moment of panic when she thought it had all been a dream: when she got into her rooms there would be no one there, she was convinced of it. She had run the last few steps along the landing to her door.

'Have you eaten?' she asked, eager to do something for him. 'I can make some scrambled eggs, I only have a gas ring but I can easily do that. Are you hungry?'

'I'm famished,' he said and followed her to the doorway of her tiny kitchen, watching as she whisked eggs and heated butter in a frying pan. Ada kept looking up and seeing him there, watching, and when their eyes met they smiled delightedly at each other. She prepared a tray, which he carried into the sitting room, and they ate before the fire, enjoying every single bite. Ada felt as though she had never tasted such a delicious meal before.

Ada saw for the first time the Canada emblem on his shoulder and gasped. Johnny had been out of England all this time and she hadn't even known it. She couldn't believe it.

'Canada?' she asked.

Johnny told her briefly about his life in Canada and she swelled with pride at his success. He told her that he had come back to England with the Canadian Army and she had a twinge of fear for him – would he be going back to France? Of course she knew he would; he was on leave, that was all. And he told her about his visit to his sister-in-law in Middlesbrough and finding her letter waiting for him.

'It must have been meant, my love,' he said, and her heart swelled yet again when he said, 'my love'.

For a moment, as the clock struck twelve she thought he would say he had to go, but he didn't. Instead he took her hand and drew her into the bedroom and she went with him, for the first time in her nursing career heedless of the patients in their beds below, forgetting that she might be called if anything went wrong with them.

They made love in Ada's narrow bed, urgently, with

an overwhelming passion. And at last, in the small hours, they slept, deeply and dreamlessly. It never occurred to Ada that she had not once been afraid of making love with Johnny, nor once thought of Harry Parker. At last she was free of him and the terrible fear.

Some time during the night, Johnny's hands on her body woke her and they made love again, slowly and less urgently this time but still as sweetly. And then they slept again, like two children, huddled together, arms wrapped round each other.

In the first light of dawn, Ada stirred and turned over to snuggle closer to him. She came properly awake as she failed to find him and she sat up in the bed, thinking he had gone. Fear rose swiftly in her. She fell back on her pillow as she saw him. He was up, pulling on his uniform, and her heart dropped as she saw he was getting ready to leave. Morning had to come, she knew that, but oh, why couldn't they stay here for ever?

'Darling.' He bent over the pillow and kissed her when he saw she was awake and watching him. 'I was going to wake you before I went, I couldn't leave you like that. But I have to go, this is the last day of my leave, I have to join my unit. And you, you have responsibilities too. My little Ada-Lorinda, I'm so proud of you, you've done so well.' He sat down on the edge of the bed. 'I have to go but I'll be back. We can't lose each other ever again. What fools we've been! Me in particular.'

He picked up her left hand and as he did so his gaze fell upon the third finger with its wedding band of gold.

'Tell me about this. I have to know. You can't love him, how could you – you love me, even though we were apart for so long. I know you love me, just as I love you. Tell me it was a mistake, tell me you'll be here for me when I come back. We can't waste any more of our lives.' His tone was insistent, imperious even.

'It was a mistake.'

Ada understood his meaning perfectly. She felt as he did, there was no room for anything but absolute honesty between them now, or ever.

'I never loved him, you're right. I shouldn't have married him. But he was so kind to me, his whole family too. But I shouldn't have, I knew I shouldn't have, I was engaged to him for years and I know I should have broken it off before I married him. But I thought you were dead, Johnny, I did really. I came through to Middlesbrough to see you and they told me you were dead. Oh, Johnny, I thought I would die too.'

Johnny remembered the girl who answered the door that last time he had come looking for Ada.

'I know. I came to Durham before I went to Canada, you know, I got your address from Eliza. I came to the Grays' house. And a girl told me it was your engagement party. So I left –'

Ada gave a strangled cry of distress and buried her

face in his tunic. Oh, Virginia, she thought, why did you do that? He wrapped her in his arms and rocked her to and fro.

'Lorinda, my love, don't cry for what might have been. We've years ahead of us yet. Forget all that – just tell me you'll leave him now, give me something to come back to.'

'Johnny, I owe him so much. I know I should never have married him and it has been a sham from the beginning. But there is his career as a doctor, he says, divorce is out of the question. Oh, I don't know, I really don't.'

'Well, promise you'll talk to him when you can, or write to him – that's it. Will you? For I'm telling you, I'm not going to give you up now, I swear it.'

She clung to him, emotion flooding through her. She felt the same, of course she did, how could she give Johnny up now? And Tom didn't really want her, she knew he didn't.

'He's an army surgeon now,' she said at last. 'He's in France and I don't think I'll see him, not for a while yet, anyway. And it's not something I can put in a letter, is it?'

She looked up at Johnny. His face was white and set, and she knew that if it came to a choice between hurting him or hurting Tom she would not have the strength to hurt Johnny.

'I love you, Johnny, oh, I do, and I know it's right for us to be together. I can't write to him, I can't, but I will tell him as soon as I can. I promise I'll be waiting for you, Johnny.'

Johnny was content, he could ask no more of her. The daylight was getting stronger and time was pressing, he had to get to the station for his train. And Ada too, realised she had to hurry to relieve the night staff. Their idyllic but brief interlude was over.

Shivering, more with distress than the cold, she washed, splashing cold water over her face and arms and rubbing them vigorously with a rough towel. She scrambled into her clothes and Johnny watched her as she combed her hair and piled it on top of her head, pinning on her cap, her actions becoming slower for she was reluctant to go. At the door, he took her in his arms once more.

'You'll see, my love,' he whispered in her ear, 'it will come right in the end, when this war is over. And then we'll have a new life in Canada. Ada will be gone for ever and there will only be Johnny and Lorinda.'

Ada smiled up at him, still under the enchantment of the evening before and the night after it. Of course everything would be all right – she had Johnny now, hadn't she?

They went downstairs together and Ada was glad that there was no one about in the hall, though the voices of the nurses could be heard from the main ward. She said goodbye to him at the front door, clinging to him for an instant before letting him go. Then she stood, holding the door half-closed as she watched him walk down the drive, turning to wave to her as he rounded the corner.

In her absorption she completely missed seeing Nurse Simpson and one of the young VADs as they came out of the ward into the hall, their mouths dropping in astonishment as they saw Matron bidding farewell to a Canadian officer. They glanced at each other slyly and slipped into the sluice.

'I thought she was married to a British Army doctor!' the VAD gasped.

Nurse Simpson nodded, her eyes bright with the knowledge of Matron's fall from grace. 'She is, she is indeed,' she said.

For the next few weeks, Ada went about her work with renewed energy. She felt so happy that even Private Holmes, the young boy who had lost a leg, was infected by it. He began to watch for her approach, and answered her ready smile as she entered his room; he always wanted her to change his dressing for him.

Ada wasn't worried about this. She had been nursing long enough to know that patients often fell for their nurses, and it wasn't serious. As soon as they recovered and went home, the nurse they left behind was forgotten, which was just as well. She saw Private Holmes gradually beginning to emerge from the dark depression which had descended on him when he was wounded. He actually began to talk eagerly of the day when his stump would be healed enough for him to try on the artificial leg which was being made for him.

Ada was walking with Private Holmes across the lawn at the back of the Hall one day in May when Tom came back once again. Private Holmes was walking with crutches by this time, his stump was healing nicely.

'Now, are you warm enough?' Ada said as she tucked a rug round him once he was settled on a garden bench. Though the sun was warm by now, sometimes a chilly breeze seemed to spring up from nowhere.

'Yes, I'm fine, thank you, Matron,' he answered, and peered round as something caught his attention behind her.

'Is that officer looking for you, Matron?'

Ada's heart leaped and she swung round to look. 'John –' she began before the light died in her eyes as she saw Tom, standing on the path a few yards away, watching her.

'Just call if you need anything,' she said swiftly to Private Holmes and walked slowly, reluctantly, to meet her husband.

'Hello, Tom,' Ada greeted him.

'Ada,' he answered, and Ada felt slightly sick. The time had come. Tom was here and she had promised Johnny she would tell him. But first there were the formalities to get through.

'How are you?' she asked. 'You should have let me know you were coming, I could have arranged the afternoon off. Never mind, I can spare a little while. Shall we go up to my rooms?'

Tom nodded his head gravely and fell into step with her. They went into the Hall and Ada sought out her deputy.

'Will you look after things for me, Sister? My husband has arrived, I would like a little time with him. I know you should be off duty shortly, but –'

'Oh, don't worry, Matron. I'll stay as long as you like. You go off if you like, it's not every day your husband comes home,' Sister assured her.

'Thank you, Sister.' Ada and Tom went up the stairs with Sister looking after them curiously.

'They didn't look too happy,' she said, as she confided in her friend at tea, 'not for a couple who hadn't seen each other in months. But then, there's the rumours about Matron and the Canadian officer she entertained in her room.' Sister pursed her lips primly.

'It's no business of mine, of course it isn't and Matron Gray is very good at her job, but really, when a man's at the front he didn't ought to have to be worrying about his wife's behaviour, that's what Nurse Simpson said and I agreed with her.'

Her friend nodded slowly and took a sip of tea.

'Sit down, Tom, I'll make some tea,' Ada said as she closed the door to her rooms.

'I'm not interested in tea, Ada,' he answered. He stalked over to the fireplace and took up a stance with his back to the fire and his hands behind him. He stared levelly at her and Ada's colour rose; for a brief moment she wondered if he could see the difference in her since they last met. But she kept her own voice level even as she moved towards him.

'Sit down then, Tom, you make me nervous.' She attempted to lighten the coming conversation with a little laugh. But Tom ignored her and so Ada stayed on her feet too; she had vivid memories of Tom towering over her the last time they had met. 'Er . . . How long have you got this time, Tom? You're staying at your parents', I suppose?' Ada could have bitten out her tongue after the last sentence, knowing how it infuriated Tom to be reminded that his own house was closed up.

But Tom was not thinking about that, not now. He came straight to the nub of what he wanted to say. 'I have been hearing some disturbing rumours about you, Ada. I want to know if they are the truth.'

'Rumours?'

'You heard what I said, Ada, rumours. And not only that, I have had a letter.'

Tom unbuttoned the top pocket of his tunic and pulled out a small blue envelope. He handed it over to Ada, watching her face intently as he did so.

Ada's forehead creased in puzzlement, she genuinely

couldn't think what he was talking about for a minute. She looked at the envelope; it was addressed to Tom care of Dr and Mrs Gray, and had been re-addressed from there to France. Slowly she opened it, her gaze going directly to the bottom of the writing for the signature. There was no name; the letter was signed 'A friend'. But the writing was familiar somehow, she had seen it somewhere before, she was sure. The message was short and to the point.

'Dear Dr Gray, I think you ought to know that your wife has been entertaining a colonial officer in her rooms. I don't think it right that you should be kept in the dark about this.'

Ada read the letter twice before lifting her gaze to Tom. Her heart sank, she didn't know what to say. What she did know was that she wasn't going to deny Johnny, it was the most beautiful thing that had ever happened to her and she refused to feel guilty, dirty or disloyal.

'Well?' Tom dropped the question into the small silence.

'What do you want me to say?'

'I want you to tell me the truth. Did you have a man in your rooms?'

'Yes, I did.'

Tom gave a muffled exclamation and stepped forward, raising his hands to her. Ada took an involuntary step back from him.

'I was going to tell you, I promised I would tell you,

I didn't want to write it in a letter, Tom, I couldn't help what happened, I couldn't.'

'Who is he? Where did you meet this man – a foreigner? By God, Ada –'

'He's not a foreigner, I've known him all my life! He's in the Canadian Army that's all. I thought he was dead, I did . . .'

Tom began walking up and down, agitatedly. 'So Virginia was right. She told me about him, this . . . Johnny is it? She said it would be him, she said you'd been carrying on with him years ago, behind my back, before we were even married.'

'I wasn't! I didn't!' Ada was distraught, she couldn't believe that Tom had discussed this with Virginia before he even told her. And Virginia, how could she tell such lies to him?

'Oh, don't start again, with your dirty lies! It's my own fault, I know, I should never have married you. I picked you up out of the gutter and look how you repay me. Your type has no idea of decent behaviour, you're like animals! You're a whore, you've always been a whore, no better than a common prostitute, ever since you were a child!'

Tom's voice rose as he came to a halt before her. She had put the sofa between them earlier, afraid of what he might do, but now she simply stood there, his words beating into her brain.

'Tom!' she whispered. She felt like a wounded animal, wanting only to crawl away into a corner. Something in her expression must have got through to him for he turned on his heel and walked away from her, obviously struggling to control himself. A struggle he gave up a moment later; swinging again to face her he continued his tirade.

'Well, it's true! You told me yourself. I wouldn't be surprised if you hadn't led that uncle of yours on with those so-innocent great eyes of yours. Ah, you're all alike, your kind, give out to all and sundry if you see something in it for yourselves, but me, no, with me you were the simpering miss, and God help me, I was fooled.' Tom stared bitterly at her, loathing for her in every inch of him. For a few minutes there was a silence except for the sound of his breathing, heavy and harsh. Then he took a step towards her once again.

'It was different with me, wasn't it? I was fool enough to believe you when you told me you were frightened – a good little actress you are, I give you that. And *I* felt guilty when I took what was mine by right! Why, I've a good mind –'

Ada stepped back again, ready to run for the door if he touched her but they were interrupted by someone knocking.

'Yes? Who is it? I'm busy,' Ada called, albeit shakily.

'It's only me, Matron. Cook was wondering if you

would have a word with her about the menu for dinner tonight,' Millie answered.

'Tell her I'll be down directly,' said Ada. She faced Tom again apprehensively, keeping by the door, just in case. 'I have to get back to my work,' she said to him.

'Oh, don't worry, I'm going, and I don't care if I never see you again. I wish I'd never seen you in the first place.'

She opened the door and stood with her head bowed, waiting for him to go. He paused as he got to her.

'This is the end, of course. You can go to your Canadian. As soon as the war is over I'll apply for a divorce.'

Ada was startled. 'But what about your practice?'

Tom laughed harshly, joylessly. 'No one will blame me, Ada, not after what you have done. Things are altogether different now. And I will not do the supposed decent thing, you're not worth it, Ada. No, you and your Johnny will have to bear the consequences yourselves.'

He went off down the stairs and Ada listened to his footsteps fading away, out of my life, she thought dully, out of my life. And slowly, deep within her, she began to realise she was free, or she would be as soon as Tom got his divorce. What Tom didn't realise was that Johnny was worth any price to her, any price at all.

Chapter Twenty-Four

Ada tidied herself up and went downstairs to relieve her deputy, feeling strangely calm and in control of herself. Oh, Tom had hurt her when he ranted and raved at her, all her old feelings of worthlessness had come to the fore. But only for a little while. For the first time she found she could actually shrug off those feelings which had haunted her since childhood; nothing anyone could say to her now could make her feel dirty or inferior ever again. For Johnny loved her and he wouldn't if she wasn't worthy of his love, she knew it. She had been a victim, that was all, a victim of circumstances, and no one had the right to look down on her or call her names. She felt quite light-hearted as she crossed the hall to check on the patients in the garden.

'Everything all right, Matron?'

Ada turned as Sister came out of the second ward and called after her. The other woman's face was alive with curiosity. Had all the staff been talking about her behind her back? Ada wondered, then dismissed it from her mind; it didn't matter any more, it didn't matter at all.

'Everything's fine, Sister,' Ada answered. 'You can go off duty now if you wish. Thank you for relieving me.'

Outside on the lawn, Private Holmes was still sitting on the bench. He was talking to a young VAD who sprang up as Ada approached. Ada almost sent the girl about her duties but she paused; after all, they weren't very busy and she could give a hand with the teas herself. For Private Holmes to take an interest in girls his own age was the best thing that could happen, it showed he was well on the way to recovery. So she simply smiled at them and went round to see the other patients.

Back in the hall, the afternoon post had arrived. She glanced through the official mail – notification of new admissions, letters of discharge for those unable to fight again and postings for those ready to go back to the front. Beneath them were two personal letters for her. Eagerly she scanned them – was one from Johnny? Her heart quickened momentarily but slowed again as she failed to see his handwriting.

One was from Eliza – well, that was lovely; Eliza might not be the best speller in the world but she wrote a nice, gossipy letter. The other had a London postmark and the handwriting was completely strange to her.

Well, she hadn't time to read them now, she thought and pushed them under the bib of her apron. Now she had to give out the post to the men and attend to the new-admissions sheet. For the next few weeks things would be busy as they always were when one batch of soldiers was well enough to leave and another lot of wounded came.

Later in the evening, Ada was writing up the report for the night nurses, detailing each patient, how they were and if their medicine had been changed by the doctor who had been round that day. She would be glad to get upstairs to her own little place, she thought; just as well to have a good night's rest for the new-admission sheet was long, the little convalescent home would be quite full.

Ada hesitated and turned back to the morning's report from Nurse Simpson, who had been the night nurse in charge the night before, as a thought flashed into her mind.

Of course! She should have realised immediately who it was that had written the letter to Tom. Even though some attempt had been made to disguise the writing, there was no mistaking the peculiar curl Nurse Simpson gave to the hooks of her Gs. Ada sat back in her chair, remembering. Nurse Simpson had been on duty on the night that Johnny came, she remembered it now.

Ada didn't even feel angry with her; she didn't know

why but she didn't. After all, the girl was doing her duty as she saw it by a soldier at the front. It simply wasn't worth the aggravation of making a fuss.

When Nurse Simpson came on duty Ada didn't give any hint at all that she knew about the letter even though the nurse was red-faced and apprehensive. Ada was amused as she saw it; Nurse Simpson must have heard of Tom's calling to see her.

'I'll be in my rooms if you need me, Nurse,' she said coolly, leaving the girl to stare after her as she went upstairs. Ada was grinning mischievously as she got to her door. She made herself a cup of tea, singing, 'O, tell me pretty maiden, are there any more at home like you?' She hadn't thought of that old song for years – why on earth had it come back to her now?

Sitting down on the sofa with her tea, Ada took a sip and sighed luxuriously. This was the best part of the day, when she could close her door and be on her own, put her feet up if she wanted to, do what she liked. She put the cup down and drew out the letters from the bib of her apron. Eliza's she would save for later on, she thought; first she was curious about the other, the one with the London postmark.

Ada read the signature first, a Mrs A. Carr. Carr? She didn't know anyone by the name of Carr, no one at all. Mystified, she began to read.

'Dear Lorinda,' Ada sat forward in shock – Lorinda?

No one called her Lorinda, no one but Johnny. Had something happened to Johnny, was this someone writing to tell her? She closed her eyes tightly, she hardly could bear to read on. But read on she had to do.

Dear Lorinda,
How are you? I can't tell you how surprised I was when I saw your advertisement in the paper. I was going to write to you straight away but then I didn't know what to do. I thought I would come to see you, but I'm afraid I can't afford the train fare. I'm on my own now, I'm in real trouble, if you knew how I'd been let down by everybody you would be so sorry for me. I know I don't deserve anything from you, I left you with my mam and all, but believe me, you were better off with her than with me. I've had a hard life, Lorinda, a really hard life. If I could only tell you about it. Please write back to me, you're all I have in the world now.

That was all, apart from the signature. Ada stared at it, unable to take it in at first. Her mother! It was from her mother! After all these years her mother had written to her. Mechanically, Ada took up her cup and drank the tea, and the letter fell to the floor.

Ada bent down and picked it up. She must be mistaken, it couldn't be from her mother. She read it through again. But it was months since she had written to the papers.

How was it that her mother had just seen it now. Why hadn't she written before?

What a day it had been, what a mixed-up, momentous day! Ada put down the letter and took her cup into the kitchen, rinsing it under the tap, and drying it and putting it into the cupboard. She folded the cloth carefully and hung it over the rail. And then she cried.

Going back to the sitting room Ada read the letter again. Her poor mother, she thought, she had had a hard time by the sound of it. And what had happened to her husband? She must have been married, that would be why she had a different name. He must have died and left her mother a widow, that would be it.

Well, Ada decided, she couldn't leave her mother in want. She had saved a modest sum of money and she barely touched her salary from the Hall. Ada was naturally frugal after her strict upbringing and all her living expenses were catered for by the convalescent home. She rose to her feet and walked to and fro, so excited she couldn't sit still.

She would invite her mother to stay, that was what she would do. She could have her to stay with her in the flat, for a short while at least. First thing in the morning she would go to the post office and get a postal order for the fare to Durham, plus a little extra just in case. She'd write the letter now, that would be best. Ada got out her writing paper and envelopes and composed a short letter to her mother. She felt very strange indeed as she began with 'Dear Mother', the very first time she had done so in her life.

When she had finished it, Ada picked up the other letter. Eliza had important news, too, Ada saw as she read the letter. Eliza was definitely going to marry her Emmerson Peart. Ada had a few misgivings when she read this; perhaps she should have paid more attention when Eliza was first telling her about him.

Ada put down the letter and thought about it. Was Eliza doing the right thing? In the letter she was full of what Emmerson could do for her boys: let them stay on at school, get them good apprenticeships.

'He's comfortably off,' Eliza wrote. 'We will be all right with him.'

No mention of loving him, thought Ada. But then, Eliza was not a girl to show her feelings; perhaps she did love him. Sighing, Ada decided to try to see Eliza, the first chance she got.

The chance came two weeks later. It was Ada's free afternoon and Eliza had written saying she would come to see her. The two girls sat in an area of the garden secluded from the patients and had a chat. Ada lost no time in coming to the point.

'Are you sure, Eliza? I mean, do you love him?'

Eliza nodded slowly. 'I do, I think. Oh, not like I loved

my Bert, I couldn't love anyone like I did my Bert. Don't worry, Ada, I'm right, I know I am. Now, tell me all *your* news.'

Ada gazed at her friend. Indeed, Eliza wore an air of serenity and well being which suited her, so perhaps it was the right thing for her; in any case, she'd made up her mind. Ada returned to her own news with an excited smile.

'Oh, Eliza, what do you think? My mother wrote to me. She's coming here next week.'

'Oh, Ada, I'm so pleased. So she answered one of your notices in the papers, did she? That's grand.'

They chatted on about Ada's mother and Auntie Doris for a while and then sat quietly, gazing out over the garden. In the distance, behind the house, they could hear the murmur of voices as the nurses came out to take the non-walking wounded in for tea. Ada was thinking of Johnny and on impulse she decided to confide in her friend.

'I didn't tell you, Eliza, I didn't know what you'd think. But Johnny came to see me.'

'Johnny? Johnny Fenwick, do you mean? Eeh, Ada!' 'Yes.'

Eliza stood up. 'I'll have to get the train, I've the bairns to meet. Can you walk along o' me?'

Ada nodded and the two girls fell into step. At the road end, they caught a bus to the station.

'Howay then, tell me,' Eliza demanded as soon as they were on their way.

'You mean about Johnny?'

'You know full well I mean about Johnny!'

So Ada told the story of Johnny's coming to seek her out. Holding nothing back, she told her that he had stayed the night and how he wanted her to wait for him and go back to Canada with him. She watched her friend's face anxiously, wondering if she was shocked at hearing Ada had spent the night with someone other than her husband. If she was, Eliza showed no signs of it.

'Eeh, Ada, fancy him coming back after all that time! Why didn't he come back sooner, do you think?'

And Ada told her about his coming to Durham so long ago and how Virginia had put him off.

'I never liked that girl,' Eliza said, rather vehemently for her, and Ada remembered how Virginia had treated Eliza at the wedding. Virginia had done her best to make Eliza feel like a servant among her betters, that was true. And maybe she herself could have stuck up for Eliza better.

'I'm sorry I let her be unkind to you,' she said humbly.

'Eeh, no, I didn't care about that, it was the way she talked to you, Ada, that's what upset me, like,' Eliza declared.

The bus got to the station. Bye, but it had been lovely, though. Lovely to see Eliza happy too, without that air of tiredness and worry about her, Ada mused. They went through to the platform; there was about a quarter of an hour to wait for the train.

'Let's stay out here, eh?' Eliza suggested. So they stood on the platform and Ada told Eliza again about Johnny and what she knew of his life in Canada.

'He's got his own business now, a steelworks in Toronto,' she said proudly. Now she was actually talking about Johnny she found she couldn't stop. 'He's so hand-some in his uniform, Eliza, he is. And he wants me to go to Canada with him, when the war is over, that is.'

Eliza nodded in understanding, though she said nothing. The train steamed into the station and she kissed Ada goodbye and climbed aboard, waving through the window to her.

'I'll come to see you when I can,' Ada cried. 'Give my love to Bertie and Miles.'

Afterwards, Ada went down the hill to the bus, feeling happy and relaxed. She had told Eliza about Johnny and Eliza hadn't been disapproving at all. In fact she had listened eagerly, and Ada was sure Eliza had been pleased for her. Eliza was fond of her, she wanted her to be happy, Ada knew that.

As Ada climbed down from the bus and started the walk up the drive, she began to feel a little less sure that Eliza had been pleased for her; after all, she hadn't said much about it. Maybe she had been wondering what she was going to do about her marriage to Tom, what Tom would think about it. For Ada had not told her that Tom knew all about Johnny, or that he threatened to divorce her. A cold wind had sprung up and Ada shivered as she let herself in the front door of the Hall.

'Matron?'

Ada turned to the desk as Sister looked up and spoke to her. 'Yes, is something wrong?' she asked.

'No, not wrong, I just wanted to warn you that you had a visitor.'

'A visitor? Oh, thank you, Sister.'

Ada fairly flew up the stairs. Had Johnny come back already? She couldn't think of anyone else who would come to see her. Her mother wasn't due until the next week.

She opened her door with trembling fingers and rushed into the sitting room, stopping dead in the doorway. There was someone on the sofa but the hair was greyish-black, not red. And it was a woman, not a man, a woman with a glass in her hand. There was a smell of gin in the air as the woman raised her glass to her, twisting in her seat to face her.

'Hello, Lorinda,' she said.

Lorinda? Ada stared at the woman who was sitting there smiling at her, a broad smile which showed an uneven set of teeth between bright-red lips. It took a minute or two for it to sink in that this was Mrs Carr, her own mother. It had to be, for who else would call her Lorinda except Johnny?

Chapter Twenty-Five

As Ada walked slowly forward, the woman stood up; they halted, facing each other. They were about the same height and build, and both had the same striking violet-coloured eyes, but there the resemblance ended.

'Give your mam a kiss then.' Mrs Carr held out her arms and after only a split second, Ada leaned forward and kissed her on the cheek. The older woman was not satisfied. She clutched at Ada, wrapping her thin arms round her; to Ada she felt as though she was all wrinkled skin and bones.

She could smell the gin on her mother's breath; distractedly she wondered where she had got it from. Close to, she saw that the high colour on the raddled cheeks was rouge which did not entirely disguise the broken veins beneath it. Ada drew away and her smile was wobbly as she tried to control the turmoil of emotion which was churning up her stomach.

'Mam?'

'That I am, lass.'

The traces of local accent and idiom still showed through in Mrs Carr's speech, strangely overridden with the twang of cockney.

'Bye,' Mrs Carr went on, 'what a carry-on I had getting here, I didn't know you lived out in the wilds like this. And I had to find my own way from the station, that girl downstairs had to pay the cabman. I told her you'd give it to her. And I come home after all this time and you're not even here, where've you been? I'm dying for a cup of tea, an' all.'

'I'll make one right away,' said Ada, feeling dazed. 'I wasn't expecting you till next week or I wouldn't have gone out. I meant to meet you at Durham Station and bring you here.'

'I'm used to fending for myself, goodness knows, I've had to do it long enough. But I thought, why wait till next week, I'll go now and surprise Lorinda. I was dying for a drink, though, when I got here, where do you keep it? I couldn't find any anywhere. It's a good job I had my travelling bottle with me.'

Ada moved into the kitchen, filled the kettle and placed it on the gas ring, her mind in a whirl. Her mother followed her, looking round with a critical eye.

'Mind, this is a poky place, isn't it? I reckoned anyone

with such a good job as you have, Matron like, would at least have a proper gas stove and everything. And married to a doctor, eh?'

'I get my meals downstairs in the nurses' dining room, I just make the odd snack or cup of tea up here,' Ada replied, rather defensively. She ignored the reference to her marriage, she couldn't go into that now.

The kettle boiled and Ada mashed the tea. She got down a tin of shortbread and arranged some on a plate, all without looking directly at her mother.

'Hmm.' Mrs Carr pursed her lips and went back to her seat on the sofa. After a moment, Ada brought in the tea tray. She poured tea, gave the other woman a cup and picked up her own with shaky hands.

'I'm ready for that.' Mrs Carr added milk and three spoonfuls of sugar to her cup. Then she took the bottle of gin out of her bag and added a dollop of that too, emptying the bottle. Ada wondered if it had been full when she started out that morning.

'I like the milk put in first,' Mrs Carr commented before looking up and seeing Ada's frozen expression. 'What's the matter? Oh, the gin, do you mean? Do you want some in your tea?'

Ada shook her head, feeling so shaken she couldn't answer. There's some mistake, she thought miserably, there has to be, this can't really be my mother. Someone is having me on, that's it. But as she saw the violet eyes looking over the teacup to her, she knew there was no mistake.

'Er . . . Did you have a good journey up?' asked Ada, she couldn't think of anything else to say.

'Bloody horrible, that's what it was,' was Mrs Carr's forthright answer. 'I ask your pardon, like, Lorinda, but it was enough to make a saint swear.'

'That's all right,' Ada mumbled. Oh, her mother wasn't at all the way she had always imagined her to be. She remembered her grannie telling her how bonny she was, 'like a dainty little fairy girl,' Grannie had said. 'The prettiest little thing in the street.'

Her mother must have had a really hard life, though – Ada found herself making excuses for her – it showed in her face, poor thing.

'I left my cases downstairs.' Mrs Carr broke into her thoughts. 'I couldn't carry them up here, could I? Not with my back.'

'I'll go down for them later,' Ada said.

'You want to make one of those lasses bring them up. Don't keep a dog and bark yourself, Lorinda, that's what I say. You should let them see who's boss.'

Ada was beginning to realise she hated her mother to call her Lorinda. Every time she said it, it grated on her. But for the minute she couldn't think of a way of telling her so without offending her.

'They're very busy,' she pointed out, 'and besides, they

are employed to look after the patients, not visitors.' She hesitated, then added, 'Mam', feeling very self-conscious about saying it.

'I'm not a visitor – I'm the matron's mother. That's not a visitor, surely, Lorinda?'

'You can't stay here, not for more than a couple of weeks, that is. I don't think it will be allowed.'

'What do you mean, I can't stop here? You're the matron, aren't you? Doesn't that make you the boss?' Ada's mother stared down her nose at her, her tone becoming strident. 'And why did you send for me if I can't stay here, eh? Was I supposed to sleep on the streets?'

For the first time Ada saw the resemblance between her mother and her aunt. Why, when they were angry they had the same forward thrust to the head, the same stridency and gimlet stare. She shook her head.

'No, no –'

'What then?' Mrs Carr interrupted. 'Who will tell you to put your own mother on the streets anyway?'

'The trustees run the place, Mam, they run it for the owner, who is fighting in France. But I didn't mean you would be without somewhere to sleep. You can have a nice holiday with me for a while and then I'll find you somewhere to stay, if you want to stay in Durham, that is.' Ada was beginning to feel overwhelmed by her mother's aggressiveness. She looked about her helplessly and her eyes fell on the gin bottle. Of course, that was what it was, the drink made people aggressive. She'd be all right when she'd had a rest, maybe she hadn't meant to drink so much.

'I'll show you where you can sleep, Mam,' she said gently, 'then you can have a nice rest. And afterwards I'll have dinner sent up on a tray, you'd like that, wouldn't you? We can talk things over then, when you're not so tired.'

'I thought you wanted me to stay with you. I can't go back now, I've nothing to go back to, a poor widow like I am.' Mrs Carr nodded her head, and her face sank into lines of self-pity.

'Howay, Mam,' Ada said gently, holding her hand out to her mother. 'Howay and have a lie-down. It'll do you the world of good, you'll feel better after it, you'll see.' Unconsciously she had fallen into the way of talking which she had often used with the old ladies in the workhouse hospital. Even though, she thought with a slight shock, her mother could hardly be in her fifties yet.

Mrs Carr responded to her coaxing and allowed herself to be led into the bedroom. She sniffed a little as she saw the narrow single bed but slipped off her shoes and dress and let Ada tuck her in.

'Just half an hour, that's all I need,' she said. 'The journey an' all.'

Ada closed the bedroom door and sat down on the sofa before the fire. What a way to end the lovely afternoon she had had with Eliza, she thought. She sighed; it was so sad seeing her mother like that. Once she must have been as young and full of hope as Ada was herself, and when she went off to London she must have been certain she could make something of herself. Hadn't she said to Grannie that she would send for her little girl as soon as she had a home for her? And hadn't Grannie told Ada, time and time again, that her mother loved her and would never have left her if she could have helped it?

No, it wasn't her mother's fault, Ada was sure, it was life and hardships that had ground her down, that was all. How awful it must have been to miss your baby, try desperately to make a home for her and never quite manage it. No, she thought again, it couldn't have been her mother's fault.

Ada picked up the empty gin bottle and took it into the kitchen, because the smell made her feel sick. She would take it down to the rubbish bins when she went for the cases. She washed the cups, tidied the kitchen and went back into the sitting room to wait for her mother to wake up. She stared into the fire, pondering what to do. It was obvious that her mother was going to be dependent on her from now on, and there would be lodgings to find for her. Mrs Dunne in Gilesgate, perhaps; Ada would enquire on her next half-day.

The daylight faded, the fire died down and Ada added coal to it from the scuttle. She lit the lamp and drew the curtains against the dark, and her mother slept on. Poor thing, she must be really tired, Ada thought as she listened at the door to the bedroom. There was a soft snoring sound coming from the bed, so she was still asleep. Ada decided to go down to the hall, bring up the suitcases and ask Cook to make a tray up for their supper at the same time.

'About nine o'clock, if that's all right,' she said to Cook. 'Millie will bring it up, I'm sure.'

'Nine o'clock, right then,' Cook answered. She was a plump, amiable woman who took everything in her stride, an extra tray was neither here nor there to her. She smiled at Ada now. 'How nice for you to have your mother to stay, Matron. I hope you both enjoy yourselves.'

'Thank you, we will. I just hope it isn't too much extra work, that's all.'

'Nay, what's one more, nothing at all,' Cook said stoutly.

Ada lugged the two heavy suitcases she found in the hall up the three flights of stairs to her rooms, puffing and panting by the time she got to her door. Inside, all was quiet and when she went to the bedroom door she could still hear the soft sound of snores. Smiling to herself, she sat down to wait for her mother to wake up.

'Mind, I was ready for that, Lorinda.' Mrs Carr, her hair brushed back from her forehead and pinned in a bun at the nape of her neck and with fresh rouge on her cheeks, picked delicately at a chicken bone. 'It's a long while since I could afford chicken, not since my poor Henry went.'

'You'll have to tell me about Henry, Mam,' Ada said. 'He was your husband, was he? Mr Carr?'

Her mother gave her a sideways glance. 'In a manner of speaking,' she answered.

Ada was bewildered – what was she talking about? Best not go into it, she thought, as the obvious explanation presented itself to her.

'He died, did he?' she asked instead, trying to sound suitably sympathetic.

'Yes. Leaving me without a penny, an' all.'

Ada creased her brow. 'Surely you'll have a widow's pension, though?'

'I haven't. Not a penny.'

'Oh, but –' And then Ada realised that her mother probably wasn't old enough for a widow's pension; she wasn't exactly sure how old you had to be to qualify for a Lloyd George pension.

'But how have you managed?' she asked. 'How did you earn a living?'

'Oh, this and that.' Mrs Carr had lost interest for the moment, and focused on the small chocolate cake which Cook had sent up for them. 'Will you cut me a piece of that cake, Lorinda?'

'Yes, of course.'

Ada fetched a clean knife from the kitchen and cut a good slice of chocolate cake for her mother, who was looking at it greedily, like a child. No doubt she didn't often get anything nice to eat, Ada told herself, it was a treat for her. She sipped her tea and watched her mother tuck into the cake. She did it single-mindedly, eating every crumb. Then she looked over at Ada.

'Aren't you having any, Lorinda?'

'I'm not hungry, you have another piece,' Ada answered and gave her another slice.

'I was meaning to say,' Ada said after a moment. Her mother looked up from her plate. A crumb of chocolate cake was stuck to her lower lip and she put out the tip of her tongue and licked it off.

'I was meaning to say,' Ada repeated, 'I'm called Ada now, I've been called Ada ever since I went to live with Auntie Doris when I was little. I'm used to it now, so please call me Ada.'

'Ada? What on earth for? What's wrong with Lorinda?' Mrs Carr shook her head and went back to her cake. 'No, I named you Lorinda, it's a lovely name. My auntie was called Lorinda. I've always thought of you as Lorinda and I would feel daft calling you Ada.'

Ada gave up for the moment. Secretly she wondered if her mother had thought of her at all during the long years of her growing up, never mind her name. But maybe that was being a bit unfair.

At last her mother had finished and she sat back in her chair with a sigh of content. She glanced round the room as though looking for something and failing to find it.

'Have you not got a gramophone, Ada? Surely you could afford a gramophone – liven things up a bit, a gramophone would.'

'No, not here,' Ada admitted. 'We had one at the house but I didn't think to bring it here. I don't like to make too much noise, it might disturb the patients, you know.'

'Cheer them up, more like. A nice lively song would do them good.' Mrs Carr watched her daughter as she piled the supper things on the tray and took them out to the kitchen. 'You should let the maid do that,' she said primly and Ada had trouble hiding her grin. Her mother seemed to go from haughty lady to poor destitute woman and back again to lady in the space of half an hour.

'Like I said, Mam, that's not what they are here for.'

Ada came back into the sitting room and took a seat on the chair across from her mother. 'Now we can have a nice, cosy talk,' she said. 'I'm longing to know all that happened to you in London.'

Mrs Carr sighed. 'You wouldn't believe the bad luck I've had, you wouldn't, pet. And Henry, bless his soul, well, he wasn't a good provider. He liked a good time, did Henry. So I've had to work all my life and here I am, not a thing to show for it.' She looked hopefully across at Ada. 'You haven't got a drop of gin in the place, have you? I like a drop of gin before I go to bed, it helps me to sleep.'

Ada shook her head. 'I don't keep it in, Mam, I don't drink it myself.' Privately she thought that her mother had had enough gin for one day in any case.

'Nothing? No brandy? Maybe a glass of stout?'

'No, I'm sorry . . . Though, wait a minute, there is some brandy. I keep the bottle for the patients up here, it's safer. Sometimes we have to use it as a restorative.' Ada went over to the sideboard and took out a half-bottle of brandy. 'It's for medicinal use, you know. But I'm sure it doesn't matter if you have a little, I can buy some tomorrow and fill it up.'

She took out a small glass and poured out the usual dose, watched critically by her mother.

'Bye, mind, I needed that,' Mrs Carr declared after she had thrown it back in one swallow, making Ada blink. She looked up at her daughter as though about to ask for another but she thought better of it. 'I only take it for medicinal purposes myself,' she said.

Ada put the bottle away and sat down again. 'Tell me about your husband,' she urged. 'You didn't have any more children then?'

'No, just as well an' all. We moved around a lot and it would have been no good with kids.' Mrs Carr pulled herself up when she saw Ada's face. 'Mind, I would still have sent for you, if we could have managed the fare. But somehow – anyway, you were all right with our Doris, I knew you'd be all right with Doris.'

Yes indeed, thought Ada, remembering the times she had cried herself to sleep behind the screen in the kitchen in Finkle Street, praying her mam would come and claim her. And Uncle Harry . . . best not think of Uncle Harry.

Mrs Carr was yawning openly now. 'I think I'll go to bed then, Lorinda,' she said. 'If you don't mind, that is.' She rose and stretched her skinny arms over her head. 'It's grand to see you, pet, it is, but I'm tired now, you know, and my back's giving me hell.'

'Yes, of course, you go to bed when you like and get up when you like, this is a holiday for you. I'll just get blankets and a pillow from the chest in the bedroom, and make a bed up for myself on the sofa.'

'Eeh, I thought you would have a spare bed in the place,' Mrs Carr declared.

'I'll be fine,' Ada answered, noticing that her mother didn't seem unduly perturbed about her having to sleep on the sofa. 'I'll probably be working when you get up in the morning, but make yourself some tea and I'll come up at ten and bring you some breakfast.'

When her mother had gone to bed and Ada was settled on the sofa with only the flickering light from the fire to light the room, she went over the momentous happenings of the evening in her mind, trying to settle her thoughts for sleep. She had to be up at six o'clock in the morning and a busy day lay ahead of her, so she needed to sleep.

My poor mam, she thought, what hardships had she undergone to bring her to her present state? No wonder she had turned to drink. But there would be no need for that any more, she would wean her off the gin, gradually, she thought. If there was none in the place, then her mother couldn't drink it, it was as simple as that.

Ada turned over, stretching out her legs so that her feet were over the edge of the sofa. She had told her mother she would be comfortable enough but in truth it was a bit restricting.

I'm not going to criticise her, Ada resolved, I'll think of all the nice things about her. She's my mother and it's going to be grand to be able to confide in her, tell her all my problems. I'm sure she'll understand me, it will be like having Eliza close by all the time. A quiet happiness stole over her, and her eyelids drooped sleepily. Her life was going to be so different now: she had her mother and she had Johnny, or she would have Johnny as soon as this war was over. And Johnny loved her, he wouldn't mind her mother going with her to Canada, she was sure he wouldn't.

It crossed her mind that her mother hadn't once asked her how it was when Grannie died or what it had been like living in Bishop Auckland. But she dismissed the thought, it was uncharitable of her.

It was half past ten in the morning by the time Ada was free to go upstairs with a breakfast tray for her mother. The latest group of wounded soldiers were all recovering physically by the time they got to the convalescent home, but most of them were in pretty bad shape emotionally and mentally. Nightmares were frequent despite the sedatives prescribed by the doctors and quite often one patient screaming in his sleep woke the whole ward and then the night staff had trouble settling the men down again. As a consequence the men were morose and irritable during the day.

And then there were the wet beds, sometimes worse. Ada herself had had to lend a hand in changing the beds that morning; there was a doctor's round later in the morning and she was a nurse short as a VAD had failed to report for duty after her day off.

'I'm sorry I'm late –' Ada broke off her apology as she entered the sitting room, for her mother was not yet out of bed. Ada could still hear the soft snoring from the bedroom. Putting down the tray, she went in to see if there was anything the matter.

No, Mrs Carr was lying on her back with her mouth open and traces of last night's make-up still visible on her face. As Ada went up to her, she tripped over a skirt which was dropped on the floor and had to clutch at the bedboard to save herself from falling, causing the bed to shake. Her mother woke with a start.

'What – Bloody hell, what's the matter?' She sat up, startled, and looked around her with a disoriented gaze.

'It's only me, Mam,' said Ada and went to the window to draw the curtains. A thin shaft of sunshine entered the room and Ada began picking up the clothes her mother had dropped as she prepared for bed.

'Oh, Lorinda,' said Mrs Carr, putting her hand over her eyes to shade them from the light. 'What time is it, like?'

'Ten thirty, Mam.'

'Ten thirty? Aw, that's all right then.' She lay back on her pillow, yawning.

'I've brought you a nice boiled egg and some bread and butter, and a pot of tea. I thought I'd have my break with you before I go back to work.'

'I never eat in the mornings. Take it away, I feel sick at the thought,' Mrs Carr said pettishly. 'You're going back to work, did you say? What about me? I thought you would take the time off, I don't like to be on my own.'

Ada sighed as she poured out two cups of tea and gave one to her mother. She felt a little nauseous herself, she thought. Perhaps it was the smell of stale gin which was still hanging around.

'I have to go to work, Mother, it's my job.'

Mrs Carr said nothing to that, merely looked discontented. They drank the tea and Ada rose to go. 'Why don't you go for a nice walk, Mam?' she suggested. 'It's a lovely day, you'll enjoy it.'

'It's too cold and anyway, there's my back. It's bad, it must have been the journey up yesterday. No, if you're going to leave me alone again I'll stay in bed, it'll do me more good. And pull the curtains together before you go, the light hurts my eyes.'

Ada was depressed as she went downstairs. She was beginning to think she had taken on more than she could manage when she'd asked her mother to stay. But she soon forgot about it in the rush to get the wards in order before the doctor's rounds. That was one of the cardinal rules she had had instilled into her during her training: have the wards tidy and neat and everything in order for the doctors to see.

By the end of the week, Ada was beginning to think that the sooner she had found a place for her mother to stay, the better. Every evening when she finished her work on the ward she went upstairs to find her mother the worse for drink. A new brandy bottle had to be put under lock and key downstairs in the office, the old one having been emptied that first day. But where was her mother getting her supplies? It was a mystery to Ada.

She found out by chance one day when she caught

Millie in her sitting room with Mrs Carr, when she popped upstairs for something she had forgotten.

'You'll have to give me the money, Mrs Carr,' the girl was saying. She was standing with her back to the door and so didn't see Ada come in. Mrs Carr tried to slip the bottle of gin behind her back as she saw her daughter, but she was not fast enough.

'How much does my mother owe you, Millie?'

Millie flushed guiltily and stared at the floor. 'Two and sixpence, Matron,' she mumbled.

Ada took her purse out of her uniform dress pocket, fished out half-a-crown and handed it over. 'I'll have a word with you downstairs, Millie,' she said.

'Yes, Matron,' Millie answered and ran out of the room, glad to escape.

Ada gazed at her mother, who was clutching the bottle to her breast as though she expected Ada to take it from her by force.

'Well, a woman likes a drink, and why shouldn't I have one? There's precious little else to do in this hole. You're always busy, you never have any time for me.'

'Oh, Mam,' said Ada helplessly. 'I've told you I have to work, do you want me to lose my job?'

'You'd think you'd have a bit more time off, though. Anyway, why do you have to work? I thought your husband was a doctor in the army, surely you get money from him? It's his duty to keep you, isn't it?'

Ada didn't want to talk about Tom, she couldn't bring herself to discuss him with her mother. Quickly she changed the subject.

'I have to go now, Mam, but I tell you what we'll do. I have a day off next Friday, why don't we go out for the day? We can go and look round for somewhere for you to stay. It's time we were making plans, you know.'

'Oh aye, I know, you want to get rid of me, that's it.' Mrs Carr glared at her daughter. 'Don't think I don't know when I'm not wanted.'

'Oh, Mam, I haven't time to stand here arguing.' Ada was losing her patience. There were a million things she had to do downstairs and she had to go. 'We'll talk about it tonight.'

Ada went downstairs feeling very worried about her mother. She knew the staff were beginning to talk, and it was only a matter of time before the trustees got to hear about her. And then where would her job be? It was imperative that she find somewhere else for her mother to stay. Seeking out Millie, she asked her not to run errands for her mother without asking Ada about it.

Fortunately, Ada had the ability to switch off all other worries and concentrate wholly on her work. She spent the rest of the day working tirelessly beside her nurses and when eventually she was ready to go off duty again she was humming softly to herself as she went up to her rooms.

As she opened the door, the smell of gin greeted her

once again and she stopped humming abruptly as all her problems came back to her. Her mother was lying half on and half off the sofa, the gin bottle on its side on the rug beside her.

'Oh, Mam, what are we going to do about you?' she asked.

Mrs Carr opened her eyes blearily and looked up at her, muttering incoherently.

'Let's get you to bed, then.' Ada bent and took hold of her under the armpits, pulling her onto her feet. 'Howay now, Mam, hang onto me.'

Swaying drunkenly, Mrs Carr almost fell and pulled Ada down with her, but in the end Ada managed to get her into the bedroom and laid across the bed. Immediately, Mrs Carr closed her eyes again, her mouth opened and she began to snore. Ada covered her with a blanket and went out into the sitting room, closing the door behind her.

Definitely, she had to do something about her mam and it was urgent, Ada mused as she made herself a cup of tea and sat down on the sofa. She unlaced her shoes and put her feet up, feeling very weary. She couldn't wait until Friday to find alternative accommodation for her mam, she had to do it as soon as she could. She would take a couple of hours off the next afternoon, she decided. But it wouldn't be any good getting her lodgings, she knew that now. Her mam would be thrown out within a week from any decent lodging house in Durham. She was toying with the idea of finding someone to share a house with her mother when she heard a cry from the bedroom. What now? she thought wearily and went to investigate.

'Lorinda! Lorinda!' Mrs Carr was sitting up in bed, her hair all over the place and tears running down her cheeks, making channels in the rouge.

'What is it? What's wrong, Mam?'

'Oh, Lorinda, I thought you'd put me out, I dreamed I had nowhere to go. Oh, pet, you wouldn't do that, would you?' She looked so pathetically small and helpless sitting there that Ada crossed to the bed and, sitting down, took her in her arms.

'No, Mam, I wouldn't put you out.'

'It's not my fault, Lorinda, really it isn't, none of it was my fault.'

'Henry, was it? He didn't treat you right?' Ada said mechanically, her weariness threatening to overwhelm her.

'Henry? Why, no, man, Henry was a saint, he was. Eeh, if he knew what I'd come to he'd turn in his grave, he would that.'

Ada felt vaguely surprised; yesterday evening her mother had called Henry every name she could think of. And today he was a saint? But her mother was rambling on about something or someone. Ada pricked up her ears as she heard a name she knew.

'No, it was long before that. I would never have had to leave me mam and go down to London in the first place but for that James Johnson. It was all his fault, all of it.' She began to weep noisily, burying her face in Ada's apron bib.

'James Johnson? Did you say James Johnson?'

'Aye, I did, the rotten sod. Eeh, I was only a bairn meself, I was, only sixteen, pet. I was working up at the university, minding my own business. I was a good girl, I was. And he was lovely, Lorinda, he was, a lovely man. He promised me he would marry me, he did. I wasn't the sort of girl to go with anybody if I hadn't thought he would marry me.'

'James Johnson? He worked at the university?' Ada was stunned. 'Do you mean James Johnson is my father?'

Mrs Carr looked at her with the earnestness of the very drunk and nodded her head vigorously. 'He is, pet, he is. Or mebbe I should say he was – he was a lot older than me, he's likely dead now. He took advantage of me, Ada, a poor skivvy. All presents and flowers at first but it was different later. Thought himself too high and mighty for a poor maid of all work when it came to it, though he was full of promises in the beginning. But once I had a babby on the way it was another thing altogether. He denied it was his, said I'd been with other men. He was worried about his precious position at the university then. Bye, that bloody James Johnson has a lot to answer for.'

Chapter Twenty-Six

Ada slept little that night and what sleep she did have was fitful. She woke up a dozen times during the night and thought of her mother's disclosure. James Johnson was my father. James Johnson *is* my father. The words went round and round in her head until it ached. She was filled with a furious anger with the man. He had befriended her ever since she came back to Durham and knocked on his door asking for work. She'd done his washing and ironing for months, helped him out with kitchen work, confided in him. Ada couldn't get over it.

Why had he thrown her mother off? Ada asked herself. Had he been married when he had the affair with the girl who cleaned his rooms at the university? But he had never mentioned a wife, only a brother, the one who was killed in the war.

At five o'clock in the morning, Ada was wide awake again. She decided she might as well get up, since she couldn't sleep any more; she had to be ready for work soon in any case. And first chance she got she would arrange with her deputy to have free time that afternoon. She wouldn't tell her mother where she was going; it would be easy enough to think up an excuse to go out on her own. She certainly didn't want to go to see Mr Johnson trailing Mam with her.

In the event, Ada simply did without lunch and slipped away at one o'clock. Mrs Carr would think she was working, she reckoned. She took a bus into the city and walked to the County Hospital, where Mr Johnson was still a patient.

As she walked, Ada rehearsed in her mind what she was going to say to Mr Johnson. Her anger towards him had cooled but only slightly. She was furious with him not only for the ruin he had brought to her mother's life but also because he must have known who she was herself, right from the beginning. Wasn't her name the same as her mother's had been? Surely he hadn't thought so little of his affair with Mam that he didn't even remember the name?

Thinking of how he had tried to educate her, the little kindnesses he had shown to her over the last few years, only made Ada more annoyed with him. There she was thinking he was doing it out of the goodness of his heart, because he saw she had a good brain and wanted to help her, because he liked her even, and all the time he had known she was his daughter, and had done it because she was his daughter.

And he had actually been the one to suggest that he give her away at her wedding! He had offered himself, he had walked down the aisle with her, proud to act as her father but not ready to acknowledge the relationship. He had deceived her, that was what he had done.

But when Ada got to the hospital it was to find that Mr Johnson had passed away a short while before.

'I was going to let you know, Matron, you were the only one to visit him,' the ward sister said to her. 'Though his son was listed as next of kin, his solicitor told us.'

Ada walked away from the hospital in a daze. She had got away as soon as she could, questions whirling round and round in her head. That must have been what the old man was trying to tell her that day in Old Elvet, she realised. Major Walter Johnson was his son, not his brother. She had had a half-brother and never even known.

Mr Johnson had behaved badly, very badly, towards her mother, she thought as she went on her way. But he had become just a pathetic, ill old man who had faced a lonely death.

Lifting her chin, she determined to forget about the past, for harking back did no good at all. She knew who her father had been now, and she knew her mother.

'I am stronger than either of them,' she said aloud,

startling a little girl bowling her hoop along the pavement so that the iron ring fell to the ground with a clatter. Ada didn't notice it, her mind was on other things. People have charge of their own lives, she mused under her breath. Maybe her early life had helped her be strong.

Ada thought of Johnny, her lovely man. Surely the war would be over soon and they would be together again. She was passing a corner shop and on impulse she went in and bought a packet of pear drops. When she slipped one into her mouth and sucked, the old, comforting taste of sweet and acid reminded her of Johnny. Maybe she was a fool, but she could almost imagine he was there, around the next corner, just waiting for her.

Within a week, Mrs Carr was settled in a tiny house in Gilesgate. Ada furnished it as best she could out of her small savings and tried to interest her mother in sewing curtains for the windows, for she had purchased a sewing machine from a second-hand shop. She spent all her spare time with her mother, chivvying her to take an interest in keeping the cottage nice.

Mrs Carr swung from one mood to another. At first she had been sullen and refusing to take any interest at all.

'A poky enough place,' she commented when she looked round the house for the first time. 'Still, I suppose you think, it's good enough for me, you still blame me for leaving you with our Doris.'

'I don't, Mam. I know you hadn't much choice, the way you were situated,' Ada said mildly. 'And it's big enough for you, isn't it? Why, there's even a spare bedroom if you need it.'

Mrs Carr snorted. 'Why should I need it then? I don't know anybody in this rotten hole any more.'

'You know Mrs Dunne. Why don't you go and see her? You know, she was Grannie's neighbour. I lodged with her when I first came back to Durham.'

'Interfering old cat! I wouldn't speak to her, I wouldn't. Why she practically crowed over me and me mam when I fell wrong with you.' Her mother could sound quite vicious sometimes, Ada thought.

Mrs Carr lifted the cover off the Singer sewing machine and inspected it. Experimentally, she moved the treadle up and down and sniffed. 'Never been oiled in years, I'd say.'

Ada smiled to see that her mother handled the machine as though she was well used to them. 'Have you done some sewing before, Mam?'

'I have. I worked in a dress factory when I went down to London.' Mrs Carr laughed shortly. 'I soon got out of there, I can tell you. Bloody slaves, that's all we were. Working for money that wouldn't keep body and soul together.'

Ada forbore to ask what her mother had gone on to. She had just about lost all her illusions about her now and maybe it was better not to know. But it did occur to her that her mother could perhaps make a little money taking sewing in, alterations or something like that.

'I have to get back to the Hall, Mam,' Ada said aloud.

Mrs Carr pursed her lips and yet again Ada was struck by her likeness to Auntie Doris, not so much in looks as in mannerisms and the way she spoke.

'Aye, well, it doesn't matter about me, I'm sure,' said Mrs Carr. 'I'll be perfectly all right on my own here, even though I don't know a soul.'

'There's the curtains to run up – look, I've got you some nice cheerful material from the market,' Ada said, ignoring the complaint in her mother's voice. 'I have to work, Mam, or we'll both starve.'

'Aw, go on then,' Mrs Carr said crossly.

Ada hesitated as she got to the door. Was her mam going to be all right? Fervently she hoped she wouldn't go on the gin again; these last few days she had been relatively sober.

'Goodbye for now. I'll come back when I can and bring you some oil for the machine.'

'Ta-ta,' Mrs Carr replied absently and Ada was cheered to see her fingering the curtain material, opening out the bundle on the table. As Ada opened the door she looked up. 'Don't bother, I can get some meself. I can't wait about for you all the time with no curtains at the window and nosy folk staring in,' she said.

Ada felt quite happy about her mother as she went up the drive of the Hall and let herself in the front door. As usual her eyes were drawn to the afternoon post which was laid out on the hall table. Her heart beat uncomfortably as she looked for a letter from Johnny. And there was one! There it was in its buff envelope, the stamp 'Passed by the Censor' across the front. She could hardly wait to get it upstairs, where she could open it in private. With a feeling of relief she opened the door into the silent flat: she would still worry about what her mother was up to in her little cottage but at least she wasn't creating havoc in Ada's own rooms. The situation had been getting impossible.

Shedding her coat and hat, Ada sat down on the sofa and opened the letter. There were two sheets covered with Johnny's beloved handwriting.

'My dearest Lorinda,' she read and impulsively she kissed the words. She was his dearest Lorinda. Oh, how much better her given name sounded when it came from Johnny than when it came from her mother. Though she'd tried and tried, she had never succeeded in making her mother call her Ada.

She read on, drinking in every word. Johnny said very little about what was happening to him at the front, but she supposed he couldn't say a lot or the censor would have blacked out the words. Instead, his letter was full of plans for the future – their future, his and hers. He told her of his business in Toronto and the house he had built just before the war.

'But if you don't like it, my love, I will build another, and you can have it exactly as you want it.'

Ada looked up from the letter. He would build another house just to suit her whims. Oh, Johnny, Johnny, she thought and went to the bag of pear drops which she kept in the sideboard drawer, taking one out and popping it into her mouth as she did whenever the longing for him filled her.

'My love, my Lorinda,' she read on after she sat down again, 'I can't wait for the day. I don't care if you haven't got your divorce by then, we'll still go away to Canada together, I won't go without you ever again. When I get back to you we will never, never be parted, I promise you.'

Ada sat back, contented. She felt exactly the same: she didn't care what anyone said, she would go with him wherever he wanted to go, Canada or the South Pole, she didn't care. As far as she was concerned she was already divorced from Tom, even if she didn't have the papers yet to prove it.

She was still sitting there when there was a knock at the door and Millie poked her head round.

'Matron, there's someone wanting you on the telephone,' she said.

'Thank you, Millie.' Ada rose and put on her cap, going over in her mind where she could put any extra patients. For that would be the only reason for a telephone call, she thought. So she was taken completely by surprise when the voice coming over the line, though sounding very tinny, was unmistakably Johnny's.

'Lorinda? Are you there, Lorinda?'

'Johnny!'

'Lorinda, my love, listen, I'm back in Blighty for a few days, can you come?'

'Come?'

'Yes, come to London. Oh, Lorinda, we might not get a chance like this again for months. Say you'll come, please say you'll come. Come for the weekend, I'll meet you at King's Cross on Saturday – Lorinda?'

Ada's legs felt suddenly weak, she sat down abruptly.

'Lorinda? Are you there?'

'Yes . . . yes, I'm here.'

Ada's mind was beginning to work at a furious pace. She had some time off due to her, so she could go to him, she would have to organise it but she could do it.

'I'll come,' she said.

It was just as well that there were no seriously ill patients that evening, for this was one time when Ada's mind was definitely not on her work. It was Thursday already and she had a lot to do, a lot to arrange, but she would do it. She could still hear Johnny's voice in her ear as he assured her he loved her, promising to meet the five-o'clock train into King's Cross. They would be together again. Was it all a dream, was she going to wake up and find it wasn't true?

Ada walked by the hall table later and saw there was another letter to her, which she hadn't noticed earlier in the excitement of finding the one from Johnny. She picked it up and looked at the postmark: Bishop Auckland, it said. It took her a minute or two to recognise the writing on the envelope, for it was shaky and sprawled right to the edge, but there was something familiar about it. With a small shock she knew the letter was from Auntie Doris. She tucked it under her bib front as she walked into the main ward, thinking about Auntie Doris as she went.

The old lady was still in the workhouse hospital at Auckland, as far as Ada knew. She had written to her often and sent small gifts of money over the last few months, and the hospital would have informed her if Auntie Doris had left, she was sure. And where could she have gone?

But the question of Auntie Doris was forgotten as Ada worked out how she was going to get the weekend off and find time to buy her ticket. Ada didn't even get round to opening the letter.

When Ada got down from the train as it at last steamed into King's Cross Station, her heart was in her mouth.

She couldn't believe she was actually going to see Johnny – not only see him but touch him, love him. Her face was rosy as she remembered that one night they had spent together in the convalescent home, her bones felt like water as she thought of it. Anxiously she scanned the crowds on the platform, a small crease appearing between her eyes as she failed to see the familiar figure of Johnny. The next moment, there he was, her Johnny, tall, broad and smiling and the bonniest sight she had ever seen in her entire life. Her eyes filled with tears as he lifted her up in his arms, swinging her off her feet and burying his face in her hair.

'Lorinda, Lorinda!'

'Oh, Johnny,' she said shakily. 'Oh, Johnny.' The depth of feeling as she felt his arms around her took her over completely. She was blind to every sight and sound on the station platform except for her Johnny. They were wrapped in a cocoon, a bright haze that shielded them from the rest of the world.

Ada hardly knew what was happening as he took her out to the taxi rank and somehow, out of all the crowds of people, managed to be the one who secured a cab and settled her in it, all without letting go of her hand. And then they were going up the broad staircase of a large hotel, a luxurious hotel in the West End, though for all Ada noticed it could have been a dosshouse in the East End.

As the door closed behind the bellboy and Johnny lifted her onto the bed, Ada felt sure her heart would burst. No one could be this happy and live.

Ada was woken by a knock on the door. Her eyes flew open and she gazed round at the unfamiliar room. She heard murmuring at the door; Johnny was keeping his voice low in order not to disturb her. Ada turned over on her back and stretched luxuriously, her lips curved in a wide, contented smile. Thank you, God, she thought, closing her eyes tightly, thank you for letting me wake up to the sound of my Johnny's voice.

'You look a bit pleased with yourself this morning.'

Ada opened her eyes and there he was, grinning down at her. He had a tray in his hands and there was the most delicious smell of bacon, eggs and toast. Her stomach rumbled and she realised just how hungry she was. She hadn't eaten since the sandwiches she took on the train the previous day – why, it must be eighteen hours or more.

Johnny put down the tray on the bedside table and sat down on the bed, the better to take her in his arms.

'Good morning, my love,' Ada whispered, as he buried his face in her neck. 'And I am. Very pleased with myself.'

Johnny chuckled softly, satisfied with her answer. The urgency rose in them once more and the breakfast was forgotten for a while.

Later, they sat cross-legged on the bed and ate the now cold toast and bacon, relishing every mouthful.

'What shall we do today?' Johnny wiped his fingers on his napkin and raised an enquiring eyebrow. 'Do you want to see the sights – the Tower, Buckingham Palace? Or shall we just stay here?'

'Johnny! I'm scandalised.' But Ada was laughing, her eyes brimming with love.

In the end they went out in the afternoon, walking in Hyde Park. There were lots of couples with the same idea, young lovers like them, strolling hand in hand under the trees. The light clothes of the women contrasted with the unvarying khaki of the men. There was an air of hectic gaiety: the laughter of the women was quick and nervous, and the men were holding the arms or hands of their girls tightly as though they might be snatched from them.

Ada felt in tune with them. Already the dark shadows were gathering on her and Johnny's precious weekend, for that night she had to catch the overnight train to Durham. It was the last possible train she could catch and still be on time for her duty the next day, and she would have to try to snatch some sleep on the train. Ada shivered; she didn't want to think of that, she wanted to live these few hours, get every single minute's worth from them. Her hand tightened on Johnny's arm and she looked up into his face. It too looked shadowed, he had something on his mind, she thought.

'Let's sit on the bench,' she said. 'We can watch the ducks.' But what she really wanted to do was bury her face in Johnny's shoulder, feel his strength sheltering her and smell the masculine scent of him. And she wanted to tell him that even though they parted, they would be together in the end.

'Don't go, Lorinda,' Johnny said suddenly. For a moment Ada thought she had misheard him. 'What?'

'Don't go, stay here with me. I don't have to go back for a few days, we can have that time together. Stay, please.'

Oh yes, thought Ada, oh yes, I will. The thought of more days and nights with Johnny, the desire just to leave everything and stay, was overwhelming. Impulsively she leaned against him on the bench, feeling the roughness of his uniform, the hard outline of the Canada emblem against her arm. Dear God, oh yes.

'I can't, Johnny,' she said.

There was a small silence, then he spoke again. 'But why not? You belong here with me – nothing back there in Durham can be as important as that.'

Ada struggled to keep her resolve. No matter how she felt, she couldn't stay here with Johnny. There was her work, there was a war on, the hospital needed her, and there was Tom away at the war, even now she couldn't just disappear from Tom's life. Chaotically, she tried to marshal the reasons why she had to go back. Johnny had to understand, she knew he would, all she had to do was explain it to him properly.

Johnny watched the conflicting emotions crossing her face. 'I want you here with me, why don't you want to stay?' he asked.

'Oh, Johnny, lad, I never wanted anything so much in my life, I didn't,' Ada said helplessly.

Johnny laughed triumphantly. 'Well then,' he said.

'I have to go back, Johnny, I have to. There's the hospital, my work.'

'I know your work is important. But nurses leave every day – they marry, they have children, someone takes their place. It's natural for a woman, Lorinda.'

Ada knew it was true, but how could she just walk out on her job? There were more convalescent wounded coming every day, she was trained to help them. And there was something else. If Johnny had asked her only a few weeks ago she might have done it; after all, nurses were needed in London too. And though she didn't want to cause Tom and his family any more pain by deserting him while he was in France, she would do it for Johnny. But there was something else.

'There's my mother.'

'Your mother?'

She looked up as she caught the surprise in his voice. She hadn't yet told him; there was so much she hadn't had time to tell him. Now the story of her mother

449

coming back tumbled out, how she was in Durham now and dependent on her.

'Your mother deserted you!' Johnny remembered the anger he had felt as a child when he had heard the story of Ada's early life, all the suffering she had gone through because of her mother. 'How can you put her before me?' he cried.

He saw her protest forming on her lips and he rose to his feet and walked a few feet away. He had to make her see that he meant it. Yet he knew he was being unreasonable. He struggled with his emotions, his back turned towards her. If only he could make her realise what it was like when he was at the front, plagued with thoughts of her in Durham. Tom Gray could be home on leave at any time, persuading her to go on with her marriage. Tom Gray was her husband, she must have had her reasons for marrying him. Oh, he wanted her away from there!

When he turned his face was stern, his eyes glittering. She looked up at him and faltered into speech, because she had to make him understand. All the while he wanted to take her in his arms, tell her he loved her, beg her to stay. Oh, God, this bloody war, what it did to a man! How could he act like this with his precious Lorinda? But his expression didn't alter.

'Johnny, man . . . even if I stayed, what then? I couldn't just turn up at the hospital next week some time and say,

"Right you are, I'm back, everything back to normal." Now can I? And what would I do? Maybe I could write to Mam, I don't know. And then there's Tom –'

'Ah, Tom, that's what the trouble is, is it? What is it, Ada, haven't you made up your mind yet who you want? Is it him or me?'

Ada felt his words like a blow, they knocked the breath out of her. How could he say that to her? Hadn't she left everything and rushed down to meet him, hadn't she shown him how she loved him? And he had called her Ada. Johnny shouldn't call her Ada, he always called her Lorinda. She stared at him, her face white, unable to answer him.

'Well?'

Ada got to her feet and took a step towards him. 'Johnny, Johnny, man,' she said. There had never been even a cross word between them before. What had gone wrong?

A couple walking past on the path were shaken out of their absorption in each other as they saw her. Open-mouthed they looked from Ada to Johnny before recollecting themselves and hurrying on, fearful that the discord might be catching.

Johnny stepped forward. Ada had never heard him speak to anyone as he did then, let alone to her. His voice was hard and flat, his lips a thin, determined line.

'Now, listen to me. I will tell you what I think. I think

you should ring up that hospital of yours and tell them you can't go back. Tell them anything, but understand this, you are staying here with me and when I go back to France you will go to my sister-in-law's house in Middlesbrough. You could visit your mother from there, couldn't you? Or, if you like, we'll get a small flat here for you until I come back. You will not go back to Durham. I will not go to France knowing that Tom Gray can come back and think he can make you his wife again. Do you understand me?'

Ada looked up at him, unable to make out what was happening. How had the idyllic dreams of the morning turned into this nightmare? Oh, surely he would listen to reason, surely he would! If she rang the hospital and asked for another day off, maybe that would satisfy him.

But Johnny was allowing no compromises, and simply shrugged it off when she tried to put it to him.

'Are you going to do what I say?' was all he said. 'I can't, really I can't, it's the war, I have to go back. And Tom. I owe it to him –'

That was enough for Johnny. He had surprised himself at the extent of his jealousy. Maybe it was that he felt so helpless stuck in the trenches and not knowing what was happening, but he couldn't bear the thought of her husband even being near her when he himself was in France, and he felt he would go mad at the thought of it.

Turning on his heel he strode off in the direction of the hotel, leaving her alone.

Ada stared after him. Had he actually gone off and left her there in a strange park? She watched him walk away swiftly, his head held high, not looking back at all. Her vision blurred with tears and when she finally found her handkerchief to wipe her eyes and looked again, he was gone.

Oh, but he didn't mean it, it was just because he loved her so. In a minute he would come back and apologise, tell her it was all right, he understood. She sank back onto the bench; she would sit here and watch the ducks. If she didn't move and kept her mind on Johnny, willing him to return, he would. She had to go back to her work, she had striven so hard to get her post, and she was needed there. And, after all Tom and his family had done for her, she had to tell them to their faces that she was leaving him. She would explain to Johnny that there was no marriage left between her and Tom.

In the distance Ada heard a clock chime the hour, then the quarter and the half-hour. The crowds in the park were thinning, a cool breeze sprang up from nowhere. But Johnny didn't come back.

She got to her feet, swaying a little at first so that she had to hold onto the back of the bench until the world around her steadied; she walked slowly back to the hotel. The room was empty of everything belonging to Johnny.

Panicking, she missed seeing the note propped up on the mantelpiece. She rang for the bellboy and he told her that the gentleman had left.

'The bill is paid until tomorrow, madam,' he said, watching her curiously, wondering what had caused the Canadian officer to charge into the hotel, throw his things in a bag and clear the bill before charging out again.

She sat on a chair by the side of the bed in a kind of stupor. After a while, she stood up, rinsed her face in cold water and combed her hair, before mechanically packing her bag. She couldn't stand being there any longer; she would try to catch an earlier train. By nine o'clock Ada was entering King's Cross Station, and by half past the hour she was already steaming north towards Durham.

At ten o'clock Johnny arrived at King's Cross Station. He paced up and down before the entrance to the platform where the trains left for northeast England and Scotland; he expected Ada to be leaving on the overnight train as she had originally planned, but he wasn't taking any chances. He would wait there until she arrived.

She would have got his note by now, he mused. He hadn't trusted himself to see her for a few hours, so he had written to say he would meet her at the station. 'Maybe it's my red hair, my love,' he had written. 'But how could I lose my temper with you? I promise, Lorinda, I promise, I will never do it again.'

As he waited he went over the row in his mind, over and over again. What on earth had made him act the way he did? His poor little love, she was only trying to do the right thing, he knew it really. But when she came he would beg her to understand, and assure her that he loved her so much, he would never give her up. Why could he not have trusted her when she said there was nothing left between her and Tom Gray?

Johnny looked up at the station clock – not long now, she would be coming through the entrance any minute. And she would understand, he knew she would.

Chapter Twenty-Seven

Ada remembered nothing of the journey back to Durham except for the drumming of the wheels of the train. The noise went on and on in her head, spelling out, 'Johnny has gone, Johnny has gone,' until she thought she would go mad.

She went on duty on the wards, wondering if she could even survive until the evening, but somehow the trained nurse in her took over and she got through the day: not even Nurse Simpson noticed there was anything wrong. Or if she did, she did not remark upon it.

Every time the telephone rang Ada thought it might be Johnny; every time it was not, she died another death. By evening, Ada was beginning to give up hope.

When at last she was free to climb the stairs to her rooms and collapse on the bed, she fell into a deep, dreamless sleep and did not wake until morning. By that time she couldn't bear to think of her trip to London at all, the agony was too hard to bear.

Trying to apply her mind to other things, if only for a little respite, Ada turned to the letter from Auntie Doris. It was a pathetic cry for help and Ada's conscience smote her as she read it.

'Please, Ada, take me out of here. I have my pension now and I wouldn't be a total burden to you. I know I didn't always do right by you but surely you owe me something. I'm not an invalid, not really, and if I hadn't had such bad luck . . .' The letter rambled on and on in the same vein.

Ada bit her lip as she read it. Her own dread of the workhouse rose up again in her, making her feel she had to do something. And then she had an idea. She wondered why on earth she hadn't thought of it before – it was the obvious solution. She would bring Auntie Doris to Durham to live with Mam – after all, they were sisters, weren't they? Although Auntie Doris was crippled with rheumatoid arthritis, she wasn't completely helpless, she could still do small household tasks; anyway, the two women would be company for one another, wouldn't they? There would be no need to worry about what her mother was doing if Auntie Doris was living with her, because Auntie Doris would watch out for her. Maybe it wasn't the perfect answer, but it was the best she had thought of so far.

Ada did have a few doubts about the idea when she remembered the way the sisters spoke about each other. But they would have to learn to live together, she decided, there was nothing else for it. There were two bedrooms in the house in Gilesgate, and it was the ideal solution. First chance she got she would tell Mam about it. Wasn't Mam just saying how lonely she would be in the cottage?

The letter to Auntie Doris telling her of Ada's proposal was sent by the next post and the reply was equally prompt.

Good, thought Ada as she read it. Auntie Doris seemed to have forgotten her dislike of her younger sister in her anxiety to get out of the workhouse. Her only enquiry was how soon Ada could come for her.

There was a little more opposition to the plan from Mrs Carr when Ada put it to her.

'The place is too small, Lorinda, you know it is,' she said. 'And I never could stand our Doris. We'll be at each other's throats all the time, we will.' Mrs Carr glared at Ada and turned back to the sewing machine. Curtains were already up at the window of the tiny front room and she was busy sewing a pair for the back bedroom.

'But you said you'd be lonely, Mam.' Ada tried to use reasoned argument in her answer. 'Mam,' she went on when Mrs Carr kept her head bent over the material fairly rushing under the needle. 'Mam, she's in Oaklands, it's the workhouse. Surely you don't want to leave her there?

Grannie always said she would never let any of hers go into the workhouse.'

Mrs Carr sat back in her chair and the whirr of the sewing machine fell silent.

'I suppose you've made your mind up anyway,' she said. 'I can't really stop you, can I? You pay the rent and that's it.'

'Oh, Mam! That's not it at all, I don't want you to be unhappy. But Auntie Doris –'

'Aye, well, it's natural, I suppose, you're bound to think more of her than me. She brought you up, like.'

Something that had been niggling at the back of Ada's mind came to the surface. 'Mam,' she said, 'how do you know Auntie Doris brought me up? I never heard anything about you all the time you were in London. Grannie was sure you would come back, she used to tell me you would, but you never did and you didn't write to me either. Howay, Mam, how did you know?'

Mrs Carr looked uncomfortable. 'I didn't know you must have told me –'

'I didn't. You said it, that very first day at the Hall,' Ada asserted.

'Aye, well, if you must know, I did find out about your grannie being poorly. When she first took bad she wrote to me.'

'But how did she know where you were? I thought you'd lost touch altogether.'

'Aye. But she wrote to the place I'd gone to in the beginning and it was just by chance that I happened to see someone and –'

'You knew she was poorly and likely to die? And you didn't come back? Oh, Mam! If you didn't care about her, what about me? What about me, Mam? Why didn't you come for me?' The appeal in Ada's voice came straight from her very soul. Emotion was churning up in her; she couldn't believe her mother hadn't cared if she was left to go into the workhouse or an orphanage or whatever happened to her.

Mrs Carr looked at her, her face working. 'Aw, Lorinda, pet, you have to understand. I was just getting on with my Henry, and he would never have stood for a little lass trailing after me. I've told you what he was like, he liked a good time, Ada, man, it was a chance for me, I loved him, can't you see that? And anyway, I wrote to our Doris, I knew she would take you in if I asked her. She's not so bad, our Doris.'

Ada couldn't think of anything to say, she was stunned. Auntie Doris had known where her mother was and she hadn't let on. She hadn't said a word. And why? Ada cried inside, knowing the answer: because Auntie Doris wanted a little slave, a skivvy for her kitchen. Ada felt she would never understand the callousness of it. She walked to the door, feeling she had to get away. No one had cared about her, no one thought of her needs – not her mam, not her father and not Auntie Doris. Her aunt had at least fed her well and clothed her after a fashion. And she had kept her out of the workhouse. In fairness, Ada had to admit that.

She went out of the cottage without another word to her mother. She would wash her hands of both of them, her mother and her aunt, she told herself. Why should she lift a finger to help them? They didn't deserve any help, either of them, they had rubbed her face in the dirt, they hadn't cared about her at all. They were just interested in their own selfish needs, that was the truth.

I won't go back. They can both of them go to hell for all I care, she thought. Why should she? They weren't interested in her until they needed her.

But of course Ada had calmed down by the time she got back to her rooms. She just didn't have it in her to abandon Auntie Doris or her mother. And anyway, she thought as the familiar ache descended on her mind, blotting out everything else, she didn't care about anyone but Johnny, and he was gone. Only let him write to her or telephone her, saying it was all a mistake, he hadn't meant any of it. Oh, why had she left the place for such a long time? He might have been trying to get in touch with her while she was out.

But when she asked Millie if there had been any calls the answer was no, no messages at all.

*

Johnny did not call because he was already back in France. There was a big push coming up and his regiment was recalled to take part in it. But he found time to write to her in those few hours before dawn on the morning of the great offensive. In his letter he tried to explain to her how his emotions had suddenly boiled over, how he couldn't bear to think of her being in Durham if Tom came home. 'My love,' he wrote, trying to infuse his words with the feelings he had for her,

My love, I'm not trying to excuse what I said and did. But believe me, I love you so much. I can't bear to be here, imagining things, stupid things, oh God, Lorinda, I'm sorry, I do trust you, I do. And I will make it up to you. I went to the station that night but I was too late, or I missed you somehow, and I couldn't telephone you then for you weren't there. And I had to go back to the front.

Lorinda, my Ada-Lorinda, I'm sorry, sorry. Tell me you forgive me.

Your ever loving Johnny.

He put the letter in an envelope and addressed it. He would post it as soon as he got back. Meanwhile he put it safe with his personal papers, leaving them in the dug-out as the others did, just in case. But it was something he refused to contemplate: he was going to get back, he had to clear up this thing between him and his little love.

*

Auntie Doris was waiting for Ada with her bag packed, sitting in the entrance to the ward dressed in a rusty black coat and hat. Ada could remember the coat well: Auntie Doris had bought it when they moved to Tenters Street. Before that she had always worn a shawl, but she had thought a proper coat was more suitable to her position as theatrical landlady.

'Mind, I've been waiting long enough,' Auntie Doris said with some asperity when Ada turned up to collect her. 'I thought you were never going to get here. Dawdling about, I suppose you were; I always had to clip your ear for that.'

Ada ignored the last bit. 'It was Eliza's wedding, Auntie Doris, you know, Eliza who used to work for you in Tenters Street. I've been to her wedding, I told you I was going.'

Ada thought momentarily about the wedding. She still wasn't sure that Eliza had done the right thing. Emmerson Peart was older than Eliza and had daughters of his own. Did he simply want a maid of all work to look after them? She sighed; they were married now, anyway. Ada turned her attention back to Auntie Doris.

'Well, of course I remember her,' that lady was saying. 'What do you think I am, in my dotage? You'd think she would have had enough the first time round, never mind trying it again, like. I know I wouldn't chance it.'

Ada thought briefly that if she had been married to a man like Uncle Harry she wouldn't chance it either, but she didn't say so. Instead she picked up her aunt's shabby Gladstone bag. The weight of it surprised her.

'Are you ready, Auntie?'

'Like I said, I've been ready an age.' Auntie Doris stumped to her feet and followed Ada along the corridor. 'Don't walk so fast, man, what do you think I am?'

Ada paused. 'Do you want to say goodbye to Matron?' she asked.

'I've said goodbye, what do I want to say it again for? Let's away, out of this hole.'

'Well, I'd better have a word with her.'

'Well, you can't, she's not in,' Auntie Doris said triumphantly. 'There's nothing to see her about, any road. I said goodbye, I told you I did. And I gave her a piece of my mind while I was about it.'

Auntie Doris's thin nose quivered with obvious satisfaction as she stuck it in the air, remembering what she had told the matron, no doubt, Ada thought and laughed inwardly. How she must have enjoyed being in a position to do it! Ada thought about the other old women in the ward, and how Auntie Doris must have crowed over them when she could tell them her niece was coming for her. It didn't happen very often in a workhouse, Ada knew.

Doris Parker kept up a complaining monologue all the

way back to Durham and even in the cab which Ada took for the journey from the station to Gilesgate. After a while, Ada stopped listening, merely interjecting the odd 'Yes, Auntie' or 'No, Auntie'. Poor Auntie Doris, she must have been bottling it up all the time she was in the hospital: it would have been no use complaining in there. All the hospitals were short-staffed while the war went on.

Briefly Ada remembered Meg Morton, the nurse she had trained with so long ago, it seemed now. Meg was a sympathetic girl right enough, but she was away in France, working as an army nurse now. Ada had had a card from her last Christmas, with a picture of a hospital which had been bombed, the walls all falling down. 'Having a grand time working here,' the irrepressible Meg had written across it. Ada's reminiscent mood was interrupted as the cab drew up in front of the little house in Gilesgate.

'Is this it?' Auntie Doris asked. 'I thought it would have been a bit bigger, like, you earning good money an' all and married to a doctor, like.'

Ada could remember her mother saying something very similar when she first saw the house. 'It's big enough,' she said, paying the cab driver and taking Auntie Doris's bag to the door. 'Come on in, then.'

She opened the door, sniffing anxiously, fearing to smell gin, but though the air was a bit fuggy, she couldn't smell any alcohol. Breathing a sigh of relief, Ada put down the bag.

'Mam?' she called. 'Mam, where are you?'

'All right, there's no need to shout, I was only in the kitchen.' Mrs Carr came into the room, wiping her hands on her apron. Ada looked round, pleasantly surprised, for her mother had obviously gone to a bit of trouble to get the house ready for her sister. A big fire burned in the grate and the furniture shone with polish. But if Ada thought this meant her mother was reconciled to Auntie Doris coming and was going to give her a big welcome, she was soon disillusioned. Her mother was staring primly at the sister she hadn't seen for twenty-odd years. She folded her arms across her chest and nodded curtly to her.

'You got here then,' she said.

'It blooming well looks like it, doesn't it?' Auntie Doris countered. 'I'm dying for a cup of tea an' all. I suppose I'll have to make it meself, you would never think of having a pot ready.' She peered at the rouge on her sister's face. 'Too busy tarting yourself up, I can see well enough.'

'Bye, our Doris, you never did give anybody credit for anything. Always thought the worst of folk, you did, especially me. How the hell did I know when you would get here, any road? But as it happens, the kettle is about boiling and I've got some scones in from the corner shop.'

'Too lazy to bake your own, like,' Auntie Doris snapped. 'Bye, I'd be ashamed to death to give any visitor of mine shop-baked scones, I would that.'

'Aye, but you're not a visitor, are you? You live here now, and by God, you can make all the scones you like because I'm not.'

'Mam, Auntie!' Ada looked from one to another; they were facing each other like two bantam cocks squaring up before a fight. 'Behave yourselves. I'll take your bag up to your room, Auntie Doris, then we'll all sit down and have a cup of tea.'

'Aye, go on then,' Doris said. 'I'm fair gasping for a cup. But this one would rather stand and argue than get on with things as needs doing.'

'Here, you watch what you're saying about me,' snapped Mrs Carr, but her tone was mild and she moved into the kitchen to make the tea.

Ada carried the Gladstone bag up to the back bedroom and put it down on a chair. Glancing round the room, she saw that the bed was made up and everything was neat and tidy, there was even a potted plant standing on the chest of drawers. She smiled to herself; so much for her mother's reluctance to have Auntie Doris to stay, she thought.

Downstairs she found the sisters had moved into the kitchen. The fire was burning cheerfully in the grate of the range and sparkling off newly black-leaded surfaces and the brass fittings of the tidy betty shielding the ash pit. The table was set with a checked cloth, and besides the scones there were daintily cut sandwiches. Oh yes, she thought, Mam has indeed gone to a lot of trouble to welcome Auntie Doris, even if she wasn't prepared to admit it. Her mother was already pouring tea into the cups and Auntie Doris was sitting at the table watching.

'Howay, lass, don't let the tea get cold,' Mrs Carr said. 'I suppose you'll be rushing off to that hospital of yours.'

'I do have to go in this evening, but I can spare an hour or two,' Ada replied. She wanted to linger a little while, if only to make sure they would be all right.

'Our Lorinda has a very responsible job, you know,' Mrs Carr said to her sister, informatively. 'She's a clever lass, our Lorinda.'

'I like to be called Ada now, Mam,' Ada put in without much hope. 'I'm used to it.'

'Oh, aye, I know. And who was it called you Ada in the first place? That's what I want to know.' She spoke sharply now and cast a meaningful glance at Auntie Doris.

'There's nowt wrong with Ada,' Auntie Doris snapped.

'There was nowt wrong with Lorinda,' her sister retorted.

Auntie Doris took a piece of buttered scone and took a bite, chewing carefully before swallowing. She put down the scone and glared at her sister.

'Aye, well, I had the bringing-up of the lass, and I

would have felt daft shouting Lorinda all over the house. And another thing, don't you go boasting because our Ada has done so well. It's the bringing-up that counts and *I* brought her up, like I said.'

Mrs Carr compressed her lips and bit into a pressed meat sandwich. She crooked her little finger and lifted her cup to her lips before she thought of an answer for Auntie Doris and then she spoke with the cup in mid-air.

'It's blood that counts, our Lorinda has good blood. And a good brain an' all.'

Ada jumped in before Auntie Doris could say what was obviously in her mind about Ada's blood and brain. 'Hand me the scones, please, Auntie Doris,' she said, successfully taking her aunt's thoughts off what she was going to say.

'Yes, of course, pet.' Auntie Doris's face changed, the glare she was giving Mrs Carr turning to a smile as she handed the plate of scones to Ada. 'You eat up, you could do with a bit of meat on your bones. Though next time you come I'll have some proper scones for you, aye, and mebbe a nice Victoria sandwich cake. I know you like Victoria sandwich cake.'

Ada stared at her in stupefaction. When she was a small child Auntie Doris had made cakes for the boarders' teas, but when she caught Ada taking a piece she had belted her. Cakes weren't good for bairns, she had said.

'I don't care for cakes myself,' Mrs Carr declared before she too turned a brilliant smile on Ada. 'I tell you what, pet, I'll give you a nice meat pie for your supper. I got them from the butcher's, dripping with gravy, they are. And it'll be a nice change from that hospital food. It's not the same food when it's cooked for a lot of people, is it? I'll wrap it up for you.'

Ada wondered why butcher's pies were not considered to have been cooked in bulk, but her mother didn't seem to notice the inconsistency in what she was saying.

'Aye, but not like my meat puddings. I'll do you one next time you come, Ada. You like them, don't you?' Auntie Doris said triumphantly.

Looking from one to another, Ada was having difficulty in not bursting out laughing. Here were her mother and her aunt vying for her affection; it was such a novel experience for her that she couldn't believe it. It certainly made things more pleasant for her, though, she mused. And she was beginning to realise that the insults the two sisters hurled at each other all the time didn't mean anything much at all. Perhaps they had simply picked up where they had left off the last time they had met, it was natural for them. But it was all too much for her.

'I'll have to go now, I think,' she said, draining her cup and rising to her feet. 'It's been a long day and I still have things to do at the Hall.'

'Righto, hinny,' said Auntie Doris, confounding Ada even more; never before could she remember Auntie Doris calling her 'hinny'.

The sisters accompanied Ada to the door, Mrs Carr pressing on her the meat pie wrapped up in brown paper. Both of them insisted on kissing Ada on the cheek.

'I forgot to ask, did Eliza's wedding go off all right? I was real pleased for the lass, I always liked her. The best worker I ever had, apart from you, of course, Ada.' Auntie Doris nodded her head to emphasise her words.

'Fine, it went off grand,' Ada managed to choke out before she went out of the door and up the street, turning at the corner to wave at them as they stood in the doorway. Then she rounded the corner and collapsed into fits of laughing. All the way home, walking to the bus stop and riding out to the Hall, she kept chuckling to herself. Wait until she told Eliza what Auntie Doris had said! She'd never believe it.

Ada was in a very good mood as she went up the drive of the Hall. As usually happened when she had been away for the day, her eyes were drawn to the hall table as soon as she opened the front door. Always her pulse quickened as she wondered if there was a letter from Johnny. Now she picked up the pile waiting for her and quickly flicked through them, but without seeing his beloved handwriting. Most of them were official letters, none private. The sharp disappointment lasted only for a minute: there was always tomorrow, she told herself. Johnny would write, he loved her, he couldn't just forget her, she knew he couldn't. 'Matron?'

Ada turned as she heard the voice of Nurse Simpson, who was coming out of the main ward. 'Yes, Nurse? Is something wrong?'

'Dr Gray is here to see you, Matron, he came about half an hour ago. I told him you wouldn't be long and he said he'd wait. He's in your rooms now.'

'Thank you, Nurse. I won't be long, I'll relieve you as soon as I've changed and had a word with Dr Gray,' Ada answered, her happy mood disappearing altogether. What did Tom want now? Surely he had said all he had to say the last time he came?

'There's no hurry. I don't mind staying on a little,' Nurse Simpson said. She gave Ada a funny look as she turned back to the ward, but Ada didn't see it. She went on up the stairs to her rooms.

She hesitated before opening the door, gathering her courage to face Tom. Then, lifting her chin, she went in. But it was not Tom who turned to greet her, it was his father.

Chapter Twenty-Eight

'Oh! I thought it was Tom when she said Dr –' Ada broke off and moved forward; of course, she thought, Nurse Simpson would have said Captain Gray if it had been Tom.

Dr Gray stood by the fireplace looking at her. He didn't say anything at first.

'Won't you sit down, Dr Gray?' Ada kept her tone formal.

'I think perhaps you should sit down, Ada. I have some bad news.'

And then Ada knew that something had happened to Tom. 'Tom?' she asked and Dr Gray nodded, his face working.

'I came over as soon as I could. The telegram came for you and Sister rang me, she thought I'd better see it as you were away for the day.'

Ada nodded dumbly. Of course, as Tom's wife it

would be she who got the telegram. What a shock for his poor father to come out here to the Hall and receive such news! She sat down on the sofa, her legs suddenly very shaky.

'But . . . I thought he was safe, I thought he was in a hospital away from the front,' she said.

'The hospital was a field hospital, Ada. It took a direct hit from a stray shell, or so it says here.' Dr Gray held out the telegram and Ada took it, though her hands were shaking so much that at first she couldn't read the words. She handed it back to Dr Gray but he shook his head.

'It's yours, Ada. You were his wife, no matter the trouble between you.' He turned away from her and put out his hands to the mantelpiece, leaning forward and staring at the dead coals in the grate. His voice was harsh with both grief and something else. His shoulders were shaking and his head bent.

'I'm sorry,' she said; what else could she say? She would grieve for Tom, for the young life lost and the brilliant future gone to nothing. But she couldn't pretend to the inconsolable grief of the bereaved wife, it would be altogether hypocritical of her. 'I really am, Dr Gray, I'm so sorry.'

Dr Gray straightened up. He seemed to have gained some sort of control of his emotions as he turned to face her.

'Yes. Well, I thought it only right that I wait for you to

tell you myself. Now I will have to go and tell my wife.' He picked up his hat, and walked to the door. 'I think we will leave it at that now. I will of course get in touch with you later, there will be things to see to.'

Now he had told her, he seemed in a hurry to be gone. Ada rose and went with him to the door. 'I'll see you out,' she said.

'Don't bother,' he answered, turning to her before going down the stairs. He gave the appearance of having come to a decision about something. 'I hope you will respect Tom's good name in this town,' he said.

Ada was taken aback. 'Of course, doctor, I –'

But he interrupted her. 'I mean, you will not talk about any estrangement between you and Tom and you will allow a decent interval before you see other men.'

Ada felt as if he had slapped her. She gazed up at his set face.

'Yes, of course,' she said again. 'Whatever you say.'

He nodded curtly and went down the stairs. Ada walked slowly back into her rooms. She sat on the sofa for a few minutes, remembering Tom, feeling guilty, sad and all mixed up about him. Then, mechanically, she went into the bedroom and changed into her uniform, ready to go down and relieve Nurse Simpson.

Ada left the Hall as soon as she could next day and walked down to the river. She had a couple of hours to spare before she had to go back on duty and she felt the need for fresh air and solitude to get her mixed-up emotions under control. She found a quiet seat and sat looking out over the waters of the Wear. It was a cold day, dry but with heavy, sullen clouds in the sky and a cold, relentless wind blowing. But down there by the water, with the towering green cliff behind her crowned by the ancient stonework of the cathedral and castle, she was sheltered from the wind.

She was a horrible woman, she told herself. Today, with Tom dead such a short while, she had woken up to the realisation that she was free now, free to marry Johnny and go with him to Canada, if he still wanted her after the row they had had last time they met. But he would, he surely would, he couldn't just forget her, could he? There had been a swift rush of delight at the thought, she couldn't help it. Then the memory of Tom had returned, the way he had looked on the day he had asked her to marry him, his bright, intelligent face and warm nature. My God, she thought, distressed that she should even think of her freedom or Johnny at such a time.

Ada watched the water as it rushed downstream, grey and leaden as it reflected the sky above it. A few drops of rain fell, spotting her brown coat but she sat on, hating herself. And all of a sudden she began to mourn for Tom, forgetting everything else but her sorrow at his untimely death. The rain was coming down in earnest now, great sheets of it, blown across the waters of the Wear in drifts which rippled with the wind. But it was a while before Ada noticed it; she sat on, her hands clasped together and the tears streaming down her face and mixing with the rain.

When at last she rose to her feet and climbed the steep path to North Bailey, she was soaked to the skin. On impulse she turned into Palace Green and crossed over to the cathedral. She went in, took a seat near the back and just sat there, letting the atmosphere of the ancient church of St Cuthbert soak into her as she had the rain. And at last she came to a sort of peace with herself.

Shivering suddenly as she became aware of how wet and cold she was, Ada hurried out and went down the hill to the marketplace, where she caught a cab back to the Hall.

The following Monday there was a letter awaiting her on the hall table, a letter from Virginia, Ada recognised the handwriting. She opened it during her mid-morning break, reading it through carefully, deliberately keeping her emotions under control.

It was vitriolic. Virginia blamed her for Tom's death, and all the old accusations which she had thrown at Ada before were now repeated, this time in black and white. It was Ada's fault, Tom would never have gone to the war if he had had a proper wife, there had been no need for it, he was needed at home, Ada might as well have killed him herself. Ada was an ungrateful wretch, she had killed Tom and ruined the lives of his parents. And all for what she could get out of it.

Ada read it through, almost as a penance. Then she put it back in the envelope and put it on the fire, watching it burn to a black sheet which crumbled into nothing. It was simply Virginia's grief for her brother, she told herself. She was sorry that Tom's sister felt the way she did, and she was even sorrier if his parents felt that way too. But it was done; there was nothing she, Ada, could do about it.

The convalescent home was full to bursting. Besides having the usual maimed limbs and injuries caused by shrapnel, the patients coming in were often burned, blind or coughing up their lungs, or sometimes a combination of all three. For the victims of gas attacks were now seeping through to the convalescent homes.

Ada was fully occupied both mentally and physically, coping with the victims, and at night she fell into bed and into a deep sleep immediately. The staff were forgoing the little off-duty time they were due, and Ada didn't have any time to visit her mother and auntie for a few weeks. For a while the Hall had to take patients at an earlier stage in their recovery as the acute hospitals overflowed.

So Ada was feeling ready for a rest by the time she managed to get a couple of hours free and visited the two old ladies.

'And about time, our Ada.' Auntie Doris stood back for her to go into the house. 'We were beginning to think you had forgotten about us altogether.'

'Hello, Auntie Doris,' Ada answered. 'No, I didn't forget. I've been busy, that's all.'

'Busy doing what, like?'

Ada sighed. 'We've had a lot of extra patients at the Hall,' she said, keeping her voice mild. 'Where's Mam?'

'She's just gone out to deliver some sewing she's been doing. She won't be long. I dare say she would have put it off if she'd known you were coming.' Auntie Doris sniffed. 'If it wasn't for me hands being so twisted I could help her with that, we'd make a tidy sum, I can tell you. But being held as I am – do you fancy a cup of tea? I'll just put the kettle on, there's fresh scones just out of the oven. Better than those ones from the shop, I can tell you.'

'Why don't I go to meet Mam and we can all have some tea together when we get back?' Ada suggested. 'It's early yet.'

Auntie Doris's face fell. 'But I thought we could have a natter about old times, just me and you,' she said, smiling at Ada as though she was offering a treat.

Bye, thought Ada, Auntie Doris must certainly have

a short memory if she thought her niece wanted to reminisce about old times in Auckland. But she didn't say so, there was no point.

'I could do with the fresh air and we can talk later. Like I said, it's still early,' she replied, trying to be diplomatic. She had to catch her mother on her own, for she had finally decided to tell her about the death of James Johnson.

'Aw, gan on then, if that's how you feel!' Auntie Doris snapped, her smile slipping and a waspish expression taking its place. 'She went up to John Street if you want to know.'

'We won't be long,' Ada promised as she made her escape, thinking she would have to do a lot of treading on eggshells if she wanted to get on all right with both her mother and Auntie Doris. She gave a rueful grin as she set off, keeping on the lookout for her mother coming.

She was almost to John Street when she saw her mother walking slowly towards her, swinging her empty basket.

'Eeh, hello, our Lorinda, I didn't expect to see you. Where are you off to then?'

'I was coming to meet you, Mam. I called to see you and Auntie Doris said where you were so I thought I would catch you on the way back. You're doing a bit of business, then? That's good, isn't it?' Ada fell into step with her mother.

'Aye, I've got a few orders, like.'

Ada glanced at her mother. There was no doubt she was looking better and there was no trace of gin on her breath. She was more self-assured, too; being able to earn a little money for herself must have helped her self-esteem, Ada reckoned.

'Our Doris wouldn't like you coming out to meet me and leaving her,' Mrs Carr commented, not without a little satisfaction in her voice. 'You know, she thinks you should think more of her than you do of me, like.' She looked sideways at Ada as though she was wondering herself if that was how Ada felt, but her daughter was not to be drawn.

'I wanted to see you on your own, that was why I came to meet you, Mam,' Ada said. 'I have something to tell you.' She paused for a moment and turned to face her mother.

'Mam, Mr Johnson died a short while ago.' Ada couldn't think of any way to say it differently.

'Mr Johnson?'

Ada saw by the mystified expression on her mother's face that she couldn't think who it was Ada meant. 'You know, Mam,' she prompted, 'you told me once. James Johnson was my father, you said.'

'Eeh, our Lorinda, I never! I never said anything of the sort.'

'You did, Mam, you told me one night when you'd been drinking.'

Mrs Carr leaned against a house wall, her jauntiness all gone now. 'Did I, pet? Eeh, the drink'll be the ruin of me. I always swore I would never let on. I'm sorry, Lorinda.'

'Sorry you told me or sorry about him dying?' Ada asked, baldly.

Mrs Carr stood up straight and started to walk down the street. 'Howay, let's be going, I'm fair dying for a cup of tea,' she said and Ada followed her.

After a few minutes, Mrs Carr said, 'I'm sorry I told you. I didn't mean to tell you. I'm not sorry he's dead, I thought he was, any road, long ago.' They rounded another corner and went on quietly, both lost in thought, until something struck Mrs Carr.

'How did you find out, Lorinda? I mean about him dying, like.'

And Ada confessed that she had known him for years, though not as her father. She told her mother about his befriending her when she had first returned to Durham City, and helping her with her education so that she could enter nursing. And she told her about the day he had taken his first seizure when the telegram came informing him of his son's death.

'Aye, lass, I knew he had a son but he was always away at school when I knew James,' Mrs Carr said thoughtfully. 'Mind,' she continued as Ada looked at her, 'I wasn't carrying on with a married man, I wasn't. His wife was dead by then, long before I met him. So you see, there was no reason at all why he couldn't marry me, none at all.' Lifting her head in a gesture which Ada recognised as almost one of her own, she carried on walking. 'I'm glad he's dead, and that's a fact,' she said defiantly. 'Howay, now, let's have that tea.'

The following week, Ada received a letter from a solicitor requesting her to make an appointment to see him, 'with regard to the estate of the late James Johnson'.

Ada found herself the chief legatee in her father's will. When she came out of the solicitor's office, she was in possession of two houses: the one in Hallgarth Street which had belonged to her and Tom, and Mr Johnson's cottage overlooking the racecourse, or cricket ground as it was now. Mr Johnson, as she called him still in her mind, for she had difficulty in thinking of him as her father, had also left her the surprising sum of £8,000. She almost went back into the solicitor's office to ask him again how much, for she couldn't believe she had heard him aright.

Before she went back to Crossgate Hall, Ada went down the hill to the cottage and looked around it. It smelled a little damp since it had been empty for so long, and she opened all the doors to let in the cold but dry air.

Sooty came in and wound himself round her ankles, purring softly. Ada bent and picked him up, holding his glossy fur against her cheek.

'What are we going to do with you, Sooty?' she said softly to the cat. Sooty purred even louder in reply, sounding like a miniature engine in his pleasure at seeing her. She carried him out to the back door and saw Mr Johnson's neighbour peering over the hedge.

'Sooty still likes to sleep in the shed,' he said. 'I don't know what he'll do now the poor old man has gone. I suppose the house will be sold?'

'No,' Ada answered slowly as an idea came into her head. She owed it to Mr Johnson that his cat came to no harm, and Sooty had shown he didn't intend to move away, not even next door. The chances of any new owner keeping him were poor – you couldn't sell a house with the stipulation that the buyers kept the cat, now could you?

'No, it won't be sold,' she said. 'My mother and her sister are going to come to live here and I'm sure they will be delighted to have Sooty. If you don't mind keeping him until then? It will only be for a week or two now.'

After all, Ada told herself, what could be more fitting than that her mother should benefit from her father's will?

Chapter Twenty-Nine

Ada was in the main ward when she looked out of the window and saw the postman coming up the drive on his bicycle. Once again she felt the familiar quickening of her pulsebeat – surely there would be a letter from Johnny today? It was so long since there had been a letter, so many days and weeks and months. She refused to believe that Johnny was finished with her, it just wasn't possible. No, there had to be a good reason, she knew there had.

'Take over for me here, please, Nurse,' she said quietly. 'I'll just attend to the post.'

'Yes, Matron.' Nurse Young, a seasoned VAD by now with two years of service behind her, left her bedmaking and took over bandaging the leg of a soldier with a shrapnel wound in his calf.

Ada went into the hall and met the postman as he was about to place the letters on the table.

'Afternoon, Matron,' he said cheerfully. 'A nice lot you've got today.'

'Good afternoon,' Ada replied, taking the bundle from him. She could hardly bear to wait to skim through the bundle but she forced herself to smile at him. 'It's hot today, isn't it?' she said. 'If you'd like a cup of tea or a cold drink of lemonade, I believe Cook has some freshly made in the kitchen.'

'Grand. Thank you, Matron, I will. Just go through, should I?'

As he shut the baize door at the end of the hall, Ada quickly went through the letters. There were quite a few for the patients and these she put aside to give out later. And there was one official envelope – the lists of the new intake, she supposed. Ada picked up the bundle of letters that were addressed to the patients and looked again – maybe she had missed Johnny's letter.

There was no letter from Johnny. Her heart thudded with the disappointment. For some reason she had built up in her mind the thought that there would be one that day. The fear for his safety, which was always at the edge of her thoughts, threatened to take over, a dark, terrifying fear. But no, she was sure she would have known if Johnny had been killed. For the thousandth time, Ada tried to convince herself that he hadn't written because he was so busy.

After all, she read the papers, she scanned the

casualty lists. It was true he was in the Canadian Army and the English papers didn't always publish the names of Canadians who were killed. But Johnny came from an important Teeside family, surely if anything had happened to him it would have been in the *Northern Echo!*

Disconsolately, Ada went back into the ward and relieved Nurse Young to go back to her bedmaking. Though she tried not to think that perhaps Johnny had really meant what he said, that he didn't want her any more, she couldn't help the thought coming into her mind to plague her. Dear God, no, she prayed silently as she went round the ward. But better that than that he had been killed.

'Matron's a bit quiet today, isn't she?' a patient whispered to Nurse Young. 'She looks sad. She hasn't had bad news, do you think?' Bad news these days meant bad news from the front, and Nurse Young shook her head.

'Oh, no. Well, I mean, not lately. Her husband was killed last year.'

Ada went off duty that evening at six o'clock for it was her early turn. The wards were quiet and most of the patients were almost ready to go home, either to stay or for a few days' leave before going back to France.

Collecting a supper tray from the kitchen, she took it up to her rooms. As always before she settled down for the night, she thought of Johnny, imagining him in France, praying he was safe.

*

Johnny was not in France. He was in a hospital in the south of England and an orderly was packing his bags, for he was leaving the next day.

Johnny was going to Dinah's house in Middlesbrough to convalesce. He had thought long and hard before deciding to go there, but in the end a letter from Dinah had persuaded him.

'You have to come, Johnny,' Dinah had written. 'I couldn't bear it if you went off to Canada without coming to see us. We are the only family you have left, Johnny. If you don't come, I swear I will follow you to Toronto.'

So Johnny was leaving on the ten-thirty train for Darlington from King's Cross the next morning, where Dinah was going to meet him and take him to Middlesbrough.

The orderly closed the second bag and put it by the door with the other one, carefully placing it to one side so that it wouldn't form an obstruction. He looked across at Johnny, sitting in the armchair.

'Is there anything else, sir?'

'No, thank you, private, that will be all,' Johnny replied. 'I can manage to get into bed myself. Put out the light as you go.'

For Johnny was blind. His eyes were still covered with a light bandage though the wounds were healed by now.

'Very good, sir.' Obediently, the orderly went out,

switching off the overhead light as he did so. Johnny sat on in the dark, thinking back over the last few months.

The letter he had written to Lorinda had never been posted and now it never would be. It had been in the breast pocket of his uniform when the gas attack came and he and the whole platoon were caught in it. Norman, he thought, Norman had been with him from the beginning and now he was dead somewhere out in no-man's-land.

Best not think of it, it brought on the nightmares, or so the doctors said. And sometimes the nightmares were worse than the real thing. Instead, Johnny forced himself to think of the coming journey. There was nothing to worry about, a nurse would be with him and the other blind soldiers who were travelling north with him. And Dinah would be there to meet him at Darlington.

The trouble with Middlesbrough was that it was too close to Durham City, he mused. And it would take all his willpower not to go to Durham and seek out his little Ada-Lorinda. But he couldn't, he refused to saddle her with a blind man. No, better by far that she become reconciled to her doctor. Johnny felt fairly sure that Tom would come out of the war in one piece; after all, he worked in a hospital, not the trenches.

Johnny climbed clumsily down from the train to the platform on Darlington Station and stood patiently waiting in the hubbub for Dinah to see him. He had not long to wait.

'Johnny! Oh, Johnny, my dear, I'm so glad to see you.' Dinah threw her arms around him and kissed him on the cheek, wetting it with her own ready tears. 'I'll have you out of here in a trice, just come along with me, I'll look after you.'

'Oh, Dinah, you don't know how grand it is to hear your voice,' he said shakily, his tone almost as emotional as hers.

'Just come along and sit down here,' Dinah said, leading him to a bench seat at the back of the platform. 'I'll find your baggage, the porter's putting a pile out now – Porter!' And Dinah was off in search of his luggage. Johnny sat there, feeling as helpless as a baby. His eyes itched and prickled under the bandages.

'Here we are, I've got them. Just two, weren't there, Johnny? Arthur, take them out to the car.'

'Righto, Mum.'

So Arthur was with her, thought Johnny. Still not in the army, then. Dinah took his arm and they left the station.

Arthur had parked the car just outside and they were soon on their way up Yarm Road and out of Darlington, heading for Teeside. Johnny enjoyed feeling the wind in his face as he sat in the back seat with Dinah beside him. At least Arthur seemed to be a fairly steady driver, he thought. Dinah chattered on beside him.

'I've given you your old room,' she said. 'It's best for you, I thought, you'll be more familiar with it. Oh, Johnny, it's going to be all right, you'll see, everything will be fine. Just a little time, that's all you need.'

'And a new pair of eyes,' said Johnny, and was immediately sorry as he heard her swift intake of breath and felt her grip on his arm tighten. 'I'm sorry, Dinah, I didn't mean to distress you.' What a boor he was! It wasn't Dinah's fault he had lost his eyesight.

'That's all right, Johnny,' she was saying. 'It must be awful for you, I know. I understand how you feel, I do.'

Johnny was quite glad when the journey was over and he had successfully negotiated the front steps of the Beeches and was in the hall. The last half-hour had been a bit of a strain, both Dinah and he being careful of what they said and Arthur, in the driver's seat, saying nothing at all.

'Come into the drawing room. I'm sure you could do with some tea,' said Dinah.

'If you don't mind, I'd like to go straight up to my room. I am rather tired. It's a long way up from Sussex, and I've been on the way since early this morning.'

'Of course, Johnny, anything you say.'

Johnny could tell by her voice how nervous she was, how eager to please him, anxious not to say or do the wrong thing. Funny what one could tell from people's voices when one couldn't see them, he thought.

'I'll send some tea up, shall I?' she asked.

'Not for me, no. I think I'll just have a rest on the bed.'

Dinah went up the stairs with him and he could sense her anxiously watching his every step, even though he took them slowly, tapping before him with his white stick. When he finally reached his room, he turned to her. 'I can manage on my own, Dinah. Please don't bother any more. I have to learn, you see.'

He knew that Dinah was about to protest but he resolutely opened the door and went in, closing it behind him. All he wanted was to be alone, he didn't want anyone, not even Dinah, fussing over him. After a few false moves he sat down on the bed, removing his jacket and shoes and lying back with a sigh of relief. Perhaps it had been a mistake to come here after all, he thought wearily, it could only distress Dinah. And then he was so achingly aware that there were only a few miles separating him from Lorinda; the temptation to get in touch with her and ask her to come to him was almost overwhelming, especially when he was overtired as he was now.

It wasn't fair to burden her with a blind man, he told himself for the umpteenth time. But all the same, there was nothing he could do to stop the longing, it was lodged just below his breastbone like a lump of lead. He sighed and impatiently pulled the bandage from his eyes, throwing it on the floor. That damnable itch, he thought savagely, would it never go away?

There were just the two of them for dinner that evening, which was just as well, for Johnny had been dreading Stephen being there, perhaps talking of the steel business. That was another sore point: how could a blind man run a steel mill?

'Stephen has rooms near the works, he often stays there now. He's rushed off his feet with work, poor boy. And Arthur is staying at his friend's tonight so we'll have the whole evening on our own,' Dinah had said as they sat down to the meal. 'The house is quiet nowadays, I'm often on my own,' she continued. 'Not that I'm complaining, I know the work has to be done. But it's lovely to have you, Johnny.'

'It's nice to be here, Dinah,' Johnny said gently, wishing himself miles away. He wasn't ready to be sociable, not even with Dinah. All he wanted was to be left alone to think about what might have been; he felt his life was over. As soon as the meal was finished he excused himself, pleading tiredness. He would make an effort with Dinah, he told himself, but not tonight, his thoughts were too dark. Tomorrow, though, tomorrow he would.

The next few weeks were difficult ones for Johnny. Dinah was good to him and eager to please him but her fussing got on his nerves so that it took a real effort of will for him to stop himself snapping at her. And then there was Stephen.

A few days after Johnny had arrived in the house, he went down to breakfast one morning to find Stephen was there. He heard his voice as he tapped his way across the hall to the dining room. He braced himself as he entered the room, but Stephen's greeting was mild enough.

'Morning, Uncle John,' he said. 'I trust you're feeling better?'

'Oh, morning, Stephen,' Johnny replied. 'Yes, thanks, I am.' He felt for the back of his chair carefully and hung his stick on it before pulling the chair out and sitting down.

'I'll get your breakfast,' Dinah said quickly. 'I won't be a tick, I have it keeping hot in the oven.' There was a silence as she went off to the kitchen to bring his plate. Stephen rustled the pages of the paper he was reading.

'Are you here for long, Uncle John?' he asked at last.

Trust you, my lad, thought Johnny. Can't wait to get me away again. But Dinah was back with his bacon and eggs and she heard the question.

'Stephen! Johnny's just arrived. You make it sound as though we want rid of him and I'm sure that's not true.' She put the plate down before Johnny and dropped him a kiss on the forehead before going back to her own seat.

'I want you to stay as long as you like, Johnny. I'm sure Stephen does too, he didn't mean anything. I would say stay and live with us, but I know you want to get back to Canada, though what you will do –' Dinah broke off, realising what she had almost said. 'Well, I mean, stay as long as you like. You're not fully recovered yet, in any case, and the best place to be if you're not well is with your family, that's what I say.'

Johnny put his napkin over his lap and felt for his knife and fork, beginning to eat slowly and carefully, mindful of the sloppy egg yolk. He particularly didn't want to make any mess for Stephen to see, even though he knew it was foolish to think like that.

'Uncle John will be wanting to go back to his own home, Mother,' Stephen said reasonably. 'He's made a life for himself in Canada now.'

'Yes, I know, but I still think he doesn't have to go,' she answered, sounding quite snappish for her, especially when she was talking to her beloved son.

Johnny cut himself off from the conversation and let their voices drone over his head, it was a trick he had learned since he became blind. He didn't want to make any plans, he didn't want to think about staying here or leaving for Toronto, all he wanted was to be left alone, to come to terms with his blindness in his own way. He chewed stolidly through the bacon, eggs and fried bread and drank the coffee in his cup. Then, thankful to have got through the meal without disgracing himself by making a mess, he pushed back his chair.

'If you don't mind, Dinah,' he said, 'I think I'll just go back up to my room.' He took a step away from the table and fell flat on his face as he tripped over Dinah's cat.

'Johnny!' Dinah pushed back her chair and rushed over to him. 'Oh, Johnny, are you all right?'

'I'm fine, Dinah, really, it was stupid of me. Please, I can manage.'

'That's what the white stick is for, Uncle John,' Stephen drawled.

Johnny didn't answer. He took his stick from the back of the chair and left the room, feeling that if he opened his mouth he would yell and shout his rage at Stephen, at Dinah, at the world which had done this to him.

It was Ada's day off and she went down Old Elvet early to visit her mother and aunt, for Eliza was coming to see her during the afternoon. It would be the first time she had seen Eliza since her wedding and Ada was looking forward to a pleasant afternoon with her old friend.

Auntie Doris and her mother had just moved into the cottage the week before. Ada had not been able to get the time off to help with the move so she felt she had to go today to make sure they were settled in all right.

Even the outside of the cottage looked different, she saw as she opened the front gate and walked up the path. There were fresh curtains at the windows and the flowerbeds underneath were newly weeded and ablaze with colour, the bright gold of marigolds contrasting with white snow-in-summer and many-hued pansies. The brass of the front doorhandle and knocker gleamed and the step was freshly scrubbed with sandstone.

'Oh, it's you, our Ada.' Auntie Doris opened the door to her knock. There was a lovely smell of new-baked bread coming from the back of the cottage. A bunch of marigolds in a glass vase stood on the hall table, Ada saw, as her aunt stood back for her to enter. 'Howay in, then, I'll just pop through to the kitchen and get the teacakes out of the oven.'

Auntie Doris hobbled back to the kitchen and Ada trailed along behind her. On the way she glanced into the sitting room, where the furniture gleamed with polishing and there were new covers on the armchairs and frilled cushions on the sofa. The two women hadn't been long putting their mark on the place, she thought.

Mrs Carr was sitting by the kitchen table, turning up a skirt hem by hand. She got to her feet and offered her cheek for Ada's kiss.

'Well,' she said, 'what do you think of it?'

Ada looked round the spotless kitchen, the floor covered with blue-and-white-checked linoleum and a blue and white tablecloth on the table. 'It's grand, Mam,' she said.

Mrs Carr gazed round in satisfaction. 'Aye, it is, isn't

it?' she said. 'A bit better than Gilesgate, eh? Mind, we have a lot more to do yet, like, but it's coming on.'

'Eeh, I don't know how you can say *we've* a lot more to do,' Auntie Doris put in, but her voice had lost some of its usual sharpness. 'She means, I have a lot more to do, it's me that does all the graft.'

'I made the curtains and cushions and things, didn't I? And any road, I'm busy, earning a living for us both, aren't I?'

'I've got me pension, I don't need –'

'Anyway, it all looks very nice,' Ada intervened before the argument could get any more heated. 'I just called in to see how you were getting on. Eliza's coming to visit me this afternoon and I want to be back for her.'

'You never do come but what you're rushing off again,' said Mrs Carr, but Ada didn't rise to this. She was getting used to such remarks by now and just ignored them.

She stayed for an hour and then left, satisfied that everything was going well for her mother and her aunt, and taking with her a newly baked teacake which they pressed upon her.

Eliza was as pleased to see Ada as Ada was to see her. The two girls hugged each other and then, as the older girl stood back to look at her, Ada saw with a start of surprise that Eliza was pregnant. Eliza laughed and put a hand over her stomach which was just beginning to swell.

'Don't look so surprised, Ada. It does tend to happen when a lass gets wed, like.'

'I don't know, I just never thought – Are you pleased about it, Eliza? Because I'm pleased too if you are.'

'Why, man, it'll be grand having another baby, mebbe a little lass this time. Oh, aye, I'm pleased and Emmerson is an' all.'

The two girls were soon settled down to an afternoon of catching up on each other's news, though afterwards Ada realised that Eliza hadn't said a lot about her new husband. She chatted on about Bertie and Miles, however.

'Have you heard from Johnny Fenwick?' Eliza said casually and the next minute wished she hadn't, for Ada's composure crumbled.

'No,' she said, her voice hardly above a whisper. 'Eeh, Eliza, I don't know what to think. If he'd been killed I'm sure I would have found out; anyway, I would have known inside myself.' Ada lifted her face to Eliza, her eyes wide with fear and tears close. 'Eliza,' she asked, 'Eliza, do you think he just doesn't want me any more? Eeh, Eliza, it's months since he wrote to me, months.'

Eliza rose to her feet and moved swiftly to Ada's side. 'Nay, lass, it won't be that. No, I'm sure there'll be another reason.' She put her arm around Ada's thin shoulders and fell silent for a while.

'I tell you what,' she said at last, 'you have the address of those relations of his in Middlesbrough, don't you?

They'll still live there, I'm sure they will. Why don't you write to them, like? It can't do any harm, just ask them if they know how he is getting on.'

'Oh, Eliza, I don't know –'

Eliza tutted softly. 'There's no reason why you couldn't, Ada, man. Say you're an old friend, nothing could be easier.'

Before Eliza went back to West Auckland, she had succeeded in getting Ada to compose a letter asking for details of Johnny's whereabouts and how he was.

'Address it to Mrs Fenwick,' she advised. 'Someone will open it and a woman would understand better.'

Chapter Thirty

Dinah was very worried about Johnny. He was so withdrawn; he spent most of his time in his room, just sitting there doing nothing, even though she tried to coax him to spend more time downstairs with her. He came down to the dining room for meals, but Dinah knew that if he hadn't thought it would be too much trouble for her, he would have asked for a tray in his room.

When he does come down, he speaks less and less, she thought to herself one morning as she watched him across the breakfast table. Oh, he was unfailingly polite to her and to Stephen and Arthur too, even when Stephen began asking him pointed questions about how long he was staying.

Dinah had spoken to Stephen about that; she stirred uncomfortably in her chair as she thought of it. He was just a little thoughtless, she told herself, he wasn't really uncaring. And he probably thought that having Johnny in the house was too much extra work for her, now she had only a daily to help.

But Dinah was alone with Johnny this morning. Stephen and Arthur had both gone off to the office early, to do something about a new defence contract. Dinah put down her coffee cup with a sigh. She would try to get Johnny to go out with her, she decided.

'Johnny?' she began tentatively.

'Yes, Dinah?' His voice was remote as though his thoughts were miles away.

'Johnny, why don't we go for a walk in the park this morning? It's a lovely day, the sunshine would do you good and I'm sure I would be glad to get out of the house.'

'Oh, you go, Dinah, I think I'll just stay in my room.'

'But you'll have to go out sometime,' Dinah persisted. 'If not walking, why not take a cab down to Saltburn?' She warmed to this idea – Saltburn would be lovely, she thought. 'We could sit on top of the cliff, the sea air will do us both the world of good. Do come, Johnny.'

Johnny smiled gently. 'You go, Dinah. Believe me, I won't be very good company for you, I'm not good company for anyone nowadays. No, I'd rather just stay in today, if you don't mind.'

Dinah stared at him, feeling frustrated. Really, she was getting to the end of her tether, she didn't know what to do or what to say to him either, to make him snap out of his depression. Poor boy, she thought, compassionately, it wasn't surprising really, of course it wasn't.

Idly Dinah looked through her post. There was a letter from her bank manager informing her of the state of her account, and there was a letter from an old friend from her schooldays in Hartlepool. The third envelope had a Durham postmark. She turned it over in her hand, but the handwriting was unfamiliar. Who on earth could be writing to her from Durham? She took up her letter opener and slit the top of the envelope, taking out the single sheet of notepaper. A good-quality notepaper, she saw as she looked at the bottom of the letter to see the signature.

'Ada Gray,' it read. Dinah's puzzlement deepened. She read the letter through from the beginning.

I hope you do not mind me writing to you like this, but I could not think of anything else to do.

I am looking for any information concerning the present whereabouts of John Fenwick, a captain in the Canadian Army. You do not know me but my name is Mrs Ada Gray, I was a childhood friend of Johnny's. I am writing to you as I believe you are a relative of his.

I would be very grateful if you could help me, I haven't heard from him for some months and I am worried about him.

Yours sincerely,
Ada Gray.

Dinah put down the letter and looked across at Johnny again; he was sitting with his elbows on the table and his coffee cup in his hands. If he had been able to see she would have said he was staring into space.

'Johnny, what did you say that girl's name was, you know, the one you knew in Bishop Auckland?'

Johnny pushed his chair back abruptly and rose to his feet. He took his stick and started to leave the room.

'Johnny?'

Johnny halted with his back to Dinah. After a moment he said, 'I'm going up to my room, I feel a little tired.'

Dinah was left looking after him as he crossed the hall and went up the stairs, his white stick tapping in front of him all the way. Was that what was the matter with him? she wondered. Not just the fact that he was blind, but this girl. She looked again at the signature.

'Mrs Ada Gray,' it read. Had she married someone else? Thrown Johnny over when she found out he had been blinded? But if that was the case, why ask for news of him?

It was all very puzzling. Dinah tapped the letter thoughtfully with her fingers; she was very tempted to write to the girl and if she had thrown him over, she would give her a piece of her mind.

During the morning, Dinah could think of nothing else but the letter as she dusted the furniture and wrote out the shopping list for the evening meal. In the end she went upstairs and tapped on Johnny's door.

'Johnny? Can I come in for a moment?' After a pause, Johnny came to the door and opened it. 'Come in, Dinah, did you want something?'

'Yes.' Dinah waited until he sat down in the chair by his bed before she sat down herself, facing him. 'Johnny, was that girl's name Ada?'

Johnny frowned. 'Dinah, I don't want to talk about it,' he said.

'But Johnny, why not?' she persisted. 'Did she hurt you, Johnny?'

'No, she didn't. She wouldn't hurt anyone.'

Johnny kept his face expressionless, but Dinah could see he was worked up emotionally; a tic appeared at the corner of his eye and he clasped his hands tightly together.

'You love her, don't you, Johnny?' she said.

'Love? What does it mean? No, of course I don't love her, I don't love anyone. What good would it be for me to love anyone, Dinah? What use is a blind man to a girl?'

So that was it, thought Dinah. 'Oh, Johnny, if she loved you it wouldn't matter, no injury would matter. Believe me, I know.'

'In any case, she's married, she's married to a doctor. She's better off with him – what future could I offer her compared with that? And even if she wasn't, I wouldn't saddle her with a blind husband.'

'Oh, Johnny,' Dinah said helplessly. She looked at him, seeing the young boy she had mothered when she had first married his elder brother, remembering his bright, eager zest for life. Now he was pale and withdrawn, except for the flush of emotion on his cheeks as he talked about the girl. His voice was so flat and bitter, in contrast to the ever-ready enthusiasm which had coloured it before this catastrophe had befallen him. Even the bright red of his hair was dulled, lank and lifeless.

'What made you think of her this morning?' Johnny asked suddenly.

'Er . . .' Dinah was taken off guard, she didn't know whether she wanted to tell him about the letter just yet. 'I don't know, I was just thinking of something to cheer you up,' she answered lamely. And I've done anything, but that, she thought to herself; if anything, I've unsettled him.

'I'll go now, Johnny.' Dinah rose to her feet and walked to the bedroom door. 'Are you sure you wouldn't like to come out for a walk? As I said, it's a lovely day.'

'No, thank you, Dinah. Perhaps this afternoon I'll go into the garden for a little while.'

And with this Dinah had to be content. She went back to the dining room and read the letter again before coming to a decision. She would write to this Mrs Gray and tell her where Johnny was and what had happened to him. There was no need to tell Johnny anything about it at all.

Going to her bureau, Dinah took out paper and pen and wrote the letter immediately, before she could change her mind. She found a stamp in her drawer, stuck it on the envelope and took it straight out to the pillar box at the end of the road. Good, she thought, it was just in time for the midday post.

Back in Durham City, Ada felt lonelier than she had ever felt in her life. She was very busy on the wards, where the steady flow of convalescent wounded seemed to go on for ever. As fast as the beds were freshly made up after a batch of patients left, they were filled up by a new lot. That evening she climbed wearily upstairs to her rooms and fell into bed thinking she could sleep for a week. But every night lately she lay awake for hours, thinking of Johnny and worrying about him.

Ada half wished she hadn't sent the letter to Middlesbrough now. What if Johnny simply didn't want her any more, what if he had fallen out of love with her? The letter could only be an embarrassment if that was the truth of it. Ada tossed and turned in bed, one moment so hot she threw the bedclothes off and the next feeling chilled and shivering so that she pulled them up under her chin.

It occurred to her that if Johnny didn't love her

any more, it served her right. She was filled with compunction as she thought of Tom: this was how he must have felt when he realised she was not in love with him. Ada turned on her back and stared at the shadows on the ceiling, watching the pale beam of moonlight which filtered through a gap in the curtains as it flickered there.

She had to get some sleep, she told herself, otherwise she would be tired out the next day and her work would be twice as hard. She had to put it out of her mind. The main thing was that Johnny hadn't been killed or injured, she scolded herself. Nothing mattered but that; she didn't care if she never saw him again if only he was safe, she thought. And believed it too.

Next morning, there was a letter from Middlesbrough on the hall table. Ada's heart thudded painfully as she saw it. She couldn't believe she had got an answer by return of post – surely it must be good news? Her fingers trembled as she picked it up, hardly daring to open it, the horrid thought coming into her mind that whoever had answered the letter had done it so quickly because Johnny was dead.

Ada stood by the table, turning the letter over and over in her hands, rosy colour coming and going in her pale cheeks.

'Are you all right, Matron?'

She looked up, startled. It was Nurse Simpson

standing in the doorway of the sluice and staring at her with open curiosity.

'Bad news, Matron?'

Dear God, no, thought Ada and snapped at the nurse, uncharacteristically. 'Get on with your work, Nurse Simpson. It's none of your business what's in my post.'

Nurse Simpson pressed her lips together and her eyes flashed in anger. For a moment Ada thought she was going to retort but the other girl recollected herself enough to mumble an apology.

Ada pushed the letter into her bib front. She would open it upstairs during her break, she thought. But then she found she couldn't wait that long, she couldn't keep her mind on her work at all. Sitting down at her desk, she took out the letter and opened it, her heart pounding in her ears and her mouth suddenly dry. It was covered with the copperplate script Dinah had learned at the National School in Hartlepool.

Dear Mrs Gray,

In answer to your query about my brother-in-law, I am writing to tell you that he is at present here in my house in Middlesbrough.

Ada dropped the letter on the floor from nerveless fingers and had to bend down to pick it up. For a moment the world went dark as she came upright again.

She waited until her vision returned to normal, her heart singing.

Johnny was not dead! Oh, she had known he wasn't. Hadn't she just said to Eliza that she would know if he had been killed? She felt like getting up and dancing around the hall, the rush of joy was so great. At last she composed herself enough to read on.

I am afraid I have to tell you that Johnny has been injured, it was his eyes. In fact, Johnny is blind. Though the doctors say there might be some chance of him regaining some sight in his right eye, I'm afraid his left eye is permanently blind.

All the elation drained from Ada. She sat back in her chair, staring at the words, unable to believe them. Johnny, her vital, athletic, vibrant Johnny couldn't possibly be blind. It was a mistake, it had to be. She read the words over and over, seizing on the one shred of hope in them. He might regain the sight in his right eye. That was good, wasn't it? Ada read on to the end of the letter.

I have to tell you that Johnny is in a very depressed state of mind. He refuses to go out, he sits in his room for most of the day and I am at my wits' end what to do about it. If you are the girl he used to talk about, the one he knew during his time in Bishop Auckland, I would like you to write back to me. I know you are married now, at least I gather so by your letter, but if you ever had any affection for my poor Johnny, I beg you at least to try to help him. If he goes on as he is doing I fear for his very sanity.

Ada felt as though someone had punched her in the stomach. For the first time in her nursing life she let her private life interfere with her professional one. She couldn't stay on duty, she simply couldn't. She looked round for a nurse, but there was not one in sight. Stumbling to her feet, she went to the door of the main ward. Hanging onto the doorjamb, she searched for a nurse, any nurse.

'Matron? Are you ill?'

Nurse Young was right behind her, a look of concern on her face.

'Ill?' Ada stared at the girl. 'No, no, I'm not ill. That is, I don't feel too good, that's the truth. Would you find Sister for me?'

'But Sister's not on duty until one o'clock, Matron,' Nurse Young replied. 'Look, why don't you sit down and I'll fetch Nurse Simpson?'

Ada nodded slowly. 'Yes, that will be best.' She returned to her desk and sat down, struggling to maintain her equilibrium. Her mind was in a whirl, she didn't know what to do.

'Matron?' Nurse Simpson was at her elbow. 'Nurse

Young says you're not well. How do you feel? Should I ring for Doctor?'

Ada made a great effort and pulled herself together. 'No, don't do that, Nurse, there's no need. If you could just take over for me for half an hour, I'm sure I'll be all right. I had a bit of a shock, that's all.'

Nurse Simpson nodded knowingly. 'Ah, I thought there was something in that letter. Look, why don't you go on upstairs and I'll get Cook to send you up a cup of tea. I'm sure you'll feel better after a little rest.' She wasn't going to ask again what was wrong, but Ada could see she was alive with curiosity, and she felt she had to get away from her.

'Thank you, Nurse, I think I will,' she said shakily and rose to her feet. The room swam around her but she forced herself to walk across to the foot of the stairs.

'Are you sure you can manage?' Nurse Simpson called after her.

'Quite sure, Nurse,' Ada replied without looking round. 'If you can just take over for half an hour –' Her voice was becoming faint so she broke off, using all the energy at her disposal to make her unwilling legs take one step at a time until at last she was up the three flights of stairs and could open the door to her rooms, breathing a sigh of relief when she could close the door behind her.

She sank down in her armchair and read the letter over again. Johnny was not dead. Now that she knew he was alive, she could admit to the secret fear which had smouldered away at the back of her thoughts for so long. Johnny was alive and needed her.

There was a knock on the door, but Ada didn't hear it. After a moment, Millie opened it and poked her head round. 'I've brought your tea, Matron,' she said.

'Thank you, Millie. Put it down on the table, that'll be fine.'

Millie brought in the tray and stood hesitating before her.

'What is it, Millie?' Ada was impatient to be alone again, she had to get her chaotic thoughts in order.

'I was to ask you how you were, Matron.'

'I'm all right, Millie, I'll be back downstairs shortly.'

After Millie went out, Ada tried to decide what to do. Her instinct was to drop everything and go to Johnny, she couldn't bear to wait another minute. But she knew she had to: she had to see if her deputy would relieve her this afternoon, she had to arrange for so many things before she could go flying off to Middlesbrough. Nurse Simpson, now, could she persuade Nurse Simpson to stay on and help? There were the beds to prepare for the new admissions, the treatment sheets to write up, the medicines to check.

Ada picked up her tea and added two spoons of sugar, drinking it hot and sweet. New energy flowed into her. She would get everything ready for her deputy, there was plenty of time if she hurried. She would send a telegram to Mrs Fenwick, saying she would be arriving that afternoon. Then she would catch the two-o'clock train to Middlesbrough.

It was after four o'clock by the time Ada arrived in Middlesbrough. She had left everything in order at the convalescent home; the rest of the staff had willingly agreed to cover for her even though they weren't sure what it was about.

And it's my free morning tomorrow, too, she told herself, marvelling at how the way seemed to have been smoothed out for her. But as she walked up the road to the Beeches, she was stricken with sudden doubts. Maybe she was being a silly fool, she thought dismally, maybe Johnny didn't want her, she would only embarrass him. Her footsteps dragged as she began to feel very unsure of how he would react to her arrival.

'Mrs Gray?'

The woman who opened the front door to her was middle-aged, her fair hair was flecked with grey. But her blue eyes looked kind, and she smiled at Ada as she stood aside for her to enter.

'Hello, I'm Dinah Fenwick, Johnny's sister-in-law. I was so pleased to get your telegram, thank you for being so prompt,' she said and held out her hand. Dinah's handshake was firm and reassuring to Ada.

'Come on through to the drawing room, will you?' Dinah led the way across the hall and Ada glanced around at the room as they entered. It was a large, pleasant room, furnished comfortably with armchairs, sofas and occasional tables – a family room, she thought.

'I came at once,' she said and added, because she couldn't help herself, 'Where is Johnny?'

'He's in the garden just now,' Dinah answered, not in the least put out by Ada's abruptness. 'I wanted to have a talk with you before you saw him, though. I'll ring for tea, shall I? We don't have any live-in staff now – the war, of course – but my daily girl is still here.'

They sat over tea and Ada forced herself to drink it and eat a tiny cucumber sandwich, but she was on the edge of her chair, dying to go into the garden and see for herself that Johnny was there.

'I understand you knew Johnny in Bishop Auckland, Mrs Gray,' Dinah began at last.

'Yes. He was a boarder in my aunt's house in Finkle Street. I was a small girl and he was kind to me and we became friends.' Ada put down her cup. She couldn't bear any more small talk, she had to go straight to the point.

'I loved him, Mrs Fenwick. I still do love him.'

'But yet you married someone else. You are a married woman, Mrs Gray,' Dinah said, simply stating the facts as she knew them.

'Yes, but it was a mistake –' Ada jumped in, then

stopped. 'No, no, Mrs Fenwick, I am a widow. My husband was killed in France.'

'Oh, I'm sorry,' Dinah said, looking anything but sorry. 'This terrible war . . .'

'Yes, thank you,' Ada said formally. She looked towards the french windows which opened out on the garden, but she couldn't see Johnny for the heavy lace hanging there. She turned back to Dinah.

'I thought Johnny didn't love me any more.' There was the unspoken question in her voice and Dinah rushed to answer it.

'Oh, my dear, I think he does. But you will have to be careful with him. Poor Johnny, he thinks his life is finished, he doesn't want to saddle any girl with a blind man.'

'I don't care if he's blind, I don't care what's wrong with him, I just want –'

Dinah got to her feet. 'Yes, my dear, of course you do, and you're right. Any girl in love would think the same. Come then, I'll show you where he is, then leave you alone with him.'

Johnny was sitting in a garden chair, his stick by his side. The house was casting a long shadow over the grass and almost to his feet as the sun sank lower in the sky.

Ada came out of the house and saw him straight away. She stood still, just looking at him. The garden was quiet; a cricket chirped insistently in the long grass over the hedge and in the distance behind them there was a muffled roar as a car chugged down the road.

Ada moaned softly, feeling her heart would burst, it was so filled with love for him.

'Dinah? Is that you?' Johnny lifted his head and turned towards the sound. 'It is getting a little cooler now. I think I will come in.'

Ada moved forward as the last rays of the sun glinted on his hair, bringing back the fiery bright colour. She stood before him, drinking in the sight of him, and he raised a questioning face to her.

'Dinah – It's not Dinah, is it?'

And Ada put out her hand to his face, touching his cheek, her hand moving in a caress to his chin, his lips.

'No, Johnny,' she said. 'It's not Dinah.'

Johnny rose to his feet with a strangled cry. Flinging his dark glasses away from him, he clasped her to him, burying his face in her hair.

'I will not let him go, not now, Dinah,' said Ada.

Dinah smiled. 'I didn't think you would, dear.' She was sitting on an armchair facing the sofa where Johnny and Ada sat close together, hands clasped and fingers intertwined. 'Oh, Johnny, I'm so happy for you! I'm so happy for you both.'

'We have to talk it over, Lorinda, I don't think you

know what you'd be taking on.' But Johnny didn't sound at all sure he meant what he said.

Ada smiled a secret smile; she smiled at Johnny and squeezed his hand to let him know she was smiling, and she smiled at Dinah. And Dinah smiled back in full understanding.

It was late evening, dinner was over and for the first time in her life Dinah was glad that her two sons hadn't made an appearance for the meal.

'I am a little confused,' she said now. 'I'm not sure what to call you: why does Johnny call you Lorinda when your name is Ada?'

'Her name is Lorinda,' said Johnny and raised her hand to his lips and kissed the fingers, one by one.

So Ada gave Dinah a brief explanation of how her name had come to be changed when she was taken to the house in Bishop Auckland to live with her aunt. Dinah tut-tutted at the idea of it.

'But that's where I met Johnny,' Ada said. 'Johnny was my hero in those days.'

'And still am, I hope,' said Johnny. Ada looked up into his face with her love shining in her eyes, and even though he couldn't see it, he knew it was there.

'But surely,' said Dinah, 'you could have reverted to your own name long ago.'

'That's true,' said Ada, nodding her head. 'But Johnny was the only one who called me Lorinda for such a long time. I couldn't bear to hear it spoken by someone else while we were parted. Silly of me, I know.'

Dinah rose to her feet, she was beginning to feel very much the gooseberry in her own drawing room. 'Not silly, I don't think so,' she said. 'I think I'll go to bed now. You know where your room is, dear.'

As she climbed the stairs, her eyes were misted. The sight of the two lovers together brought back poignant memories to her: they were just as she and Fred had been, she thought. And if in the morning the guest room should prove not to have been used, then what did that matter? They had wasted enough time already.

Ada stood at the bedroom window of the cottage which had been her father's. Downstairs she could hear the voices of her mother and her aunt raised in some argument over the wedding breakfast which they were laying out in the front room. It was such a familiar sound now that she could ignore it altogether, it was just her mam and Auntie Doris going on as they always did.

Both of them seemed to thrive on it, she thought as she gazed out of the window at the frost-laden bushes in the garden. In the distance the trees over the other side of the Wear were spangled with frost too, the black branches showing through to provide a contrast.

Ada was already dressed for her wedding; she had been ready for half an hour but she was reluctant to go downstairs and join her family. She was treasuring this short time alone, thinking of how her whole life seemed to have led to this. In less than an hour she would be Mrs Johnny Fenwick. Sometimes she could hardly believe it was actually happening.

Sooty came in and wound himself round her ankles, purring. She picked him up and held him to her, relishing the feel of his warm, furry body. Funny, she thought, how all the small everyday pleasures of life had suddenly acquired something more: the woods were more beautiful, the red roses of her bouquet somehow softer and a deeper shade than any red roses she had seen before, and Sooty's fur, too, was extra soft and warm.

There was a knock at the door and she turned to see Eliza putting her head round the door.

'Eeh, Ada, you look grand!'

Eliza's down-to-earth tones and the uncompromising accent of west Durham made Ada smile, bringing her out of her fanciful imaginings.

'Eliza! I'm so pleased you've got here early. Where's Emmerson and the bairns?'

Ada went forward and kissed Eliza, and the two girls hugged one another.

'Emmerson's gone straight to the church and the bairns with him. The baby's downstairs, Emmerson reckoned he had enough on his plate without a baby an' all.'

Eliza stood back and gazed critically at Ada's dress.

'Aye,' she said, 'that's just the right shade of blue, just a touch lighter than your eyes, I'd say. Eeh, lass, I'm that pleased for you, I am that.'

'Ada! Eliza! Howay, man, the pair of ye, you'll be late if we don't get set off now.'

Eliza and Ada grinned at each other. The strident tones of Auntie Doris Parker hadn't altered one little bit since the times she caught them gossiping together in the boarding house in Tenters Street. Together, they went downstairs, arms linked in the old companionship.

'Bye, I tell you, you two've never changed. Still the pair for getting away by yourselves into a corner, forgetting altogether what's still to be done.'

Auntie Doris was standing at the bottom of the stairs with arms akimbo and they burst out laughing. For a minute her eyes snapped and Ada thought she was going to go off into a tirade, but she collected herself and gave a reluctant grin herself.

'Aw, hadaway with you,' she said. 'The cars are here, our Ada, are you going to get married today or have we been wasting our time making all this food?'

At the church gates, when Johnny arrived with Arthur, whom he had prevailed upon to act as his best man, there was a gang of urchins hanging about in hopes of a 'hoy-oot', the traditional throwing of pennies and ha'pennies. Any bridegroom foolish enough not to bring a handful of change in his pocket was inviting cries of 'Shabby wedding!' Johnny knew this, feeling the weight of coin in his trouser pocket.

'Good luck, mister!' one or two of them called sympathetically when they saw his dark glasses and stick, and Johnny waved the stick in acknowledgement.

'Thanks, lads,' he said.

And then he was in the church, waiting by the altar as the organ was playing. He heard the rustle as the congregation stood for the bride and he stood too, turning his head unerringly to the aisle down which she was coming.

The next moment he felt her hand in his and they were repeating their vows. For the first time since she was a small girl, his bride was claiming her given name as she said in a low, clear voice,

'I, Lorinda . . .'